Millie's Escape

MARCIA CLAYTON

In loving memory of my dear son, Paul Michael Clayton.

Also by Marcia Clayton

The Hartford Manor Series

Betsey: The Prequel

The Mazzard Tree

The Angel Maker

The Rabbit's Foot

Millie's Escape

A Woman Scorned

Annie's Secret

Acknowledgement

There are a number of people that I want to thank for their help in producing this book. Without their input and support, it would never have been published.

Firstly, my family. I want to thank my husband, Bryan, for his patience and encouragement and for letting me monopolise the desktop computer for hours on end! Thanks to my talented daughter-in-law, Laura, for producing another fantastic cover and her patience when I kept changing my mind! Thank you to my eldest son, Stuart, for converting my files into PDFs and to my youngest son, David, for sorting out any problems relating to my computer and I.T. in general. Also, thanks to Bryan, my sister Gill, and my niece, Sharon, for being the first family members to read my book.

My heartfelt thanks to author Celia Martin for editing my book and providing me with many valuable suggestions and excellent constructive criticism. My sincere gratitude to authors Marlene Cheng, Laura Lyndhurst, and Shiv Saywack for beta-reading my book and providing useful comments and tips. I must also thank the many other authors and readers who have befriended me on social media, providing help, advice, and much-needed moral support.

Last, but not least, the biggest thank you goes to my readers. I have received some wonderful feedback from readers, who have told me how much they have enjoyed my books. Their reviews and messages encourage me to continue writing. A simple message, particularly from a stranger, saying they loved my story, means so much to me.

Thank you.

The Main Characters of Hartford

The Carter Family

EDWARD CARTER (b1812)
Married **BETSEY LOVERING** (b1814)

Their children:

1. **EVELINE CARTER** (b1837)
Married **Charlie Chugg** (b1835)

Their adopted children are:
- Twins Joseph and Matthew (b1875), children of Eveline's late brother William
- Amelia (born 1876) daughter of Eveline's late brother William.
- Martha, (born 1884) orphan, parents unknown.

2. **GEORGE CARTER** (1840)
Married (1) Alice Brown (1840 – 1880)

Their children:
- Harriet (b1860)
- Francis (b 1862)
- Alfred (1865 – 1869)
- Theresa (b 1868)

Married (2) Mary Ann Brown (b1848)

Their children:
- Nellie (b 1883)
- Sophie (b 1884)

3. **FREDERICK CARTER** (b1841)
Married (1) Lucy Fuller (1843 –1881)

Their children:
- Llewellyn (b1872)
- Rosella (b1876)
- Alfie (1877 – 1877)
- Grace (1879 – 1879)
- Eddie (b1880)

Married (2) **CHARLOTTE MACKIE** (b1860)
- Illegitimate daughter Doris (b1884)
- Nicholas (b1885)

4. **TOM CARTER** (1841 – 1880)
Married **SABINA BAILEY** (b1846)

Their children:
- **ANNIE** (b1864) married (1) Harry Rudd (1851 - 1881)
  (2) **ROBERT FELLWOOD** (1863)
- Mabel (1866 – 1866)
- Willie (b1869)
- Mary (b1871)
- John (1872 - 1880)
- Emma (1874 - 1880)
- Edward (b1876)
- Stephen (b1878)
- Helen (b1880)
- Danny (b1880)   Foundling (Son of Charles and Eleanor Fellwood)

5.   **WILLIAM CARTER** (1845 – 1881)
Married (1) Lottie Chang (1850 – 1880)

Their children:
*   Identical twins Joseph (b1875) Matthew (b1875)
*   Amelia (b1876)

Married (2) **SARAH MARTIN**(b1845)
Their son:
*   Bentley (b1882)

The Fellwood Family of Hartford Manor

Ephraim Fellwood (1770 – 1840)
Married Helena Thompson (1775 – 1820)
Their children:
a)   Joshua (1803 – 1868)
Married Marianne Simpson (1805 – 1825)

Their son;
*   **Charles Fellwood** (b1825)
Married: **Eleanor Chichester** (b1838)
Their children:
    1.   David Fellwood (1861 – 1881)
    2.   Lily Fellwood (1862 – 1864)

    3.   Robert Fellwood (b1863)
Married **Annie Rudd** (b1864) nee Carter

Their children:
*   Selina (b1881) (Annie's daughter)
*   David and Thomas (twins b1885)

    4.   **Victoria Fellwood** (b1863)
Married Frank Eastleigh (1863 - 1885)

Their children:
- Caroline   (b1882)
- Joshua (b1884)

5. **Sarah Fellwood** (b1870)

6. **Danny** (b1880) (Adopted by Sabina Webber)

b)   Thomas Fellwood (1805 – 1823)
Married Gypsy Jane (b1805 – 1841)
Their son:
- **Sam Fellwood** (b1821) married Gypsy Jenny (b1824)

Their son
- **Marrok Fellwood** (b1840) married Laura Smith (1842 – 1885)

Their children:
- Jinnie and Elizabeth (twins) (b1876)
- Martin (b1880)
- Paul (b1882)

c)   George (1807 – 1833)

d)   **Margery** (b1814)
Married Clarence Montgomery (1810 – 1870)

The Chugg Family

Alfred Chugg (b1815)
Married Jane Watts (1820 – 1884)

Alfred's brother:

CHARLIE CHUGG (b 1835)
Married: EVELINE CARTER (b1837)

Their adopted children:

- Identical twins Joseph and Matthew (b1875)
- Amelia (b1876)
- Martha (b1884)

The Rudd Family

Benjamin Rudd (1815 – 1881)
Married Matilda Yeo (b1820)

Their children:

- Harry Rudd   (1851 – 1881)   Married ANNIE CARTER (b1864)
- Jacob Rudd   (b1855)
- Francis Rudd   (b1860)

The Webber Family

PETER WEBBER (b1815)
Married Mary Jane Watson (1818 – 1866)

Their son:
ARTHUR WEBBER (b1836)
Married Drucie Reynolds (1840 – 1866)

Their children:

- Christopher Webber (b1856)
- Dudley Webber (b1858)
- Elsie Webber (b1863)
- Maria Webber (b1866)

Married (2) **SABINA CARTER NEE BAILEY** (b1846)

CHAPTER 1

BRAMPFORD SPEKE

Taking a knife from the drawer of the old kitchen dresser, Millie Gibbs cut two thick slices of bread from the crusty loaf sitting on the table. She then retrieved the remainder of the slightly stale cheese from the larder and cut it in half. Putting the cheese to one side for the moment, she took the bread and two toasting forks and went to sit beside her younger brother, Jonathan, in front of the stove. Using a cloth, Millie carefully opened the door of the Bodley, revealing the glowing coals inside. She spiked one piece of bread onto a fork and handed it to her brother.

"Here you are, Jonnie; hold that in front of the fire to toast it, and I'll do mine. Then we can spread it with butter and eat it with some cheese for our tea."

The boy did as he was bidden and held the fork before the roaring fire. It was only a few seconds before he had to swap hands as the heat was so intense. When one side of the bread was toasted, Millie expertly turned it over using a cloth, and together, they toasted the other side. When the bread was browned to their liking, Millie put it onto two plates, spread it liberally with butter and sliced the cheese onto it,

"That will stop us being hungry for a while, and there's a glass of milk for you, Jonnie."

"What about Mum and Granny, Millie? Shouldn't we do some for them?"

"I would if I thought they'd eat it, but they can't keep anything down and don't feel like eating anyway. There's enough bread left for breakfast, but most of the food's gone. I'll have to ask Granny if I should go shopping tomorrow."

"Do you think they'll get better, Millie? You don't think they'll die, do you?"

Jonathan was five, and Millie, fifteen, and in recent weeks, both had become accustomed to seeing their neighbours die one by one as the typhoid epidemic swept through the village. Speaking with a confidence she did not feel, his sister answered him cheerfully.

"No, of course not. I think Mum and Gran are on the mend. I've heard people say it gets worse before it gets better. I reckon they'll turn the corner tomorrow and start to improve. I hope so, anyway. When we've eaten this, we'll see how they both feel before we go to bed."

With their supper eaten, Millie carefully added more logs to the fire to prevent it from going out during the night. She checked that the front and back doors were locked and followed Jonnie up the stairs to bed. They entered the first bedroom, where their mother, Rosemary, lay asleep. Her gaunt face was pale, glistening with perspiration, and her lank brown hair was damp. Millie poured water from the pitcher into the bowl and moistened a cloth to bathe her forehead. She was concerned when her mother did not stir but said nothing to Jonnie, and she pulled the bedclothes up around her mother's neck to keep her warm. She kissed the sick woman's forehead and encouraged her brother to do the same. The air in the room was stale, and there was an unpleasant smell. Reaching under the bed, Millie grasped the handle of the pink chamber pot and pulled it towards her. Trying to ignore the contents, as her supper threatened to reappear, she suggested Jonnie go and see their granny whilst she emptied the receptacle. Jonnie didn't need to be told twice, and he hurried to the next bedroom, leaving his sister to her unpleasant task. When Millie returned from the outside lavatory, she found Jonnie snuggled under a thick blanket in the ancient armchair beside Emily's bed.

"Hello, lass. Are you going to cuddle up to Jonnie and get warm, too? What have you been doing?"

"Yes, I will; my feet are frozen. I've emptied Mum's pot because she still has diarrhoea, and she'd been sick again."

"Oh, my dear, I'm so sorry you must deal with all this at your age. If I had the strength, I'd see to it myself. Have you given your hands a good wash? How is your mother? I haven't seen her today, for neither of us has had the strength to move from our beds."

"Yes, I've washed my hands, and Mum's still poorly. I've bathed her forehead like I've seen you do and pulled the clothes up around her, but she didn't even stir, and I thought it was better to let her sleep. How are you feeling?"

"Not good, my dear, but hopefully, we might see an improvement tomorrow. Anyway, let's hope so. Now, I was going to tell Jonnie a story; do you want to listen, too?"

"Yes, please, but only if you feel up to it."

"Aye, I don't have to move to do that; now, snuggle up together. I'd like to cuddle you in bed with me, but I don't want you to catch this horrible disease. That's it; is everyone comfy? Jonnie, which story would you like tonight?"

"Can you tell us again about when you were a little girl, Gran, and all the games you used to play with your friends? I like hearing about that."

Emily kept them entertained for fifteen minutes or so and then told them to go to their beds, for she needed to sleep. Millie led Jonnie into the third bedroom, which they shared and tucked him into bed.

"Night, Jonnie; see you in the morning."

CHAPTER 2

BARNSTAPLE

The young man's straggly brown hair needed a wash, and an unkempt beard covered much of his face, but his hazel eyes were bright enough as he scrutinised his unexpected visitor. He glanced down, first at the rabbit's foot he was holding and then at the matching foot clutched in the gnarled hand before him. For a few moments, he remained silent, the only sound the hailstones rattling on the workhouse window, and then he spoke in a whisper, so quietly that he could barely be heard.

"Dad? Is it really you, Dad?"

Sam nodded, finding it difficult to speak, and impatiently brushed away the tears from his wet cheeks.

"Aye, lad. It's me. I'm your dad, and I'm sorry it's taken me so long to find you, especially here in the workhouse. I can't believe we still have the rabbit's feet after all this time. It must be over forty years since I shot that rabbit. They were supposed to be good luck charms, but they didn't work very well, did they? "

Then Sam was on his feet, his arms embracing the son he had abandoned so many years ago. Robert Fellwood watched the scene unfolding before his eyes in disbelief and was not ashamed of the tears running down his own cheeks. For several minutes, father and son clung to each other in silence until, at last, Sam released his hold on the younger man and searched for the right words.

"Oh, Marrok, I'm so glad we've found you, though not in these terrible circumstances. I'm sorry to find you so down on your luck, but all that's about to change, I assure you." A mischievous smile played around Sam's lips. "I have some amazing news, son. It's a long story and not one we have time to tell you now, but it turns out that my dad, Thomas Fellwood, was a gentleman and the brother of Robert's grandfather, Joshua. We're of noble birth, lad; what do you think about that?"

Sam and Robert laughed out loud at the incredulous expression on Marrok's face.

"You're joking!"

"No, no, I'm not, but all you need to know for now is that your days of hunger are well and truly over. I'm a wealthy man, and I'm delighted to be able to help you and your family; in fact, I can't wait. I see you're on crutches, though. What's wrong with your leg?"

"I broke it falling off a roof, and it should have mended by now. It doesn't seem any better now than when I had the accident, and it's still very painful."

"Oh dear, that's not good at all."

All this time, Robert had remained silent, but at this point, he laid his hand gently on the older man's arm and intervened.

"Sam, I'm sorry to interrupt, but we must discuss what we should do now. The light's fading fast, and we must return to Hartford; it's quite a journey in the pony and trap on such a cold winter's day."

"Aye, you're right, Master Robert; sorry, Robert."

"Marrok, everything your father tells you is true, but I would keep it to yourself for now. Sam, I suggest we go back to Hartford Manor and return here tomorrow with my carriage to collect Marrok and the children. It will be a long and uncomfortable journey for you, but it's either that or we get you admitted to the North Devon Infirmary. You can think about that overnight. On the one hand, you might be able to get treatment for your leg in the hospital, but the food will be better at Hartford Manor, and it looks to me like you need it. Also, if you can face the journey, I can get my doctor to examine your leg and suggest what might be done, and I'm sure your children would prefer to have you with them."

"I can't believe any of this; I feel I'll wake up in a minute, and it will all have been a dream, but I can tell you now, sir, I would much prefer to come home with you. I've had enough of institutional food, or rather the lack of it, to last me a lifetime, and I long to spend time with my family," the young man smiled, "and, of course, my father."

"That's settled then. We'll explain to Mr Jenkins that you and the children will be leaving tomorrow, and we'll take you to Hartford Manor. It's a long journey, but not as far as Enderby, where your father now lives."

Leaving the two men alone for a few minutes, Robert spoke with the beadle. Mr Jenkins was hovering outside the door, discreetly trying to overhear their conversation. Without explaining too fully, Robert advised him that Sam was Marrok's father and that they would be collecting him and his children the following day. They agreed on a time of two o'clock. The door to the office opened, and Marrok limped out on his crutches. The beadle shook his hand warmly.

"Congratulations, young man; I'm pleased for you. It's not often folk come here to rescue their relatives; it's normally the other way around, and they can't wait for us to take them off their hands. You are indeed fortunate."

Leaving Marrok to limp back to the men's dormitory, Robert and Sam left the gloomy building and, with some relief, breathed in the cold, fresh air. Robert drove the pony and trap home, and occasionally, he glanced at Sam, who was grinning widely.

"Sam, I've never seen you so happy, not even when you discovered you were a rich man."

"No, I've never been so happy, and that's a fact. Now, don't get me wrong, hearing I'd inherited all that money was unbelievable, and at my age, it will allow me comforts I've never known, but it has more meaning now. What could be better than finding your long-lost son in such dire straits and knowing you have the means to set him and his children up for the rest of their lives? I'm the luckiest man alive."

It was a long, cold journey back to Hartford despite the warm blankets the two men shared across their knees. The bitter temperature bothered Robert far more than Sam, who had slept under the stars for decades and knew what being cold meant. Luckily, however, the hailstones and the rain had cleared up, and there was a full moon as they travelled across the bleak moorland. As they passed the spot where Frank Eastleigh, Robert's brother-in-law, had recently been found with severe stab wounds, Sam asked if they had caught the culprits.

"No, I've heard no more. Do you know, Wilf Folland, the police constable, was convinced I'd had something to do with it; he was so persistent with his questions."

"And did you?"

"Oh, not you, too, Sam. No, I did not! Mind you, although Frank was once my friend, I have to say he brought it all on himself. He was never faithful to Victoria, but I never thought he'd stoop so low as to have a young girl abducted for his pleasure."

"How is the young maid?"

"Theresa's handled it remarkably well since her escape. She's Annie's cousin, of course, and she was lucky to be rescued before any real harm came to her. Annie never did like Frank, for he made a pass at her, too, more than once. Like I say, he brought it on himself, but I didn't wish him dead."

When they arrived at Hartford Manor, Robert drove the pony and trap around to the stables, and Dodger appeared and took the reins.

"Good evening, sir; it must have been a cold journey back from Barnstaple."

"Yes, Dodger, it certainly was, thank you. Please take care of the pony; he's had a long day and deserves a rub down and perhaps a little extra food." Robert patted the animal fondly.

"Aye, sir; don't worry, I'll take care of him."

"I know you will, Dodger; goodnight."

Robert led Sam into the West Wing of the Manor House, where he resided with his wife, Annie, and their family. The two men entered the hallway and hastened towards the large fireplace where a cheery log fire was burning. As they held their hands to the welcome heat, Annie appeared from the sitting room.

"Oh, there you are; I was beginning to get worried. Was it any good? Was the man your son, Sam?"

With a broad smile on his face, Sam took her hands. "Yes, I've found my son and what a state he's in."

"Why, what's wrong with him? And how can you be so sure? Come into the sitting room and tell me all about it. I'll ring for some food; you must both be starving."

When they were comfortably seated in front of another roaring fire, Annie rang the bell, and when the young kitchen maid, Molly, appeared, Annie instructed her to bring food for the two men. Then they told her all that had happened, and Sam once more reached into his coat pocket and displayed the lucky rabbit's foot.

"That's quite a story, Sam. I've never believed in lucky charms, but that one certainly came good."

"Aye, it did, though I wish it hadn't taken forty years or more."

"Never mind, at least it's turned out all right now. You must be so excited, Sam, to find you have four grandchildren."

"I am, but do you mind them all coming here? It's quite an imposition. I can take them to Enderby tomorrow if you prefer, although it's a long way for Marrok to travel with a broken leg."

"No, we don't mind at all, Sam. I think you should all stay for Christmas. It's only ten days away, and Selina will be delighted to have some children to play with. Robert, do you think we could invite Aunty Margery as well? After all, these are new relatives for her, too, and it would be so lovely to celebrate Christmas together."

"Yes, that's an excellent idea. I'll ride over to Enderby first thing in the morning. She insisted I tell her the outcome of our visit as soon as possible anyway."

Sam had tears in his eyes once more as he took Annie's hand.

"You're such a kind young woman; you always have been. You even helped me to escape the law when I'd stolen that pair of boots from your Uncle George's shop; do you remember?"

"Yes, I do, Sam. Mind you, I'd got a bag of stolen vegetables from the Manor House garden with me, so I was no better than you."

"I don't know; I'm surrounded by thieves." Robert's wide grin took the sting out of his words as he offered them a celebratory glass of Madeira wine.

CHAPTER 3

HARTFORD

It was early the following morning when the lusty cries of the twins awoke Annie. Thomas and David were now nearly six months old, and although they usually slept through the night, they were always wide awake and hungry by five o'clock. Annie knew she could safely leave Naomi, their nursery nurse, to feed and care for them, but seldom did. Annie loved being a mother and still breastfed her babies once a day. Quickly, she slipped from the bed and pulled a cosy dressing gown around her, hoping not to disturb Robert, whom she knew was tired. He stirred but turned over and snuggled down again as she quietly left the room.

She quickly walked along the corridor to the nursery, where Naomi was lifting David from his cot.

"Good morning, ma'am. I have a bottle ready for Master David, as I thought you'd probably feed Master Thomas this morning."

"Yes, that's right, Naomi, thank you; feeding one myself in the morning and the other in the evening seems to work. I haven't heard them; did they sleep through the night?"

"Yes, ma'am; they seem more content now that they're having some solids and a bottle."

As Annie settled down in a comfy armchair to feed her son, Selina, her daughter, peered around the door, rubbing her eyes sleepily.

"Good morning. Did you sleep all right?" The child nodded and tried to climb up beside her mother.

"Fetch your dressing gown and put it on; it's cold this morning."

Selina returned with a warm red dressing gown clutched around her, climbed into the roomy armchair, and snuggled up to her mother.

"I have some exciting news to tell you, Selina. We're going to have some visitors over Christmas. Daddy will invite Aunty Margery today and possibly her friend, Peter Webber. Uncle Sam is already staying here, and yesterday he found his son, Marrok, whom he hasn't seen for a long time. Marrok has four children. There are nine-year-old twin girls, Jinnie and Eliza, and two boys, Martin, six, and Paul, three. They are all going to stay here for a while over Christmas. What do you think about that?"

Selina's green eyes shone as she pushed a stray curl back from her face. "Oh, that's good; will I be able to play with them?"

"Yes, of course. You must be kind, though, and let the children share your toys because they don't have any."

"Why don't they have any?"

"Unfortunately, they're not as lucky as you. They've been living in the workhouse, where poor people live if they have no money. Life's hard there, so we must make them all welcome."

"Do you think Father Christmas will bring them some presents here?"

"Yes, I expect he will. He'll come to you, too, but only if you behave and be a good girl."

"I will; I promise. I want him to bring me a new spinning top because mine doesn't work anymore."

"We'll have to wait and see, won't we?" Now, climb down a minute while I move Thomas to the other side; then, you can climb up again."

When the twins had been fed and changed, Annie left them with Naomi, and she and Selina went to wake Robert. He was stirring as they entered the room, and Selina bounded onto the bed and climbed in beside him.

"Papa, we're going to have visitors for Christmas, and there are four children. Mummy says I can play with them."

"Yes, that's right. I'll visit Aunty Margery this morning and see if she would like to come too."

"That's good; I like Aunty Margery. She gave me her best dolly when we saw her last time. Do you think she would like to see her again when she comes?"

"Yes, I'm sure she would. Now, you go with Mummy, get dressed, and have breakfast because I need to get moving. I'll see you again later." He kissed the top of her head as she left the room with her mother.

Within the hour, Robert was cantering over the frozen ground to Enderby House, some ten miles away. His Great Aunt Margery had lived there for many years, and he was fond of the old lady. After discovering that Sam was her nephew, she offered the old man a large cottage on her estate. Sam was unsure at first, as he had lived all his life as a gypsy and a tramp, but had taken surprisingly well to his new-found wealth and now enjoyed all the comforts that it brought. Sam shared the dwelling with his close friend, Peter Webber. A former miner, Peter had lost his hands in a mining accident many years earlier and felt he had nothing to live for. However, thanks to Annie's mother, Sabina, he now had a harness around his shoulders, allowing him to use various tools, including a paintbrush. Peter also used his mouth to hold his paintbrush and became a talented artist, selling many paintings. Margery shared his passion for painting, and together with Sam, the three of them had enjoyed several expeditions in the previous year.

When Robert was shown into Enderby House, he was taken to the dining room where his aunt was enjoying a late breakfast, and she urged her nephew to join her.

"Thank you. I've had my breakfast already, but I might pinch a slice of toast and a cup of tea."

"Do that, lad; you must eat plenty to keep the cold out in this weather. So, don't keep me in suspense; how did Sam get on? Was it his son in the workhouse?"

"Yes, it was. It was incredible. He's called Marrok, and he showed us a rabbit's foot that Sam gave him as a lucky charm when he was four. Then Sam reached into his pocket and found the other matching foot; it was so moving, and I don't mind admitting it had me in tears. Sam's made up, as you can imagine, and it turns out he has four grandchildren."

"Oh, I'm so pleased for him. Will he be bringing them all back to Primrose Cottage?"

"I expect he will eventually, but Marrok has a broken leg, and it would be too far for him to travel here. We've decided to take them all to Hartford Manor to feed them up and give them time to recuperate. With Christmas so close, it makes sense for them to stay until the new year, at least. I thought I'd get Doctor Luckett to take a look at all of them, particularly Marrok's leg. So, I'm here to ask if you would like to join us for Christmas. You don't have to decide today, but you'd be more than welcome, and it would give you a chance to meet them all."

"That would be wonderful; thank you. I don't need to think about it. I'd love to come. May I ask if Peter could come too?"

"Yes, that's no problem; we have plenty of room."

"Thank you. He may not want to come because his grandson, Christopher, and his wife, Clarice, live with him and take care of him, as you know. I want to give him the choice, though."

Yes, please ask him. Selina's looking forward to seeing you; she wants to show you that she's caring for the doll you gave her."

"Aw, bless her; she's adorable. She'll enjoy having some extra friends to play with over Christmas."

"Yes, she will. I must get going because I'm taking Sam to collect his family from the workhouse later. I'll see you soon."

Robert galloped back to Hartford Manor, where he found Annie deep in conversation with Mrs Potts, the housekeeper, and Maisie, the cook.

"Oh, hello, that didn't take you long. Does Aunty Margery want to come for Christmas?"

"Yes, she was delighted to be asked. She may bring Peter Webber with her, but she'll let us know about that. What are you three hatching up now?"

"We're discussing which bedrooms to put our guests in. With his broken leg, it would be best if Marrok sleeps downstairs; then, he can wander about on his crutches. I thought perhaps he could use the study. The bed's still in there from when we were nursing Frank Eastleigh; do you think that would be all right?"

"Yes, I should think so. What about the children?"

"There are two spare rooms along the corridor from the nursery, and they're next to the one that Sam used last night, so I thought we could put them in there. They'll be near us and their grandfather. It's not practical for them to sleep downstairs near their father, but they haven't been living with him recently. If we put the two boys in one room and the two girls in the room next to it, hopefully, they'll be all right. Oh, here's Sam now."

"Good morning, Sam; we're discussing where Marrok and his family will sleep."

The old man smiled, his blue eyes lighting up his wrinkled old face. "Thank you. I'm sure they'll be grateful wherever you put them."

"In that case, Mrs Potts, may I leave all this in your capable hands?"

"Yes, ma'am, I'll get the servants to light the fires and air the rooms; it won't take long to make up the beds. Don't worry; it will all be ready before your visitors arrive."

"Thank you, Mrs Potts; what would I do without you? Now, Maisie, there will be a lot of us to feed over Christmas, but I know you're more than capable of dealing with it all. I'll come to the kitchen later, and we'll talk about how many guests there will be and what dishes you need to prepare. In the meantime, can you bake some pies and cakes so there's something for Sam's son and his family to eat as soon as they arrive? No doubt they'll be hungry."

"Of course, ma'am, it will be a pleasure."

"Good; thank you both for your time."

"Right, Sam, are you ready to collect this family of yours? I've ordered the carriage to be made ready, and I'll ride alongside to leave more room in it."

"Aye, I can't wait."

"Come on, then, let's get going."

CHAPTER 4

HARTFORD/BARNSTAPLE

Dodger Watkins was sitting patiently on the carriage outside the front door of the West wing of the Manor House, waiting for Robert and Sam to emerge. Despite the bitter wind, he raised a cheery smile as the two gentlemen appeared, and another boy led Robert's horse, Prince, from the warmth of the stable. Having seen Sam comfortably seated inside the carriage, Robert mounted his horse and told Dodger to meet him at the workhouse in Barnstaple. Knowing his journey would be quicker on horseback, there was little to be gained from trotting alongside the carriage in such inclement weather. He had a couple of errands in the town and intended to ensure that Marrok was ready when Sam arrived. Sam was a bundle of nerves inside the carriage, and he reprimanded himself, for there was nothing to fear, and he couldn't wait to see his son again and meet his four grandchildren.

Usually, Robert enjoyed a horse ride, but found this one intensely unpleasant. Within minutes of leaving the Manor, the rain came down in torrents, quickly soaking him to the skin despite his warm clothing, and the chilly north wind made matters even more unpleasant. It was with immense relief that he reached Barnstaple and, having dealt with his other business, hammered on the door of the workhouse. He was kept waiting five minutes in the rain, something he was not pleased about, for there was no shelter. However, he was delighted when the carriage drew up and realised that he and Sam could enter together.

When the maid answered the door, she apologised for keeping the two men waiting but advised that they were short-staffed owing to so many being stricken with typhoid, and Robert decided to make their visit as short as possible. He was pleased to find that Mr Jenkins was expecting them, and they were shown into his office, where Marrok and the four children were waiting.

"Good afternoon, gentlemen; I fear you've had an unpleasant journey, particularly you, by the looks of it, sir."

"Good day, Mr Jenkins. Yes, Sam travelled in the carriage, but I came on horseback as I thought the journey back might be a bit cramped. Now, Marrok, won't you introduce us to your family?"

"Yes, of course; this is Jinnie and Eliza, and although they're not identical, they're twins. This is Martin, and this little nipper is Paul. Children say hello to your grandfather, and er, I'm not quite sure what relation you are to them, Mr Fellwood."

"No, that's a tricky question, Marrok; please call me Robert, and the truth is, I'm not sure either. I think I'm probably your first cousin, once removed, so maybe your children are my first cousins, twice removed? I'm not sure, but given the age difference, shall we settle for me being their Uncle Robert?"

"Yes, that sounds like an excellent idea, Robert."

"Then I suggest we get on our way, for the sooner we get back to the Manor House and into the warm, the better it will be. Do you have any luggage to bring with you?"

Marrok shifted uncomfortably, and the beadle stepped in.

"I'm afraid that with Mr Fellwood being unable to work with his broken leg, their few possessions have been sold to contribute to their keep. This institution runs solely on charity, and I can assure you there is never a penny to spare."

"What about coats? Do you at least have coats to put on?"

"No, all we own is what we stand up in. We had to give up all our possessions when we were admitted here, but I'm thankful to Mr Jenkins for taking us in; otherwise, I'm sure we would have all perished. Sadly, my wife, Laura, succumbed to the terrible cholera epidemic sweeping through the workhouse as we speak."

"In that case, bear with me whilst I fetch some blankets from the carriage. Fortunately, my wife, Annie, suspected this might be the case and had the foresight to provide some warm coverings."

"Thank you, sir, that is fortunate."

When Robert returned with the five blankets, he and Sam wrapped them around Marrok and the children, but the beadle once more hindered their departure.

"I'm sorry, but you'll have to leave the crutches behind, Mr Fellwood; we'll need them for another inmate, you see."

With a deep sigh, Marrok thrust the rough wooden crutches towards the man and stood unsteadily on his one sound leg, but Robert put out his hand to stop him.

"We need the crutches, sir. What if I donate to the workhouse coffers? Would that solve the problem?"

"Yes, sir; it would. I'm sorry to appear so mean, but every penny counts in a place like this."

"Will this suffice?" Robert thrust a crisp white five-pound note towards the beadle.

"Yes, indeed, sir, thank you."

They left the gloomy building with Sam carrying Paul snugly wrapped in a warm blanket and Robert carrying Martin. Neither child weighed much, for they were so thin. The two girls pulled their blankets around them as Dodger climbed down and lifted them into the relative warmth of the carriage. Between them, Dodger and Robert lifted Marrok into the carriage, making him as comfortable as possible on one seat with his leg stretched out in front of him. Sam held Paul on his knee, and the other three children squashed into the seat beside him.

As Mr Jenkins watched their departure from his window, he chuckled. He was genuinely pleased for the family, but that was not the main reason for his good humour. He quickly slipped the five-pound note into his back pocket, anticipating his young wife's smile when he told her she could purchase the new dress she coveted. With any luck, the change would cover the cost of a bottle of brandy for himself.

Fortunately, the rain had eased, and Robert galloped off into the distance, keen to get home and change into some dry clothes.

There was a slightly awkward silence in the carriage as Sam and Marrok tried hard to think of something to say. Then Sam remembered something that Annie had thrust into his hands at the last minute, and he reached under the seat and retrieved a tin.

"I was wondering if any of you might be hungry?"

The children stared at him with renewed interest, and the old man beamed at them.

"Ah, I thought that would get your attention, and I'm pleased to tell you that I have no less than six pasties in here, all baked by Maisie, the cook at Hartford Manor. They might still be warm if we're lucky, for they were fresh out of the oven. Would anybody like one?"

Sam lifted the lid, and immediately, a mouth-watering aroma assailed the nostrils of the starving inmates of the carriage. The ice was broken as the children took a pasty each and ate it immediately. Sam then offered one to his son.

"I think they're enjoying them; what about you, son? Have you got room for a pasty?"

Marrok grinned widely at his father, reached for a pasty, and eagerly took a massive bite.

"You have no idea how delicious this tastes … Dad …" He hesitated as he spoke.

"Ah, but I have, lad. I've spent more years of my life being hungry than not, but hopefully, those days are behind all of us now."

Robert made record time on the journey home and, after handing his horse over to a stable lad, thankfully entered the back door as quickly as possible. He was pulling off his wet coat and boots when Annie appeared.

"Oh, Robert, you're so wet; you'd better get changed, or you'll catch your death of cold. Are Sam and his family on the way?"

Yes, they should be here within the hour. I've told Dodger to drive slowly to avoid jarring Marrok's leg. Thank goodness you sent those blankets, love; none of them had coats or any possessions other than the clothes they stood up in. I'm glad Sam has this time alone with them before they get here; it will give them all a chance to get to know one another. It's bound to be a bit awkward to start with."

Robert had a hot bath to thaw his frozen hands and feet and was descending the stairs when he saw the carriage pull up outside. Pleased he had arrived in time to greet the visitors, he opened the door and helped to lift the children and then Marrok out of the carriage. With some difficulty, he and Dodger gently carried Marrok up the steps to the front door, and Sam followed with his crutches.

Annie was waiting at the door with Selina as the children scrambled up the steep steps. Dodger and Robert set Marrok down on his sound leg, and Robert steadied him whilst Dodger retrieved the crutches from Sam.

"Thank you, Dodger; when you've seen to the horses and put the carriage away, get yourself to the kitchen and tell Maisie to cook you something warming; you must be frozen. I know I was."

"Thank you, sir; I'll do that."

Turning his attention to his guests, Robert made the introductions.

"This is my wife, Annie, and our daughter, Selina. And this is Marrok, who needs to sit down as soon as possible. Now, I know this is Paul and Martin, and these young ladies are Jinnie and Eliza, but I'm afraid I've forgotten which is which."

"Hello, Annie, I'm pleased to meet you, and thank you so much for inviting us to stay over Christmas, though we don't wish to impose."

"Hello, Marrok; it's a pleasure, and Selina is so pleased to have some children to play with. Her two brothers are still babies, and she'll enjoy the company. Come in and get warm."

Annie led the way through the hall with Marrok limping on his crutches, followed by Sam and the children. They gazed around them in wonder at the ornate furnishings. A cosy fire burned in a massive fireplace, and Sam led them all to it to warm themselves.

"It's all right, Sam; there's another fire in the sitting room, so we'll go there until lunch. Did you enjoy the pasties?" Maybe you won't have room for any lunch? I know Maisie's pasties are enormous."

"Don't worry about that, ma'am; I'm pretty sure the children will eat anything you put in front of them for a few days at least."

The children sat nervously on the sofa, huddled close to their father. They surveyed their surroundings, taking in the warm carpet on the floor, the heavy midnight-blue velvet curtains, and the oak panelling. In one corner, a giant Christmas tree, some six feet high, was decorated with shiny baubles and candles, and some beautifully wrapped presents were underneath. Selina saw Paul, the youngest child, gazing at the tree.

"Do you want to come and see the tree, Paul? You can touch the shiny balls if you want; they're ever so pretty, and you can see your face in them. Some presents are for me, but I expect Father Christmas will leave you some on Christmas Eve now that you're staying here. You have to be good, though."

"Selina, why don't you let the children have a closer look at the tree and then take them to the nursery to play until you hear the gong for lunch?"

"Yes, come on, I've got lots of toys to play with, though not so many for boys; do you want to come and see? I've got a puppy called Lady, too, so we can play with her in the kitchen later. She's not allowed in here yet because she still has little accidents sometimes."

Four pairs of eyes stared hopefully at Marrok, and he nodded.

"Yes, go on, go and play and enjoy yourselves; I'm not going anywhere."

When the children had left the room, there was a slightly awkward silence, and after a moment or two, Annie rose to her feet.

"Robert, I think we should let Sam and Marrok have a little time to themselves. They've been separated for a long time and must both have questions."

"Yes, of course. Gentlemen, if you will excuse us, we'll leave you to get to know each other again. Lunch will be served in about an hour, so we'll see you then."

When the door had closed, Sam rose to his feet and went to sit next to Marrok.

"They're right, son; you must have many questions to ask me. Let's try to catch up."

"I have to ask, why didn't you take me with you all those years ago or come back for me? Mum would never talk about you; she said you couldn't wait to get away from her and me, that you wanted your freedom and had never been faithful. When I was older, I asked other people in the camp about you and if they knew where you'd gone, but no one would tell me anything."

"I'm afraid your mother was unfaithful, lad, not the other way around. She took little interest in you right from the day you were born. I always looked after you far more than she did; she had no time for you. Then, when you were two, she got pregnant again and miscarried twins at about six months. They were two little girls, and I was heartbroken, but your mother was pleased, and I found it hard to forgive her. I don't think she had a maternal bone in her body. Anyway, after that, we grew farther and farther apart, and she had one affair after another. She kept saying it wouldn't happen again, but it always did."

"That makes sense, for she never showed me any love. I ran away from the gypsies when I was about fifteen, and no one came after me. I expect she was pleased I'd gone, and she could have as many men as she wanted. That's what she did after you left, you know, she sold her body. Perhaps it was the only way for her to make money to support us, but I saw little of it, I can tell you. I had a miserable childhood, always cold and hungry, and I knew I wasn't wanted. A constant stream of men visited the wagon; some stayed for a few weeks until they got fed up with her. Many were cruel to me, and she never intervened if they chose to beat me. I used to dream that one day I'd run away and find you, and we'd live happily ever after, but of course, it never happened."

"I'm so sorry, son. I planned to take you with me, as you know. Do you remember me telling you I would leave in the middle of the night and come and get you? I told you, you must be quiet."

"Yes, I do remember, and I stayed awake as long as I could waiting for you, but you didn't come, and in the morning, you'd gone. Mum said I'd never see you again, and it was good riddance to bad rubbish; I can see her saying it now."

"Aye, I can picture her saying it too, no doubt with a wide smile. I couldn't take you with me because I was lying in a ditch, badly beaten. Many of the gypsies were members of her family, and their leader, Bart, was her father. I don't know how they found out I was planning to leave or why they minded, but they lay in wait for me and gave me such a beating that I almost died. If the local vicar hadn't taken pity on me, I wouldn't be here to tell the tale. It took me weeks to recover, and by then, the gypsies had moved on. I knew where they were headed, and I followed and watched you from a distance, but I knew if they saw me, they would finish the job this time. Finally, I realised it was hopeless and would have to leave you where you were; I'm so sorry, lad. I should have tried harder."

"No, I understand. I've seen the beatings they used to hand out, and I can quite believe they would have killed you. I remember my grandfather, too. He was a nasty piece of work, and he beat me black and blue more than once for little reason. I don't know why they didn't let you take me, though, for no one there wanted me, and things were even worse after you left, and there was no one there to protect me."

"No, I'm sure they didn't want you, but it would have been a matter of pride not to let me take you. I don't know who betrayed me, but they have much to answer for."

CHAPTER 5

HARTFORD

The Lodge House was situated at the entrance of the driveway to Hartford Manor. It had been occupied for many years by Tom Canning, the gatekeeper, but when he passed away, it was decided that a gatekeeper was no longer required, and the house lay empty and forgotten for twenty years or more. Following his marriage to Annie, Robert Fellwood had taken it upon himself to make it fit for his mother-in-law to move in with her family, and it was now Sabina's pride and joy.

However, the lady of the house was not in the best spirits as she shuffled in her armchair, trying to get comfortable.

"I don't know, Liza, this will be my tenth child, and I never remember being this uncomfortable with any of the others. It must be because I'm getting too old for this."

"Not much longer now, my love; only a couple of weeks, and it will all be over. I think you're bigger this time than I've seen you before."

"Yes, and don't I know it. I can't wait to see my feet again."

The older woman laughed. "I don't think it's quite that bad, but as I say, not much longer. Now, you wanted to talk about Christmas Day, I believe? Are you going to the Manor House to spend Christmas with Annie this year?"

"No, I thought I'd leave them some time to themselves. Annie did invite us, but I've agreed we'll all go there on Boxing Day. Willie and Mary are coming here for their Christmas dinner, so having them home for a few hours will be lovely. Willie says Mr Houle has some geese fattened up for Christmas, and I've ordered one for our dinner. We could cook a bit of belly pork with it to make it stretch further; there's not a huge amount of meat on a goose; they're so big-boned. Speaking of poultry, Eveline asked if we'd like to go to Hollyford Farm to help her pluck her chickens, geese, and ducks. I want to go. How about you?"

"Yes, I've always enjoyed helping out on the farms at Christmas; it's a bit of extra money and a friendly atmosphere and a bit of a laugh. Do you think you'll be all right to travel there, though, in your condition?"

"Yes, I think so; it's only a few miles, and I think Annie wants to come with us, so she'll ask Robert if we can use the carriage. I won't be sorry if the jolting makes the baby come sooner. Is that someone at the door?"

"Yes, it's probably Louis from the inn; if you remember, I told you I'd asked him to tea."

"Oh yes, that's right. I'll say hello, and then I'll leave you to it. I know you like to talk to him about the past."

Liza answered the door and held it open for her visitor to enter. The pair had known each other for only a short time but had become close. A few months earlier, Louis Blaquiere had been discovered lying unconscious on the beach at Hartford, and with the incoming tide threatening to cover his body, he was lucky not to have drowned. He was taken to The Red Lion Inn to recover, but when he regained consciousness, he was dismayed to find he had lost his memory. As the young man had no idea where to go or what to do, Betsey and Ned Carter, the owners of the inn, had offered him work for a few weeks. Louis had fitted in well, and one day, when their paths crossed, Liza thought she knew him. It turned out she had once known his parents and recognised Louis from his strong resemblance to his father. Liza was able to tell him that, sadly, his entire family had been wiped out by smallpox, and he had been raised in the workhouse. She took him to see his family's grave, and the memories came flooding back. The old lady surveyed him closely and was pleased to see he had fully recovered from his recent ordeal of being beaten and robbed. He handed her a bunch of holly and some mistletoe.

"Here you are, Liza; I thought perhaps you'd like some of this to decorate the house for Christmas, or maybe you could put some on Isaac's grave. I've just put a bunch of holly on my family's grave."

"Oh, thank you, Louis; come into the sitting room, and we can have a chat. It's warmer there, and I've baked a batch of scones for us to enjoy."

Having exchanged a few pleasantries with their visitor, Sabina went to the kitchen to make a pot of tea for Liza and Louis. Her son, Edward, was chopping up meat to feed three young hedgehogs, now residing in a wooden crate in the dairy. She went to him and put her arm around his shoulders, peering at the tiny hedgehogs he had found beside their dead mother. For some reason, all animals were attracted to Edward. He had been deaf since birth and made little progress at school, but was never happier than when caring for animals. Over the years, Sabina's kitchen had hosted a menagerie of creatures. She hugged him and kissed his cheek, thinking, not for the first time, that one day he would make a splendid farm hand.

Her other son, Stephen, burst through the door with the puppy he had been playing with in the garden. The dog was a bundle of energy and required a lot of exercise, and Sabina's biggest fear was that he would kill the hedgehogs and break Edward's heart. However, the children were careful not to allow the dog into the dairy, and there had been no problems so far.

"Hello, Stephen. Have you tired Piper out? It doesn't look like it."

"He should be tired, Mum; I took him for a long walk, but he has so much energy."

"Yes, I can see. Why don't you feed him, and then perhaps he'll settle down for a nap in his basket?"

By this time, the kettle was boiling, and Sabina made the tea and laid a tray with plates, scones, cream and jam. She carried it into the sitting room, where Liza and Louis were deep in conversation. The young man rose to his feet and took the tray from her.

"Oh, Sabina, I would have done that. You don't need to wait on us. We just got talking."

"I know that, but it's my pleasure. I'll leave you to enjoy your tea."

"Thank you. Now, where were we, Louis? Are all your wounds healed from your beating, and what about your memory? Have you remembered anything else?"

"Yes, I'm fine now, thanks, and I think most of my memory has returned. Could you tell me any more about my parents, please? As far as I know, you're the only person living who knew them, and it's such a comfort to talk to you."

"I don't think there's much more I can tell you. They were honest, god-fearing folk, and I was so sorry when they and your younger brother, Pierre, died of smallpox. Looking back, I wish we could have taken you in and raised you as our son. Sadly, Isaac and I were never blessed with a family, and it would have been better for you than going to the workhouse. Of course, we'd moved away from the hamlet where they lived before they were taken ill, and by the time we found out they'd died, you'd already been taken to the workhouse. Still, never mind, we can make up for lost time now, eh? I'll spread these scones with some cream and jam, and we'll have a little frawsie."

"I've never heard that before. What on earth is a frawsie?"

"Oh, it's a treat; have you never heard that before? I think it's an old Devon saying. Anyway, get that down you; you're still as skinny as a rake. How are you getting on at The Red Lion?"

"I love working there, and Ned and Betsey treat me like one of the family."

"Yes, they're a kind couple, and I know they speak highly of you. Now, did I hear you're courting their granddaughter, Theresa?"

The young man blushed, and Liza laughed.

"There's no need to be embarrassed; you'd be a fine catch for any maid."

"I think it's the other way around, and you know it, but yes, we are seeing a bit of each other. It's early days, and I'm not sure what her father will make of it when he finds out. He'll probably think I'm too old for her, and my prospects aren't rosy enough. Still, once I've saved enough to repay Willie Fisher the money I owe him, I'll be able to get some savings behind me. Betsey and Ned feed me, and I'm comfortable enough sleeping in the loft of their barn, so I save most of my wages."

"You might be surprised. It's true George Carter is not an easy man to please, but he was so worried when Theresa was abducted that I think he's mellowed a bit. You never know; he might be glad to see her happily married to an honest, hard-working man. Anyway, I'd like to invite you here for your Christmas dinner. You can ask Theresa to come if you like?"

"Thank you, Liza; I'd love to. I'll check if it's all right with Betsey and Ned, and if so, I'll ask Theresa; she can only say no."

In the kitchen, Sabina was peeling potatoes and carrots for their tea. She knew Liza would grumble at her when she found out, but she didn't like the old lady doing too much. Liza was in her late seventies, and although fit and healthy, she needed to take life a bit easier. As she continued with her chores, Sabina surveyed her back garden through the kitchen window. The garden was her pride and joy, though, at the moment, there was not much to see. However, along one of the hedges, she spied a swathe of snowdrops about to open, and the winter jasmine was in full bloom. She smiled to herself, thinking that spring was just around the corner. Farther down the garden was her vegetable plot, and she decided to pick some sprouts and curly kale.

She had just put on her coat and boots when her daughter, Helen, and son, Danny, burst through the back door. They were rosy-cheeked from the bitter cold and laughing loudly. Helen, at five, was Sabina's youngest child, born after her father, Tom Carter, succumbed to consumption after suffering for several years. The little girl had straight blond hair and clear blue eyes, and she smiled happily at her mother. Danny was as dark as Helen was fair, with brown curly hair and hazel eyes. The same age as Helen, Danny was a foundling, discovered by Annie in the woods five years earlier and taken in with no hesitation by Sabina. Few knew, including Danny, that he was the son of Eleanor and Charles Fellwood, Robert's parents, who rejected him at birth because of his disabilities. Born with a cleft palate and deformed feet, he had endured two operations in London with remarkable results. His cleft palate was now barely noticeable, and one foot had been straightened. He was waiting to see if a further operation was required on his other foot.

"Slow down, you two; you nearly knocked me over. How were Granny and Grandad?"

"Granny Betsey was fine, but we didn't see Grandad Ned. He's poorly, and Granny has made him stay in bed. We wanted to see him, but he was asleep, and Granny didn't want to wake him."

"Oh dear, I'm sorry to hear that; I must visit them tomorrow. Now, listen, Liza has a friend she's talking to in the sitting room, so don't disturb them. You can play in your room until the tea's ready. It's your favourite, Helen; roast pork."

"Oh, good. Will there be some apple sauce?"

"Yes, I think there are one or two Bramleys left in the store room. Help yourself to a scone and a glass of milk if you're hungry now."

CHAPTER 6

BRAMPFORD SPEKE

The following day, Millie awoke and was surprised to find that dawn was breaking. For the last few nights, she'd been disturbed by her granny or her mother vomiting or needing their chamber pots to be emptied, and she hoped this signalled the start of their recovery. It was a cold morning, and gently pulling the corner of the curtain back, she rubbed the ice from the inside of the window. A wintry scene was revealed; it had snowed during the night, and icicles hung from the thatched rooftops lining the street. Quietly, she pulled her dressing gown around her and slipped her feet into her slippers before tiptoeing into her mother's room, for she didn't want to wake Jonnie if she could help it.

Her mother was in the same position that she had left her, and, as before, she poured a little water into the basin to bathe her forehead. However, sensing something was different, she moved to the window to pull back the curtains. It was impossible to see much in the dim light, but as soon as she touched her mother's face, she knew the poor woman had succumbed to the terrible illness during the night. Her face was cold, and her eyes were eerily half open. Millie pulled back in horror and ran into her granny's room, silently praying that her granny was all right. To her immense relief, she could hear gentle snores coming from the bed, and she tugged at the woman's shoulder.

"Gran, Gran, wake up. Mum's died! Gran, wake up."

Emily opened her eyes and slowly focused on the frightened face before her.

"It's all right, Millie, it's all right. Are you sure?"

The girl nodded, the tears now running down her cheeks.

"Help me out of bed, then, and I'll come and see. Is Jonnie still asleep?"

Millie nodded again and helped her granny to sit up. Pulling back the heavy covers, she lifted the old lady's feet out over the side of the bed and put on her brown slippers.

"My word, it's cold this morning. Pass me my shawl, and we'll see what's what."

The old lady rose unsteadily and swayed as the room spun. Leaning heavily on her granddaughter's shoulders, she slowly shuffled to the next room where she could see that, sadly, Millie was right, and her daughter had passed away during the night. She sat heavily on a chair next to the bed and told Millie to go downstairs and light a candle from the fire so they could see better. Emily wept as she waited for her granddaughter to return.

When Millie returned with the candle, they silently surveyed the motionless body. Then they heard Jonnie moving, and Emily urged Millie to make sure he went straight downstairs.

"Tell him to fetch some logs for the fire and to pull the kettle forward so we can have a cup of tea. Then come back here and help me to bed; I feel so weak I fear I may not make it on my own, and falling over won't help matters. Don't let him come in here, my love. I'm sorry you've had to see your mother like this, but he doesn't need to see her too."

When Millie returned a few minutes later to help her grandmother to bed, she was relieved to find the old lady had pulled the sheet over her mother's face, hiding those haunting eyes. With difficulty, she helped Emily back to bed, firmly closing the door of her mother's bedroom as they left.

"Now, Millie, you'll have to be very brave today. I want you to get yourself and Jonnie some breakfast; is there any food left?"

"Aye, Gran, some bread and butter. How about you? Could you manage some toast?"

"No, not for me, my love. I can't keep it down, and I don't feel hungry; it's more important that you eat. When you've had breakfast, I want you to send Jonnie to me, and I'll tell him about his poor mother. Then I want you to go next door and fetch Agnes; tell her your mother's passed away, and I want to see her. I'm sure she and Ollie will help us to sort things out. Go on now."

Emily sank back against her pillows, feeling exhausted. Fighting the desire to sleep, she wrestled with her dilemma. Convinced she would soon join her daughter, what would happen to her grandchildren? Not a religious woman, she now prayed to the Almighty, begging him to spare her so she might raise the two children for a few more years.

Half an hour later, Agnes and Ollie Dallyn entered the bedroom to find Emily consoling a sobbing Jonnie. Millie was sitting white-faced on the chair beside the bed. The fact that her granny, too, may succumb to typhoid had not escaped her, and she was distraught. Emily dried her grandson's tears and told him and Millie to go outside and get some fresh air. She reached under her pillow and retrieved a leather purse containing a few shillings.

"Here we are; buy eight rashers of bacon at the butcher's, and then a dozen eggs, two loaves of bread, a chunk of cheese and some milk at the grocery shop. Take the can with you to carry the milk home in, and don't forget to wrap up warm; you can buy a gobstopper each if you like. Take your time because I want a chat with Ollie and Agnes. I don't want you back until dinnertime, so play with your friends for a while before you do the shopping. Perhaps you could have a snowball fight; I noticed plenty out there."

When Millie and Jonathan had gone, Emily thanked her neighbours for coming to her aid.

"I'm sorry to ask you both to come here and risk catching this awful disease, but I've no one else to turn to. Do you think you could go to the undertakers and ask if they will collect poor Rosemary's body?" She looked at them knowingly. "We've been expecting Sir Edgar to call for the last couple of weeks or more, but he hasn't been, so I don't know how I can pay them. That clock downstairs is worth a bit, so hopefully, they'll take that and get the job done."

"It's all right, Em; we both had typhoid last week and got over it, so I doubt we'll catch it again. It's a nasty thing, though, and as you know, several in the street have died." Agnes hesitated before she continued. "I'm afraid I have more bad news for you, Em; we heard this morning that Edgar Grantley also died last night. It seems even the rich can't avoid catching typhoid."

Emily gasped as the impact of her neighbour's words hit home. "Oh, my God, what will we do now?"

A little later, Ollie Dallyn returned to tell Emily that Mr Wardle, the undertaker, was so busy he could not collect Rosemary's body for a few days. With so many folk dying of typhoid, he was running out of coffins and space to put the bodies and the vicar was also rushed off his feet.

After her neighbours had left, Emily lay in her bed, wondering what to do for the best. Agnes had insisted on bringing her some broth, telling her she must eat to give her body the strength to fight the illness. However, within minutes, she was racked with violent stomach cramps and, to her embarrassment, had to use the bedpan urgently. Agnes was a true friend, for she treated everything in a matter-of-fact manner and even emptied the bedpan.

After much thought and deliberation, Emily decided the time had come to tell her grandchildren the truth, hard though that would be. Once she had made her decision, her mind felt less troubled, and she fell into a restless sleep until she became aware of Millie and Jonathan's presence in the room. Slowly, she opened her eyes and even managed a faint smile when she saw the huge swelling in their cheeks caused by the gobstoppers they were enjoying.

"Hello, my lovelies; did you get all the shopping?"

"Yes, Gran, can I get you something to eat now?"

"No, it's all right. Agnes brought me a bowl of broth earlier, so I've had something."

"Oh, that's good; perhaps you'll feel better soon."

"Yes, I hope so. Now, I was going to tell you to have your dinner, and then I wanted to talk to you, but I can see your mouths are busy with those enormous gobstoppers, so we'll chat first. Cuddle up together in the chair to keep warm because the time has come to tell you a few home truths. I'm afraid Mr Wardle, the undertaker, can't collect your mother's body for a few days as he's so busy, so keep that door shut and don't go into your mother's bedroom again. The dead never look good, and it's far better for you to remember your dear mother as she was; if she were here, she'd tell you the same. Millie, my dear, could you please let me have a sip of water? My throat is parched."

The girl obliged, and then Emily divulged her story.

"Now, you've always been told that your father died just after you were born, Jonathan, but I'm afraid that's not the truth. Have you never wondered why you have no memory of him, Millie?"

"I've never thought about it, Gran, but I don't remember him at all."

"No, and that's because the man we told you about never existed. When your mother was a girl, she and several of her friends used to stray into the grounds of Grantley Manor to play in the woods. Old Lord Grantley didn't seem to mind, so their presence was ignored. However, the

Grantley family was unaware that Edgar Grantley, the eldest son, used to enjoy playing with them, which would have been frowned upon had the gentry known. When he was ten, Edgar was sent to boarding school, so the problem went away, but when he was seventeen, he returned home to live, and by that time, your mother was a kitchen maid at the Manor. They'd always been attracted to each other, even as youngsters, and before long, their feelings turned to love.

"They knew the relationship had no future, for Edgar had long been promised to Lady Lilliana Thompson. Her family was fabulously wealthy, and the Grantleys were keen to bolster their finances with the enormous marriage dowry offered. Likewise, with the Grantley family able to trace their lineage back to the Domesday Book, it was a desirable match for all concerned. Edgar pleaded with his parents not to force him to marry Lilliana, but to no avail, and when he was twenty-one, the wedding took place.

"I warned your mother time and again that nothing could come of the relationship, but they were besotted with each other and kept hoping they could find some way of being together. When Edgar and Lilliana married, I was relieved, for I thought that would be the end of the matter, and at last, Rosemary would find another suitor, but 'twas not the case. They continued to meet in secret until, eventually, their luck ran out, and Rosemary found herself expecting you, Millie. I was worried sick and didn't know what would happen. Around the same time, your grandad, Lenny, had an accident at work and died.

"As you know, he worked on the Grantley estate as a labourer, and this cottage came with his job. When he was killed, I thought Rosemary and I would be thrown out to make room for the next worker, but it never happened. Folk were intrigued to know why we were allowed to stay and who the father of her baby was, but Rosemary always refused to say, though most people guessed the truth."

"So, what happened? Because we're still living here."

"Yes, to give Sir Edgar his due, he took full responsibility for his actions. He came here and admitted he was the father of Rosemary's baby and that we could continue to live here for as long as we liked. Naturally, his wife was curious why we were allowed to stay in the cottage. She'd always had her suspicions that he had a mistress, and he told her the truth and said she'd have to live with it, for he would never give Rosemary up. Naturally, Lilliana was furious, particularly when she found out he'd fathered Rosemary's baby, for theirs was a childless marriage, but there was nothing she could do about it. I must confess I felt sorry for the woman."

"I know Sir Edgar calls here occasionally, so why didn't he tell us he's our father?"

"He had enough respect for his wife to be discreet, and he and your mother were well-liked enough in this village that folk were willing to turn a blind eye. It's not as if we live in London or even Exeter. Out here in the countryside, people get on with their own business and are usually of the opinion to live and let live. So, the relationship continued, and although they tried to avoid any more pregnancies, eventually, you were born, Jonathan. You're named after Sir Jonathan Grantley, Sir Edgar's late father, though you'll never be recognised as a Grantley.

"Now, I'm telling you this because Agnes and Ollie from next door have heard that Sir Edgar died last night, too. Typhoid is no respecter of persons, it seems, and it will take the rich as well as the poor. So, sadly, you not only lost your dear mother yesterday but your father, too, though you didn't know it. This is terrible news for us, for Sir Edgar has provided us with enough money to live on for years and has allowed us to live here rent-free. The money your mother earned cleaning would never have been enough for us to survive.

"I'm afraid Lilliana will be ruthless and wreak revenge on this family at the first opportunity. I can even understand it. Your mother was the cause of the failure of her marriage, and you two are living proof of her husband's continued affair. It doesn't help that even before she knew of her husband's infidelity, their marriage was childless, and I've heard she was desperate to have a family. I presume that, since she found out about your mother, she and her husband have lived separate lives. Anyway, I suspect that in the next day or two, we'll be evicted from this cottage, and unfortunately, apart from a few shillings, we have no money to rent anywhere else. Sir Edgar was generous, but we didn't need much and were never greedy; it would have been foolish to flaunt our money and attract attention. Rosemary was puzzled why she hadn't seen him for over a month, and now we know why: the poor man was ill himself."

"Oh, Gran, what are we going to do?"

"You won't like this, and neither do I, but you two must run away."

"No, you're not strong enough to go anywhere, Gran; it's bitter outside, and you can barely walk."

"I'm not coming with you, my dears; I shall stay here and face the music. Shh, now, hear me out. I know this is hard, but I've given it much thought and think it's the only solution. When Lilliana sends the bailiffs, and send them she will, I'll have to leave here, though I hope she'll grant me a few days to gain a bit more strength. You know little about my past, but it was troubled, and I'm used to facing hardship.

"Now, I'm exhausted with all this talking, so I'd like you to get yourselves some dinner and leave me to snooze. Millie, fry all the bacon and two eggs and be careful not to burn yourself. Put the eggs on some thick slices of bread and have two rashers of bacon each, and eat it all up. While that's cooking, put on a pan of water and boil the rest of the eggs for ten minutes, then throw that water away and leave the eggs in cold water. That will make it easier to remove the shells. After that, cut more bread and butter and make sandwiches with the rest of the bacon. Make some thick jam sandwiches as well; there's still some gooseberry jam left in the pantry. Wrap the sandwiches in a clean cloth and leave them ready for later. You can take the hard-boiled eggs and shell them as you need them. Go on now; I'm tired, so leave me in peace for an hour, and I'll tell you the rest of the story later."

Millie did as her granny told her, and although she and Jonathan were upset about their mother and terrified at the thought of leaving the only home they had ever known, they were hungry and ate every morsel of the delicious bacon and fried eggs. When they had finished, Millie washed the dishes and made Jonnie dry them, and then they tiptoed upstairs to see if their granny was awake.

Emily heard their footsteps on the stairs and the familiar creak of the loose floorboard on the landing, and she tried to rouse herself, wishing she could find some energy from somewhere. Seeing them peer around the door, she beckoned them in.

"Did you enjoy your dinner?"

"Aye, it was lovely, but I wish you'd have some; will you try to eat a bacon sandwich?"

"No, I'm still full from the broth Agnes made me, thank you. Now, sit in the chair and snuggle back under your blanket again. I need to finish my story.

"My father died when I was a little girl, and he left my mother, Greta, with me to support and no money, so we ended up in the workhouse. She'd been ill for a long time, and within a year, she passed away, leaving me all alone in the world.

"I was raised in the workhouse, and it was a miserable existence. When I was twelve, I was sent into service on the Grantley estate as a scullery maid, and there I met your grandfather, Lenny, and married him ten years later. He worked as a farm labourer, and that's how we got this cottage. Before she died, Greta, my mother, told me that my father came from a village called Hartford, near Barnstaple in North Devon and had a family there. She was an orphan, so she had no other kin that she knew of. Anyway, she told me all this, in case I might want to find my relatives one day. I know little more than that, but the best thing now is for you two to make your way to Hartford, find these relatives, and see if they will take you in. You're strong and healthy, so maybe they can put you to work."

"But Gran, they won't even know us, and it's so long ago that our great-grandfather left. You're always saying how times are hard; they're hardly going to be pleased to see us, are they?"

"No, it's a long shot, but if it doesn't work out, you'll have to try to earn enough to get by as best you can. I agree; it's a desperate plan, but I know how bitter Lilliana Grantley is. A few years ago, she came across me picking blackberries and beat me black and blue with her riding crop. I didn't tell Rosemary what had happened because I didn't want her to tell Sir Edgar. I pretended an old tramp had robbed me. Lilliana is a scorned woman, and I reckon she'll make up all manner of charges against the pair of you. Her father's a magistrate and a powerful man, and it would be easy for her to get you sent to jail. No, at least this way, you'll have your freedom and stand a chance."

"What about you, though? Can't you come with us? We don't know the way to Barnstaple; it would make more sense for you to come with us."

"It's no good, Millie; I'm not strong enough. I lived in the workhouse for many years when I was young and hungry, and it will be far easier to endure now that I'm old and with a poor appetite. I don't want you to worry about me, for I can take care of myself; I've always had to. I'd much rather go there and send you on your way than let that evil woman take her spite out on you. I'm glad your mother didn't know her beloved Edgar was ill, and I'd like to think that after all these difficult years of snatching a few odd moments together, perhaps they're finally reunited.

"What I want you to do later is to put on as many of your clothes as you can and take a few spare ones with you.

My old workbag is on the bottom shelf of the larder, so fill that with as much food as you can carry. There's also a hessian sack there, so put your Sunday clothes in that. Take a warm blanket from your bed, and you can wrap it around your shoulders to save carrying it."

"We must leave some food for you, Gran."

"No, I can't eat at the moment, and tomorrow I'm going to ask Ollie to take me to the workhouse in Exeter, so you take it; you'll need it more than me. I want you to leave when it gets dark and fewer folk are around. I can give you directions to the next couple of villages, and then you'll have to ask the way. Follow the track from the village towards Cowley Bridge and then keep heading north. I think the same road will take you to Barnstaple, and hopefully, you might get a ride on a cart. Now, Jonnie, go downstairs to the dresser and open the drawer on the right. You'll find an old pipe inside, and I want you to bring it to me."

Jonathan ran off and soon returned with the pipe. He peered inside, where a few tobacco flakes still clung to the bowl.

"Why do you want this, Gran?"

"This is the only thing my mother kept that belonged to my father. He used to smoke a pipe, and that's one of my few memories of him. Anyway, I'm hoping he brought the pipe with him when he ran away from his family. See, it has his initials carved there on the bowl. I hope that if you show this pipe to folk, they may remember him, and you may find your long-lost relatives."

Even as she spoke the words to her two round-eyed grandchildren, Emily knew the chances of them finding their distant relatives were ridiculously slim, and for them to be willing to take on two extra mouths to feed in these challenging times, even less likely. However, she was determined to send them away and out of the reach of an understandably bitter and twisted woman who would stop at nothing to wreak vengeance on her husband's two bastards.

CHAPTER 7

BRAMPFORD SPEKE

The church clock had just struck ten o'clock, and Emily was hunched in front of the fire with a blanket wrapped around her shoulders as she supervised her two grandchildren, preparing for their long journey. Although she was putting on a brave face, she felt terribly ill and was keen for them to leave as soon as possible. She feared she might soon be joining her daughter and had no wish for the two children to find she had passed away come morning.

"Now, have you put on as many clothes as possible?" The two children nodded. "Good. Millie, have you cut the bread into sandwiches?"

"Yes, I've packed all the food like you said, but I'd rather leave some for you. You need to eat to get your strength back, and perhaps you could follow us when you feel better?"

"Yes, I'll try to, my dear, as soon as I can, but don't worry about me. Agnes and Ollie will let me have a little to eat, and I'm going to the workhouse in a day or two. I don't intend to let Lilliana Grantley have the pleasure of throwing me out of my home. I'll recuperate for a few weeks in the workhouse and then come and find you. Don't worry; this is not goodbye. We'll all be together again soon, but it's safer for you to leave now."

Millie and Jonathan felt happier knowing their granny would be following them, and Millie lifted the sack she had packed with their clothes and handed the workbag to Jonathan.

"Here you are, Jonnie. You carry this bag. It's the lighter of the two and will become less heavy as we eat the food. Now, I'll wrap this blanket around your shoulders as it's easier than carrying it. Give Granny a hug first."

Jonnie was drawn into Emily's embrace, and she hugged him tightly, concentrating hard on hiding her distress from the child.

"Now, Jonnie, you're the man of the family, and I expect you to behave yourself and look after your sister, all right?" The boy nodded as she tightened the blanket around his neck and fastened it with a pin. "Good, now, you do as she tells you, for she has a wise head on her shoulders, and I know she'll take care of you." She kissed him on the cheek and pushed him from her. "Come here then, lass; it's your turn."

Millie put her arms around the old lady and hugged her tightly. Tears ran down her cheeks, and Emily gently brushed them away with her thumbs.

"Now then, lass, that's enough; you're off on an important mission, and it's up to you to care for your brother and find him somewhere safe to live. Promise me you'll do that."

"I will, Gran; you can rely on me. I'll take care of Jonnie."

"I know you will, and like I say, as soon as I feel strong enough, I'll catch you up. Now, that's right, put your blanket around your shoulders, for you'll be glad of it; 'tis bitterly cold outside. Here's another pin to hold it on. Few folk will be around on a cold night like this, so hopefully, no one will see you leave. Head for the church and take the path towards the inn. It might be a bit creepy, but you'll have to get used to that. If you hear anyone, hide in the bushes until they pass. From the inn, follow the lane to Cowley Bridge, walk through Half Moon village, and then on to Newton St Cyres. If you walk fast, you'll keep warm, and you should be there in a couple of hours, for 'tis only about five miles or so. You've been there once before when we visited my friend, Hubert March. Do you remember, Millie?"

"Yes, I think so; was it where we saw the horses in the field, and the man let me feed a baby lamb?"

"Yes, that's right. I've known Hubert all my life. We were raised in the workhouse together as children, and I've been friends with him ever since. It must be a couple of years since I last saw him and his wife, but as far as I know, they're still there at Hilldale Farm, and I'm sure they'll make you welcome. If we had more time, I'd let them know you're coming, but I'm confident they'll let you stay the night, even if it's in the barn. Go on, now, before we all start to bawl."

Forcing a bright smile onto her face, Emily waved goodbye through the window and then struggled up the stairs to bed. On the landing, she hesitated outside the door to the room where the body of her only daughter still lay. However, she did not enter the room but gently placed her palm on the door and begged her daughter's forgiveness for sending her two children out into the night on a dangerous journey. "I beg God and you to forgive me, lass, but I don't know what else to do."

Millie and Jonathan crept through the village. There was already a hard frost, and icicles hung from the thatched roofs, sparkling eerily in the weak moonlight. They were soon at the lych gate leading to the church, and Millie opened it and urged Jonnie through. For the benefit of her younger brother, the girl displayed confidence, but in truth, she, too, was frightened. As they wandered through the deserted tombstones, an owl suddenly screeched loudly, sending them both into a panic. Millie chuckled as they clutched each other.

"Come on; it's only the old owl we hear screeching every night. He won't hurt us."

Taking her brother's arm, they left the churchyard, walking past two ancient Scots pine trees and down a narrow path lined with yew trees and holly bushes, which brought them to The Agricultural Inn. They saw lights inside the inn and realised some customers were still enjoying an ale or two. Millie put her finger to her lips to ensure Jonnie knew to be quiet as they crept past without anyone seeing them.

Fortunately, their father, Sir Edgar Grantley, had provided his beloved Rosemary with sufficient money to ensure she and her family were well-dressed. Unable to acknowledge his offspring as his own, he had done all he could to ensure their well-being and comfort. Thus, they were lucky to be wearing thick coats and boots. Nevertheless, their hands and feet were quickly frozen, and their bags seemed heavier with every step. Their granny's directions were accurate, and within three hours, they saw the name of Hilldale Farm painted on a weathered sign. Millie vaguely remembered the lane to the old farmhouse.

Not knowing the time but thinking it must be after midnight, they wondered whether they should knock on the front door. Emily had offered no advice on this, and Millie thought the farmer and his wife would not be best pleased to be disturbed in the middle of the night. However, quietly opening a gate and picking their way across the farmyard, they noticed a lantern flickering in the barn.

"Look, Jonnie, I think someone's still up."

Cautiously, they pulled the large barn door open, and as it squeaked in protest, a farmer peered over his shoulder at them. Despite the cold, the sweat stood out on his brow as he tried to assist a cow with a difficult birth. Millie and Jonathan approached nervously and thankfully lowered their bags to the ground.

"Hello, Mr March; do you remember me? I'm Millie Gibbs, and this is my brother, Jonathan. I think you know my granny, Emily?"

The man ceased his struggles and dropped his arms to his sides, glad to rest them for a moment. He peered closely at the two visitors.

"Aye, I know your granny, but what are you doing here at this time of night?"

"It's a long story, Mr March, but our family's in trouble, and we're on our way to North Devon. Granny thought you might let us sleep in your barn for a few hours."

"Did she now? Well, I'm afraid she was wrong about that."

Millie and Jonathan lowered their eyes and picked up their luggage.

"Oh, I'm sorry to have bothered you then, sir, and we'll be on our way. I hope the cow is all right."

"Nay, lass, don't be silly. I don't mean you can't stay. What I mean is I'm not letting you stay out here in the cold barn. I'm fond of your granny, so you'll be sleeping in the farmhouse in the warm just as soon as I've helped this calf into the world. This would happen tonight of all nights. My son and daughter-in-law are visiting her folks in Plymouth for a few days, and the cow wasn't due to calf until next week."

"Thank you, Mr March; is there anything we can do to help?"

"Aye, go into the farmhouse and fetch the soap by the sink. Take that bucket with you, and pour the hot water from the kettle into it. Be careful not to burn yourself, mind. I'll have to examine this cow and find out what the problem is. Now, you lad, what's your name?"

"It's Jonathan, sir, but most people call me Jonnie."

"Right, Jonnie, you go with your sister, and in the dairy that's just off the kitchen, there's a big cupboard. Have a rummage around in there and see if you can find a thin piece of rope. I think it's on the bottom shelf. Perhaps between us, we'll save this calf. Take that lantern with you."

Millie lifted the lantern, and they hurried to the farmhouse. Pushing the back door open, they found themselves in a large kitchen. With only one light, they had to work together, so Millie swung the lantern around, and they located the door to the dairy. As the farmer had described, they found a long piece of rope on the bottom shelf. Back in the kitchen, they collected the soap, and using a cloth to hold the hot handle, Millie carefully poured water from the kettle into the bucket. She put the kettle by the sink, knowing she must not put it back on the stove empty. She handed the lantern to her brother.

"Here, Jonnie, you carry the lantern; this bucket's heavy and I don't want to spill any water."

The farmer smiled as the two youngsters returned to the barn with the items he had requested.

"Thank you; have you ever seen an animal born before?" They both shook their heads. "Well, you're going to now, so I hope you're not too squeamish. I think this calf's lying wrong, and that's why the cow's having so much trouble. I need to help things along a bit."

The youngsters watched, wide-eyed, as the old man wet his hands and soaped them. He soaped up his right forearm, splashed some water onto the cow, and soaped her, too. They were shocked as he inserted his hand and arm into her vagina, wincing as she endured a strong contraction and tried to push. He grunted as he tried to ascertain how the calf was lying.

"Ah, yes, I think I know what the problem is. One of the front feet is lying wrong, but I think I can move it."

He soaped his arm and the cow again and repeated the process, this time clutching the thin rope in his fingers. Some minutes passed, and they could see the farmer was tiring. However, with a broad smile, he eventually withdrew his arm, the rope clutched between his fingers.

"Right, I've looped the rope around that foot, so with any luck, we can pull the calf into the right position. Young man, do you think you can help me to pull on this rope?"

The boy nodded, and together, they pulled hard on the rope. The cow cried out in anguish as she pushed, and they pulled, and eventually, they were rewarded with the sight of two tiny hooved feet. The farmer heaved a sigh of relief.

"Ah, that's good; the calf's in the right position to be born now. We'll keep a hold on this rope, Jonnie, and hopefully, nature will take its course."

The children were fascinated as, repeatedly, the cow pushed as contractions seized her body. Each time she pushed, the feet and legs appeared, and eventually, with one almighty effort, the calf was born. Hubert March caught the animal and lowered it gently to the ground. He cleared its mouth and nose of mucus and massaged its body with straw. After a moment or two, it gave its first cry and struggled shakily to its feet. Hubert beamed jubilantly.

"There, what do you think about that, then? Come on, Mum, say hello to your baby."

The cow nuzzled her offspring, and within minutes, the newborn calf was seeking her udder and enjoying its first meal.

"There, we can leave them to it now; thank you so much for your help. Now, come with me, and let's get into the warm and have a hot drink; then, you can tell me how you came to be here in the middle of the night."

CHAPTER 8

NEWTON ST CYRES

Having watched the newborn calf suckle for a few moments, Hubert picked up the lantern and led the way into the farmhouse, where he lit a couple of candles and placed a large pot on the stove.

"There, that's better; we can see what we're doing now. This rabbit stew was left over from dinner time, and I reckon a bowl of that will warm our insides and help us to get off to sleep; are you hungry?"

"Yes, sir, I'm always hungry and cold, too."

"Aye, I bet you are, lad. I was always hungry at your age. Come over here by the fire and warm yourself; you too, my dear."

The old man opened the stove door, and Millie and Jonathan held their frozen fingers to the fire blazing merrily. Whilst Hubert busied himself, refilling the kettle from a bucket and cutting shives of bread, they took the opportunity to survey their surroundings.

Along one wall of the comfortable room was a large oak dresser, sturdily built and blackened with age. Stacked in the cupboards were plates and mugs, and Hubert reached into one of the drawers to find some spoons. The floor was laid with flagstones, uneven and rough, but scrubbed clean and covered with several rag mats. A long kitchen table was in the centre of the room, and on each side were two benches. Bright blue curtains at the window excluded the night outside and made the room feel cosy. After a few minutes, Hubert ladled stew into each of the three bowls and carried them to the table.

"There, that didn't take long. Come and eat your supper, and tell me what brings you here in the middle of the night."

So, they told Hubert their sad tale of how their mother had died of typhoid and how their granny was sick.

"Granny wanted us to leave because she said Sir Edgar Grantley was our father, and his wife is angry about it. She was worried Lady Grantley might seek revenge; now he's also died of typhoid."

"Oh, dear, I see. Yes, I knew he was your father, though I suggest you keep that information to yourselves. It's not something you want widely known. Your granny must have been desperate to send you out into the night alone. Where are you heading?"

"Gran said her father used to come from Hartford and that he still has family there. She wants us to find our relatives to see if they will take us in. She'll follow us as soon as she's better, so we can all be together again and away from Lady Grantley. Mr March, where is your family? Gran said you have a wife, and your son lives with you. I remember Mrs March from when we once visited with Gran, but it was a long time ago."

A sad expression flitted across the old man's wrinkled face. "Yes, my dear wife, Mary, and I were happily married for over fifty years, but sadly, she passed away last year. My son, Vivian, his wife, Angela, and my four grandchildren, Gertie, Albert, Rosie, and Walter, are away for a few days visiting Angela's family in Plymouth, but they'll be back before Christmas. I assured them I could manage on my own for a few days, but to be honest, I was struggling a bit.

I certainly didn't expect this cow to have such a difficult time birthing her calf. Still, thanks to you, everything is all right. Now, have you had enough to eat? Good; in that case, I'll fill a couple of hot water bottles to keep you warm, and you can sleep in Gertie and Rosie's beds; they won't mind."

Hubert filled the two stone bottles from the large kettle and wrapped them in cloth covers. He led his unexpected visitors upstairs to a room with two single beds and told them to make themselves comfortable. Warm and cosy at last, Millie smiled at the kindly man.

"Thank you so much for letting us sleep here; we were dreading sleeping outside in the cold."

"You're welcome, my dear; now you two get some rest, and I'll see you in the morning. I'm only in the next room if you want anything. Goodnight."

Millie wished she could let her granny know they were safely tucked up in a warm bed, but it didn't worry her for long, for she was fast asleep within minutes.

In the morning, the smell of bacon frying awoke Jonathan, and he gazed across the room to where his sister was stirring.

"Oh, Millie, can you smell that delicious smell?"

"Yes, I can, but hurry up and get your clothes on; we'd better get on our way and out from under Mr March's feet. We mustn't take advantage of his generosity. Granny said we mustn't outstay our welcome. Bring your bag."

They trooped down the stairs and into the kitchen, where they had eaten the night before.

Hearing their footsteps on the creaky old stairs, Hubert turned from the stove and regarded them.

"Good morning. Did you sleep well?"

"Oh, yes, thank you. I've brought the hot water bottles down for you, and we'll be on our way; thank you so much for your kindness."

"Don't be silly; sit yourselves down at the table and have some breakfast. I want to ask you something."

Deftly, Hubert cut three thick slices of bread and put them onto large plates. He placed two rashers of bacon and two sausages onto each plate and returned to the stove to fry three eggs, which he then deposited onto the bread.

"There, eat up, and then we'll have a chat. There's some milk there for you, all fresh from the cow this morning."

"Have you milked the cows already?"

"Aye, of course, I have; 'tis nearly nine o'clock; I thought you two were going to sleep until dinner time. I reckoned the smell of the bacon frying might do the trick, though."

There was little conversation for the next ten minutes as all three enjoyed their breakfast, none leaving a single morsel on their plates.

"Thank you so much, Mr March; that will set us up nicely for the day. We need to head for the next village and see if we can find some work for a few days. Can you tell us what it's called and point us in the right direction?"

"If you carry on along the road you were on yesterday, in a couple of miles, you'll come to the town of Crediton, and about four miles farther on from that is the village of Copplestone, but I'd like to suggest that you stay here for a couple of days. I've always been fond of your granny, and I'd like to help you. If Lady Grantley is on the lookout for the pair of you, it might be best to lie low for a couple of days. I must confess that I have my reasons for wanting you to stay. For one thing, I could do with a bit of help around the place until my family return, and I don't mind admitting it; I don't like being here on my own, and I'd enjoy your company. The place is usually full of chatter and laughter, and I miss it. Would you consider staying here for a few days to please me?"

Jonathan stared hopefully at his sister, and she nodded her head.

"Yes, please; that's a wonderful idea, and it makes sense. If Lady Grantley calls on Gran, she'll point her in the wrong direction towards Somerset, but you never know; she might be crafty enough to search in both directions. We'd love to stay until your family returns, so tell us what you want us to do; we're grateful that you've fed us and given us a warm bed."

"Excellent, I can't afford to pay you, but I can keep you fed and warm. In that case, Millie, can I leave you to make the beds, wash the dishes, and tidy the kitchen? My daughter-in-law likes things clean and tidy and won't want to come home to a mess. Mind you, I'm of the same opinion because Mary always kept the house spick and span, and she'll haunt me if I don't keep to her high standards."

"It will be a pleasure. You don't need to pay us; we're grateful if you can feed us and let us stay here for a few days. We don't have much money, so Gran said to find a few jobs along the way so that we could buy food. I'm used to doing chores around the house, and while Gran and Mum have been ill, I've had to see to everything."

"What about me, Mr March? What do you want me to do?"

"I thought you could help me feed the animals, Jonnie. I must carry hay to the cows and horses and chop some mangolds for the pigs. Then there are the chickens and ducks to feed. There aren't so many now because most of them have been slaughtered and sent to the market for Christmas. Have you had enough to eat?"

"Yes, thank you."

"Right, get your coat on then, lad. Millie, we'll be back at lunchtime. Now, you'll find a ham, some cheese, and another loaf of bread in the larder. There are some jars of pickles and, in a red tin, a new fruit cake Angela baked before she left. It will save me a job if you can lay the table and get everything ready."

Hubert and Jonathan pulled on their coats and left the warm kitchen. It was cold outside, and the first job Jonnie was tasked with was to break the ice on the water troughs to allow the cows to drink. He enjoyed smashing the thick ice with a hammer and then scooping out the large shards. He watched as Hubert opened the shippen door and let the cows into the yard to drink their fill.

"Right, Jonnie, our next job is to clean the shippens while the cows are outside. They always make a mess overnight, and I like to clean it up as soon as possible. Bring that wheelbarrow over here, and we'll shovel the dung into it and take it to the dung heap."

Jonnie's hands, frozen from breaking the ice, were soon glowing as he worked hard shovelling the dung into the wheelbarrow. When it was full, Hubert wheeled it to the bottom of the yard, where there was a large pile of manure. He tipped the barrow up, and the dung fell out, steaming in the cold air. They repeated this process several times until the shippens were clean. Next, they spread clean straw and filled the mangers with chopped mangolds and hay. Then, they opened the door, and the cows returned to eat their fill.

"Don't the cows go into the fields during the day?"

"They do when the weather's warmer and sleep outside too, but now, in December, while it's so cold, they prefer to be in the warm. If we get a mild day, I let them out for a few hours, but they're content inside. It's much easier for us farmers when they can go out during the summer, for we don't have to keep cleaning the shippens. Now, we'll feed the pigs with slops and a few mangolds. Eat anything; pigs will."

Fascinated, Jonnie leaned over the pigsty wall as Hubert poured the food into the trough. The pigs were eager to eat, and squealing loudly, they jostled each other for the best position.

"I'll just take a closer look at that sow; I think she's cut herself on something, or maybe one of the other pigs nipped her."

Hubert cocked his leg over the pigsty wall and examined the wound on the pig's shoulder while she was busy eating.

"Can I come in and scratch their backs?"

"Aye, come on. Pigs can give you a nasty bite, and some can be vicious, but these are too busy eating to bother you. I like pigs, so I treat them kindly, and they don't give me much trouble. Come through the gate; the wall's too high for you."

Jonnie entered the pigsty and scratched the backs of a couple of the pigs. They completely ignored him, as they were too busy ensuring they got their fair share of the food. At last, satisfied that the cut on the sow's shoulder was nothing to worry about, Jonnie and Hubert moved on to muck out the stables and groom the two horses.

In the farmhouse, Millie was enjoying herself. She poured water from the kettle into the sink and washed the dishes, leaving them to dry on the draining board whilst she went to the well outside and drew a bucket of water to refill the kettle. The girl wondered if the well would be frozen, but thankfully, the bucket smashed through the ice, and she puffed and panted as she turned the handle to raise it to the top. With some difficulty, she heaved the bucket over the side of the well, slopping a little over her leg, and then struggled back to the house, trying not to spill any.

When the dishes were wiped and put away, she swept the kitchen floor and cleaned the table. Satisfied that the room was all in order, she mounted the stairs and made the three beds. Having had no time to observe the room she had slept in the night before, she now investigated more closely. In one corner were a few toys: a spinning top, a skipping rope, and a couple of dolls. On the window ledge was a pack of cards, and Millie wondered if Mr March would let her and Jonnie play a game later.

When Hubert and Jonnie came in for their dinner, the table was laid, and the kettle was boiling. Hubert beamed at them both.

"Thank you for your help this morning. You've both worked hard, and I'm grateful. Now, let's eat this delicious lunch that Millie has prepared for us."

CHAPTER 9

HARTFORD

Annie arose early the following day and hurried to the nursery to feed the twins. She paused to peer into Selina's bedroom, and, for once, the little girl was still fast asleep. Annie tiptoed away quietly and gently opened the door of the room in which Jinnie and Eliza were sleeping. She was pleased to see that they had not yet awoken. Paul and Martin were in the next room, and the sound of sobbing reached her ears before she even opened the door. Annie found three-year-old Paul in tears and Martin trying to comfort him.

"Hey, good morning, boys; what's the matter, Paul? Do you feel poorly?"

The toddler shook his head, clung to his brother, and wouldn't meet Annie's eyes. She looked at Martin, wondering why the boy was so distraught.

"What's wrong with Paul? Has he had a bad dream?"

"No, ma'am, but I'm afraid he's wet the bed. I'm so sorry. I'll help him take the sheets off and wash them; we don't want to be any trouble."

"Oh, don't worry about that; Selina still has an accident now and then. It happens, and I expect you were tired last night. Thank you, Martin, but there's no need for that; I'll ring for a servant, and they'll change the bed and put fresh sheets. It's not a problem."

The younger boy lifted his face and stared anxiously at Annie in bewilderment. The tears were still flowing down his cheeks, and his nose was running; his frail body shook with sobs.

"Are you going to beat me?"

Annie was shocked.

"Goodness me, no! Of course, I won't beat you; why would I do that? You didn't wet the bed on purpose, did you?"

"No, ma'am; I didn't know it was wet until I woke up."

"No need to worry then. Do you ever have little accidents like this, Martin?"

"No, ma'am, luckily I don't, but you see, if this happened in the workhouse, Paul would get a hiding, so he didn't tell anyone if he could help it; he'd just sleep in the same wet bed the next night."

"Now, we need to get some things straight here, boys. Firstly, you can't keep calling me ma'am; could you call me Aunty Annie?" The two boys nodded. "Good; the other thing is that from now on, if you should wet the bed, Paul, no one here will beat you, and the servants will change your bed if they need to. What I suggest, though, is that just before I go to bed every night, I'll lift you out of your bed to have a wee, and then, hopefully, we might have a dry bed in the morning. Would that be all right with you? I usually do the same for Selina, and it makes a big difference. Shall we give it a try?" The boy nodded his head. "Good, now, I'll find you a dry nightshirt and then take you both to the kitchen, where I'm pretty sure Mrs Potts will find you something to eat and a drink of milk."

Annie quickly lifted the wet garment over the child's head and popped on a dry nightshirt. He suddenly grinned at her, and his broad smile and bright blue eyes brought tears to her eyes. Instinctively, she drew him to her and hugged him tightly, then wondered if she had gone too far. However, he relaxed into her embrace, and after a few moments, she pulled back to arm's length.

"That was a lovely cuddle; I'd like a few more of them, please. How about you, Martin? Are you too big for a hug?"

"No, ma'am; sorry, I mean, Aunty Annie. Our mum used to cuddle us all the time, Dad, too."

"Come here then because I love a cuddle myself, and as my mum used to say, at least they don't cost anything."

Annie escorted the two boys to the kitchen, where Maisie was already busily kneading some dough, and Mrs Potts was pouring boiling water into a large teapot. The women regarded the two nervous youngsters.

"Whom do we have here, then?"

"This is Paul, and this is Martin, and they're staying with us until their daddy is better. They're Sam's grandchildren, and I think they might like some breakfast; do you think you can help them with that, ladies?"

"Aye, we can certainly do that; come on, lads, sit up to the table, and we'll see what we can find. Maisie, you carry on with what you're doing; this sort of job is right up my street."

"This is Mrs Potts, and this is Maisie, and there's nothing they like better than spoiling boys like you, so I think you'll soon be firm friends with them. Now, will you be all right here for a while? I must feed my twin boys, for they're making quite a racket."

The two boys nodded happily, and Annie hurried up the stairs to the nursery from where loud wails could be heard. On the landing, she found a slightly bewildered Jinnie and Eliza, and Selina tugging them both by the hand.

"Good morning; did you sleep well?"

The two girls nodded.

"That's good; now, Selina, I've taken Paul and Martin to the kitchen, so if you show Jinnie and Eliza the way, you can all have breakfast there this morning. When you've finished eating, get dressed, and then play in the nursery, and I'll come and find you later when I've fed my noisy babies."

After feeding and changing the twins, Annie left them in Naomi's care whilst she went and had her breakfast. Robert, Marrok, and Sam were in the dining room, and she helped herself to some scrambled eggs and bacon from the sideboard and went to sit next to Robert.

"How are you this morning, Marrok? Did you sleep all right?"

"Yes, thank you; what a comfortable bed. I had a better night's sleep than I've had for a long time."

"I'm pleased to hear it, and just in case you're concerned, the children are all awake and in the kitchen with Selina, eating their breakfast. They would normally have it here with us or sometimes in the nursery, but I wanted to introduce them all to Mrs Potts, our housekeeper, and Maisie, our cook. I can tell you now; they're being spoilt as we speak."

"That's so true. Mrs Potts has spoilt me all my life."

"She still does, Robert. I know she has a soft spot for you."

"Were the children all right through the night?"

"Yes, they slept well, though Paul was upset because he had wet the bed, something he was punished for in the workhouse, I understand. I've reassured him that it isn't a problem and nothing to worry about. When I retire tonight, I'll lift him out for a wee, like I do, Selina. It makes all the difference, I find. I hope you don't mind?"

"No, of course not; thank you for taking care of them."

"So, what are you gentlemen going to do today?

"I'm going to see Arthur Webber at the Lodge House this morning, and Sam and Marrok are welcome to come along if they want to. I know it's only at the end of the driveway, but we can take the carriage to make it easier for Marrok. I've arranged for Arthur to visit some friends of mine in Cornwall in March. They have an immense market garden with lots of glasshouses, and I think spending a week with their gardeners would benefit him. I've already mentioned it to him, but it's definite now. Marrok, Arthur, is married to Annie's mum, Sabina, so you'll be able to meet her. It's a second marriage for both of them, and they have a large family between them already, but Sabina is due to give birth any day now to their own child. After that, we'll come back here for lunch, and then this afternoon, I'm going to ride to Cullompton to talk to Doctor Turner about Danny's other foot. What do you think, gentlemen? Would you like to accompany me to the Lodge House?"

"Yes, please, that sounds interesting, but what about the children? Shouldn't I stay here and take care of them?"

"I thought I might take them for a walk into the village with me this morning, Marrok, if that's all right with you? I want to visit my granny and grandad at The Red Lion Inn and then see my mother at the Lodge House, so we might all bump into each other. My grandad's a bit under the weather, so I want to make sure there's nothing he needs, and whilst I'm out, I'll call in to see my mum. Perhaps they could spend the afternoon with you?"

"You're so kind; I don't know what to say, but that sounds splendid. Thank you."

They had barely finished speaking when their peace was disturbed by the sound of the five children arriving. Annie took them back to the nursery to find warm clothing for the two boys and girls to walk to the village. An old coat of Selina's fitted Paul, and she provided the two girls with a shawl each. She smiled to herself as one of the shawls, a grey one, stirred a distant memory. It had been given to her long ago by the Fellwood family when she was a kitchen maid. It was her Christmas present, which became known as her 'Granny Annie' shawl at the time. She struggled to find something to fit Martin, but eventually, Mrs Potts came to the rescue with an old coat that had belonged to one of the estate manager's sons. Finally, Annie collected the twins from Naomi and settled them into the large pram Robert had bought for her. They were sitting up now and loved going outside. Heaving a sigh of relief, the party set off, with Annie ruefully thinking that the next time she took seven children out with her, she would be a bit more organised.

It was a chilly morning, and the grass was white and crisp with frost. The children ran ahead of Annie, laughing as they could see their breath in the air. The twins and Selina were wrapped up warmly and wearing woolly hats and mittens, but Annie could see that Marrok's children were still cold despite her attempts to find them warm clothing.

"I think our first task this morning will be to visit my Uncle George's shop in the village and see if he has any warmer clothing for you; I can see you're frozen, even though you aren't complaining. Martin was intrigued. He was a handsome boy of six with brown curly hair, and he stared at Annie with wide hazel eyes.

"Are you going to buy us some clothes, Aunty Annie?"

"Yes, if there's something in the shop to fit you, would you like that, Martin?"

"Will they be new clothes or old ones from a jumble sale?"

"They'll be new ones, though, when there is a jumble sale, we could certainly take a look because I think you all need several things."

"Do you have enough money to buy clothes?"

"Yes, I can afford to buy you some new clothes, and I'm hoping my uncle will give me a generous discount, seeing as we'll be giving him quite a bit of business. Would you like some new clothes?"

"Aye, that would be grand; we've never had new clothes, and we're always cold."

"Here we are at the shop now, so let's see what we can find."

Annie told Eliza to hold the door open as she negotiated the step and pushed the pram into the shop. It was too cold to leave the twins outside, although she knew they would be safe enough. Her cousins, Theresa and Harriet, were busy serving customers.

The shop had expanded quite a bit in recent years, as George Carter had purchased a plot of land from Matilda Rudd and had an extension built. After a disastrous fire at the smithy a few years earlier, Matilda, wanting to finance the rebuilding of her business for her sons, Francis and Jacob, had put the land up for sale, and George had been quick to spot the potential. His shop was twice the size it had been, with one half being given over to groceries and the remainder to clothing and shoes. Annie turned to the left, where Theresa was in charge.

"Good morning, Annie; you have quite a tribe with you this morning."

"Hello, Theresa, yes, I have. These are Sam Fellwood's grandchildren. You know, Sam, who used to be a tramp but turns out to be a long-lost Fellwood relative? These are the children of his son, Marrok, and Robert and Sam found them recently in the workhouse. Marrok is recovering from a broken leg, and they're all staying with us for now. They only have the clothes they're wearing, and they're threadbare, so can you show me what you might have that would fit them all, please?"

"Yes, of course. If you'll excuse me for a moment, I'll see what we have in the store cupboard, and you can see if anything is suitable. Oh, here comes Dad."

George Carter had been checking the stock and preparing an order when he overheard the conversation between his daughter and his niece, and his curiosity was piqued. A rather pompous man, he had always disapproved of Annie's family when they lived on the breadline, though since her marriage to Robert Fellwood, the heir to Hartford Manor, his manner had changed somewhat hypocritically. However, his behaviour had improved recently, especially since the abduction of his daughter, Theresa. He was so relieved to have her home safe and sound; he had finally realised that some things are more important than money.

"Hello, Annie. I thought I heard your voice; how are you?"

"I'm fine, thank you, Uncle George. Now, I must introduce you. These are Sam Fellwood's grandchildren, and they all need new clothes and shoes; I'm hoping you'll offer me a discount, seeing as we need so much."

"Yes, Annie, I'm sure I can do you a good price. Perhaps I can address the needs of the boys and leave Theresa to see to the girls."

It was over an hour and a half later before Annie had selected everything they needed. By the time they left, all four children had new coats, boots, gloves, hats and scarves and were beaming from ear to ear, for they had never been so warm. It didn't stop there; Annie also purchased underwear, socks, and additional clothes. George agreed to have them all delivered to the Manor House that afternoon, along with the discarded jumble of clothing they had removed.

By this time, the twins were grizzling because they were hungry, and Selina was getting up to mischief. Feeling pleased with her morning's work but somewhat exhausted, Annie left the shop and walked to The Red Lion Inn.

CHAPTER 10

HARTFORD

Annie walked to the back of the old coaching inn and past a queue of people waiting to be served at Betsey's Kitchen, another food outlet of the inn. Here, folk could buy food to take away or eat inside the old shippen at a few roughly made tables. Betsey's Kitchen had been opened way back in the 1830s when Hartford was full of the many workers employed to build Lord Fellwood's new canal, and indeed, it had helped to save the old inn from financial ruin. Annie frowned, for there was talk that the canal might soon be closed as the railway was cheaper and much quicker. She decided she must remember to ask Robert about this, for it would be his decision, the canal having been built by his great-grandfather, Ephraim Fellwood. However, Betsey's Kitchen was well-established and as busy as ever. It still sold the pasties, pastry squares, rabbit stew, and cakes that Betsey herself had produced from the day it opened and for which it was famous. The portions from Betsey's Kitchen were known to be generous, tempting folk to buy a bowl of stew rather than cook it themselves.

The Red Lion was always busy with the large number of stagecoaches and carriages that passed through Hartford on the way to Exeter and London. The inn offered a change of horses and a bed for the night or a hearty meal for the travellers before they resumed their journey.

Annie knocked briefly on the back door and then let herself in, pushing the pram inside the kitchen. Her granny, Betsey Carter, was sitting at the table peeling potatoes. A wide grin spread across her wrinkled face, and her grey eyes lit up when she saw it was her eldest granddaughter.

"Hello, Annie, how nice to see you, and my goodness, how many people do you have with you today? Our family seems to grow larger by the day."

Annie quickly explained and made introductions. "Gran, it's a bit of a cheek, but do you think we could have lunch here with you, please? I know there are a lot of us, but I can pay for it. The twins are ravenous, and I want to call into the Lodge House and see Mum and Liza before we go home."

"Don't be silly, I'd love you to stay to lunch; nothing would please me more, and you certainly will not pay for it. Sit yourself down, and I'll make us some tea. There's a fresh batch of rabbit stew on the old Bodley, so perhaps you'd all like a bowl of that with some of my fresh, crusty bread. Can the twins manage some of that if we mash it up?"

"Yes, that would be perfect. Can I get the two highchairs from the dairy?"

"Aye, you fetch them. Now, please take off your coats, everyone; you can hang them on the hooks in the passageway. My goodness, you are smart. What's your name, my dear?"

"I'm Eliza, and Aunty Annie's bought us new clothes from a shop in the village. We've never had new clothes before. Do you like my coat?"

"I do, my love; it suits you, and how lovely that you and your sister have chosen the same style but in a different colour." She turned to the other girl. "Now, I think you must be Jinnie, is that right?" The child nodded. "I don't know, yet another set of twins in the family, but at least you two are not identical, so I may stand some chance of telling t'other from which."

Annie quickly dished up a plate of stew for the babies and put it to cool whilst putting them into the highchairs she and her siblings had all sat in over the years. The rest sat around the huge kitchen table and gazed appreciatively at the bowl of stew and large shive of bread Betsey put in front of them.

"There you are, get that lot down you; there are plenty of dumplings, and they'll stick to your ribs and keep out the cold."

She placed a bowl of stew in front of Annie and then sat beside her with a bowl for herself.

"I'll bet Sam's over the moon to discover all these grandchildren. How's his son? Did I hear he has a broken leg?"

"Yes, Sam's overjoyed to have found all these relatives; I don't think he can quite believe it. Marrok fell off a roof and broke his leg, and it's not mending properly, so Robert will get the doctors to look at it soon. Anyway, more importantly, how's Grandad?"

A brief shadow passed over Betsey's face.

"He's not too good, my dear, and I've insisted he stays in bed for a rest. We have plenty of help these days; it's not like it was in the past when we worked all hours of the day to survive. Louis Blaquiere is a godsend, and I'm so thankful he came to Hartford when he did. William's widow, Sarah, has also fitted in well, and Bentley is so much like William was at that age. Having him here makes up a little for losing our William before his time; your dad, Tom, too. Ned probably has the flu, but I'm worried something else might be wrong. He's not been himself for a few months, but never complains. You can see him when we've eaten."

"Yes, I will; thanks. Where are Louis, Sarah, and Bentley?"

"Oh, they're serving food in The Kitchen. Bentley likes to help, and Sarah's quite strict with him; she has him running to and fro carrying things. He's a clever lad, just like his father was; he'll go to school after Christmas, but he can already write his name."

When the children had finished eating, Betsey showed them into the parlour and let them play with a box of ancient toys she always dragged out on such occasions. Annie changed the napkins of both babies and laid them side by side in the pram for a nap. Now, with their bellies full, they were content and sleepy, and leaving Betsey rocking the pram, she climbed the ancient, creaky stairs to visit her Grandad, carefully carrying a bowl of stew and some bread for him.

She peered around the bedroom door and, at first, thought he was sleeping, but his eyelids fluttered open, and he smiled at her.

"Hello, Annie; how lovely to see you."

"Hello, Grandad. How are you feeling today?"

"Not great, if I'm honest, my love, but don't go worrying your granny."

"Can you manage some stew? I'll prop your pillows up, and then you can have the tray on your lap."

"Perfect, thank you. Now, tell me all your news. I miss being in the bar and hearing all the gossip, but I did hear you had found Sam's family, and I'm so pleased for him."

"Yes, I have his four children downstairs with the twins and Selina. I've just taken them to Uncle George's shop and bought them loads of clothes. They only had what was on their backs, and that was threadbare."

"Oh, no doubt, you've made George's day. He loves making money."

"Has the doctor been to see you yet?"

"Aw, don't you start, Annie. Your Granny's nagging is more than enough; I don't think he can do anything for me."

"What do you mean? It's only the flu, isn't it?"

"It might be, but the last time I saw Doctor Luckett, he thought there was something wrong with my heart. I'm always tired and so breathless, and that was before I caught this awful cold or flu or whatever it is. There's nothing he can do anyway; it's just one of those things, I'm afraid." Ned regarded her intently with his watery blue eyes. "Actually, between you and me, I intend to have a serious chat with your granny later when the rush is over. It's time we moved aside and let someone else take over the inn; we're getting too old for all this. It's not only me; it's your gran, too. You know what she's like; everything has to be done to her high standards, but we're in our seventies now, and it's time we had a rest."

Annie was shocked to hear her grandad talking like this. He and her granny had always been there for her, but she realised he was right, and it was time they took life easier.

"I'm pleased to hear you say that, and I think it's an excellent idea. I'd love you both to enjoy your old age without working so hard, but who will take over the inn?"

"Ah, now, that's the question. Whom, indeed?" I've given it a lot of thought over the last few days lying here, and I have a few suggestions. Keep all this to yourself for now, love, won't you? I had no intention of telling you any of this, but for some reason, I've always been able to confide in you; it's the same with your mother. Over the years, I've often told her things I never intended to."

"Yes, Mum has that effect on people, Grandad, and me too. She can always tell when I'm hiding something. I'm going to see her when we leave here because her baby's due any day, and I want to make sure she's all right. Don't worry; your secret's safe with me, and I hope you get something sorted out. I want Doctor Luckett to take a look at you, though, so I'll arrange that." Her grandfather opened his mouth to protest, but she wagged her finger at him. "Now, what would you do if I were lying there? Please humour me and let the doctor examine you, and I hope you'll feel strong enough to come to the Manor House on Boxing Day. I can send the carriage to pick you up, so you won't have to walk anywhere. Now, let me take that tray, and I'll leave you to get some rest." Annie leaned over and kissed the old man on the cheek before making her way thoughtfully down the stairs.

"Right, it's time we were on our way. Gran, are you coming to Aunty Eveline's tomorrow to help pluck the poultry, or do you want to stay here with Grandad?"

"Ned says I must go because he knows I like doing it, and I would like to see Eveline; I haven't seen her for a week or two. Louis and Sarah have assured me they'll care for Ned, so I'll see how he is in the morning and decide then."

"Fine, we're all going in the carriage because Mum wants to come, though she probably shouldn't in her condition. We'll call for you at eight o'clock in the morning, but if you decide not to come, then it won't matter. Bye, for now, Gran."

After giving Betsey a big hug, Annie gathered everyone together, left The Red Lion, and walked to the Lodge House. On the way, they called into Mrs Scott's shop, and Annie bought some sweets. She could have purchased the sweets at her Uncle George's shop, but she liked to support all the local businesses. Mrs Scott was, as always, delighted to see Annie and enjoyed watching the children select their favourite sweets. Jinnie, Eliza, Martin, and Paul had never been taken to a shop to choose sweets before, but Selina, knowledgeable on the subject, soon advised them on the best ones to buy. As Annie left the shop, she glanced over her shoulder and waved at the old lady, wondering how old she was. Now tiny and wrinkled, she had seemed old when Annie was a child, but her smile was as bright as ever, and Annie left the shop feeling pleased to have seen her.

They arrived at the Lodge House just in time to see Robert, Sam, and Marrok before they left in the carriage, and Annie apologised to Marrok for keeping his family out for longer than she had intended.

"Oh, that's all right, Annie; as you can see, we're only just going home ourselves. I enjoyed chatting with your mum and Liza while Robert and Dad walked around the gardens with Arthur. But where did all these clothes come from? They must have cost a pretty penny; I'm afraid I can't repay you."

"That doesn't matter; they needed warmer clothing in this cold weather, and I thoroughly enjoyed spending money on them. When you feel up to it, we must buy you some new clothes too."

"I'll pay for all the clothes, Annie, but thank you so much for sorting it out. I wouldn't have known where to start. I must say, they all look very smart, though."

"Thank you, Sam, but that's all right. Uncle George gave me quite a healthy discount; he knows which side his bread is buttered and likes to keep me sweet. I was tempted to ask him for a new pair of boots for you, Sam, but I wasn't sure how he'd feel about that."

The old man roared with laughter at Marrok's puzzled face. "I'll explain it to you later, lad; it's a tale from my not-so-innocent past."

"Robert, are you still going to ride to Cullompton to see Doctor Turner about Danny's foot?"

"No, I've spent far longer here than I intended, and it's a bit too late now, for the days are short, and I don't want to be riding in the dark. We've sorted out the details for Arthur to visit Cornwall in a couple of months, though, so I'll ride to Cullompton tomorrow morning."

"When you do, could you ask him if he'll examine Grandad while he's here? I'm worried about him, and it wouldn't hurt to have a second opinion, although I have every faith in Doctor Luckett."

"Yes, I will; now we'll be on our way. Thank you for the tea and scones, Liza; they were delicious."

When the three men left, Annie introduced Marrok's family to Sabina and Liza and her siblings, Helen, Edward, Stephen and Danny. Hoping for a quiet chat with her mother, Annie suggested the children go upstairs to play.

"There, that's better; we can hear ourselves speak now. You didn't mind me telling them to go upstairs, did you?"

"No, of course not. They seem well-behaved, but they're so thin."

"Yes, being in the workhouse for a few months has taken its toll, but they'll soon pick up with some good food inside them. After all, we did. How are you, anyway?"

"As you can see, I'm big and fat and can't wait for this baby to put in an appearance, but other than that, I'm fine."

"And how about you, Liza? Do you want to come to Hollyford Farm tomorrow? I'm sure Arthur can watch the children for a few hours. He'll only be in the gardens working, and it's not like they're babies anymore."

"Yes, I'd like to come, and Arthur's already said he'll mind the family."

"Good. I hope you'll join us on Boxing Day, too."

"Yes, thank you. I'm looking forward to it already."

"Good, I'm going to invite Tilly Rudd, Francis, and Jacob, too; I know you like a natter with Tilly, Mum, and at least she'll be on hand if your pains start. I like to include her because I still treat her as if she were Selina's other granny, although they're not related."

CHAPTER 11

HARTFORD

When Annie left The Red Lion, the kitchen was strangely quiet after the hubbub of seven children chattering and laughing. Betsey had enjoyed their visit, for she loved to have her family around her. Knowing these were precious times, she never took them for granted. Having lost two sons, Betsey learned to enjoy every moment spent with her loved ones long ago. She decided to make another cup of tea and put her feet up for half an hour. However, her peace was short-lived when Sarah and Bentley returned from The Kitchen.

"Granny, Granny, guess what. I've been serving customers all on my own, and I even took the money because I can count the pennies now."

Betsey studied her grandson fondly. He was the spitting image of his father, William, and a constant reminder of the son she had lost, but she loved him dearly, and though she would never admit it to anyone, even herself, he was something of a favourite. She pulled him towards her and sat him on her knee, pushing his mop of curly red hair out of his eyes.

"Aren't you a clever young man, then? Whom did you serve?"

"Mum said I could serve all the children with a square of sugary pastry and charge them a ha'penny each."

"That's very smart of you. What did you do if a customer gave you a penny?"

"Oh, that's easy; I gave them a ha'penny change. I know there are two ha'pennies in one penny."

"That's right. You'll be running the place before we know it."

"Do you know, though, Granny, there were three who didn't have any money, and Mum told me to give them a pastry square each anyway."

Bentley seemed puzzled by this.

"I see. Did you want to give them some food?"

"Yes, they were thin and dirty and looked cold and hungry, so I think they needed something to eat."

"You did the right thing then, and I hope you'll always be kind to folk less fortunate than yourself. Do you know, when I was a little girl, I was like those three children because I never had enough to eat, and I was always cold? But for the kindness of some folk, I probably wouldn't be here at all."

Bentley was astounded at the thought of his granny being cold and hungry.

"Oh, I'm so glad someone was nice to you, Granny. I'll always remember that."

Sarah glanced at her mother-in-law, thinking there was a lot about this remarkable woman she didn't know.

"Is The Kitchen busy this morning, Sarah?"

"Aye, we're rushed off our feet as usual. I've come to fetch this extra batch of pasties you baked earlier, and I'm sure they'll be sold in no time. Come on, Bentley, back to work; we'll leave Granny to have a bit of peace."

Betsey quickly kissed her grandson's cheek and sent him on his way. She put her feet up on a stool for fifteen minutes and enjoyed a hot cup of tea, for her lunchtime brew had gone cold with so much going on around her. Whilst sitting there, she reflected how glad she was that Sarah and Bentley were now a part of her life; if she'd continued to hold a grudge against her daughter-in-law, it could have been a different story. It just shows it pays to forgive and forget, she thought to herself. Feeling better for a rest, Betsey poured another cup of tea and mounted the stairs to see how Ned was feeling.

Her husband was pleased to see her, and having helped him to sit up a bit better, she plumped up his pillows and handed him his cup of tea.

"Have all the visitors gone now, love?"

"Aye, it was a bit hectic for an hour or so. I don't know; Annie and Sabina seem to attract extra children like magnets; their family gets ever bigger. I'm pleased for Sam, though; he must be made up to have found his son and four grandchildren. They're polite and well-mannered, though they need feeding up, and I know how that feels. They made short work of the bowl of rabbit stew that I gave them, and they didn't leave a drop. Anyway, more importantly, how are you feeling?"

"Not too bad, thanks; just tired. Do you have to rush off, or is everything in hand?"

"Yes, we're on top of things at the moment. I'd attended the midday stagecoach before Annie and her tribe arrived, thank goodness, and Sarah and Louis are serving food in The Kitchen, so I can sit with you for an hour before the four o'clock stagecoach, and then it will only be snacks for them."

"Good, because I need to talk to you about something." Ned took her hand, kissing it fondly. "Don't look so worried, my love, but we must face facts. Much as we like to think we're still twenty-one, I'm nearly seventy-four, and you'll be seventy-two in January, and I think it's time we passed the inn on for someone else to worry about. We must take it easy and enjoy our final years; the doctor says my heart's failing, and it's likely to last longer if I do less, so what do you think?"

"Oh, Ned, you didn't tell me the doctor said that."

"Oh, he said it years ago, and until now, I've ignored him, but I must confess I'm feeling my age recently, and I'd like you to do less, too. We've worked hard our entire lives, and it's time we thought of ourselves and let someone else pick up the reins. By the way, Annie has insisted on sending for the doctor, but there's nothing he can do because he told me so last time. This bout of flu has laid me low for a few days, but once that's better, I'll be up and about again."

"I'm glad the doctor's coming, and I want a word with him this time. You certainly need to stay in bed until that cough's better; I know you aren't getting much sleep. I suppose you're right, but it's difficult, isn't it? Whom would we pass the inn on to?"

"We'll need to give it careful thought, but it must be a Carter, for the inn's been in this family for generations. Mind you, that's only thanks to you and your inheritance from Thomas Fellwood. It's funny how our lives are intertwined with that family. And now our granddaughter is married to the heir of Hartford Manor; who would ever have seen that coming?"

"The other thing to think about is where we would live, Ned?"

"The obvious answer is the cottage next door, where you were born. Bluebell Cottage, as it's called now. How would you feel about that, my love?" I know you didn't have a happy childhood there."

"No, it was far from that, but it was a long time ago. Yes, I think I could live there happily enough now. Fortunately, the Bevans are moving out after Christmas. We'll have to see what needs to be done there, though. That family's lived there for several years, and we've not spent any money on the place lately."

"We can easily get the cottage spruced up before we leave here; there's no particular rush. I've been giving all this much thought, and I suppose George, as the eldest, will probably feel the inn should come to him. What do you think about that?"

"I expect he will think that because he's so money-orientated, but it would never work. I mean, for a start, he's teetotal and frowns on anyone else who likes a drink, but not only that, he's so strictly religious. I've nothing against folk following their beliefs, but the regulars would not take kindly to George berating them for not going to church. In any case, we bought the shop premises for him and set him up in business, giving him a good start in life. He's worked hard, mind, I know."

"What about his son, Francis?"

"He's settled in Barnstaple now, running George's other shop, and the last time I saw him, he told me he was courting, so I wouldn't be surprised if we don't hear wedding bells in the not-too-distant future. I doubt he'd want to take on the inn; he knows nothing about running it. There are George's daughters, Theresa and Harriet, but they'll marry eventually and no longer carry on the Carter name. I suspect Theresa may marry Louis, and he knows this business, having worked here for a while, but as fond as I am of him, I don't want the inn passing to a Frenchman."

"I don't think you can call him a Frenchman, Betsey; his family have lived in Devon since his grandfather fled France, and that was years ago."

"That's as maybe, and he's an honest lad and a hard worker, but I want it to stay in the Carter family and carry on the tradition."

"Yes, I agree with you, so that rules out Eveline, too, then, doesn't it, because she's been Mrs Chugg since she married Charlie."

"Yes, and anyway, Eveline's happy at Hollyford Farm, especially since she and Charlie adopted William's three children and Martha, that poor orphan. No, I'm sure Eveline has never expected to inherit The Red Lion, though she'd do as good a job of running it as anyone. She's an excellent businesswoman and has a wise head on her shoulders. I'm sure George has missed her since she left the shop; I think his success was largely due to her ideas. That takes us on to Fred, then. He's the next eldest; do you think he'd be interested?"

"I admit Fred would be my choice. He's a hard worker and has built a sound business with his carpentry yard. Now that he's married to Charlotte, he's settled down, and she's a good wife. Not a liability like his first wife, Lucy."

"Oh, Ned, that's unfair; the poor lass couldn't help it. She was mentally ill."

"Aye, I know, but it's hard to forgive her for what she did to those poor babies. I'm fond of Charlotte; I liked how she nursed you when you broke your leg, and she lived here long enough to understand the business. Before he took to carpentry, Fred also knew what was entailed with running the inn, and he's the next in line, anyway, so it seems right that the inn should be handed down to him. With Tom and William no longer with us, it could only pass to one of their sons, who aren't old enough. Tom and Sabina's eldest lad, Willie, knows nothing about the inn. No, he's settled working on the farm for Mr Houle, and I think he loves it there, though, by all accounts, he needs more help. William's lads, the twins, Joe and Matthew, are only ten, so again, not old enough."

"What about Sarah and Bentley, though? I wouldn't see them turned out."

"No, nor me, but I think Charlotte and Sarah get on all right, don't they? I don't see why they couldn't carry on living here as they are, and, anyway, Bentley's William's son and I think he'd like to know he was here."

"He's a canny lad, you know, Ned. He came in to see me earlier and was full of himself because he'd been serving customers and taking money in The Kitchen."

"I'm glad we've had this chat, and, as usual, we've come to the same conclusion. I suggest we invite Eveline,

George, Fred, and Sabina to come and see us, and we'll tell them what we're thinking. If Fred likes the idea, he can always carry on doing his carpentry here at the inn, and we can either sell his cottage or rent it out. We could move there if you prefer. It's bigger than Bluebell Cottage."

"One step at a time, eh, but I agree that we should ask them all to come here, and they can hear our news together. If you feel all right in the morning, I'm going to Hollyford Farm with Annie, Sabina, and Liza to pluck the poultry, so I can ask Eveline and Sabina then. I expect George and Fred will call in to see how you are tomorrow, so you can invite them then. Shall we say Sunday afternoon? Christmas will be over by then."

"Yes, and I'll be fine tomorrow, so you go to Hollyford Farm. I know you enjoy a get-together with all the other ladies, and Sarah and Louis will see to me."

"There is one other thing, Ned. There's something I want to tell you, too."

"Go on, then. It seems to be a day for getting matters off our chests."

"Yes, and it's exactly that. Annie's invited us to the Manor House on Boxing Day, and Sam and Lady Margery will also be there. I still have Thomas Fellwood's watch, and I need to give it back. I have to do that before I pass on, and none of us knows when that will be. In any case, now that Sam's found his son, he might like to give it to him. I want Sam to enjoy it for a while first, though."

"Yes, you should do that; I know it's been on your conscience for too long. I doubt I'll come to the Manor with you, but I want you to go. You don't mind, do you? I'd rather stay here and have a quiet day."

Betsey kissed him on the lips and hugged him.

"Sensible as always, my love. Now, you must need forty winks after all that talking and thinking, so I'll see you later when I've dealt with the next stagecoach."

CHAPTER 12

HARTFORD

When Annie joined them the following day, Robert, Sam, Marrok, and the children had nearly finished breakfast. She had fed and changed the twins and left them in Naomi's care. Marrok contentedly pushed back his plate and sighed deeply.

"Aw, that was delicious and more than I would have eaten in days in the workhouse. I'm already feeling much better for having some decent food inside me. I've never seen my family eat so much, either. I'm forever in your debt, Robert."

"Nonsense, you're more than welcome, Marrok, and it's a pleasure to see you all enjoying your meals. I must ask you to excuse me as I'm off to Cullompton to see Geoffrey Turner. I was at public school with his son, Stephen. It was Geoffrey who operated on Annie's brother, Danny, and made such improvements to his cleft palate and club foot. He's a renowned doctor and has a practice in Harley Street in London, and he's been so generous with his time to this family. We think Danny might need one more operation on his other foot, and I want to find out when that might be."

"Don't forget, Robert, can you ask Geoffrey if he'll visit Grandad while here?"

"No, I won't forget, and I want him to examine your leg, too, Marrok. Annie, we might need to invite him to stay overnight."

"Yes, that's not a problem; maybe Clara will come too. I enjoyed her company the last time she came."

"Right, I'll say goodbye because I want to have a word with Jack Bater before I leave. He's the manager of the Hartford Estate, Marrok, and he does a wonderful job. I want to look at the bullocks with him this morning and select one to be slaughtered for Christmas. Times are hard, and I like to give the local families at least one decent meal to enjoy over the festive season. I used to give them ale, but the meat is more appreciated by the women, though perhaps not their husbands. What are the rest of you doing today?"

"I'm off to Hollyford Farm to help prepare the poultry for Christmas. Aunty Eveline has quite a few orders to fulfil, and she'll take the rest to the pannier market in Barnstaple for the Christmas market."

"Yes, I remember now; are you taking the carriage?"

"Yes, if it were only me going, I'd enjoy the ride, but Mum, Liza, and Gran want to come, and it will be better for them in the carriage. There's no way they can ride, particularly Mum, in her condition, and Gran and Liza are too old. I'm not sure Mum should come at all, but she's determined. I think she's hoping the journey might bring things on. She's uncomfortable and wants the baby to be born soon. What about you, Sam? Would you like to come to the farm? I know you like to see everyone, particularly Martha."

"I do like to see them, it's true, but no, not this time. I want to spend the day with Marrok so we can get to know each other better."

Leaving the others to enjoy the rest of their breakfast at leisure, Annie and Robert left the room together. In the boot room, and out of sight of the prying eyes of their servants, Robert pulled his wife to him and kissed her.

"Now, Mrs Fellwood, don't you go doing too much today, will you? I know what you're like."

She put her arms around his neck and returned his kiss.

"No, I'll be fine; it's the others I'm worried about. I'm glad Marrok's children are here because Selina will enjoy playing with them. We'll have to think about them all going to school after Christmas. Selina, too, unless we get a governess, but we don't need to think about that today; I'll see you later."

Leaving Robert conversing with Jack Bater about which bullock was the best to slaughter, she went to the stables where Dodger had the carriage waiting for her.

"Good morning, Dodger. Can we call at the Lodge House to collect my mum and Liza, please, and then onto The Red Lion to see if my granny will come?"

All the women were ready and waiting, and as Ned had assured Betsey he was fine, she was looking forward to her day out. The journey only took half an hour, and the women chatted nineteen to the dozen. When they arrived, Dodger helped his passengers alight from the carriage, and Annie asked him to return at three o'clock to get home before it was dark. They entered through the back door, and a noisy scene greeted them.

"Hello, Aunty Eveline; my goodness, it's noisy here. You can't hear yourself think."

"I'm afraid Martha fell and bumped her head a few minutes ago, and she doesn't want to forget it. Martha, look who's come to see us."

The toddler, still sobbing, removed her head from snuggling in Eveline's neck and surveyed the visitors warily. When her eyes alighted on Betsey, a wide grin spread across her face, and she held out her arms.

"I think someone's pleased to see you, Mum; here you are, have a cuddle."

Betsey took the distressed toddler and kissed her plump cheek.

"Hello, my darling. You come and have a cuddle with me, and we'll soon put everything to rights."

Betsey sat down heavily on a chair next to the table and held out her other arm to Amelia, Joe, and Matthew.

"Come here, then, you three, give your old granny a kiss and a cuddle. How are you all?"

Nine-year-old Amelia snuggled into her granny, enjoying the attention, but her twin brothers, ten-year-olds Matthew and Joe, gave the old lady a peck on the cheek and disengaged themselves as soon as possible.

"Ah, these two are getting too grown up for kisses from a sentimental old woman like me, but I'm pleased to see you're all well. And how are you, Eveline? You're a bit pale."

"I'm just tired; it's such a busy time of year leading up to Christmas, and I'm so glad to see all of you. I'd never get all this poultry ready on my own, and I'd like us to get started as soon as possible, please. I've put everything ready in the linhay, and Charlie's lit a fire so we won't freeze; it's bitterly cold this morning. If you follow me, we'll get started. Maria, can you bring a pot of tea and some biscuits, please? You, youngsters, must amuse yourselves today and not get up to mischief, or Father Christmas won't come."

"Aunty Eveline, can I come and help, please?"

Eveline glanced at her niece in surprise.

"Yes, if you want to, Amelia. Are you sure it won't upset you?"

"No, I want to be a farmer's wife like you, so I need to get used to it. I don't want to watch Uncle Charlie and Uncle Alfred killing the birds, though."

Eveline led them all outside to the linhay, where Charlie was adding some logs to the fire, and his father, Alfred, was placing chairs around a leaky old tin bath.

"Morning, ladies; thank you for coming to help us. Eveline, shall I kill the first lot of chickens now?"

"Yes, please, Charlie, then we can get started. It's always easier to pluck the feathers when the birds are still warm. Alfred, are you going to join us?"

"Aye, I'm a dab hand at plucking poultry, and I'll enjoy a chinwag with all you ladies."

Within minutes, Charlie brought the first plump hens inside and handed three brown ones to Liza, Betsey, and Sabina. They had spread sacks across their laps to prevent the blood from the hens' mouths from dripping onto their clothes, and around their heads, they had tied headscarves.

"Why must we cover up our heads?"

"There will be fluffy down and feathers flying everywhere in a few minutes, Amelia, and it's easier to take off a scarf than get it all out of your hair."

Charlie returned with four white hens and handed one each to Annie, Eveline, Alfred, and Amelia.

"There we are then, Amelia; watch Aunty Eveline and copy what she does. Pluck the feathers away from you, and be careful not to rip the skin on the breast. If you do, the bird doesn't look so appetising, and we'll have to sell it cheaply. As you pull out the feathers, let them fall into the old tin bath, and then we can sort through them later."

"Why will we sort through them?"

"We'll discard the bigger feathers and keep the soft downy ones for pillows and mattresses. There's nothing like a soft feather pillow to rest your head on. We'll keep the tips of the wings because they're ideal for dusting and removing cobwebs."

Sabina and Liza chuckled at this remark.

"Not that Annie ever remembered to glance up when she was dusting, did you, Annie?"

"No, I must confess, I was always getting told off for that at the Manor House when I was a maid there. I never remembered to remove the cobwebs on the ceilings, but then, it was hard to reach them, and there was always more than enough dust lower down."

They worked hard all morning, moving on from hens to geese and then turkeys. Their fingers became sore, especially Amelia's, but she soldiered on, and the others were impressed by her perseverance. After a few birds had been plucked, Eveline left the others to continue while she began drawing the birds. Amelia was intrigued and studied her every move.

"What are you doing now?"

"I have to draw the birds. I draw out their insides because we don't eat most of that."

As she worked on the first chicken, Eveline expected Amelia to vanish, for it was a gruesome sight. However, the girl was fascinated and keen to watch and learn. Deftly, Eveline washed out each bird, turned the wings underneath, and spread the creamy fat from inside the chicken across its breast. She tied the legs together with string and placed the neck, gizzard, and heart between its legs and body.

"There, that one's all ready for the market now. Do you think it looks nice?"

"Yes, it does. I'm sorry for the poor chicken, but I know people must eat. Can I do the next one?"

"No, I think you'd better carry on with the plucking, my love. You need to pull quite hard to get all the insides out, and I don't think you're strong enough yet. If your fingers are getting sore, you can go and play, though; you don't have to spend all day out here."

"No, I like doing it."

"All right then; we're glad of your help. In any case, we'll stop soon to have some dinner. Maria is cooking us a 'schooner on the rocks'.

"Oh, lovely; I haven't heard it called that for a long time. A joint of belly pork, I presume?"

"Yes, that's right, Liza. It should be delicious and cooked on top of potatoes, sage, and onions. Maria's an excellent cook. I think she's roasting some parsnips to go with it, and she's made a junket with cream for afters."

At ten minutes to one o'clock, Matthew came to tell them that dinner was ready. They trooped into the kitchen and washed their hands, their stomachs rumbling at the delicious smell of the roast pork. Over dinner, Eveline told them she had also been busy making twenty rag dolls for the shop in London.

"Oh, you're still making your dolls, then?"

"Yes, and the shop owner would take more if I could make them faster, Sabina, but there's always so much to do. They sell like hotcakes in London, and I think they make quite a price, far more than I'm paid. Mind you, Amelia is becoming skilled with her needle, and she helped me with the last batch. Fortunately, they've all been delivered now, and I can forget about doing any more until after Christmas."

"Do you still have the doll that your Aunty Eveline made you, Amelia?"

"Yes, she sits at the bottom of my bed, and I shall keep her forever. She even went to the workhouse with me, and I'm so glad Lizzie didn't sell her; she's very special."

"Whilst we're all here together, there's something I need to ask you, Eveline, and you, Sabina."

"Yes, Mum, what is it?" Eveline glanced at Betsey. "Is everything all right?"

"Yes, it's just that your father and I want to see all of you together to talk to you about something, and we thought perhaps the Sunday afternoon after Christmas would be a convenient time for everyone. Can you come to the inn, then? Ned's going to invite George and Fred when they visit him today. It will be nice to have you all together for a while; it doesn't happen often."

Betsey would not be drawn on the reason for the get-together and told them it was nothing to worry about, and they would find out soon enough. After lunch, the group returned to the linhay for another hour before Dodger reappeared with the carriage to take them home.

CHAPTER 13

BRAMPFORD SPEKE

Emily was unable to sleep that night. She tossed and turned as her troubled mind worried over her grandchildren. At last, in the early hours, she finally lost consciousness, but it seemed only a few minutes later that a loud hammering on the door rudely awoke her. Wearily, she sat on the side of the bed for a moment, trying to gather her strength, whilst the commotion downstairs continued. Emily couldn't for the life of her think who could be making so much noise. Shakily, she rose to her feet, but the room swam before her, and she sank back onto the bed, afraid she might fall.

By this time, the noise had alerted her neighbours and Agnes and Ollie came out of their front door, curious to find out what was happening. A young man was hammering on Emily's door, and behind him, a lady dressed all in black urged him to continue. Their horses were tethered to a nearby tree, one a handsome chestnut stallion and the other a roan cob.

"Can I help you, ma'am?"

The young lady looked down her nose at Ollie. Her clothing was of the finest quality, her boots highly polished, and she wore sparkling earrings. The only thing that marred her beauty was the sour expression on her face.

"Is this where that whore, Rosemary Gibbs, lives?"

"It's where Rosemary used to live, ma'am, but I'm afraid she's lying dead in her bed, awaiting collection by the undertaker."

The woman glared at him. "How typical of the woman to die before I even had a chance to give her a piece of my mind. What about her two bastards? Are they here?"

"Yes, ma'am, they live with their granny, Emily Gibbs, but I should tell you she has typhoid. I would not advise you to enter the cottage for fear of contracting it yourself."

The woman pushed the young man aside. "Get out of the way, Henry; I'll deal with this myself. I've recently recovered from typhoid, so I'm not worried about that."

Slamming the door open, the woman entered the cottage and surveyed her surroundings distastefully. She proceeded through the living room and mounted the stairs. Still lying in bed, Emily was astounded to see Lady Grantley enter the room. She struggled to sit up.

"Why, Lady Grantley, what brings you here? I'm sorry I couldn't answer the door, but I'm so weak I couldn't get out of bed. I'm ill with typhoid, you see. Please don't come near; you don't want to catch it."

"Touching though your concern is, you do not need to worry about me, for I've had the beastly disease, though it managed to see off my unfaithful husband and serve him right. Now, I understand from your neighbours that his trollop, Rosemary Gibbs, has joined him. How typical that they should even leave this world together."

Although incensed at the woman speaking about her daughter in such a way, Emily could think of nothing useful to say, so she lay back on her pillows and regarded her visitor with baleful eyes.

"So, where are your grandchildren? Where are my husband's bastards?"

"They're not here, ma'am. With their mother deceased and me likely to join her soon, I've sent them to seek out distant relatives in Somerset."

"A likely story, as if you would send two youngsters off alone on a long journey in this weather. I expect they're hiding somewhere; tell me, for I will find them."

The woman turned on her heel, went across the landing, and opened a door that led into the room usually occupied by Millie and Jonathan. Seeing it was empty, she opened the next door and recoiled at the awful smell which assailed her nostrils. Putting her handkerchief to her nose, she surveyed the body lying on the bed, covered with a sheet. Unconvinced that the children were not hiding, she forced herself to peer under the bed but found nothing. Angrily, she called down the stairs to her groom.

"Henry, search everywhere downstairs and all the outbuildings. Then search every house nearby; I want them found."

She walked back to Emily's bedroom.

"I will find them, so you might as well tell me where they are."

"I've told you the truth, ma'am. I've sent them on their way, for I don't want them to find my dead body like they found their mother's. Have you no compassion? Whatever wrong their father and my daughter have done you, 'tis hardly their fault; they did not ask to be born."

"Maybe not, but there is a serious matter your granddaughter must answer for. A valuable brooch has gone missing. It's a blue sapphire surrounded by diamonds and belonged to my mother-in-law; I inherited it recently following her death. I've made enquiries, and a servant saw your granddaughter sneaking out of our house a few days ago. Obviously, she came to see what she could steal now that her father can no longer support you all. So, where is she? If you don't tell me, I shall refer the matter to the police."

"You do that, ma'am, but you'll find no brooch here. My granddaughter is no thief, and I think you've made the story up to wreak your revenge on this family. Now get out of my house!"

"Ah, and there we have it. It's not your house, is it? It's my house, and I'll kindly ask you to vacate it. You've lived here rent-free for years enough, sponging off my husband."

Emily was white-lipped with anger. "Don't worry, ma'am, I wouldn't stay here if you paid me. As soon as I'm strong enough to get out of my bed, I intend to make my way to the workhouse in Exeter, and then you can have your house and much pleasure may it give you."

"No, I want you out of the house now. You're a squatter; you pay no rent and have no business here. Now, stop your malingering and get up. I'll give you fifteen minutes to grab your belongings, and then I want you gone."

Emily was shocked. "Ma'am, I beg you, please give me a few days. I'm so weak I couldn't answer the door. I promise you, one way or another, I'll be gone within a week."

For an answer, Lilliana left the room and stormed down the stairs. By this time, there was quite a gathering of neighbours outside their cottages, as an embarrassed Henry insisted on searching their homes. Lilliana spotted him leaving a dwelling a short distance away.

"Henry, leave that and come here."

The young man hurried towards his mistress, looking most uncomfortable.

"Henry, I want you to carry the old woman from her bedroom and put her outside the cottage."

"But ma'am, 'tis bitterly cold, and I understand she's ill with typhoid."

For an answer, Lilliana raised the crop she still held in her hand.

"Are you disobeying me, Henry? Do you want to feel my crop across your face?"

"No, ma'am."

Reluctantly, the young man entered the cottage and went up the stairs. The neighbours gathered around the newly widowed woman.

"Ma'am, you surely can't mean to throw Emily out onto the street? She's an old lady and seriously ill, and she has nowhere to go."

"That's not my problem; if any of you want to grab a few of her belongings for her, then do it now, but be quick, for in a few minutes, I intend to lock that cottage and take away the keys. If any of you dare to question my orders again, you'll find yourself in the same boat. Do I make myself clear?"

Quickly, Agnes, Ollie, and a couple of the other neighbours entered Emily's cottage and gathered a few of her belongings while Henry struggled to carry the sick woman down the stairs. He had wrapped her in two blankets, and leaving the cottage, he gently sat her on the ground outside. Tears ran down the old lady's cheeks, but she raised her face defiantly to the woman before her.

"You're an evil woman, Lilliana Grantley, and I can see why Sir Edgar preferred my Rosemary. He loved her, you know; loved her until the day she died. What sort of woman are you that you can't keep a man? You may have a beautiful face, but inside, you're rotten, through and through, and I hope you get your comeuppance one day."

Before the furious lady could respond, a voice behind her drew her attention.

"May I ask what is going on here? Why is Mrs Gibbs sitting outside her cottage on a day like this?"

The vicar wore an angry expression as he took in the situation at a glance.

"It's none of your business, vicar; I'm evicting this woman for non-payment of rent, as is my right. Now, be on your way."

"Even if that is the case, ma'am, surely you can give her a few days to gather her belongings and find somewhere else to live. As far as I know, she has done you no wrong, and surely, you're not so much in need of the dwelling that she has to leave today?"

"As I said, vicar, mind your own business. If you wish to continue enjoying the living of this parish, be on your way, or you may find yourself out on your ear like these folk."

The man hesitated at the lady's harsh words as Ollie, Agnes, and the others came out of the front door clutching Emily's few personal belongings.

"I see." He crouched down beside the terrified old woman. "Emily, is there somewhere I can take you, my dear? I'm sorry to see you in this predicament, but it seems there's little I can do. Would you like to stay at the vicarage for a day or two until you recover?"

"There's no need for that, vicar. Emily can stay in our house until she sorts something out." Agnes put her arm around her friend. "Don't you worry, my love; let's get you into the warm."

However, Lilliana rounded on both of the well-intentioned neighbours.

"No, don't you dare offer to take her in. I own all of these houses, including the vicarage, and if I find any of you have offered shelter to this woman, you, too, will be evicted. Do I make myself clear?"

"Crystal clear, ma'am, and may God forgive you." Before the furious young woman could retaliate, the vicar scooped Emily off the ground and deposited her, blankets and all, into the back of his cart. "Come on, Emily, I'll take you to the workhouse in Exeter."

"Yes, thank you, vicar, but what about my Rosemary? Her body's still upstairs. She has to be buried."

"Oh, my goodness, I'd forgotten. Ollie, can a couple of you take Rosemary's body to the church, please? Lay her in the vestry, and when I return from Exeter, I'll see that everything is attended to. Is that all right with you, your Ladyship?"

"Yes, now get that woman out of my sight. Henry, I'll leave you to lock the cottage and then bring me the keys and the rest of you; remember, if you do anything to upset me, you'll find yourselves out of work and home, so be careful. My husband has been far too soft on all of you, but you have me to deal with from now on."

As the bitter woman galloped off, Emily's neighbours gathered around her in dismay, but she smiled up at them bravely.

"It's all right; don't distress yourselves, and thank you for trying to help. You all know of the situation with my Rosemary and Sir Edgar; the woman does have reason to be upset, but I didn't think she'd go this far. Vicar, thank you so much for helping me; take the clock on the mantelpiece and sell it to pay for Rosemary's burial. It was a gift from Sir Edgar and should fetch enough. I would have liked to be there to say goodbye to my daughter, but it can't be helped. Agnes, could you hold on to my things for now? If I take them to the workhouse, they'll sell the lot, and if you hear I've died, sell them and keep the money; you've earned it."

Having said her goodbyes to her friends and neighbours, Emily lay back on the pillow that someone had thoughtfully donated for her comfort on the journey. She gazed at the grey sky above her and thanked God she'd had the foresight to send Millie and Jonathan on their way before all this happened. She would have hated for them to witness the events of the last hour. Not only that, but she knew Millie had escaped jail by the skin of her teeth. Emily had recognised Lilliana's description of the brooch, now pinned to Millie's bodice, below all her other clothes and safely out of sight.

The story of her granddaughter stealing the brooch was a complete fabrication, with a servant, no doubt paid or threatened to testify to seeing Millie in Grantley Manor. The wealthy baronet had given the brooch to Rosemary the last time he visited, and Emily had scolded her daughter for accepting it, telling her it would never be safe to wear it. Sir

Edgar's mother had recently died, and Lilliana had inherited all her jewellery. However, this particular brooch had been the old lady's favourite, and Sir Edgar had told his wife, in no uncertain terms, that he wished to give this one item to Rosemary to pass on to his daughter, Millie. His wife had, naturally, been furious, and the couple had rowed bitterly. Emily hoped and prayed that Lilliana would never find the two children and wished with all her heart that she had not let her granddaughter take the brooch. She could then have returned it to the bitter woman.

CHAPTER 14

NEWTON ST CYRES

Millie and Jonathan had enjoyed staying at Hilldale Farm with Hubert March for a few days, but Millie knew they must continue their journey, so one morning, she asked him when he was expecting his family to return.

"It's funny you should ask that this morning, for I think they'll be home later today. I don't know if you've realised, but today is a Thursday, and not only that, it's Christmas Eve."

Both of the youngsters went quiet, and Hubert realised they were remembering other, happier Christmases with their mother and granny, and he was dismayed to see tears on the boy's cheeks.

"Oh, is it? No, I didn't know; I'd forgotten all about Christmas. In that case, we'll be on our way today. We've been thankful for your hospitality, but we'll leave you in peace to welcome your family home."

"Now, there's no rush, and I'd like you to meet my family; they'll be pleased to hear you've kept me company and helped out around the farm. Gertie and Rosie will need their beds, but you could sleep on a few blankets in front of the fire. Perhaps you might like to stay for Christmas Day and Boxing Day and continue your journey the day after. What do you think?"

"If you're sure your family won't mind us being here, we'd love to; thank you. We'll have to find work along the way to buy food, and probably no one will want to be bothered over Christmas."

"That's settled, then. Now, Jonnie, I can see you eyeing up that spare sausage; do you have room for it before we clean out the shippens?"

"Aye, I've got room unless you or Millie want it?"

"No, I think we've had enough; thank you, lad, you eat it up; you've got a lot of growing to do. Now, Millie, I hardly need to say this, but can you make sure everything is sparkling clean in the house before Angela gets home, please? She's a bit of a fusspot, and she'll be pleased if it's neat and tidy when she arrives."

"Yes, sir; I'll give everywhere an extra clean this morning, and if you can show me where the clean sheets are, I'll change the beds for Gertie and Rosie. Jonnie and I have slept in them for several nights now."

"No, don't worry about that; they won't notice, and Angela changed all the bedding a day or two before she left. No need to wash the sheets; it takes them so long to dry at this time of year, and we don't want them draped everywhere over Christmas."

Vivian, Angela, and their family arrived back at the farmhouse just as Hubert, Millie, and Jonathan were about to eat their dinner. Millie felt embarrassed to be sitting at their table when they all trooped into the kitchen and stopped in surprise at seeing two children sitting with Hubert.

"Goodness me, what do we have here? Dad, what have you been up to? Have you kidnapped two children whilst we've been away?"

"No, not quite, lad, but these two have kindly kept me company for a few days, and they've worked hard around the place. I must confess I found it a struggle here on my own; I think it must have something to do with getting old. This is Millie and Jonathan Gibbs, and they're the grandchildren of my dear friend, Emily Gibbs. You may remember she's visited me several times over the years. Their family's fallen on hard times, and they're on their way to North Devon to find some relatives they're hoping will take them in."

"I see. Hello, you two; I'm glad you've helped my dad while I've been away. I'm pleased to meet you. I'm Vivian March, and this is my wife, Angela, and this is Gertie, Albert, Rosie, and Walter; I should think you and Gertie are about the same age, Millie."

"We're pleased to meet you, sir; I'm fifteen, and Jonnie is five. Mr March has been so kind to us for the last few days, and it's been a pleasure to stay here with him."

"Oh, yes, you are the same age as Gertie. Albert's ten, Rosie's seven, and Walter's five, like you, Jonathan, and I'm sure you'll get along like a house on fire. Now, let's sit down and have some dinner; we're all starving. The journey from Plymouth took ages, although we travelled part of the way yesterday. We left on the stagecoach early this morning, and it seems a long time since I had my breakfast."

Millie swiftly rose from the table and fetched six more plates from the dresser. She then went to the larder and brought another loaf of bread as Angela watched her in amazement.

"Millie, I can see you've been a godsend to my father-in-law, for I think this place is cleaner than when I left, and that's not usually the case when I come home, is it, Dad?" She glanced at Hubert.

"I do my best, maid, but I know tisn't quite up to your high standards."

"I know you do, Dad; I'm only teasing, but thank you, Millie; the place looks lovely, all spick and span. Now, why are you two wandering the roads on your own?"

Millie told their sad tale about why they were travelling to North Devon.

"Oh dear, I can understand how that poor lady must feel, but none of it is your fault. Do you know where to find these relatives of yours?"

"No, not exactly, but we know they lived in Hartford, and we have a pipe that belonged to my great-grandfather. It has his initials carved on it, so we're hoping someone will remember him. Gran said it was a long shot, but she didn't know what else to do, and when she's better, she'll follow us. I'm hoping she'll catch us up on the journey."

"I see. Well, you're welcome to stay here for another couple of days over Christmas. I wouldn't like to think of you travelling on your own over the festive period, for there'll be few folk around, and no one will want to be bothered with you."

"Thank you so much, Mrs March. What would you like us to do this afternoon?"

"It sounds to me like you've both been working hard, even helping to deliver the new calf, so I'd like you to take the afternoon off and relax. Gertie will be glad of your company, Millie, and I expect Albert, Rosie and Walter would like to see the new arrival. Would you like to take them to see the new calf, Jonathan? Have you given her a name?"

Jonathan admitted he had taken to calling the new calf Holly.

"I hope you don't mind, but Mr March told me to think of a name for her, and I liked Holly."

"It's a perfect name at Christmas time. Go on, get your boots on and go out to play. Perhaps you could show Jonathan your den when you've seen Holly."

That evening, Angela made a bed on the floor for Millie in Gertie and Rosie's room and another for Jonathan in Albert's and Walter's. She gave them both a hug before she tucked them in cosily.

"There, do you think you'll be able to sleep all right down there on the floor? I've put down a couple of quilts, so it shouldn't be too uncomfortable for you. I know Hubert told you to sleep in the kitchen in front of the fire, but that would have meant you couldn't go to bed until we all did, and I'm sure you're tired. The fires are lit in the bedrooms anyway, so you should be warm enough."

"Yes, we'll be fine; thank you so much for letting us stay another few days. I'll be out early in the morning to help you prepare the Christmas dinner; I always used to help Mum and Granny."

Millie's voice trailed off at the end of the sentence as she remembered happier times.

"Thank you, Millie; I'd like that. Goodnight, now."

In the morning, the March children were awake early. Their stockings were hung in the kitchen, and they stampeded down the stairs at the crack of dawn, eager to find out if Father Christmas had left them anything. To their delight, the stockings contained new socks, gloves, an orange, and some sweets, and beside them was one larger present each. The gifts were homemade, for Hubert, Vivian, and Angela had been busy for weeks, making them as soon as the children were safely fast asleep. Gertie had a smart new shawl and Rosie a rag doll, both beautifully made by Angela. Albert was delighted to find his present was a kite, something he had wanted for a long time, and Vivian had carved a boat from a piece of wood for Walter.

Millie and Jonathan sat quietly at the side of the room, watching everyone open their presents. Millie took Jonathan on her knee and whispered in his ear.

"Next year we'll have presents too, Jonnie, you see if we don't. It doesn't matter this year because we couldn't carry any more things with us, anyway."

The boy nodded and stared enviously at the kite and the boat.

"Goodness me, what's this?"

"What is it, Grandad?"

"I've just noticed two more stockings near the door; wait a minute, they have a note on them. Let me see what it says." Hubert read the note out loud. "To Millie and Jonathan for being such good children this year. I couldn't find you in Brampford Speke, but the elves reminded me you're staying at Hilldale Farm, so I brought your presents here. Happy Christmas and love from Father Christmas."

Jonathan's eyes were as wide as saucers, and a wide grin spread over his face. "Are they for us, Mr March? Are they really for us?"

"It looks like it, lad. How clever of Father Christmas to find out you were here. You'd better come and see what he's left you. Nothing too heavy, I wouldn't think, because he knows you're travelling. Come and sit down beside me and see what there is."

They rummaged in the large brown stockings and discovered nuts, sweets, and an orange, the same as the March children had received, and at the very bottom, wrapped in coloured paper, was a bar of chocolate.

"Is it chocolate, Millie?"

"Yes, I think so, Jonnie; I've only ever tasted it once."

"Oh, I wonder why Father Christmas didn't leave us some chocolate, too?"

Walter looked upset, and his mother reminded him he had a new wooden boat to play with, but Millie and Jonathan had no toys.

"No, that's true; I suppose Father Christmas thought they could carry the chocolate with them, but not heavy toys."

"Yes, I'm sure that's what he thought, though funnily enough, I bought a couple of bars of chocolate for us all to share over Christmas, and I think they're the same as the ones that Father Christmas has left for Millie and Jonathan. They cost quite a lot of pennies, so I could only afford two bars, but we can share them later."

Walter brightened up, and Millie regarded Angela curiously, thinking it was quite a coincidence, but the farmer's wife smiled and headed for the kitchen to make a cup of tea.

CHAPTER 15

HARTFORD

It was snowing heavily on Christmas Eve when Lady Margery arrived at Hartford Manor. Annie and Robert were enjoying a cup of hot chocolate in the drawing room with Sam and Marrok, and Robert, seated by the window, saw his great-aunt arrive in her carriage.

"Oh, here's Aunt Margery now, and I think she's on her own; perhaps Peter didn't want to come."

"No, I thought he'd rather stay at Primrose Cottage with Christopher and Clarice; after all, they're his own family."

The couple wandered into the hallway just as Sid Hobbs, the butler, opened the front door and welcomed their visitor inside. As always, Lady Margery was impeccably dressed. Sid Hobbs took her warm cloak from her shoulders, revealing an elegant navy blue dress with cream lace at the neck and cuffs. She wore a sparkling string of pearls around her neck, complemented by matching earrings.

"Aunty Margery, how nice to see you." First Annie, and then Robert, hugged the old lady.

"Hello, my dears; what a cold day, and look at all the snow; a real blizzard. It isn't lying on the ground yet, but I suspect it will. I'm glad to have arrived safely; I was a bit dubious about making the journey in this weather."

"Did Peter not want to come with you?"

"No, he appreciated the offer but wanted to spend Christmas with his family. Your Aunty Eveline has kindly agreed to Maria having a couple of days off, so she and Dudley will join him, Christopher, and Clarice. Elsie has Boxing Day off, too, so she'll ride over then for the day. Peter will enjoy having all his family around him, and I know Clarice and Christopher will make them welcome. I hope the weather doesn't spoil their plans. Do you have many guests arriving for Christmas Day?"

"No, only Geoffrey and Clara Turner, and they should be arriving any time soon. Annie's family is joining us on Boxing Day. I rode to Cullompton a few days ago to see Geoffrey because we want him to take another look at Danny's foot; he may need one more operation. Anyway, it turned out that the Turners would have been on their own for Christmas, as their son, Stephen, is still working in Italy, so I invited them here."

"Oh, that's good, Robert, thank you. As you know, I've been friends with Clara for years and love catching up with all her news."

"Yes, I thought you'd be pleased, and it seemed sensible as we have a few more patients for Geoffrey to examine now."

"Oh dear, is someone else ill?"

"Yes, Ned Carter, Annie's grandad, is unwell at the moment. You know, he and Betsey keep The Red Lion Inn."

"Yes, that's right; what's wrong with Ned?"

"Doctor Luckett is convinced there's a problem with his heart, and we'd like a second opinion. The second casualty is Sam's son, Marrok, and if you come into the drawing room, you can meet him. We're all enjoying a cup of hot chocolate; would you like some to warm you up?"

"Yes, that would be delightful, thank you."

As they entered the room, Sam rose to his feet and embraced the elderly lady. His son, Marrok, struggled to rise from his chair, using his crutches, but Lady Margery waved her hand at him to stop.

"No, please don't get up. I can shake your hand just as easily sitting down. How are you?"

"I'm feeling much better, ma'am; thank you for asking. Robert and Annie have spoiled me and my family for the last few days; we've never eaten such delicious food."

"Marrok, as I'm your great aunt, we'll have less of the ma'am, if you please. Call me Aunty Margery, like everyone else. Now, perhaps you could introduce me to your family. I already know this young lady; how are you, Selina?"

"I'm fine, thank you, Aunty Margery, and I brought your dolly downstairs to see you; look."

"So you did, and I think she likes living with you; I can see you're looking after her."

Marrok had just introduced his family to his aunt when Geoffrey and Clara Turner arrived, and within no time, Annie, Clara, and Margery were enjoying catching up on each other's news. It was not long before they heard the gong for lunch, and Robert and Annie led the party into the dining room.

When everyone had eaten their fill, Annie took the children to the nursery. She would have liked to take them out for a walk to burn off some of their energy, but that was impossible in such atrocious weather. Instead, she let Eliza give Thomas his bottle, and Jinnie fed David. The two girls were fascinated by the babies, and leaving Naomi to keep an eye on them, Annie rummaged in one of the cupboards to see if she could find some toys suitable for Martin and Paul. Knowing the boys would be coming to stay, Robert had visited the nursery in the main part of Hartford Manor and retrieved some of his old toys. Before long, she found a box of tin soldiers and a clockwork train, complete with a track to be assembled. Annie, Martin, Paul, and Selina knelt on the floor, trying to figure out how it went together, and eventually, they succeeded. Annie wound up the slightly rusty train, hoping it would work, and gave it to Martin to put on the tracks. To their delight, the red train sped around the track, and Annie left them, taking it in turns to have a go. Passing them a box of bricks, she suggested they make a tunnel for the train to travel through.

Downstairs, Lady Margery and Clara Turner had found a quiet corner in the library and were enjoying a pot of tea. Robert led the men into the study that Marrok used as a bedroom.

"Let's have a look at this leg, then, Marrok. Why don't you lie on the bed so I can examine you properly? How long is it since you fell and broke it?"

Robert took the crutches from Marrok and helped him onto the bed.

"Oh, it must be over two months by now."

"Hmm, that's a long time; it should be on the mend by now. Is it feeling any better?"

"No, not really; I still get a sharp pain if I try to put it to the ground."

"Has anyone taken off the dressings and examined it?"

"No, no one in the workhouse was interested, and Robert thought it was best to wait until you arrived before we did anything."

"I see; let's take a look, then."

The doctor removed the soiled bandages that were holding the two splints together. He pursed his lips as he carefully felt down Marrok's leg. Although he tried to be as gentle as he could, the examination was clearly causing the young man considerable discomfort.

"I'm sorry to have caused you pain, Marrok, and I'm afraid your leg hasn't mended at all. I can still feel the rough edges of the break on the larger bone in your leg. The problem is that the leg wasn't plastered, and the splints weren't bandaged tightly enough to hold the two broken edges together. They have to be held firmly to knit back together, you see."

"Oh, so after all this time, I'm no further forward? Is there anything to be done?"

"Oh, yes, it can be put right, but I'll have to reset the leg and encase it in plaster. Fortunately, we can use chloroform to put you to sleep these days. It would be agonising to do if you were awake. I would prefer to carry out the operation in a hospital, but given that it's Christmas and snowing heavily, that's not an option. Would you like me to reset it for you?"

"Yes, please, if you can, sir; I was beginning to think I'd never walk again."

"I could ask the local doctor, Luckett, I think he's called, to assist me, but again, given the circumstances, do you think Annie would help, Robert? I believe she's practical, and I can instruct her."

"Oh yes, Annie will help you; she has some nursing knowledge and is not squeamish. When would you like to carry out the operation?"

"The sooner, the better, but as we've recently eaten a large meal, I suggest we tackle it first thing in the morning. We've found that chloroform often makes patients sick, and there's a serious risk if food has been eaten within the last few hours. It can be dangerous if the patient vomits whilst unconscious."

"Do you have everything you need to carry out the operation?"

"Yes, fortunately, I carry a lot of my medical equipment with me these days. As new cures and methods are found, it becomes necessary to have a supply as little is available in the countryside."

"'Tis generous of you to help my son, doctor, but tomorrow is Christmas Day; are you sure you want to operate then?"

"Oh yes, Sam, of course it is; I forgot. I don't mind doing it then unless you'd rather we put it off for a few days. What do you think, Marrok?"

"If it wouldn't hurt to leave it for a few more days, I think I'd prefer you to do it after Christmas, sir, but only if you're happy with that. My children have had a difficult time of it lately, and they're excited about Christmas, but I think it will be hard for them as it's the first year they'll be without their mother. I need to be here for them, not asleep, having my leg fixed."

"Yes, no problem; I think that's sensible, and a few days will make no difference."

By Christmas morning, the snow was six inches deep outside, and despite the roaring fires lit in every room, there was a distinct chill in the air as the bitter wind rattled every window pane. Paul Fellwood was the first to awake and was distraught to find he had again wet the bed. His brother, Martin, heard him crying and guessed what had happened.

"Paul, have you wet the bed?"

"Yes, can I get in with you?"

"Yes, take off your nightshirt and put on a clean one. There's one on the chair beside your bed, isn't there?"

"Yes."

"Don't cry. You know Aunty Annie won't smack you."

"No, I know, but I wish I hadn't done it."

"Never mind, you haven't done it much lately; climb in here and get warm. My goodness, your feet are like ice."

The boys and their sisters in the next room usually stayed in their beds until someone came to fetch them. They were not yet confident enough to wander around the large house on their own, and their father had instructed them to cause no one any trouble. Indeed, they had no intention of doing so, for every day, they thanked their lucky stars that they were warm, well-fed, and no longer living in the workhouse.

However, the boys did not have to wait many minutes before they heard Selina running along the landing and into her parents' room.

"Mummy, Mummy, is it Christmas?"

Annie was awake and enjoying lying in the warm for a few minutes before getting up to feed the twins. She nudged her husband.

"Come on, Robert; it's Christmas Day."

Her husband groaned, for he liked his bed, especially when it was so chilly outside the covers.

"What time is it?"

"I heard the hall clock chime six o'clock not long ago; come on, I can't wait to see everyone open their presents."

There was no time to say more before Selina threw herself onto the bed and crept between them.

"Papa, can we see if Father Christmas has been?"

A short while later, the family gathered in the sitting room, where the kitchen maid, Molly, was stoking the fire to encourage it to burn more brightly. With the glow from the coals and the many lamps, the room was cosy and warm. Annie settled comfortably in one armchair to feed Thomas, and Robert sat in another, giving David his bottle. Annie wanted all the family to be present. Marrok sat on the sofa, his leg stretched out before him, and Sam cuddled Paul on his lap.

"Molly, can you bring us all some hot chocolate, please?"

"Aye, ma'am."

On the floor surrounding the Christmas tree were seven bulging pillowcases. Selina fidgeted, inching ever nearer to the intriguing packages.

"Papa, can we open them now?"

"Yes, now, that pillowcase on the end is yours, Selina, and then, next to it, in order, are the ones for Jinnie and Eliza, Martin, and Paul. The two smaller ones are for David and Thomas, but they're more interested in their breakfast for now."

"How do you know about the presents, Papa?"

"Father Christmas explained it to me last night."

"Did you see him?"

Yes, but he didn't stay long because he had many toys to deliver. Go on, then; see what he's brought you all."

The children were thrilled with their presents, especially Marrok's family, and the morning sped by. Annie had purchased some toys and a few more warm clothes for them, and Marrok had tears in his eyes as he watched them joyfully handle each gift. In the midst of it all, Lady Margery joined them, enjoying the chatter and laughter, and Sam had never been happier.

After a delicious lunch cooked by Maisie, the family, Geoffrey and Clara retired to the drawing room, where Robert's sisters, Sarah and Victoria, joined them with Victoria's children, Caroline and Joshua. Lunch in the main part of Hartford Manor had been a subdued affair with their parents, Eleanor and Charles, and the two young women had escaped as soon as possible. Victoria's baby was a week overdue, and she shuffled around in her armchair, trying to get comfortable.

"Here, Victoria, put your feet on this stool; you might be more comfortable."

"Thanks, Robert. Goodness, it's such a relief to join you this afternoon; it was pretty gloomy next door, and it's a pleasure to meet you and your family, at last, Marrok."

"Thank you. Why didn't your parents come with you? I'd like to meet them."

There was a short silence until Robert spoke.

"I'm afraid they don't mix with us in this household. It's a long story, which we won't go into today, but Mama and Papa don't approve because I married Annie, and she used to be a servant here at the Manor."

"I see; I'm so sorry. I didn't mean to pry. They probably won't approve of me and my family, either."

"I'll tell you everything soon, but not on Christmas Day. As you are a Fellwood, I suspect they will want to meet you. They've welcomed Sam, after all, but time will tell."

"Have you heard how Frank's father is, Victoria?"

"I had a letter from Catherine last week, Annie, and she said Monty was desperately ill and not expected to be with us much longer. I've tried to keep in touch with her since Frank's death because she has little else, and I'm hoping she might move to Devon eventually. Sarah, do you think you could pass my shawl, please? It's on the chair, look. I'm feeling slightly chilly." Victoria pulled the warm blue shawl around her shoulders. "Thanks, that's better. I wondered if we might persuade you to play us a few tunes on the piano."

"Yes, I'd like that too, Sarah; would you mind? I haven't heard you play for ages."

Sarah was fifteen and had grown into an attractive young woman. "Yes, it would be a pleasure, Annie, if you'd like me to."

After a few carols and well-known songs, Sarah was persuaded to play some nursery rhymes for the youngsters to sing along to, and Robert rose to his feet.

"Ladies, would you mind if we men retired to the library for a game of whist? I haven't played for a long time, and I thought I could pair up with Marrok and Geoffrey with Sam to have a game."

The women nodded their agreement, content to chat with each other and watch the children singing and playing with their new toys.

"Do you two gentlemen know how to play?" Both men shook their heads. "Not a problem; Geoffrey and I can soon teach you."

CHAPTER 16

HARTFORD

At the Lodge House, Sabina was looking forward to having her family under one roof for Christmas dinner, all except Annie, and she would see her on Boxing Day. She rose from her bed quietly, not wanting to wake Arthur, for he did not often lie in bed. Her baby was due in less than a week, and she wondered if it would be a girl or a boy; maybe a boy, for she had carried five girls and four boys, and another boy would even it up. It didn't matter as long as it was healthy; that was the main thing. She opened her bedroom door and descended the stairs. It was early, and she intended to prepare the goose and belly pork for dinner before breakfast. However, as she entered the kitchen, she saw Liza sitting at the table enjoying a cup of tea.

"Liza, what are you doing up so early? It's only about five o'clock, I think?"

"Aye, it is, but I wanted to prepare the dinner. It'll take a while for that goose to cook; 'tis a big bird."

"Great minds think alike then, but you could have left it to me; I'm too uncomfortable to lie abed these days; the sooner this baby is born, the better."

"It's the same for me; I can't stay in bed in the mornings anymore, and I think this is the best time of day. Sit down, and I'll pour you a cup of tea."

"Thanks; let's think about how many there will be for lunch before we prepare the vegetables."

"I've had a quick count, and I reckon there will be eleven of us: me, you and Arthur, Stephen, Edward, Helen and Danny, and then later, Mary and Willie, and Louis and Theresa. I think that's eleven; we'll need plenty of teddies anyway, for if I remember rightly, Willie loves his teddies."

"Yes, he does. It's a good job that Arthur grows so many. When I've had this cup of tea, I'll start peeling the teddies, and perhaps you can do the parsnips and carrots. Have you put the goose and pork in the oven already?"

"Yes, the meat's been in for half an hour. We can take it out and let it rest while we roast the teddies and parsnips; we're spoilt having such a spacious oven these days. What about the sprouts? Have they been picked?"

"Yes, Arthur gathered them yesterday, and they're in a basket in the dairy. They've had some frost on them, so they should be full of flavour. I'm glad he picked them yesterday, for today, we'd have had to brush the snow from them; have you looked out?"

"Yes, it looks so pretty. I love seeing the snow, but only when I don't have to go out. I hope Willie can get here all right. It will be a long, cold journey from Sugworthy Farm."

"It will; I expect he'll borrow one of Mr Houle's horses and ride over; I hope so, anyway. I hear Arthur moving; I didn't think he'd stay in bed long."

Arthur Webber rubbed the sleep from his eyes as he entered the kitchen.

"Oh, it's nice and warm in here. I'll fetch a few more logs before breakfast and put them on the fires in the bedrooms; we don't want them to go out in this cold weather. The children are moving, so I reckon they'll be here in a minute, hoping for some presents. Shall we let them open them in the sitting room?"

"Yes, the fire's burning nicely there, for I stoked it earlier." Sabina smiled as Stephen entered the room, followed by Edward, Helen, and Danny.

"Good morning. You're all awake early this morning; is there any particular reason?"

"It's Christmas, Mum. Have we got any presents?"

"Let's go into the sitting room and see, shall we? I think Father Christmas may have left them around the Christmas tree."

As she led the way into the comfortably furnished room, Sabina reflected on how, just a short time ago, no one in her family would have even asked about presents; they would have been content to have something to eat for breakfast. She would never cease to be thankful for how their lives had changed since Annie had married Robert Fellwood, the heir to Hartford Manor. Tom would find it hard to believe that his beloved daughter was now a lady and Sabina was living in the Lodge House.

Just as at Hartford Manor, there was much excitement as the presents were opened. In each pillowcase were some nuts, an orange, a new toy, gloves, socks, and warm clothes. Although she could afford to buy gifts these days, Sabina had been poor long enough not to want to waste her money, preferring to spend it on practical presents rather than frivolous toys. Nevertheless, Stephen, Edward, and Danny were delighted to share a box of toy soldiers, some marbles, and a Noah's Ark, complete with wooden animals. Helen was overjoyed with a new doll and the doll's clothes, carefully knitted by Sabina and Liza when she was not around.

At eleven o'clock, Mary arrived. Aged fourteen, she had been in service to an old gentleman in the village for two years. She was content there but treasured time with her family and was pleased that leave had been granted for Christmas Day.

"Hello, Mary; come in and get warm, and I'll get you a cup of tea. Please take off your boots and put them near the fire to dry. You can borrow a pair of my slippers for today. Oh, I love your dress. Is it a new one?"

The girl hugged her mother and Liza and smoothed her hands down over the knitted bottle-green dress.

"Yes, fairly new. Annie bought it for me when I went into Barnstaple with her, Aunty Eveline, and Charlotte. I haven't had an opportunity to wear it until now, but it's ideal for Christmas Day. How are you all?"

"You look beautiful in it, and yes, we're all fine, thank you. Oh, here's Willie."

The door opened, and a tall young man entered, grinning at everyone. He was over six feet tall and broadly built. His curly red hair was almost down to his shoulders, and his deep green eyes surveyed the room in appreciation.

"It's so cosy here, Mum; I'm glad Annie persuaded you to move here."

"I didn't take much persuading, lad; wild horses wouldn't have kept me away. I'm pleased to have you here, though; how on earth did you persuade Mr Houle to give you Christmas Day off?"

Willie frowned. "It wasn't easy, but I've worked there for a few years and never get the time off I'm owed. This time, I put my foot down. Mr Houle's still grieving and doesn't pull his weight; we desperately need more help. The farm's barely paying its way because there's only one young lad and me, and we can't do everything, but Mr Houle insists he can't afford more labourers. Anyway, I persuaded him to pay one of the Chuggs to do the milking tonight so I could have the whole day off. It will be fair near breaking his heart to part with his money, but there it is. He can't take it with him, and as far as I know, he has no living relatives; I've never seen any, anyway. I don't know why he doesn't give up the tenancy and retire to a cottage somewhere."

"I think he's lived there for fifty years or more, so I can understand his reluctance to move. I expect he and his late wife, Lettie, hoped to have a family to carry on after they'd gone, but sadly, that never happened. Still, at least you're here now, lad, and you get taller every time I see you. Come and give your mother a hug."

Willie obliged by hugging not only his mother but Liza and Mary, too.

"Something smells delicious, and my belly's rumbling. What time are we having dinner?"

"Not until two o'clock, but sit down and have a slice of the bacon and egg pie I made yesterday; it will tide you over until dinner. How about you, Mary? Would you like some?"

"Oh, yes, please, Mum; I love your pie, and it's a long time since my breakfast. I had lots of chores to do this morning before I could get away."

Once the children realised Willie and Mary had arrived, they hurried into the kitchen, keen to show off their new clothes and toys. Sabina reached under the Christmas tree and retrieved a few presents for Willie and Mary.

"Here we are; it gives me such pleasure to give you a present; 'twas never possible when you were younger."

Mary opened her gift, revealing a warm grey shawl, a skirt, and some mittens, and Willie found he had a new jacket, boots, and socks. Both were delighted and presented Sabina and Liza with small gifts, too. Edward, deaf from birth, observed all that was happening and pulled Willie's arm. He pointed into the dairy.

"What is it, Edward? Do you have something to show me?"

"He's adopted some young hedgehogs that he found a month or two ago. They should be hibernating, but I think their mother must have died, for they're too skinny to survive the winter. Anyway, Edward's taken them under his wing. He has such a way with animals, and they're thriving. Go and see them, but make sure you don't let Piper in. It's my biggest worry that the dog will kill them. Here, Edward, give them some of this meat; I trimmed a few scraps off the pork, but they'll eat it." Sabina chuckled. "It's lucky for those hedgehogs we have enough to eat these days; there was a time when I would probably have made them into a stew!"

Edward led Willie and Mary into the dairy and proudly showed them three tiny hedgehogs in an open-topped wooden crate. Willie reached in and gently picked up the largest hedgehog, which promptly rolled into a ball. However, when Edward gathered the smallest animal into his hand, it nuzzled his fingers, and he beamed at his brother.

"How does he do that? He has such a way with animals. This one doesn't like me holding him at all, but that one is quite at home in Edward's hands."

Edward offered the hedgehog a piece of meat, and it gratefully ate it in no time. He returned the tiny creature to the crate and put the rest of the food on a slate for them all to share. Willie, too, replaced the hedgehog he had been holding, and after a few minutes, it uncurled and began to eat.

"I think if Edward feeds them well, they should survive now; they seem healthy, anyway. At least if he lets them go in the garden, they'll help to keep the slugs and snails down. Let's go back to the kitchen, where it's a bit warmer."

Louis Blaquiere arrived with Theresa Carter just before lunch, and Liza opened the door.

"Hello, Louis, I'm pleased to see you, and you, my dear; your father let you come, then?"

"Hello, Liza; thank you for inviting us to dinner. I love spending time with you; you're the nearest thing I have to a family."

"It's the same for me, Louis, and I think of you as my adopted son these days; I hope you don't mind?"

"No, on the contrary, I love you telling me about my real parents and brother. I was going to visit their grave on the way here, but with all the snow, that job will have to wait for another day."

Theresa Carter joined the conversation. "Hello, Liza, thanks for inviting me, and yes, amazingly, Dad agreed. He's not even grumbled about me seeing Louis and him so many years older than me. Since I went missing and he thought he'd lost me, it's changed him, or something has. Maybe it's being married to Mary Ann. I don't know, but George Carter has changed for the better, and I'll enjoy spending the day here with all of you."

CHAPTER 17

HARTFORD

Victoria Eastleigh had felt uncomfortable throughout Christmas Day and longed for her labour pains to start so she could get the birth over and done with. Although her husband, Frank, had never been an attentive father, often out drinking and gambling when he should have been by her side, or at least waiting anxiously outside the delivery room, it felt strange and more upsetting than she had thought possible to know he would never see his third child. Frank had been unfaithful to her, virtually from their wedding day, and had done nothing to hide his infidelity. He often assured her she was the only woman he loved but would never change, and, in that, he had been correct. Unfortunately for him, however, someone had taken exception to his behaviour, and a couple of months earlier, he had been found stabbed and fatally injured on the road from Barnstaple to Hartford. For a gentleman like Frank, the police had made every effort to bring the villains to justice. However, they knew there was probably a long queue of fathers, brothers, and uncles, all seeking revenge for the girls Frank had taken advantage of over the years and, in many cases, literally left holding the baby. The culprits had never been found.

Despite her discomfort, Victoria had enjoyed Christmas Day in the company of her siblings and was pleased to see Caroline and Joshua playing with their cousins. As she drifted off to sleep, she consoled herself that, already more than a week overdue, by the laws of nature alone, it could not be long before her baby was born. She was right and woke up at three o'clock with a backache. By four o'clock, her pains were coming every five minutes, and Ethan, one of the servants, was dispatched to fetch Doctor Luckett. After a short and trouble-free labour, he announced that the baby was a healthy boy.

Victoria lay back on her pillows, exhausted from the birth but delighted to have a healthy child. Even with her first two children, Frank had not seen them until several hours after their birth, but this baby he would never see, and a few tears slipped down her cheeks as her mother, Eleanor, tapped on the door and entered.

"How are you feeling, darling?"

"Tired and glad it's all over, but sad that Frank will never see his child."

"No, and that is a shame, but, my darling, you're better off without him; surely you know that."

"I know I should be, for he was consistently unfaithful, but for all that, I loved him, Mama, and I miss him. Can you send Sarah to tell Robert and Annie that I've had the baby, please? At least Robert can come to see me, though I don't suppose I'll be able to see Annie until I'm up and about. It does annoy me that you won't receive her. She's such a warm-hearted and generous person, and if you get to know her, you couldn't fail to like her."

"I'm not discussing that now, Victoria; it's all been said before, and you must rest. As if life isn't difficult enough with Robert's unfortunate choice of wife, we have Sam, your father's long-lost cousin and a tramp all his life, suddenly on the scene, and now his son and grandchildren have been found in the workhouse. I don't know where it will end; I really don't. Not many of our friends want to receive us now, and when this latest scandal is known about Marrok and his family and where they were living, I suspect there will be even less."

"I wish you wouldn't worry about it so much, Mama. Don't concern yourself with what people think; I don't. Anyway, you're right about one thing, and that is, I must get some sleep. Tell Papa I'll bring the baby to see him when the doctor lets me out of bed."

When Robert Fellwood arose on Boxing Day, his first task was to pull back the heavy damask curtains and peer out of his bedroom window. Beneath him, the snowy landscape stretched as far as the eye could see, and he grimaced. It was the meet of the Hartford Manor hounds that day, and people from far and wide would be arriving later to take part in the hunt or at least follow its progress. He decided to consult Jack Bater, his farm manager, about whether the hunt could go ahead in such wintry weather.

He was pleased when Jack assured him that the snowy weather could work in their favour, for it would likely draw the foxes out of their burrows in search of food. Thus encouraged, he joined Sam and Marrok for a hearty, cooked breakfast and reflected on how his father, Charles Fellwood, his brother, David, and his twin sister, Victoria, would have joined him in years gone by. However, that would not be the case this year, for his father was an invalid and, sadly, would never ride again; poor David had died in the Boer War, and Victoria was due to give birth at any time. Although a proficient horsewoman, his younger sister, Sarah, was not a lover of blood sports and had never taken part, for she believed it to be cruel. He was finishing his breakfast when, to his surprise, Sarah appeared.

"Good morning, Sarah. Have you decided to join us for the hunt, after all?"

"Certainly not. I think you know me better than that, Robert; it's a beastly sport, and I shall never take part, but we won't start that argument again now. No, I've come to tell you that Victoria gave birth to a healthy son in the early hours of the morning. Doctor Luckett delivered the child, and I believe she will call him Frank, after his father, though, goodness knows why, after his terrible behaviour."

"Oh, that's good; I know she was uncomfortable yesterday, and I'm glad the child's well. I'll come back with you and visit her. I should have time before everyone arrives for the hunt."

Given the inclement weather, Robert and Sarah took a shortcut through the kitchens of the west wing, where Robert and his family lived, to the kitchen in the main part of Hartford Manor. It was the only connection between the two dwellings and was left in place for the odd occasion when the servants had to cater for both establishments.

Sarah accompanied him to Victoria's bedroom, where they found his mother, Eleanor, cuddling the new arrival. Robert embraced his twin and duly admired his new nephew.

"Well done, Victoria; was it an easy birth?"

"Yes, it was the easiest yet, I have to say. I might call the baby Frank; do you think that's silly given the circumstances?"

"No, I'm sure Frank would be thrilled, and for all his many faults, I think he genuinely loved you. It's best not to bear a grudge, for he is the father of your children, and Caroline and Joshua adored him, for all they saw little of him."

"I knew you'd understand, Robert; thank you. Are you hunting this morning?"

"Yes, there's quite a bit of snow, but Jack assures me it won't matter and, if anything, will encourage the foxes from their burrows. They certainly need to be culled; we've recently lost several chickens to them. It's a pity you can't come with us today."

"Hmm, yes, well, you know I'd love to, but I can assure you I don't feel like sitting on a horse at the moment."

"No, I guess not. Mother, the huntsmen and the hounds will be here shortly to enjoy the stirrup cup before we set off, and I'm sure Father would like to see the gathering; can you put his wheelchair near his bedroom window? He should be able to see everything from there."

"I think he'd like that, Robert, but if you can spare the time, why don't you go and see him and do that? You don't visit him often, and I'm sure he'd be pleased to see you."

Visiting his father was the last thing Robert wanted to do, but his mother knew nothing of his bitter feelings towards the man, and he had no intention of enlightening her, so he forced a smile onto his face and agreed with her suggestion.

Charles Fellwood was a shadow of his former self since the severe stroke that had left him paralysed down one side, and he spent much of the day in his wheelchair. His speech had also been severely affected but had slowly returned, although he still struggled with some words. A side room had been converted into a bedroom, well equipped to deal with the disabled man's needs, and a bathroom had recently been installed in the adjacent room. Charles had two full-time carers who could push him in his wheelchair to different rooms on the ground floor. It was lucky he was a wealthy man, for such care did not come cheaply, and many in his situation would have spent the rest of their days bedridden. His bedroom had patio doors that led out onto a terrace, and when they were opened wide, he could be pushed outside in his wheelchair in pleasant weather.

Although the atmosphere was strained between the two men, Charles was pleased to see his son and grateful for the suggestion of viewing the hunt through the double glass doors. Having positioned the wheelchair where his father would have a good view of the proceedings, Robert welcomed his guests.

At the Lodge House, Sabina and Liza were busy preparing the family for their visit to the Manor House. They had intended to walk the short distance along the driveway, but as the snow was already some eight or nine inches deep, Robert had sent Dodger on horseback earlier in the morning to tell them a carriage would be provided. Having imparted the message to Sabina, the stable boy rode on, first to The Red Lion to tell Betsey and Ned the carriage would return to collect them and then to the smithy to give the same message to Matilda Rudd.

Annie was pleased that her guests had arrived in time to witness the gathering of the hunt, and there was quite a crowd in the courtyard outside Hartford Manor. For some present, it was the first time they had witnessed a hunt, and there was much excitement. The many hounds were yapping and barking, and the horses, their coats shining, were impatient to be off, having been cooped up in the stables for a few days because of the poor weather. The huntsmen, dressed in bright red jackets and creamy white trousers, made a colourful spectacle against the snowy landscape. As they put their feet into the stirrups and mounted their steeds, Robert took the stirrup cup from Sid Hobbs and, as tradition demanded, passed it around the crowd to enjoy a sip of port and brandy. Seeing his father peering through the glass doors of his bedroom, Robert took pity, dismounted, and took the stirrup cup to his father to allow him a sip. The older man smiled his lop-sided smile at his son gratefully and wished him luck.

Within minutes of emptying the cup, a huntsman blew hard on his trumpet, and with cries of 'tally ho', they were off.

After the huntsmen had departed, the visitors trooped back inside, and Annie ushered them all into the drawing room, where a cosy fire was burning. Having introduced everyone to Marrok and his family, she rang the bell and instructed

Molly to bring tea, coffee, hot chocolate, and some of Maisie's best cakes.

Danny smiled shyly at Geoffrey Turner, and the doctor shook the little boy's hand.

"Hello, Danny, I'm pleased to see you again. How are you?"

"I'm very well, thank you, sir. Are you going to mend my other foot?"

"Would you like me to?"

"Yes, please. I can walk much better since you mended one foot, but I still limp and can't run fast."

"I'll tell you what, then; I'm going to keep an eye on you today and watch how well you walk, and then, in a day or two, I'll come to your house and examine your other foot, and we'll decide what to do. Is that all right with you?"

"Yes, sir, thank you."

Sabina had been listening to this exchange, and she thanked the doctor.

When everyone was seated comfortably, Annie handed out Christmas presents to her family. She enjoyed watching their faces light up as the wrapping paper was torn off and the contents revealed. She then urged Selina to take the children to the nursery to play with their new toys and leave the adults in peace until lunchtime. Selina was delighted to have so many people to play with, and before long, she and Helen had organised a game of hide and seek, which was likely to take some time.

As the adults chatted amongst themselves, Annie took the opportunity to speak with her granny.

"How's Grandad today, Gran? It's a pity he didn't come with you. I thought he might, seeing as Robert sent the carriage."

Betsey smiled fondly at her eldest granddaughter. "I would have liked Ned to come, but he didn't feel up to it, and it's better for him to rest quietly in bed. He insisted I come, though; he knew it was important to me to be here today, as I wanted to get something off my chest. He's in safe hands with Sarah, though I would have liked her and Bentley to be here today."

"They could have come; I invited them."

"Yes, I know you did, but Sarah, bless her, knew I wanted to come and that I'd feel happier if she stayed with Ned."

"What did you mean, Gran, when you said you had something to get off your chest? What is it that's worrying you?"

"I don't want to go into it now, but later, I want a quiet word with Lady Margery, Sam, and Marrok, and I'd like you to hear what I have to say, too."

"Very well. After lunch, we'll sit quietly in the library, and you can have your say."

"Splendid, it's nothing to worry about, but I need to pass my knowledge on before it's too late."

"I don't want to hear that sort of talk. I hope you'll be with us for many more years."

"Yes, I hope so too, my dear, but none of us know when our time will come, and I'll feel happier when I've had my say."

CHAPTER 18

HARTFORD

Maisie had prepared a delicious lunch of cold turkey, goose, and pork, accompanied by pickled red cabbage and piccalilli. On Christmas Day, she had purposely cooked far too many roast potatoes, knowing they would be tasty, fried in goose fat the next day. She was not mistaken, and they went down a treat. She had made lemon posset, a sherry trifle, a jam roly-poly pudding and custard for dessert.

Sabina pushed back her plate and groaned contentedly. "Oh, that was so delicious; I think I enjoyed that meal almost more than my Christmas dinner yesterday, and that's saying something. Do you think I could take Maisie home with me?"

"Not a chance, Mum; not even for you would I part with Maisie or Mrs Potts."

"Oh, well, it was worth a try. How about you, Tilly? Did you enjoy your lunch?"

"It was wonderful. Thank you for inviting us, Annie. I'm so grateful to you for letting me spend time with Selina; I wish Harry could be here, too."

"Aw, yes, I'm sure you do, Tilly. We all have loved ones we're missing today, but Harry would love to think you were here, enjoying your dinner in the Manor House with your granddaughter."

"Yes, he would."

"How about you, Francis and Jacob? Did you enjoy your lunch?"

Jacob Rudd, fully recovered from the horrific burns he had suffered in a devastating fire at the smithy a few years earlier, grinned happily. He had always been a little simple-minded and seldom had much to say, but he enjoyed life and was a hard worker. As usual, Francis answered for him.

"It was a tasty meal, and I'm so pleased to see Mum here enjoying herself. It's not been easy since we lost Dad and Harry, but you've never forgotten us. As for Maisie and Mrs Potts, if they ever want a job, I'd love them to come and cook my dinner at the smithy, a good cook, though my mother is."

"You can all forget it because Maisie and Mrs Potts are going nowhere. Now, children, if you dress up warmly, I thought you might like to go outside and play in the garden to get some fresh air. Maybe Arthur, Francis, and Jacob would like to go with you to build a snowman? What about you, Geoffrey? Do you feel like some exercise?"

"Yes, I think I do. It's been years since I played in the snow, and it would help that enormous dinner to go down."

Arthur got to his feet. "Come on, you lot, let's have a snowball fight, and you'd better watch out because I'm a pretty good shot; how about you, Francis?"

"Aye, I'm pretty handy with a snowball, myself. I reckon Jacob would enjoy that too."

Leaving Clara, Matilda, Sabina and Liza to sit with David and Thomas in the drawing room, Annie invited Lady Margery, Sam, and Marrok to join her in the library with Betsey. They were all puzzled, and when they were seated comfortably, Annie explained that she had got them together at Betsey's request. A little nervous at first, Betsey thanked Annie and then faced her audience.

"Thank you for getting everyone together, Annie. I expect you're all wondering what I want to talk to you about. It's a secret I've kept for over sixty years, and I think it's time I shared it, for it's something that all of you in this room should know. The only other folk who know about this are Ned, his brother, Silas, and his wife, Josie, and they, too, vowed to keep their silence all that time ago.

"I had a difficult life as a little girl. My father was called Adam Lovering, and he drank heavily, and sometimes, when he'd had one too many, he'd beat my mother, Ellen. He was always sorry the next day, but that didn't put it right. Seven of my siblings died at birth or in infancy, and I think the losses drove my father to seek refuge in the bottle. I don't think he was a cruel man at heart, but he had a difficult life. I only knew two of my siblings: Barney and Norman.

"My eldest brother, Barney, lives in Wales with his wife, Bronwen, and their family. Barney was four years older than me and did his best to care for me and my younger brother, Norman, who was three years younger than me. When Barney was ten, my father took him to the mill one morning to get a job, so he left home. After he left, life was even harder for me. My father did little around the house, and my mother was expecting her tenth child. She was a wonderful mother, but she received barely any money from my father, and we were always hungry and dressed in rags.

"We lived in the cottage next to The Red Lion Inn, owned by Ned's parents, Mal and Keziah Carter. It's called Bluebell Cottage now, but it didn't have a name back then. Barney and I went to school with Ned and his brother, Silas. Auntie Kezzie and Uncle Mal, as we called them, were kind to us, often feeding us when we had no food, and Mum did washing for them to earn extra money. One night after Barney had gone to live at the mill, Dad came home even more drunk than usual and beat my mother again. Norman and I could hear it all going on, but there was nothing we could do. I pulled the clothes over our heads and sang to Norman to drown out my mother's screams. She was so seriously injured that she couldn't get out of bed the next morning, and I ran next door to fetch Auntie Kezzie. Sadly, the beating brought Mum's labour on, and she died giving birth to a premature baby boy."

"Oh, Gran, that's awful. Why haven't you told us all this before?"

"I've never seen the need to burden anyone with it; what's done is done. I'm sorry if I'm rambling on a bit, but you need to understand the circumstances, and I'll get to the point in a minute. After Mum died, things went from bad to worse for Norman and me, and if it weren't for the Carters, we would have starved. Then Dad fell out with Mal and Keziah and forbade them to come to our cottage any more, and we really were on our own then. Dad was carrying on with a woman called Becky Chown and had no interest in us. The only people I could turn to were the gypsies on the common. An old lady called Gypsy Freda had delivered me at birth and always had a soft spot for me. She was a clever woman who knew all sorts of herbal cures and taught me many of them. She had a granddaughter called Jane."

At this point, Betsey glanced at Marrok and Sam and smiled.

"Yes, you've guessed; Jane was your mother, Sam, and Gypsy Freda was your grandmother. Your father, Thomas Fellwood, was about seventeen when he discovered the gypsy camp one day while riding. I happened to be there at the time, begging for bread, and young though I was, I could see that he was taken with Jane from the first time he saw her. The miller, Jasper Morris, was there too, delivering flour, and he had designs on Jane himself, though it was clear she wasn't interested in him.

"From then on, Thomas made every excuse under the sun to visit the gypsy camp. The gypsies never made him welcome, for he was one of the gentry and not one of their sort, but Jane used to meet him in secret. With Thomas trying to see Jane at every possible opportunity and me going there to beg for food most days, our paths often crossed, and he was always kind to me."

Betsey glanced at Lady Margery.

"Margery, I don't know if you remember, but one day, when you were riding with Thomas, he stopped and helped me because I'd fallen and skinned my knees. I've never liked to mention it to you when we've met with Annie because I didn't know if you realised I was that little girl."

"Yes, I do remember, Betsey, and I guessed it was you, although your name had changed. How funny; I've never wanted to mention it to you, either, in case it embarrassed you, for times were hard for you back then. If I remember correctly, Thomas gave you a ride to the gypsy camp on his horse, and we played with some puppies there; he bought one for me a few weeks later, and I called him Gyp after the gypsies."

"Yes, that's right, and I suspect I provided Thomas with the ideal excuse to visit the camp that day and the opportunity to see Jane again."

"Yes, I think so, too."

"A few weeks after that, Thomas came across me again on my way to beg for food from the gypsies. It had snowed heavily, a bit like today, and my feet were frozen as my shoes were full of holes. I'd left Norman at home while I went in search of something to eat, for his shoes were in an even worse state than mine. Thomas was out for a ride, hoping to see Jane, and again, he lifted me onto his horse to take me to the gypsy camp. I was shivering with the cold, and he wrapped his cloak around me. I can remember the heat from his body as Thomas held me close and from the horse beneath me, and I tried hard not to cry as my feet and hands began to thaw. He urged his horse towards the camp, but we hadn't gone far when we heard screams from up ahead. He kicked the horse, and it galloped to the next clearing, where we saw Jasper Morris handling Jane roughly. He was trying to kiss her, and she was having none of it. In no time, the two men were fighting, and I didn't know how it would end. Mr Morris was much the stronger of the two, but Thomas was agile and light on his feet and mostly avoided Mr Morris's flailing arms. Suddenly, Mr Morris stumbled backwards over some rough ground and fell heavily, and he just lay there. Thomas took the opportunity to catch his breath, but then we all wondered why the miller hadn't got up.

"Thomas was worried he was feigning injury to lure him closer, and eventually, when Jane investigated, she found he had cracked his head open on a stone half hidden under the snow, and he was dead! Thomas was horrified and was all for going to the police and owning up to the fight, but Jane persuaded him not to. At first, we thought about leaving Mr Morris there and going on our way. It was a cold day, and no one was around, so no one would know we'd been there, but Jane was worried that his body was so near the gypsy camp that they would get the blame, as they often did for anything that went wrong."

"So, what did you do?"

"Thomas and Jane heaved him back onto his horse and lay him on his belly across the saddle. Then I led the horse to Shebworthy Pond and shoved him off so people would think he'd had an accident and fallen from his horse."

"You did? But Betsey, you were only a small child; how did you manage it?"

"Thomas rested the body on the horse so that most of the weight was on one side, and it was easy to push him off; I was more worried his body would fall off before I got a decent distance from the camp."

"So, what happened next?"

"Thomas went home, Jane went back to the gypsies, and when I'd got rid of the body, I went to the camp too, and Jane gave me some rabbit stew and some for Norman. Then I went home. The waiting was awful, and we all expected the police to be knocking on our doors at any moment, but nothing happened until the next day when Barney came to our house and asked us to help find Mr

Morris, for he had gone out on his horse the day before and not returned. The whole village was involved in the hunt for him, and my father found him. Doctor Abernethy said it appeared Mr Morris's horse had thrown him, and he'd knocked his head on a stone and died of the cold. We were so relieved but still worried in case the story didn't stick."

"This is quite a tale, Betsey. Why have you kept it a secret all this time, and why are you telling us now?"

For an answer, Betsey reached into her bag and withdrew a small tin with her swollen and misshapen old fingers. It was prettily painted with bright blue forget-me-nots, red poppies, and yellow buttercups.

"Apart from my family, this tin holds my most treasured possessions." Carefully, she opened the lid and delved inside. "I don't know where it came from, but my mother used to keep her housekeeping money in this tin. She would carefully plan how to spend every penny to get the most for her money, and then my father would take the lot back and spend it on alcohol.

"Aunty Kezzie bought me this red ribbon in the Barnstaple pannier market one day. I was so thrilled because I'd never owned anything so pretty." Lying it carefully on the arm of the chair beside her, she reached into the tin again. "And these are my brother, Norman's, baby curls." A tear slid down her wrinkled cheek. "He died, you see. My father abandoned us, and we all but starved and froze to death in that cottage next to the inn. If the schoolteacher had not come to check on us when he did, I would have died, too, but fortunately, I was saved. Poor Norman was not so lucky, and he perished, poor lad. Aunty Kezzie cut off his curls for me to keep; he's buried with my mother in the churchyard in the village."

The small group of people in the room were horrified at the sad story unfolding before them, and they waited for Betsey to continue her tale.

"This cheap brooch was one my mother used to wear; I think it's the one thing my father gave her when they were courting that he didn't sell. I believe he won it at the Barnstaple Fair." She reached into the tin again. "And here is the reason you're all here. This is Thomas Fellwood's watch. He lost it during the fight with Jasper Morris, and Jane asked me to search for it. I found it in the middle of a gorse bush, and luckily, it wasn't damaged. Not long after the fight, Thomas and Jane hitched a ride to France on a boat with a local smuggler, an old man called Raymond Chugg. He was Aunty Kezzie's father and a relation of Charlie Chugg, who married my daughter, Eveline.

"Lord Fellwood had found out about Thomas and Jane's relationship and forbidden Thomas to see her again. They knew they could never be together in this country, for Jane would never be accepted into Thomas's family, and the gypsies would never allow Thomas to be one of them. I didn't find the watch until after they had left for France, and I kept it, hoping to give it back one day, for I know it meant a great deal to Thomas; I believe it belonged to his grandfather. Unfortunately, I never saw either of them again, but I'd like you to have this watch, Sam, because it's what your father would have wanted, and it gives me a lot of pleasure to give it to you. No doubt in time, you'll want to pass it on to your son, Marrok."

Betsey handed the golden watch over to Sam, who turned it over and over in his hands. His eyes were full of tears as he took her hands in his.

"Oh, Betsey, I'm so grateful to you for this; it means so much to hear about my father and what happened. Thank you for never selling it; you must have been tempted over the years."

"More than you will ever know, Sam."

"But Granny, what happened to you after Norman died? Did your father come back?"

"No, Annie, I never saw him again. The woman he ran away with, Becky Chown, returned a few months later. She'd found out the hard way that he was not the catch, she thought. Her mother owned the butcher's shop where my

Dad worked, and she went back and lived with her mother again. She never married and died before her mother, and she's buried over in the churchyard. I never spoke to her again.

"No, luckily for me, Uncle Mal and Aunty Kezzie took me in and gave me a home. I was raised with Ned and Silas, and they were like brothers to me. It was so generous of the Carters to provide me with a home, for they were in a lot of debt trying to pay off a bank loan they'd taken out to finance a new roof for the inn. At one point, just before I was twenty-one, the bank manager called in the loan, and The Red Lion Inn was put up for sale. It seemed certain Uncle Mal would be sent to a debtor's prison, and that's when I was sorely tempted to sell Thomas's gold watch."

"So, why didn't you? No one could have blamed you."

"To be honest, I didn't know who to sell it to, and I was worried folk might think I'd stolen it. If anyone asked where I got it, I couldn't say without betraying Thomas and Jane, and I would never have done that."

"What happened? Did your Uncle Mal get sent to jail?"

"No, on my twenty-first birthday, I received a letter inviting me to attend a solicitor's office in Barnstaple. It was on my wedding day, actually, and I was worried to death. A few days after the wedding, Ned went with me, and we were shocked to discover Thomas Fellwood had left me one hundred guineas. Bless him, he repaid me times over for keeping his secret, and the money saved the day. I used it to pay off Uncle Mal's bank loan and repair Betsey's kitchen, which had been damaged in a thunderstorm. After that, Uncle Mal and Aunty Kezzie moved into the cottage, and Ned and I lived at the inn, and we've lived there happily ever since."

It was early evening before all the guests left the Manor House and were transported to their homes in the comfort of the Fellwood carriage. Annie asked Dodger to drop Betsey off first, for she knew her granny was exhausted with divulging her long-held secret. The old lady entered through the bar of the Red Lion, where Sarah and Louis were busy serving a large crowd.

"It's busy in here tonight."

"Yes, we've been rushed off our feet. It's mainly the huntsmen, enjoying a pint or two since the meet; I'm afraid one or two are a bit the worse for wear."

"Right, I'll check on Ned, and then I'll be back to help you."

"No, Betsey, we can manage; you look exhausted. Go and sit with Ned; he's missed you today. Master Robert's over there if you want to say hello first."

Betsey chatted with Robert and heard they had eventually caught a fox, but not before he had led them a merry dance. Wishing them goodnight, she thankfully mounted the stairs and climbed into the bed beside Ned. They left the candle burning for a few minutes while she told him about her day. The dim light flickered on the ceiling, casting shadows around the room as she cuddled up to her husband.

"I feel much better now that I've told Sam about his father and given him the watch, and he was so pleased. Do you know, Margery knew I was that little girl she met all that time ago, but she never mentioned it, as she didn't want to upset me. Oh, and Doctor Turner is coming to examine you tomorrow morning to see what he thinks."

"Aye, that's all right, he can have his say, but I think Doctor Luckett's right; I think it's my heart, and he can't give me a new one. Anyway, this cuddle is just what I needed; 'tis the best medicine."

CHAPTER 19

HARTFORD

The following morning, Robert awoke with a blinding headache, which he endeavoured to hide from his wife. Annie, however, knew her husband well, and with one glance at his tired, pale face, she knew he had imbibed rather too much alcohol the night before. She teased him because he was known to be no drinker, and if he had more than one or two drinks, he always felt the effects the next day. Annie mixed him up a potion, the ingredients of which had been passed down to her by her granny. She stirred the concoction, wondering if the recipe had originated from Gypsy Freda, a woman she had never heard of until the previous day.

Having forced down a couple of slices of dry toast, much to the amusement of Maisie and Mrs Potts, Robert felt well enough to accompany Geoffrey Turner to The Red Lion Inn to examine his father-in-law. The two men decided to walk to the village through the slushy snow that still lay on the ground, and the fresh air did much to revive the younger man.

The inn was closed when they arrived, and Robert led Geoffrey around to the back door, where he knocked and entered. Sarah was in the kitchen kneading some dough, and Betsey was chopping onions.

"Oh, good morning, Robert. Good morning, sir; thank you for coming to see Ned. I'm afraid he had a restless night; his cough was troublesome."

"Now, Betsey, may I call you Betsey?" The doctor raised his bushy white eyebrows questioningly.

"Yes, sir, of course."

"Right, I thought you'd say that, so could you call me Geoffrey, please, Betsey? We're friends now, after all."

"I'll try to remember, sir; sorry, Geoffrey, but it doesn't seem right, a silly old woman like me calling a doctor by his first name."

"However, I insist; now, where's the patient?"

Betsey led the way upstairs, leaving Robert sitting at the kitchen table and chatting with Sarah over a cup of tea. Before long, Bentley arrived and, in no time, climbed onto Robert's knee and enjoyed looking at a picture book with him. In the bedroom, the doctor withdrew a stethoscope from his bag and asked Ned to lift his nightgown.

"Goodness me, what caused these terrible scars? Were you in a fire?"

"No, not exactly, but I was struck by lightning when I was young. The cow beside me was struck dead, and I was not expected to survive either. It was only due to Betsey's skills as a herbalist that I pulled through."

"I see; well, the burns are extensive, so yes, you're lucky to still be with us. Now, I want to listen to your heart, if I may."

The doctor carefully listened to the front and back of Ned's chest, then sat beside the bed and took his patient's pulse.

"Tell me how you feel, Ned. What symptoms make you lie in bed when you've worked all your life?"

"I don't want to lie here; I can tell you. I've always worked hard and would like to continue doing so, but it's impossible. I'm always tired, and the slightest thing leaves me gasping for breath. Then there's this troublesome cough that keeps me awake half the night; 'tis no wonder I'm tired. What do you think's wrong with me, doctor?"

"I agree with Doctor Luckett that your heart is causing the trouble. It's beating fast and irregularly, and I can hear your lungs wheezing. It's called heart failure, and I'm afraid there's no cure; some folk get it with age. How old are you?"

"I'm nearly seventy-four."

"That's a good age, and I'd say it's high time you gave up work. Now, it's not all bad news. If you have complete rest, with no stress or worry, you could have several years yet. To have survived those burns, you must have a strong constitution and a determination to live, and that's important, but you must heed my words and let others take the load from your shoulders. It's time to retire, my friend."

"Oh, dear, I know what you're telling me is right, and to be honest, I don't think I have a lot of choice. I appreciate your honesty, Doctor; you've confirmed what Betsey and I have been thinking. Could I ask you to keep my diagnosis to yourself for now? We've invited several family members to come here this afternoon to discuss the future of The Red Lion, and I'd rather tell them the news myself."

"Yes, I will, and I wish you a long and happy retirement. You and Betsey have worked hard all your lives, and it's time to enjoy a rest and let others take up the reins."

Betsey escorted the doctor downstairs and thanked him for his trouble. She enquired how much she owed him, but Geoffrey assured her that any more talk along those lines would make him angry, and so, with a grateful smile, she waved him and Robert on their way.

Fred Carter was the first to arrive that afternoon. The third eldest in the family, he was happily married to Charlotte, his second wife, and just before Christmas, they had welcomed their son, Nicholas, into the world. Nicholas was their first child, though Charlotte had a daughter called Doris from a previous relationship. Fred was the father of Llewellyn,

Rosella, and Eddie, the offspring of his first marriage to his late wife, Lucy. He was a carpenter, and his business was prospering, so much so that he had recently taken on thirteen-year-old Llewie as an apprentice and was teaching him the trade. Fred could turn his hand to any job involving wood. He supplied the rafters for new roofs and made staircases and numerous coffins, but his main love was making high-end furniture. He lived in a cottage not far from The Red Lion Inn, where he grew up, and although he had a decent-sized yard and workshop behind his property, until recently, he had nowhere to display the exquisite furniture he crafted. He entered the kitchen, put his arm around his mother, and kissed her cheek.

"This is all very mysterious; is everything all right?"

"Your dad and I will tell you our news when everyone's here, Fred; there's no point in us going through it all several times. Why don't you go into the sitting room and chat with your father while we wait for the others? He's been in bed for days but insisted on coming downstairs to see you all. See if he needs anything; the others won't be long."

Fred's elder brother, George, also lived in the village, where he kept a grocery shop. He, too, had remarried recently, having sadly lost his first wife, Alice, in the terrible diphtheria outbreak a few years earlier. He was now married to Mary Ann, his wife's sister, and they had two daughters, Nellie, aged two, and Sophie, aged one, and Mary Ann was expecting another baby in the spring. Given a choice, George would have preferred not to start a second family at his age. Still, nature had taken its course, and Mary Ann, previously resigned to being an old maid, was delighted to become a mother. George had three grown-up children from his first marriage to Alice. His eldest son, Francis, managed a new shop in the larger town of Barnstaple, and it was there that some of his Uncle Fred's finest furniture was on display and in some demand. George's two daughters, Harriet and Theresa, both worked in the shop in Hartford, and it was Theresa who had spent Christmas Day at the Lodge House with her young man, Louis, and her Aunt Sabina and Uncle Arthur.

George arrived at The Red Lion Inn ten minutes after Fred, with his sister, Eveline, and sister-in-law, Sabina, on his heels. Eveline, Ned and Betsey's first-born child was a keen rider, and she had made the most of the occasion by riding from Hollyford Farm to the Lodge House and then walking into the village with Sabina. On their way to the inn, the two women had speculated why the family had been summoned, but neither knew the answer.

Betsey welcomed her family into the sitting room and asked Sarah to bring them all a drink. Fred and Eveline opted for a tankard of ale each, whilst Sabina and George enjoyed a pot of tea with Betsey and Ned.

"Now, Ned, will you tell them what we wanted to see them for, or would you like me to do it?"

"You tell them, Betsey. I'll sit here quietly and put in my pennyworth if you forget anything."

"All right. Now, I'm sorry for all the mystery, but we thought it was best you all hear this together to avoid any misunderstanding. Your father and I have decided the time has come for us to give up The Red Lion Inn."

There was a shocked silence around the room, and before anyone could interrupt, Betsey continued.

"It's not been an easy decision, for we've both lived here all our lives and been involved in running the inn right from when we were teenagers, but the thing is, we're not getting any younger, and your dad needs to rest. Doctor Luckett and Robert's friend, Doctor Turner, have examined Ned, and they agree he's suffering from heart failure, and there's no cure."

Amid gasps around the room, Betsey reassured her family.

"It's all right; he won't be leaving us just yet, but he needs complete rest and no stress, and neither of that is possible running this place."

"So, what will happen? Are you going to sell up?"

Ned and Betsey gazed at George in horror.

"No, George, of course, we won't sell the inn. It's been in this family for hundreds of years, maybe ever since it was built. No, it has to continue in the Carter family, and we've given this much thought. George, as the eldest son, you may feel it should pass to you, but it's not practical. You're a strictly religious man, and the locals would not tolerate you preaching to them. Not only that, but you're teetotal and frown upon folk imbibing alcohol, so again, you're hardly going to make an ideal innkeeper. Now, I hope you won't feel hard done by, but we won't leave the inn to you. We bought the shop for you when you were twenty-one and set you up in business, and you've made an excellent success of it. Indeed, so much so that you now have a second shop in Barnstaple. We considered whether Francis could run the inn, but he knows nothing about the business and is doing a great job managing your shop, so we've ruled him out, too."

George appeared disappointed, but one glance at his father's stern face made him realise it was useless to protest, and indeed, all that his mother had said was true.

"Now, Eveline, you're the eldest in the family, so you may feel the inn should come to you. However, I'm afraid we've decided against that, too, though we know you'd do an excellent job of running it, for you have a wise head on your shoulders. I reckon we're right, though, in thinking you're happily married to Charlie Chugg. We don't think you'd want to leave Hollyford Farm and come here to live and run the inn, are we right?"

Betsey regarded her only daughter anxiously.

"Yes, you're right. I love living on the farm, and I'd never ask Charlie to leave there. When anything happens to his brother Alfred, Charlie and Alfred's son, Jimmy, will continue running the farm together. It's already been discussed. Beyond that, I don't know, but unless Jimmy marries and has a family, then probably one of William's sons, Joseph or Matthew, might want to take over the tenancy, but that's years ahead. In any case, The Red Lion has been in the Carter family for many generations, and, as you say, it has to pass to a Carter, and as I'm now a Chugg, that's not me. I guess it only leaves you, Fred."

"As usual, Eveline's hit the nail on the head, and yes, that's what we're thinking. Fred, we'd like you to take over running The Red Lion."

Ignoring the shock on Fred's face, Ned took his daughter-in-law's hand in his.

"Sabina, you and I haven't always seen eye to eye over the years, but we think of you as our daughter, even more so since we lost poor Tom to consumption. I hope you won't be put out that we're not considering you or your family to take over the inn. Willie's your eldest and a fine young man, but I think he enjoys his work at Sugworthy Farm and knows nothing about running an inn."

"Ned, please don't give it a second thought and thank you so much for your kind words; they mean a lot. Arthur and I are so lucky to be living in the Lodge House, and Annie will never see us in want again. Arthur loves his market gardening, and I have to pinch myself most days to make sure I'm not dreaming. Not only that, but now I've remarried, I'm no longer a Carter, and I agree it must be a Carter to take over the inn and keep up the tradition. I think Fred's the ideal choice."

Betsey took her son's arm. "And what do you think, Fred? You seem shocked. Had you never considered what would happen when your dad and I finally gave up the inn?"

"No, not really, Mum. I'd always assumed it would pass to George as the eldest son, and maybe it should. George, you might not want to run the inn, but you could employ a manager. I don't want this to cause any trouble between us. I've already lost Tom and William, and I certainly don't want to become estranged from my third brother."

All eyes rested on George, known to be fond of money, but he had a thoughtful expression.

"No, I was a bit disappointed when Mum first had her say, but I've thought more about it whilst I've been sitting here, and I think it's right you have the inn, Fred. Putting in a manager wouldn't be the same; a Carter needs to live here, and you and Charlotte know more about running this inn than I ever will. Mum's right; the church is important to me, and I've never approved of drunkenness, so yes, I would be a terrible innkeeper. I make a decent living from the two shops, and that's the business I know, and, believe it or not, since losing Alice and nearly losing Theresa, I realise now that some things are more important than money."

His mother rose to her feet and hugged her eldest son. "George, hearing you say that pleases me so much. The last thing we wanted was for there to be any bad feelings in the family. Now, Fred, you seem bemused, but what do you think of taking over The Red Lion Inn and seeing your name over the door?"

A wide grin spread across Fred's face. "To be honest, I'm shocked; delighted, but shocked. I need to see what Charlotte thinks of the idea, but I don't think she'll mind. Will you still live here, Mum and Dad? If so, we won't be able to offer as much accommodation to travellers as we do now, and I'll have to consider what to do about the cottage and the carpentry business."

"No, we shall move out; it wouldn't be fair on you and Charlotte to have us here looking over your shoulder, and as you say, you need the rooms for the travellers; a lot of our profit comes from that. We haven't quite decided where we'll live yet. We may move back to the cottage next door, as luckily, the Bevans are moving out soon, and it will be empty. Your mum thinks that will be all right, but I'm not sure; she endured an unhappy childhood there, and it holds too many unpleasant memories for her. The other option would be for you and your family to move here and for us to live in your cottage, but it's probably a bit too big for just the two of us. Anyway, these are details that we can iron out later; I'm pleased that you all approve of our suggestions."

"There is one more thing, Fred."

"What's that, Mum?"

"We haven't discussed what will happen to Sarah and Bentley, and I wouldn't want to see them turned out. I suppose if we went to live in your cottage, they could go with us, but there wouldn't be much for Sarah to do."

"I need to talk it over with Charlotte, but she gets on all right with Sarah, and I don't think it would be a problem, and it would be fitting for William's son to live here, wouldn't it?"

"Yes, it would, and that's what we think too. Now that we've got that off our chests, will you all stay for some tea?"

Seeing the hopeful expression on Betsey's face, none present had the heart to say they had other things to attend to, for they knew she loved nothing better than getting all her family together under one roof.

CHAPTER 20

NEWTON ST CYRES

Under the circumstances, Millie and Jonathan enjoyed Christmas and would be forever thankful to the kind-hearted folk at Hilldale Farm for making them so welcome. Angela and Hubert were all for offering the two runaways a permanent home, but Vivian was firm.

"No, we can't do that. I want to ask them to stay, but money's tight, and we have enough mouths to feed as it is, especially as there's another on the way."

Hubert raised his eyebrows and glanced at Angela. "Oh, I didn't know. Congratulations, my dear. Are you pleased?"

"I'm a bit shocked, to tell you the truth; I didn't expect to have any more babies now that Walter's going on six, but there it is, and we'll love it just like the rest. Are you sure we can't afford to keep Millie and Jonathan, though, Viv?"

"No, their relatives in North Devon may be far better off than us and able to offer them a decent home, and anyway, their granny's following them there, so we shouldn't interfere. What I will do is take them as far as Crediton; we need some supplies, so I might as well get them tomorrow and help them on their way."

"Hmm, I'm not sure their granny will be joining them. The last time I saw Emily, she was suffering from arthritis, and I can't see her being able to travel all that way. She's the same age as me, for we were in the workhouse together, and it's not a journey I'd want to undertake at my age. She must have been desperate to send the two of them out on a winter night on such a journey. She doesn't even know if these relatives exist, far less whether they'll be willing to take on two penniless children. It all seems a bit of a mystery to me, and if Emily's father never kept in touch with his folk, it begs the question why. Why did he turn his back on his kin in the first place? No, I fear Emily knew she was not long for this world and wanted them to leave Brampford Speke and get away from Lady Grantley whilst they could."

Hubert's words did nothing to ease Angela's concerns, but she could not persuade her husband to change his mind, so in the morning, she put a cheery smile on her face.

"Now, have you got everything, Millie? I've packed some food to keep you going for a couple of days, and you have a good breakfast inside you to keep you warm. Here, let me pin those blankets around you again. Your granny was right; it's the easiest way of carrying them, and they'll give you an added layer of warmth. I hope you find somewhere warm to sleep tonight."

Unable to say more, Angela hugged them both and tried hard to keep a smile on her face. Her children, too, would have liked their new friends to stay, but they had been told it was impossible. Hubert followed them out and lifted Jonnie onto the cart. Vivian was busy harnessing the old horse, and as Hubert helped Millie on board, he held her hand in his and whispered a few words to her.

"It's been a pleasure to meet you and Jonnie, and I've enjoyed your company. Thank you for helping me whilst the family was away; now I told you I don't have much money, but here's a florin for you. It will buy you a pasty or two when all Angela's food's gone. Now, listen to me; if you can't find your family in North Devon, or they don't want to know you, make your way back here, and I'll sort something out. That's our little secret, mind, but don't forget, will you?"

Millie hugged the old man and whispered back. "Thank you so much, Mr March; that makes me feel better."

It was another cold morning, and the weak sunlight glistened on the sparkling frost that coated the grass and the bare branches of the trees. The north wind chilled them to the bone within minutes, and Millie and Jonathan huddled together next to Vivian, trying to keep warm. It was about four miles to Crediton, and the town was busy. Vivian tied the horse up outside the grocery shop in the High Street and lifted his passengers down.

"Here we are then, carry on along here, past a large church, and then follow the road all the way to Barnstaple; that's the main town in North Devon. The next village you'll come to is Copplestone; you'll know when you get there because you'll see the Copplestone Cross. It's a huge granite pillar, and I believe it's been there for hundreds of years; it's some sort of boundary marker. Now, have you got everything? Take care then, and I hope you have a safe journey."

Vivian found it harder to say goodbye than anticipated, so he turned abruptly and entered the grocery shop. Smiling bravely to keep Jonnie's spirits up, Millie hoisted up her sack and took her brother's hand. They had only taken a few steps when they were horrified to see a policeman striding towards them.

"Good morning. May I ask your names, please?"

Jonnie started to cry, and Millie desperately tried to think of two false names. However, she suddenly heard a voice she recognised call out behind her.

"Gertie, Walter, come back here this minute. I told you to wait on the cart. Where do you think you're going?"

Vivian March strode up to the two surprised children.

"Do you know these children, sir?"

"Know them? Of course, I know them. I'm their father. Why do you ask?"

"I've been asked to keep my eyes open for two children who have run away from Brampford Speke, and I think these two are likely candidates. It looks to me as if they're set for a journey. Why else would they be carrying bags and have blankets wrapped around them? Are you sure they're your children, sir?"

Vivian replied testily. "What sort of a question is that? Yes, of course, I'm sure. Gertie's fifteen, and she's my eldest, and Walter's five and the baby of the family. They're wrapped up in blankets because we've travelled several miles to buy supplies, and it's a frosty morning. Their mother always makes a fuss about them going far, and she's packed them some food; you can check if you like."

"No, that won't be necessary, sir; thank you for explaining. Please continue about your business."

"Thank you, and you two get back on the cart and stay there this time. Why are you searching for these two children anyway, constable? The police are not usually too concerned about runaways."

"I'm not sure that's true, sir, but on this occasion, the two children in question are wanted for stealing from Grantley House. They and their granny were evicted from their farm cottage just before Christmas for non-payment of rent, and it seems the girl, the elder of the pair, stole a valuable brooch from Lady Grantley a week or so ago."

"I see. Good luck then, sir; I hope you catch the culprits. However, if you'll excuse me, I'll get on my way."

Vivian lifted his hat to the policeman, then turned sternly towards Millie and Jonathan and told them again in no uncertain terms to wait on the cart until he returned from the shop. The policeman sauntered off down the High Street, glancing back over his shoulder once or twice to see if they were still sitting on the cart. After fifteen minutes or so, Vivian, having made his purchases and enjoyed a chat with the shopkeeper, returned to the cart and grinned at the anxious pair.

"Goodness me, that was a narrow escape. I thought I'd take my time in the shop to give that nosy policeman time to go about his business. At least you know now that the word is out and people are searching for you. Lady Grantley seems determined to cause trouble for you two; your granny was wise to send you on your way. Now, what are we going to do about it?"

"Oh, Mr March, thank you so much for saving us; I didn't know what to say when he asked our names. You were quick-thinking to pretend we were your children. It's lucky he didn't know you. I'm worried about Gran now. It sounds as if she's been turned out of our cottage."

"Yes, I admit it was the first thing that came into my head, and fortunately, I think it's done the trick. Now, just in case the policeman is hanging about somewhere watching us, I think you'd better stay on the cart, and we'll move on and decide what to do. Luckily, he's walked off in the opposite direction to Barnstaple. As for your gran, it sounds as if she knew she'd be evicted and planned to go to the workhouse."

"Yes, that's true; do you think they would take her in?"

"Oh yes, especially if she'd been evicted; she'll be all right there for a few weeks until she recovers from typhoid. Workhouses aren't the most pleasant places to live, but they help the poorest to survive."

Vivian clicked his tongue and encouraged the old horse to continue along the High Street. His mind was working overtime as he tried to decide the best thing to do. He didn't want to take the youngsters back home with him, nor did he want the policeman to apprehend them for something they hadn't done. He knew someone as important as Lady Grantley could cause them much trouble and probably have them jailed for years or hanged. Suddenly, he had an idea.

"I know what we'll do. I'll put you on the train; the police will never think two runaways will be travelling on the train. It will mean going back towards Exeter to the railway station, but it's on my way to Hilldale Farm anyway, and if the policeman sees us, he'll think we've finished our business and are heading home."

"But, Mr March, how much will the train fare be? I only have the florin that your father gave us and a few pennies of Gran's money, and I need to keep that to buy food along the way."

"I don't know how much it will cost, Millie, and I certainly can't afford to pay for you to go all the way to Barnstaple, but if you ride for a few stops on the train, I doubt the police will be looking for you that far from Brampford Speke. They'll think you're on foot and unable to travel very fast. Let's go to the railway station, find out what time the next train is, and see how much it will cost to ride a short way. Have you ever been on a train before?"

"No, sir, but it sounds like a good idea."

The railway station was not far, and they didn't see the policeman again. Fortunately for them, the constable had decided that, having patrolled the streets for a couple of hours, it was time he returned to the warmth of the police station for a brew, as it was such a cold morning. They arrived at the station within ten minutes and were delighted to see that a train facing towards Barnstaple was preparing to depart.

"Quickly, let's see if we can get you on the train. It will be ideal if it's about to leave, for the sooner you get away from here, the better."

Mr March quickly lifted Jonathan from the cart and held out his hand to Millie, and they ran to the station counter. In his mind, he ran through the villages along the line: Copplestone, Morchard Bishop, Lapford, Eggesford. Smiling at the clerk, he enquired how much it would cost for his two children to travel third class to Eggesford. The man surveyed them.

"I can charge them half fare, seeing as they're children; sixpence each should cover it."

"A whole shilling! They only need a single ticket; they're going to stay with relatives for a few days."

"Nevertheless, sir, that is what it will cost; now make your mind up, for the train will leave in four minutes."

"Oh, all right, here you are. Where should they sit?"

The clerk smirked. "It's unlikely they'll be sitting anywhere, sir, but take them to the far end of the train, where they'll likely have to stand the whole way."

"Thank you; come on, hurry up."

Vivian grabbed their bags, rushed them along the platform to the last door on the train, and urged them up the step. The carriage was packed, and he had to ask folk to move along to allow them to enter.

"There, that was lucky. Now, hold on tight, and I think you'll need to get off at the fourth stop, at a place called Eggesford. It's in the middle of nowhere and surrounded by a forest, but it will take you several miles on your way. If you're not sure, ask one of the other passengers."

An elderly woman was seated on the hard wooden bench near the window, clutching a basket on her lap. She regarded the new passengers.

"I'm getting off at Eggesford, so no need to worry, my dears; just get off when I do."

"Thank you, ma'am; that's kind of you. Goodbye."

Jonathan held on tightly to Millie's arm as the train started to chuff out of the station. Fortunately, thanks to the old lady, who told them to stand beside her, they had a fine view out of the window and watched in amazement as the train gathered speed.

CHAPTER 21

EGGESFORD

Millie and Jonathan held on tightly as the train sped along the tracks. They would have enjoyed their journey at any other time, but anxiety about their circumstances overshadowed the experience. The old lady was curious why the man had quickly pushed them onto the train and then abandoned them, and she asked them where they were going.

"We're hoping to find our relatives in North Devon because Mum died of typhoid last week, and our granny is ill too; she'll follow us when she's strong enough."

"I see; do you have anyone nearer who can help you? Who was the man who put you on the train?"

"Oh, he's a farmer who let us stay on his farm for a few days over Christmas. His father is a friend of our granny, but we couldn't stay there forever. He thought a train ride for a few miles would help us on our way, but he couldn't afford to pay for us to travel all the way to Barnstaple, and we don't have much money."

"Where are you going to sleep tonight?"

"We don't know; we'll walk to the next village and see if we can find a barn to shelter in. Can you tell us what it's called and how far it is?"

"It's five miles to Coleton Mill, but there's nothing much there apart from the mill. If you walk another mile, you'll come to Kings Nympton. There's an inn there and a few houses dotted around. You'd probably have more chance there of finding somewhere to sleep, but it's nearly noon now, and it'll be dark early today; you'll have to get a move on."

"Thank you. When we get off the train, could you point us in the right direction for the mill?"

The woman was thoughtful for a few minutes as she gazed at the two anxious youngsters.

"If you like, you can come home with me for the night and set off early in the morning. I've lived on my own since my husband died last year, and I suffer something awful with arthritis. If you do a few jobs around the house for me, I'll put you up for the night and give you some tea. It would be better for you to set off on the next part of your journey early in the morning and make the most of the daylight."

Jonathan studied his sister's face hopefully.

"Yes, thank you, we'd like to do that."

"That's settled then; 'tis no weather for travelling, and I could do with your help. My name's Rosa Baker, and I'm pleased to meet you."

Rosa held out her hand, first to Millie and then to Jonathan.

"Thank you so much, Mrs Baker. I'm Gertie, and this is Walter, and we'll work hard to repay your kindness."

Millie stared hard at Jonathan, who was surprised to be introduced as Walter, but fortunately said nothing. There was no knowing if Lilliana Grantley's men might have been making enquiries in the neighbouring villages. Rosa smiled to herself, for she had enjoyed a cup of tea and a bun in Crediton, and indeed, two men had quizzed the shop owner as to whether he had come across two youngsters travelling on their own. It hadn't taken long for her to put two and two together, but she decided it was none of her business, and she hadn't liked the look of the two men, anyway.

Just before the train arrived at Eggesford Station, Rosa warned Millie and Jonathan that they would get off at the next stop. They held on tightly as the train braked and followed Rosa out of the door and onto the platform.

"My cottage is at the top of this hill. My parents lived there for many years, and it's where I was born and raised. My husband, Jim, used to work on a nearby farm and also helped with the logging, for there's a large forest in Eggesford. Sadly, our only son died young, so I'm alone now. I'll have to take my time because I get so out of breath, and my hip's that painful."

They slowly made their way up the steep hill, with Rosa stopping every few minutes to catch her breath and rest. She leaned heavily on her walking stick and had to keep putting down her heavy shopping bag. After a while, despite having her sack to carry, Millie insisted on taking it from her, and they all struggled together. As they reached the brow of the hill, a thatched cottage came into view. It was in need of repair, and the garden was overgrown. Rosa took a large iron key from her pocket and unlocked the door, and they entered the dingy cottage.

"Here we are then, home at last. Now, I'll pull the kettle forward to bring it to the boil, and then we'll have a cup of tea and some bread and cheese. The loaf's fresh, for I only bought it this morning."

"What would you like us to do for you, Mrs Baker?"

"As you can see, my dear, the place is filthy, but I'm not fit enough to deal with it. I'd like you to clean as much as you can, and in return, I'll cook you some tea."

"Do you want me to do some cleaning, too, Mrs Baker?"

"Now, Walter wasn't it? Yes, you can help your sister, but I have a special job for you. Outside, there's a woodshed with a lot of chopped logs; I paid a man back along to deliver them for me. I want you to bring in as many as you can and stack them beside the old Bodley; there are two baskets you can fill up, too. The wood will dry out nicely then and burn better, and it will save me having to go out into the cold for a few days to fetch it."

Rosa had not lied when she said her house was filthy, and Millie worked hard all afternoon. She dusted the furniture, swept the floors, and scrubbed them on her hands and knees. By the time she had finished, the water in her bucket was black. Jonathan, too, scurried back and forth to the woodshed, bringing in a few logs at a time. He stacked them one on top of the other in the space on either side of the stove and then filled the two baskets in front of it. Whilst they were working, Rosa rested to recover from her morning's shopping and then set about cooking some pigs' hearts on a bed of parsley stuffing and onions. She simmered the hearts with the onions on the stove for an hour before putting them into a dish with parsley stuffing and into the oven.

"There, that'll be delicious later, but hearts need to cook slowly, so come and have a glass of my homemade lemonade and a slice of the fruitcake I made yesterday. You've done a wonderful job, more than enough to earn your tea and a bed for the night; you don't need to do any more."

However, Millie and Jonathan were grateful not to be walking in the dark and sleeping out in the open, and after a short rest, Millie announced that they would clean upstairs if Rosa would like them to.

"Yes, please, my dear, that would be wonderful if you don't mind. I'll find some clean sheets, and perhaps you could change my bed for me; it's not been done for some time because I find it too difficult. I'm so unsteady without my stick that I can't handle the bedding. I know there's a lot of dust under the bed, too; great rolls of fluff. I see them blowing across the floor sometimes. I still manage to climb the stairs at the moment, but the day is not far away when I'll have to get someone to bring my bed downstairs."

When they had finished eating, Millie and Jonathan ventured upstairs, finding two bedrooms and a large airing cupboard. They stripped the double bed between them and made it up with clean sheets. Millie then told Jonathan to dust the furniture whilst she swept and scrubbed the floors. They found two single beds in the spare room, all neatly made with clean bedding.

Exhausted, they carried the dirty washing downstairs to the kitchen, where Rosa held out two hot bricks wrapped in rags and told them to put them in their beds.

"Those beds haven't been slept in for a long time, not since my friend came to stay last summer, so they need airing, particularly in this cold weather. Now, come and sit down and have some tea."

They sat on a bench and watched the old lady ladle the braised hearts onto their plates. She also served mashed potatoes and carrots, and then spooned gravy from the casserole dish over their meal. It smelled delicious.

"Oh, Mrs Baker, this is so tasty. It's like our granny makes; thank you so much."

"I'm glad you like it, my dear, but 'tis me who should be thanking you; you've worked wonders here this afternoon between you. It gladdens my heart to see my house respectable again. Now, there's something I want to tell you. I might be wrong, but I have a feeling your names might not be Gertie and Walter. I think you might be Millie and Jonathan; am I right?"

Millie drew in a sharp breath, and Jonathan looked worried.

"It's all right; you don't need to worry, and you don't have to tell me if you don't want to, but this morning in Crediton, I had a cup of tea and a bun in a teashop while I waited for the train and two men came in and asked if anyone had seen two children travelling on their own. They said they were called Millie and Jonathan Gibbs and were wanted for stealing."

Millie's face was white, and tears ran down her brother's face.

"Now, don't worry; I'm pretty sure you're no thieves, that's if it is you, and anyway, I'm not going to tell anyone I've seen you, but I thought you ought to know you are being pursued. You'll need to be careful on your journey."

"Oh dear, yes, we're Millie and Jonathan Gibbs, Mrs Baker. I'm sorry we lied to you, but we've done nothing wrong, though Lady Grantley of Grantley Manor in Brampford Speke would have you believe otherwise."

Millie told her tale to Mrs Baker, and the old lady shook her head sadly.

"The story these two men were telling was that you, Millie, were seen in the Manor House last week, and then it was discovered that a precious brooch had gone missing. It's made of gold and set with one large sapphire, surrounded by diamonds, and it once belonged to Sir Edgar's late mother."

Millie gasped. "Oh no, I do have that brooch, but Sir Edgar gave it to my mother recently, and before we left, Granny pinned it onto my bodice out of sight in case anything like this happened. I don't want it; she can have it back."

Millie reached under her clothing and retrieved the brooch. It was beautiful, exactly as Rosa had described, and the jewels twinkled softly in the lamplight.

"Oh my, it is pretty, and I suspect from what you've told me, it's not the brooch that's important to Lady Grantley, but getting you sent to jail or hanged, Millie. She bears a grudge for her husband's unfaithfulness, and with some justification, to be fair, but none of it's your fault. They do say hell hath no fury like a woman scorned. I forget who said that, but I know it's a famous saying."

"Mrs Baker, could I leave the brooch here with you for now? If I'm caught with it pinned to my bodice, I'm bound to look guilty, and it's more important that I stay out of jail and take care of Jonnie."

"You can if you want to, but when could you get it back?"

"I don't know; maybe if we find these relatives, they could come and collect it, but it's no use to me, anyway. I can never wear it, and I can't sell it either, so it's of no value to me. It would be safe here with you for now."

"Yes, that's a wise idea, and I'll keep it safe until you can come back and collect it. My neighbour is younger than me, so if you haven't returned for it before I pass away, I'll tell her where it is, and she can keep it for you. She's completely trustworthy and already has a key to my cottage; I've known her since she was born, and she keeps an eye on me."

"Oh, Mrs Baker, don't say that; I hope you live for a long time."

"We all get older, my dear, and we must go some time. I'm not afraid to meet my Maker and am ready to be reunited with my beloved Jim and my little boy. Anyway, have you both had enough to eat? If so, I suggest you get an early night."

They nodded gratefully, crept upstairs, and snuggled into their warm beds.

After the two youngsters had gone to bed, Rosa sat in her favourite armchair and held the precious brooch in her swollen hand. It was exquisite, and she had never seen anything so pretty. The old lady turned it over and over, enjoying the lamplight glinting on the precious stones, painting a rainbow of colour on the ceiling. She felt sorry for her two visitors, for the likelihood of them finding their relatives seemed such a long shot, and she wondered at their granny's decision to send them on such a mission. Millie and Jonathan spoke lovingly of their grandmother, so the poor woman must have been desperate to send them out into the night in the hope they would escape Lady Grantley's clutches.

She glanced around the room, thinking how nice it looked after all the efforts of her two young visitors. She hated being unable to keep the cottage clean, but couldn't afford to employ anyone to help. Fortunately, she owned a couple of fields behind the cottage, and renting them to a local farmer provided her with a modest income. She considered whether the money would stretch to offering the children a home, for she would enjoy their company and the help they could provide. However, she knew it was impossible, for she struggled to make ends meet now. She had been considering whether she should sell the fields and live off the capital they raised, for she had no family to leave her property to. The question was, how many years had she left? Would the money last?

Eventually, she decided the two runaways must continue their journey to find their relatives, but that she would offer them the chance to return if their plans did not work out. Maybe, by that time, the hue and cry over their disappearance would have died down, and Millie could find work to support them all. Either that or Rosa would sell her fields and have a nest egg for them all to live on, at least for a while.

She yawned and decided it was time for bed. Then she surveyed the brooch again and pondered where to keep it. Getting to her feet with difficulty and leaning heavily on her walking stick, she went to the fireplace and reached under the mantlepiece. Feeling for a familiar loose stone, she eased it out carefully and put the brooch inside a small leather pouch that held her life's savings.

CHAPTER 22

HARTFORD

A couple of days after Christmas, Sam, Marrok, and Margery were enjoying a cup of hot chocolate in the drawing room. They were waiting for Betsey to arrive, as, following her revelations on Boxing Day, the four of them had vowed to meet up again soon, their interest in the past piqued. Annie had taken the children for a walk, and the trio eagerly awaited Betsey's arrival. They didn't have to wait long as Betsey arrived promptly on the dot at ten o'clock, as agreed. With the snow melting, she had declined Robert's offer of a carriage to collect her, saying she needed to keep her old joints moving or they would seize up altogether, plagued as she was with arthritis. The three Fellwoods greeted her with beaming smiles.

"Good morning, Betsey; I'm pleased to see you and so glad you could come."

"Thank you, Margery; I've been looking forward to meeting with you all again. I think there are still questions about the past we'd all like answers to. How are you, Marrok? Is your leg any better?"

"No, I'm afraid not. Doctor Turner says the bones aren't knitting back together properly. He'll reset it tomorrow and put a plaster cast on, and he thinks that will do the trick."

"Oh, yes, I'm sure it will. When I broke my leg a while ago, the doctors at the hospital put on a plaster cast, and it mended fine. I can't say it's quite as good as new, for it still aches, but I think that's old age, and as they say, that doesn't come alone. I don't envy you having it reset, though; it won't be pleasant."

"I think I might be luckier than most because the doctor will give me chloroform gas to put me to sleep while he does it. I'd be more worried otherwise."

"Oh, that's good."

"Now, Betsey, we're enjoying a cup of hot chocolate, so can I interest you in the same?"

"Yes, please, Margery, 'tis some time since I had breakfast. I have a lot to sort out at the moment. As you know, Ned's poorly, and according to Geoffrey, goodness, how I struggle to call that gentleman by his Christian name; sorry, according to Geoffrey, he has heart failure and must have complete rest, so we're giving up The Red Lion Inn."

"Oh, my dear, I'm so sorry to hear that; is there no treatment?"

"No, it's a matter of age, but if he takes things easy, the doctor thinks he should have a few years yet."

"So, what will happen to the inn? I believe it's been in your family for a long time."

"Yes, it has, Sam, at least a couple of hundred years that we know of, and maybe even since it was built; no one knows. We've discussed the situation with our family and hope our son, Fred, will move in and run the place. He's discussing it with his wife, Charlotte, and coming back to see us this afternoon with his answer, but I think it will be all right. Charlotte's a competent girl; she nursed me when I broke my leg, if you remember, and her baby, Doris, was rescued from Buzzacott House, along with Eveline's adopted daughter, Martha."

"Yes, of course. Fred's not your eldest son, though, is he? I thought George, who runs the Hartford shop, was older than Fred?"

"Yes, that's right, he is, but even George agrees he'd make a terrible landlord and probably have the place closed down within a few months. We could sell up and split the money between them all when we die, but the inn's been in the Carter family for generations, and we want that to continue."

"Will you carry on living there?"

"No, the spare rooms are needed for the stagecoach travellers, for that's where a lot of the inn's income comes from, but not only that, Fred and Charlotte won't want us looking over their shoulders. If we carried on living there, it would be difficult not to interfere, and Ned needs complete rest, so it's best we leave."

"But where will you go? You won't be leaving the village, surely?"

"No, we're lucky because we own Fred's cottage and the one next door to the inn where I was born. If Fred and his family move to the inn, we can choose either of those two dwellings. The money that Thomas Fellwood left me when I was twenty-one set us up nicely. Like I told you, most of it went on clearing Mal Carter's bank loan and some to repair the roof of Betsey's Kitchen, but the rest we saved, and when the business picked up, we saw our chance and purchased the cottage Fred lives in. Until he moved in there, we rented it out and made a decent profit, so we'll have enough money to keep us comfortable in our old age. We have much to thank your father for, Sam; he was a generous and kind-hearted man, and I'd like to hear more about him."

"That sounds like a good place to start talking about the past. Let's see what we can piece together between us. I hope your plans work out well, Betsey; you and Ned deserve a few years without working so hard."

"Thank you, Margery; perhaps you would like to start? What do you remember about your brother, Thomas?"

The old lady's eyes misted slightly as her thoughts turned to the brother she had lost.

"I loved my brothers, Joshua and George, but Thomas was my favourite. Joshua was always busy because, as the eldest son, my father, Ephraim, involved him in estate matters from a young age, knowing he would one day inherit and become the next Lord Hartford. Joshua loved learning the ropes and was the right man for the job. My other brother, George, was slightly retarded and physically disabled, and sadly, he died when he was only twenty-five, though he had lived far longer than anyone expected.

"Thomas was a carefree young man who always had time for me. He used to take me riding, George too, sometimes. My mother died when I was only six; she'd had a weak heart for years, and after that, Thomas looked after me more than anyone. That was in 1820, and I believe your mother died in the same year, Betsey?"

"Yes, that's right, she did, and I believe we're the same age?"

Lady Margery nodded her head and continued.

"I often woke early in those days, and I was never allowed to creep into my parents' bed as my mother was an invalid, but Thomas never turned me away. He always let me climb in beside him and often read me several stories before breakfast. I knew he liked the young gypsy girl called Jane, for I was with him on several occasions when he went to their camp. As you mentioned the other day, Betsey, he gave you a ride there more than once, and I know he was concerned about you and Norman."

"Yes, he was, and when he left me that money, I was pleased to learn he had left it solely to me. His will stated that my husband could not use the money if I were married. He didn't want me to be in the same position as my mother. It didn't matter in my case, for Ned's always treated me right, but it was so thoughtful of Thomas to ensure I was provided for."

"He was generous with his time and money and bought me my beloved dog, Gyp. He was one of the puppies that you and I played with on that day, Betsey. When Thomas disappeared for a long time, no one knew where he'd gone, and certainly no one enlightened me. I was heartbroken, and I hoped and prayed he would return, but as the days turned into weeks, months, and years, I knew he was gone forever. I asked so many questions, and I was forbidden to mention his name again, but one day, my nanny took pity on me and told me Thomas had run away with Jane and not to worry about him, for he had probably found happiness elsewhere. That helped, for I thought he might return one day, but he never did. I know that my father, Ephraim, never gave up on him and had people searching for him for a long time. Even when, after many years, he eventually called off the search, he refused to write Thomas out of his will, and I'm glad about that, Sam; for now, you have reaped the benefit and rightly so. So, now it's over to you, Sam, to tell us more."

"Sadly, I can't tell you much about my father, for I was only two when he died in a fishing accident. Margery, when your father found out about Thomas's relationship with Jane, he forbade him to see the gypsy girl again; however, the couple had already made plans to escape to France, and when Ephraim gave his orders, they brought their plans forward and left on a boat the very next day with some local smugglers. As you say, Betsey, Raymond Chugg was in charge of most of the smuggling around here back then, and although he was in his nineties, his mind was still as sharp as a tack. He no longer sailed the boats but masterminded the whole operation, and his son, Jonathan, and grandson, Jeremy, carried out his orders."

"That's right, Sam and Ned's mother, my Aunty Kezzie, was Raymond Chugg's daughter. She became a Carter when she married Uncle Mal. They reckon most folk in this village are related, and that's not far wrong. Sorry to interrupt your tale, Sam, do carry on."

"After my father drowned in 1823, Jane didn't know what to do. Thomas could speak French fluently, but she only knew a few words, and when his money ran out, she was destitute. She had to leave the cottage they rented and was in dire straits. In desperation, Jane waited on the quayside, day after day, hoping to see one of Raymond Chugg's ships, and eventually, her persistence was rewarded. Jonathan Chugg remembered taking her to France and Thomas Fellwood's generosity when paying him, and he took her and me back to England for nothing. She struggled to survive for several weeks while trying to find the gypsies, but eventually, she moved back in with her granny, Gypsy Freda."

"Oh, that's interesting, Sam. I've often wondered what happened to Gypsy Freda. She was so good to Norman and me, but after Jasper Morris died and Thomas and Jane fled to France, the gypsies moved on and never returned to Hartford. They frequented certain places at different times throughout the year and usually spent several weeks in Hartford during the winter, but I never saw them again. What happened to Gypsy Freda?"

"Oh, she lived to a ripe old age, Betsey, and I remember her fondly. I was about ten when she died, and I think she was only a few days short of her one-hundredth birthday. She used to wear her long grey hair in two pigtails and smoked a clay pipe; she told wonderful stories, too."

"Yes, she did. I remember her pigtails and clay pipe; she used to tell me stories, too. It's thanks to Gypsy Freda that Ned's alive today. As a young man, he was burnt when he was struck by lightning, and luckily, she had taught me many of her herbal cures and potions. I'm sure they saved his life, and the doctor thought so, too. Why did the gypsies never come back to Hartford?"

"They were worried the Fellwood family would make trouble for them. It was common knowledge locally that young Master Thomas was sweet on the gypsy girl, and eventually, the story came out about them running away to

France together. When my mother, Jane, returned to England, she was keen to lie low and keep away from Hartford because of what happened to the miller and for eloping with Thomas."

"Marrok, you've not had much to say up to now. Do you remember your granny?"

"No, I don't remember her at all. I remember you, Dad, and you telling me we would run away together. You said you would come for me in the middle of the night, and I must be quiet, but you never came. I know now that you couldn't come for me because the gypsies had beaten you rather than let you take me."

"Yes, that's right, and it's the biggest regret of my life, though there was nothing I could do about it then. No, you wouldn't remember your granny, Jane, because she died when you were only one. It was one of the saddest days of my life when she passed away, for she was a wonderful mother. I don't know what she died of, but she lost her appetite, and the weight fell off her. By the time she died, she was nothing but skin and bone, and although I didn't want her to go, I couldn't wish her back, for she was in so much pain. I wondered if she died of a broken heart, for she was never interested in any other men after Thomas drowned. She warned me not to marry Jenny, but I was young and wouldn't listen. Jenny's father was the leader of the gypsies and a powerful man, but my mother was wise and never took to Jenny. Like I've already told you, Jenny was repeatedly unfaithful until I could stand it no more and decided to leave. More's the pity they wouldn't let me take you with me, Marrok. Still, at least we've found each other now."

Annie and the children suddenly burst through the door, their cheeks red from the fresh air, and Paul went straight to his father and inched his way onto his sound knee.

"My goodness, are you still talking about the olden days? I thought you'd have finished long before now. We've had a lovely morning. We walked into the village and bought some sweets at Mrs Scott's shop, and then we called in to see Mum and Liza at the Lodge House. On the way home, we walked to the lake and fed the ducks, and now we're all hungry and need some lunch. Have you all enjoyed your trip down memory lane?"

"We have, and didn't realise it was so late. I must get back to The Red Lion; your grandad will wonder what's happened to me."

"You're welcome to stay for lunch if you'd like to?"

"No, it's all right, thank you, Annie. I've enjoyed my morning, but I'll get home now because Uncle Fred's coming to see us this afternoon. Thank you all so much for sharing your memories with me; filling in some of the missing pieces has been good. I'm so glad Jane returned to England and found Gypsy Freda, though I'm sorry to hear Jane died young."

Sam and Margery got to their feet and walked to the door with Betsey.

"Thank you for telling us your side of things, Betsey; there's a lot we would never have known but for you. How strange it is that our lives are so entwined."

CHAPTER 23

HARTFORD

Betsey enjoyed her morning reminiscing, and as soon as she got home, she sat on the bed next to Ned and told him all about it.

"It was so interesting to hear all the different sides to the story and piece together exactly what happened. I was surprised Margery realised that the little girl she played with all those years ago was me. I mean, it's getting on for seventy years ago, and I've changed my name. She never mentioned it as she didn't want to embarrass me about how poor I was then."

"I'm not surprised; after all, you remember her, and she's changed her name, too, although everyone around here still thinks of her as a Fellwood. I don't think I even know her married name."

"I think it's Montgomery, but I'm not sure. Anyway, will you come downstairs to see Fred and Charlotte later, or do you want to stay in bed?"

"I'll come down for my dinner. I'm fed up with these four walls, and it'll be easier to come down to see them; I want to see the new baby."

"Yes, me too. I've only seen Nicholas a couple of times, and he must be three weeks old now; how time flies. What would you like for dinner? Sarah's made a fresh batch of pasties, or there's bread and cheese, or a bowl of stew, left over from yesterday."

"All of that sounds lovely, but I fancy some of your freshly baked bread spread thickly with butter and raspberry jam if there's any left."

"Yes, there is. We're on the last jar, though, so I'll need to make some more come the summer; raspberry's my favourite, and it's the easiest jam to make. I think I'll join you and have the same. Get yourself dressed, and I'll prepare the dinner; we can sit in the parlour beside the fire and have it on our laps for once."

A few minutes after two o'clock, Fred and Charlotte arrived with four of their children. Llewie had stayed behind to mind the yard and finish making a coffin. As usual, they entered through the back door, exchanged pleasantries with Sarah, Louis, and Bentley, and then went to find Betsey and Ned in the parlour.

Hearing them arrive, Betsey rose to her feet and hugged nine-year-old Rosella and five-year-old Eddie before turning her attention to the two younger children. Doris was eighteen months old, and although she was sturdy on her feet, Fred had carried her as it was too far for her to walk, and the pram was needed for the new baby. She held out her arms to her granny, and Betsey took the child and kissed her plump cheek.

"Hello, my beauty; how are you today? I'm pleased you've come to see us."

Charlotte entered the room and greeted her in-laws, and Bentley sidled in behind her, hoping to play with his cousins.

"Hello, Betsey, hello, Ned; Nicholas is asleep. Is there room for me to bring the pram in? It's a bit chilly out here in the passageway, and I'm hoping he might sleep another hour and give us time to talk before I need to feed him."

"Yes, there's plenty of room, my dear; bring him into the warm. Put the pram over there in the corner, look. Now, Rosella and Eddie, you can stay here with us if you want to, but our cat, Tibby, had kittens a few weeks ago, and I thought you might like to play with them before you take your coats off. Would you like that?"

"Ooh, yes, please; where are they?"

"They're out in the linhay, and I'm sure Bentley would like to show them to you. When you come back in, Sarah will find you some cake and a cup of milk. I've put the box of toys here ready for you to play with, too; is that all right?"

"Yes, thank you. Dad, can we have one of the kittens when they're old enough?"

Fred glanced at Charlotte, who nodded.

"Yes, I think so; we've got a few mice around; go and play with them and decide which one you want."

They ran off happily, and Betsey put the squirming Doris down on the floor as she was impatient to play with the toys she had spotted.

"Sit yourselves down then. We'll wait for Sarah to bring us some tea and cakes, and then we can talk. How are you feeling, Charlotte? Have you recovered from having Nicholas?"

"Yes, I'm fine, thanks; I'm a bit tired, but that's always the way with a new baby. He wakes once or twice during the night for a feed, but thankfully, he usually goes back to sleep again."

"Ah, here's Sarah, now. Thank you, my dear."

Betsey poured them all a cup of tea and handed around the plate of cakes.

"Now, how do you feel about taking over the inn? I know it's a lot to think about. Have you come to a decision?" Ned peered at the young couple anxiously.

"Yes, we've given it a lot of thought, and we're delighted; it's such a generous offer, we don't know how to thank you. There's nothing we'd like better, is there, Charlotte?"

"No, thank you both so much. It's an amazing opportunity for Fred and me, and we can't wait to move in and get started. I'm glad it will mean you can both take it easy, too; I know how hard you used to work from when I lived here nursing you, Betsey, and I think you're doing the right thing. As you know, Ned, I used to work in the Exeter Hospital, so I've nursed a few patients with heart failure, and the best thing you can do is to take it easy and get plenty of rest. It's the right decision for you to retire, and we feel honoured that we should be the ones you've asked to take over The Red Lion."

"That's such a relief. We were hoping you'd both feel that way, and when we considered everybody in the family, you were the obvious choice. Sabina and Eveline are happily married, and even George could see he would make a terrible innkeeper."

"Yes, I think the villagers would have been horrified to find my brother standing behind the bar. How are you feeling, anyway, Dad?"

"A lot better, thanks, Fred. It's so annoying; as long as I do nothing, I'm fine, but the slightest exertion leaves me feeling tired and breathless, so I'm afraid I don't have much choice in the matter. Now, when could you start?"

"We can move in any time you like, and if you want to carry on living here, that's not a problem."

"No, if we're here, we'll want to help, and it's better to leave you two to find your own way of doing things. You only have to ask if you need any advice, but we should move out, for your sake and ours. In any case, you'll need the rooms for the travellers who stay to break their journeys."

"Yes, I can see that; I'm sure if you still lived here, you'd continue working, and you need to take it easy. Have you decided yet where you'd like to live? The cottage next door or the one we live in?"

"We've talked about it a lot, and your dad says it's up to me. As you know, the cottage next door, Bluebell Cottage, as it's called now, holds some bitter memories for me, though it was all a long time ago. It's tiny but plenty big enough for us, and we'd get far more rent for the one you live in. Do you think there's room for you to continue your carpentry business here, or will you still need the yard where you live now?"

"There's plenty of room here, but I thought we might walk around later and consider what could go where."

"That's a good idea, and I think your dad and I need to do the same and wander around Bluebell Cottage and the one you live in. We could do that this afternoon if you like, because the Bevans have moved out of Bluebell Cottage a bit sooner than expected, so it's empty. Nicholas is stirring; do you want to feed him, and then we could walk around the three premises?"

Charlotte lifted the grizzling baby from his pram and put him to her breast, where he immediately went quiet and suckled hungrily.

"While you're feeding the baby, shall we call Sarah and Louis in and tell them what's happening? It will affect them too, and perhaps they could keep an eye on the children while we go for our walk. Do you mind if Louis comes in while you feed the baby?"

"No, that's all right; he can't see anything."

Betsey invited Sarah and Louis to join them, and Ned told them their news. They were concerned at first, but when Fred assured them their positions were safe and that he and Charlotte would be relying on their help, they liked the idea. When Charlotte had finished feeding the baby, Betsey changed his nappy and enjoyed a quick cuddle before putting him back in his pram. The three children had returned from playing with the kittens, and Rosella and Eddie had finally agreed which one they would like to have. Betsey and Ned, and Fred and Charlotte left the children eating cake at the kitchen table, and Doris sat in the old high chair. Sarah assured Charlotte she would mind the children and to take as long as she liked.

Leaving by the back door, they walked down the garden path, and Fred considered the various outbuildings that might be suitable for his carpentry workshop. The large stable was used for the eight horses that were kept in readiness for the stagecoaches. Often, on long journeys, the horses would need to be changed and swapped back on the return journey. That was the main business of The Red Lion Inn and could not be changed. The inn kept fewer cows than in the past, and the large shippen had been converted into Betsey's Kitchen when Ned's parents, Mal and Keziah, ran the inn. The two cows now lived in a small linhay and provided all the milk, butter, and cheese the inn needed.

"How's Betsey's Kitchen doing these days, Mum?"

"Remarkably well; it makes an excellent profit. When we started it up in the 1830s, there were scores of workers here building Lord Fellwood's canal, but, of course, that was completed years ago. I wonder how much longer it will operate now that the railway is so much quicker. The canal builders are long gone, though there are still a few who work there, but with the employees of the silver mine and the limekilns and the farm labourers, there are a lot of folk around, so we're not short of customers."

"It's a sound business, Fred; we employ quite a few staff now, and they all know what they're doing, so it should be easy for you and Charlotte to take over, and we'll be around if you need to know anything."

"Yes, I can see that, Dad. I reckon the barn would be ideal as a workshop for me. It needs quite a few repairs, but it's nothing I can't do myself. Is it all right with you if I clear it out later and make a start? I need to get things ready here before we can leave our cottage."

"Yes, do what you like. You could enlarge it if you want to. The garden beyond it is extensive, and it's never fully planted as we've never had the time, and then there's the meadow behind that. I've often wondered if we should take on a part-time gardener to make full use of it, so that's something you might like to consider. The produce could be used in the inn."

"Yes, I might do that."

"The other matter that will need your attention in the not-too-distant future is the roof. Goodness, I can't believe I'm saying that; it seems like only yesterday it was replaced, but it was nearly fifty years ago. The loan to replace it then nearly caused my father to go bankrupt and have to sell the inn, and it was only Betsey's inheritance from Thomas Fellwood that saved the day. It doesn't need to be done straight away, but probably within the next five to ten years. I know that sounds like a long way off, but you need to start saving for it as soon as possible."

"That will give us time to put some money by, and at least with me being a carpenter, I can replace all the beams and wooden trusses myself; I'd only have to pay for the materials and to have it thatched. Shall we go to Bluebell Cottage now?"

They walked through the gap in the hedge that had been there since Betsey and Ned's childhood. Betsey and her brother, Barney, had often used it as a shortcut to the inn to play with Ned and his brother, Silas. The garden outside the cottage was a bit wild and neglected, and the gate needed oiling. Ned took the key from his pocket, and they entered the kitchen through the back door. Betsey glanced around her, and in her mind's eye, she could see her mother standing at the sink doing the washing. She stared at the mantelpiece and remembered the pretty little tin, now in her possession, that once lived there and contained her mother's housekeeping money. Then Betsey thoughtfully surveyed the old Bodley stove, the same one she had fed with logs as a girl. She remembered lying on the floor in front of it, cuddling Norman, trying to keep him warm while waiting in vain for their father to return. A tear slid down her cheek, and Ned put his arm around her.

"Now then, come on, Betsey, don't upset yourself. I knew you shouldn't have come here; it stirs up too many memories. If you remember, we planned to live here just after we were married, but you found it too difficult, and in the end, we stayed at the inn, and Mum and Dad moved in here. We've seen enough, Fred; we're not living here; we'll move into your cottage."

"No, I'm all right, Ned. Moving in here and renting out the bigger cottage makes more sense. Fred can take his time moving his carpentry stuff, then. No, I need to get a grip. The place needs decorating, though. It was last done when we were all going to move in here when The Red Lion was up for sale, and that's years ago. As you say, we never did move here because I never liked it, and when I got the Fellwood money, your mum and dad insisted they would live here and leave us to run the inn. Just like we're doing now for Fred and Charlotte, it's our turn to move along now."

"We'll see, but I agree it needs redecorating and freshening up, and what a load of rubbish the Bevans have left behind; the place is filthy. I should have inspected it before they left. Fred, if you decide to employ a gardener, he could till the garden here, too, because I can't do it. Let's visit Fred's cottage now, Betsey, and see which one you prefer."

They returned to The Red Lion, where Ned decided he was too weary to walk to the village. Leaving him to rest, Charlotte and Fred gathered their family together, and Betsey walked with them back to their cottage, proudly pushing her newest grandson in his pram. To his delight, Betsey allowed Bentley to go with them.

Charlotte enjoyed showing Betsey around their home. It was a far larger cottage than Bluebell Cottage and had a spacious hallway, a kitchen, parlour, and sitting room, and upstairs, four bedrooms. Betsey had not visited the cottage for some time, as the family usually came to her, and she exclaimed at the improvements Fred and Charlotte had made. The kitchen had some beautiful oak cupboards, and a large table and six chairs, all hand-crafted by Fred. Charlotte had made pretty green curtains for the windows, and rag mats were scattered on the roughly flagstoned floor. It was a warm and comfortable room. As they wandered from room to room, Betsey noticed that everywhere was clean and tidy. Eventually, when they had surveyed the entire cottage, they went outside to the backyard, where Llewie was putting the finishing touches to the coffin he was making.

"Hello, Gran. I didn't know you were coming today. Hello, Bentley."

"Hello, Llewie; you've done a splendid job there. What do you think, Fred?"

Fred ran his hand over the joints of the coffin and inspected the well-fitting lid.

"Yes, you've done a good job there, Llewie; we'll make a carpenter of you yet."

Betsey glanced into Fred's workshop and admired a new tallboy he was making for someone.

"I should think all of this will fit into the barn at The Red Lion, Fred. You could make the repairs to the building and extend it before you think about moving. There's no rush; the move can wait a few weeks, and that will give us time to get Bluebell Cottage decorated."

"Which cottage do you really want to move to, Mum? Money's not everything; I'd rather you were happy, as would Dad."

"Bluebell Cottage, definitely; this one's far too big for your dad and me, and it has such a large garden. No, renting it out to a family and bringing in more money would be far better. Besides, Bluebell Cottage is next door to the inn, and it would be nice to live next door to you and Charlotte. If it's not too cheeky, I wouldn't mind pinching one or two of your cupboards unless you want to take them with you. The inn already has a lot of cupboards, so you'd have to get rid of them."

"You'd be more than welcome, Mum; it's the least we can do, and I wouldn't want to leave them here for strangers. They can bring their own furniture."

"Thank you, Fred; I think we can see the way forward then, can't we? We need to get on with it and make it all happen. Oh, there is one other thing I'm hoping you can help me with."

"Of course, Mum, what is it?"

"It will be Ned's seventy-fourth birthday in a couple of weeks, and I'd like to organise a surprise birthday party for him; I think he's fit enough now. It will only be family and one or two friends, though, mind you, that will be enough of us. We could hold it in Betsey's Kitchen and have a buffet on a trestle table along one wall. The piano's already there, so we'll persuade Eveline to play a few of Ned's favourite songs. I'd like you to write to my brother, Barney, and his wife, Bronwen, and Ned's brother, Silas, and his wife, Josie, and invite them all to come and stay for a few days. Ned, Silas, Barney, and I were friends as children, and I lived here at the inn with Ned and Silas after my father ran away and Norman died. It's been years since we've all been together, and as we're all in our seventies, I'd like to see them before it's too late. I could write myself, but with my eyesight, my writing's not what it was, and it would take me a while; I don't want Ned to see me writing a letter, or he'll wonder what I'm doing."

"Yes, no problem. If you give me the addresses, I'll get on with it."

CHAPTER 24

HARTFORD

Doctor Luckett arrived at Hartford Manor early the following day to help Geoffrey Turner operate on Marrok's broken leg. Annie would have been more than willing to assist, but when Doctor Luckett offered his services, she decided to take Marrok's family out for the day to spare them worrying about their father. Leaving David and Thomas in Naomi's care, she wrapped Selina and the others up snugly and set off down the drive to the Lodge House, where she knew they were sure of a welcome and could play with her siblings. It was a treacherous journey, as the snow that had fallen over Christmas had partially melted but was now frozen again, making the ground exceedingly slippery. The children, of course, saw no fear, and the twins, Jinnie and Eliza, and their brother, Martin, took great pleasure in running, then skidding to a halt. Being younger, Selina and Paul were more cautious, but they all enjoyed a snowball fight and arrived at the Lodge House out of breath, with cheeks glowing from the cold. Annie took them to the back door and called out as she entered.

"Hello, Mum, hello, Liza; where are you?"

Getting no answer, she proceeded into the sitting room where Edward and Stephen were doing a jigsaw and Helen and Danny were looking at picture books. They leapt up in excitement when they saw Annie and the others.

"Hello, where's Mum and Liza this morning? Have they abandoned you?"

"Mummy's having her baby, Annie, and Liza's with her. Liza says we must stay down here and keep quiet. Uncle Arthur's gone to fetch Mrs Rudd."

"Oh, I see; thank you, Helen. In that case, you all stay down here while I go to see her."

Annie mounted the stairs, pausing momentarily to enjoy the view from the window, which looked out across the frozen landscape. She knocked on the bedroom door, and Liza opened it.

"Oh, it's you, Annie. Come in, my dear."

"Hello, Mum; how's it going?"

Sabina gasped as a strong contraction seized her body and smiled wanly at her daughter as the pain eased.

"All right, I think; my labour started in the early hours, and it seems to be taking a while. It's not quite like shelling peas, as your dad used to say. I'm glad you've come, though. Could you take the children back to the Manor House with you for the day? It would be one thing less for me to worry about," Seeing Annie's rueful grin, she continued, "What is it? Is something wrong?"

"No, nothing's wrong, but Doctor Turner and Doctor Luckett are operating on Marrok's leg today, and I thought I'd bring the children here to get them out of the way. They'll put Marrok to sleep with chloroform, and he'll be unconscious for a while. We didn't want his children worrying about him, as they lost their mother recently. No matter, I'll think of somewhere else to take them all."

"Oh, don't worry about it; you can stay here with them."

"Let me think about it; can I get you both a cup of tea?"

"Yes, please, thanks, love."

Annie pulled the kettle forward onto the hot plate of the Bodley stove so that it would come to a boil. She prepared a tray with cups, saucers, and a teapot, adding a couple of cakes from a tin in the larder. She then popped her head around the door of the sitting room and asked if anyone would like something to eat; naturally, the answer was yes, and in no time, all nine were sitting around the large kitchen table enjoying a mug of milk and some of Liza's freshly baked rock buns.

The back door opened, and Arthur entered with Tilly Rudd. Tilly was the nearest thing the village had to a midwife, and she had delivered many babies over the years. Annie was relieved to see her, for she knew her mother would be in safe hands. A stout woman, the walk from the village with Arthur had left Tilly breathless, and her plump cheeks were red from the exertion. Wisps of her curly grey hair had escaped from her bun, but her warm blue eyes twinkled, and she had a radiant smile. Arthur and Tilly were surprised to see Annie and the children, and she explained her presence and added another cup to the tray for Tilly.

"The water's nearly boiling, Tilly; I'll bring the tray up in a little while. Arthur, are you going to join us?"

"Yes, I'll have a cup of tea, thanks, Annie, though I must go to the hothouses then and add more straw to the fire; it's so cold out there today, I must keep the temperature up, or all the tender plants will die."

Observing Annie's puzzled face, he explained.

"The hothouses have double walls, and we burn straw in the cavity; it smoulders away for hours and keeps the temperature above freezing, but I mustn't let it go out. Are you staying here for the day?"

"I've been thinking about that, Arthur, and I think I'll call in on Aunty Charlotte. Maybe she would keep the girls to play with Rosella, and I could take the boys to Aunty Eveline's in the carriage. It would be better for them to be occupied for the day, and if we split them up, it's not quite so many to deal with."

"That would be helpful if you don't mind. I want to sit with Sabina, but Liza gave me my marching orders earlier, and I don't think it's even worth asking Tilly."

"No, I can tell you from experience that she doesn't like men around when she's delivering babies, so you'd best keep busy."

Annie washed and dried the dishes and, having said goodbye to her mother, Liza, and Tilly, walked the children to the village. As Annie expected, Charlotte was willing to help and agreed that Selina, Jinnie, Eliza, and Helen could play with Rosella for the day. Annie's Uncle Fred was there, too, and he offered to take them all home later in the evening. Pleased with the arrangements and taking Eddie with her, Annie walked the boys back to the Manor House. Having checked that no one else wanted the carriage for the day, she instructed Dodger to drive them to Hollyford Farm.

Although surprised at the arrival of their unexpected visitors, Charlie and Eveline welcomed them with open arms, and Matthew and Joe were delighted to have six more boys to play with. The only person who was not pleased with the arrangements was Amelia.

"Oh, that's not fair, Aunty Eveline. Matthew and Joe have got lots of boys to play with, and I have no girls. They won't let me join in their games."

"Oh dear, I'm so sorry, Amelia; I didn't think about that. Perhaps you and I could do something together and let the boys get on with their games."

At Annie's words, Amelia seemed slightly mollified.

"What could we do?"

"Um, let's think; I believe you like helping Aunty Eveline to make her rag dolls, so shall we do some sewing? Or perhaps we could make some cakes? You and I rarely get to spend a day together; I think we could have a nice time."

In the end, Charlie took the boys sledging, and although Amelia could have gone with them, she elected to take Annie up on her offer, and the pair had an enjoyable day sewing and baking cakes with Aunty Eveline.

Back at the Manor House, the two doctors were delighted with their efforts to reset Marrok's leg. Following his stay in the workhouse, the poor man's thighs were so thin it was easy to feel the fractured edges of his femur and set them firmly together. With Andrew Luckett holding the bones firmly in place, Doctor Turner skilfully wound the linen bandages, soaked in Plaster of Paris, around the limb and waited for the cast to harden. The two men were enjoying a chat and a cup of tea whilst waiting for their patient to awake from the anaesthetic. It was not too long before the young man began to stir, and he was surprised to see the two doctors relaxing and drinking tea.

"When are you going to start on my leg?"

"It's all done, lad, and you're on the mend. Now, you'll need to be patient because it's a nasty break in the biggest bone in your leg. The delay in setting it won't have helped either, so I reckon it might be six months or more before it's fully healed. What do you think, Andrew?"

"I don't have as much experience as you in dealing with broken bones, Geoffrey, or in setting them using a plaster cast, but yes, I think it will be at least that long."

"Once it settles down from the operation, you'll find it far less painful and easier to get around on your crutches. The bones are held firmly now, whereas before, they were moving about; it must have been excruciatingly painful for you."

"Aye, it was the worst pain I've ever known, without a doubt. Thank you so much for putting it right for me. Will I be able to travel in the carriage to Primrose Cottage with my father?"

"Yes, in a day or two, I should think. Why? Don't you like it at Hartford Manor?"

"Oh yes, I do; I've been made so welcome here, but I can't impose on these generous folk indefinitely, and I'd like to see my father's cottage where we'll be living for the time being. It will be better for the children to be settled too. I want them to go to school, and it makes sense for them to start the new term at Enderby School."

"Yes, I understand; I'll let your father in now, for I think he and your Aunty Margery are anxiously pacing up and down outside. Andrew, thank you so much for your help this morning; I'm much obliged to you. I'll walk with you as I'm going to call into the Lodge House to visit my next patient, young Danny Carter. I've already operated on his hare lip, and he's had one operation on his left foot, but I need to decide whether he needs treatment on the right one. If so, it will mean another trip to London as it's a complicated operation best carried out by my colleague, Doctor Brown. Anyway, goodbye for now, Marrok; I'll call in to see you later and again in the morning before Clara and I depart."

The two doctors walked together to the Lodge House, and then Andrew Luckett went on his way. However, Geoffrey found his journey had been in vain, for Danny had gone to Hollyford Farm with Annie, and Liza could not apologise enough.

"I'm so sorry, Doctor Turner; it completely slipped my mind. It's been hectic here this morning, what with Sabina going into labour and then Annie turning up with Selina and Marrok's family. She's taken some of them to her Uncle Fred and Aunty Charlotte in the village, and the rest with her to her Aunty Eveline at Hollyford Farm. Sabina must have forgotten, but to be fair, she does have other things on her mind. She's been in labour for twelve hours or more, and it's not like her; she usually has her babies quickly."

"Not to worry, Mrs Hammett, I can see you've had a trying morning. Do you think Mrs Webber would like me to examine her whilst I'm here?"

"If you'd like to take a seat, sir, I'll ask her."

On Tilly's advice, Sabina agreed to let the doctor examine her, and after doing so, he smiled at her.

"Now, Sabina, I think I know what the problem is; this child is not in the right position, and it's a sizable baby. How long has it been since you last gave birth?"

"Helen will be six this year, but apart from my first child, all my babies have been born easily and in far less time than this one's taking."

"Now, that makes me even more certain of my diagnosis. In the past, I suspect you had all your children within a short time of each other; am I right?"

"Yes, probably only two years apart, if that. Usually, as soon as I stopped breastfeeding, I'd be pregnant with the next; that's how it goes."

"Exactly, and because of that, your body never quite returned to normal between the births. This time, with a space of five years, it's almost as if you're having your first child again. Not only that, but like I say, this is a large baby, probably because you're eating better these days, and I expect the others were smaller."

"Yes, that's right, they were; still, being my tenth, you'd think my body would know what to do by now."

"That's not quite how it works, but if you allow me, I can help things along, though I'll have to nip back to the Manor House for my bag. Would you like me to assist you?"

"Yes, please. The sooner this is over with, the happier I'll be."

A couple of hours later, after the doctor had eased the baby into the world using forceps, Sabina happily cuddled her new daughter. Tilly weighed the baby on the kitchen scales, and Sabina was amazed to learn that the baby was nine and a half pounds.

"Good heavens, the others were all around four or five pounds; no wonder it was a difficult birth. Thank you so much for helping, Geoffrey, though it wasn't pleasant. If this had been my first, I might not have wanted any more."

"No, I can understand that, my dear, but probably in your case, and, forgive me, given your age, this may be your last child. Now, I'll give your husband a shout, for he's worn out with waiting, and then I suggest you get some sleep. Now, about Danny, as he's not returned home yet, I'll call again in the morning, and I can check on you at the same time. I'll have Clara with me, if that's all right, as we'll be on our way home."

"Oh, my goodness, I'd completely forgotten you were coming to see Danny today. I'm so sorry, and yes, that will be fine, thank you."

"No problem, and I'm sure Clara will enjoy seeing your new daughter. Goodbye for now; I'll see you in the morning."

The doctor left the room with Tilly Rudd and beckoned Arthur in.

"Congratulations, Arthur, you have a healthy baby daughter and an exhausted wife; make sure she gets some rest."

Grinning widely, Arthur took Sabina into his arms and kissed the top of her head.

"Well done, darling; now, let me say hello to this young lady who's caused you so much trouble." He leaned over the crib where the baby was fast asleep. She had plump, rosy cheeks and blond hair.

"Oh, Sabina, she's beautiful; how wonderful that we have a child of our own. Are you all right?"

"Yes, I'm fine, Arthur, just tired. It was kind of Annie to take the children out for the day; I need forty winks before they come home. Do you have any thoughts about a name?"

"You did all the hard work, my love; you name her if you have something in mind."

"I do, actually, seeing as it's a girl. Betsey and I were reading the Carter family bible a while ago and came across the name Katel. She was an ancestor of Ned's, and I think it's a lovely name; so unusual. I'd like to call her Katel."

"I like it; yes, let's call her Katel."

CHAPTER 25

HARTFORD

Victoria Eastleigh was bored, and, sighing deeply, she pushed the book she was reading off the bed and onto the floor. It had been several days since she had given birth to her new baby boy, and she longed to be up and about. However, even though the delivery had been straightforward and accomplished within three hours, Doctor Luckett insisted she stay in bed for at least another ten days. He had visited her earlier that morning before assisting Geoffrey Turner in resetting her cousin Marrok's broken leg, and he was adamant she must continue her confinement. Leaning over the side of the bed, she rang the bell, and her maid came running.

"What can I get you, ma'am?"

"Please ask Elspeth to bring the baby and Caroline and Joshua to me."

"Yes, ma'am."

Within a few minutes, Elspeth, the nanny, appeared, leading two toddlers by the hand. The girl wore a pretty pink dress with matching ribbons in her plaited brown hair. She was quite a plain child, considering her good-looking parents, but her face was transformed when she smiled widely at her mother. In contrast to his elder sister, the little boy was handsome. Dark and unruly curls framed the creamy complexion of his face, and his eyes were the same startling blue as those of his late father. Victoria greeted them.

"Hello, you two; climb in here with Mama, and I'll read you a story."

Elspeth lifted them onto the bed and passed their mother a book of nursery rhymes from the bookshelf.

"Will this one do, ma'am?"

"Yes, we like that one; shall we read some nursery rhymes?" The children nodded their approval, and with her arms around each of them, Victoria began to tell them about Jack and Jill, but after a few minutes, she paused.

"Where's the baby? I asked for him to be brought here, too."

Elspeth explained that the wet nurse was changing the baby and would bring him as soon as she was finished. Some ten minutes later, Mary, the wet nurse, arrived with the baby, and Victoria held out her arms.

"Hello, Francis; how are you this morning?" She kissed the baby on his soft cheek.

"Can I hold him, Mummy?"

"Yes, I think so, Caroline, hold out your arms, and I'll put him on your lap; that's right, now be gentle."

Victoria placed the squirming baby into her daughter's arms and put her arm around them both. However, the baby soon expressed his discontent, and Victoria took the crying child back into her arms and kissed his soft, downy head. He turned his head towards her breast, his open mouth seeking her nipple.

"Oh dear, I think he wants to be fed; Mary, is he due a feed?"

"Yes, ma'am; he'd just woken up and needed his nappy changed when you asked to see him, but I expect he's hungry."

"Oh, bad timing, then; you'd better take him but bring him back again later, please."

"Yes, ma'am."

The woman disappeared with the baby, and Victoria continued to read to Caroline and Joshua. After half an hour, her maid reappeared and asked if she would receive her Aunt Margery and Uncle Sam.

"Yes, of course. Now, I have visitors, so you two must say hello nicely, and then Nanny will take you back to the nursery to play with your toys, but you can come and see me again tomorrow."

Lady Margery and Sam greeted the children, and then Elspeth took them back to the nursery.

"They're growing up so quickly; how are you feeling, my dear?"

"Oh, I'm as right as rain, thank you, Aunty Margery, and I want to get out of bed, but the doctor won't hear of it; I'm sure I shall die of boredom."

"Oh dear; sadly, I never had any children, so I haven't been in your situation, but yes, I can imagine that must be tedious."

Victoria studied the elderly couple seated on either side of the bed with interest, thinking they could not have led more different lives. Sam had a good head of greyish-white hair, but his weather-beaten face was lined with deep wrinkles, and he was missing several teeth. His smart clothing could not entirely hide the rough life he had led as a gypsy and a tramp. However, since his relationship with the Fellwood family had been revealed, his life had changed beyond all recognition. Although Sam was Victoria's cousin, once removed, it was decided that, given his age, he would be known as Uncle Sam.

Her eyes shifted to the other side of the bed, and she surveyed her Great Aunt Margery. Every inch a lady, Margery was smartly dressed as always. Her elegant maroon dress was trimmed at the neck and cuffs with delicate cream lace, handmade especially for her in Honiton. Sparkling diamond earrings and a matching necklace completed her outfit. Her hair was elaborately styled, and she held herself erect, as she had been taught to do since childhood.

Margery was an incredibly independent woman, and indeed, since losing her husband, Clarence, many years earlier, she frequently defied convention and lived life as she liked. Unlikely as it seemed, she had warmed to her nephew, Sam, and taken him under her wing, even providing him with a cottage on the Enderby Estate, where she resided in a mansion. There was little difference in their ages, so they had become firm friends, spending much time together. Victoria dragged her attention back to her visitors.

"How are you, Uncle Sam? It must be marvellous to have found your son and his family. Have they settled in all right?"

"Yes, thank you. It's all a bit strange for them, but they enjoy having plenty to eat. Once Marrok has recovered from his operation, we'll go to Primrose Cottage. The doctors say he can travel now that his leg's in plaster."

"Oh, that's good; I'm sure Robert and Annie are happy for you all to stay as long as you like, but no doubt you'll be glad to get home. Are they all going to live with you at Primrose Cottage?"

"Yes, certainly until Marrok is back on his feet properly. We've barely had time to discuss the future, as we only found him a couple of weeks ago, and then Christmas was upon us. We'll need to make a few changes to accommodate them, but the cottage is plenty big enough. I think Marrok wants the children to attend Enderby School, and the sooner they can start, the better; I go there sometimes with my friend, Peter Webber. He talks to the pupils about his experiences in farming and mining and how he's coped since he lost his hands in an accident. They're always fascinated to hear his stories, and occasionally, I tell them about my life as a tramp," Sam chuckled. "I think the teacher considers it a lesson in how not to live your life."

"Aunty Margery, I wondered if you might be aware of any houses on the market that would suit me. I don't want to ask Mama because she'd like us to continue living here, but I'd rather have my own place, and there's no point in upsetting her until I need to. Frank's will has been read now, and he's left me comfortably off as I knew he would; he was never mean with his money, though, as you know, he had many faults."

"Yes, my dear, I know he did; are the police any nearer to catching the rogues who murdered him?"

"No, I don't think so; I've not heard anything, anyway. At least they've stopped treating Robert and Annie's uncles as suspects. Frank upset many fathers, brothers, and uncles with his womanising, and probably many were not sorry to see him dead."

The young woman's gaze dropped as she felt tears pricking her eyes. Seeing her distress, Margery took her hand.

"Leave it with me, my dear, and I'll get my estate manager on to it. He usually knows everything that's going on. Do you mind where the house is?"

"No, somewhere within ten miles or so of Hartford would be perfect. Once I've found a suitable dwelling, I'll ask Frank's mother, Catherine, if she wants to move to Devon. I had a telegram from her yesterday telling me that my father-in-law, Monty Eastleigh, has passed away. He'd been ill with syphilis for years, and sadly, for the last few months, he'd become insane. It's been so difficult for Catherine, losing both her son and her husband within a few weeks of each other, and she's not in the best of health herself."

"Are you sure you want to invite her to live with you? It's generous, but I'm not sure it's wise."

"No, not to live with me, but maybe close by. That way, she can see more of her grandchildren, for she dotes on them, and she's not even seen the baby yet. I think she'll be pleased I've called him Francis, though I want him to be known as Frank, like his father."

"Presumably, you won't attend the funeral?"

"No, I can't possibly travel to London so soon after giving birth. Perhaps the doctor's insistence that I remain in bed for another ten days might be a blessing in disguise."

"Yes, maybe, my dear. I'm looking forward to seeing the new arrival; is the baby thriving?"

"Yes, I have a wet nurse called Mary, and she says he's taking plenty of milk. You just missed him. He was here with Caroline and Joshua, but was hungry for his next feed. Never mind, maybe next time, or I'll bring them all to see you at Enderby House when I'm up and about."

"Yes, do that, my dear. We'll leave you to rest now, for Sam and I are to meet with your parents, and I think Robert will join us. As they walked down the corridor from Victoria's bedroom, Lady Margery tucked her arm through Sam's and gave it a squeeze.

"Before we meet with Charles and Eleanor, I thought this would be an opportunity to show you around Hartford Manor. I know you want to see where your father used to sleep; would you like to do that now?"

"Oh, yes, please, I'd love to."

Lady Margery led Sam back to the grand staircase that provided access to the two upper floors. Wide and spacious, it was built of solid oak, and the carpet beneath their feet was thick and luxurious, with a dull red pattern mixed with gold. The walls were panelled to dado height and then covered with an attractive turquoise wallpaper. However, there was little of the walls to be seen, for many paintings adorned them. The old lady stopped in front of a large portrait of a gentleman. The subject was wearing hunting clothes and had an amused expression. Sam gasped in amazement, and his aunt chuckled.

"Yes, I thought this painting would surprise you, Sam; now, do you see why I do not doubt your parentage?"

"Oh, my goodness, it's almost like seeing myself in the mirror; I'm so much like him. I take it this is my grandfather, Ephraim Fellwood?"

"Yes, this is my father, Ephraim, and I think he was around forty when this portrait was painted. He was a wonderful man, Sam, and heartbroken when your father left home without saying goodbye. He'd be so pleased to know you're standing here with me, admiring his picture and enjoying your inheritance. Come on, Thomas's bedroom was along here, next to mine."

They entered the large bedroom, and Sam observed his surroundings with interest. On the floor was a rich royal blue carpet, and the walls were covered with pale yellow embossed wallpaper. They, too, were covered with many paintings, all in heavy gilt frames, and a large one above the marble fireplace was of a young man in hose and doublet.

"Goodness, what strange clothes that man's wearing; I've never seen anything like that."

"I think that painting is at least two hundred years old, Sam, and I suppose that's what they wore back then."

Sam strolled around the room, admiring an ornate walnut bureau. The rich dark wood was delicately inlaid with an iridescent mother-of-pearl, which greatly enhanced its appearance. It was an elegant piece, and he reverently ran his hand over its smooth surface before moving on to observe a clock on the mantelpiece.

"Has the room changed much since my father slept here?"

"No, it's been left as it was; I don't think anything has been changed. That's the same bed that Thomas slept in, and I should know because I often used to creep into it for a cuddle with him in the mornings."

Sam moved over to the large double bed and sat on the edge. It was covered with a white bedspread, lightly patterned with pale pink and grey flowers and foliage. On the wall behind the bed, an ornate pelmet and curtains matched the bedspread, as did a panel on the wall.

"It's such a beautiful room; I'm glad he had a good life, especially as it was so short. It's strange to think of you and him lying in that bed, and I'm so grateful to you for showing me; thank you."

"It's my pleasure, Sam; now, I'll show you a few more rooms, and then we'd better present ourselves to Charles, Eleanor, and Robert, or they'll wonder what happened to us."

CHAPTER 26

HARTFORD

Lady Margery led Sam back down the stairs to the room where Charles Fellwood spent most of his time. He was seated in his wheelchair in the drawing room, and his wife, Eleanor, was sitting on a chaise longue beside him, working on some embroidery.

"Good morning, Robert; how are you?"

"I'm fine, thank you, Mama; how about you both?"

"Yes, we're all right, too; how are the family?"

Robert was surprised his mother had even voiced this question, for she never acknowledged Annie or his family, so he decided to make the most of it.

"Yes, they're all in good health, thank you for asking. Selina grows prettier and more independent by the day, and Thomas and David are thriving. They're seven months old and can almost sit up unaided, though Annie likes to put cushions around them. Are Aunty Margery and Uncle Sam not here yet?"

"Yes, they arrived about an hour ago, but they went to see Victoria and the new baby, and now I think Margery is showing Sam around the house. She wanted to show him his grandfather's portrait and where his father, Thomas, slept. Only she knows things like that. She's the last of her generation, I'm afraid."

"Yes, she is; we should ask her everything we can about the family whilst we still have her with us. Ah, I think I hear them coming now."

When Lady Margery and Sam were seated, Eleanor rang the bell, and a maid brought them some coffee and cakes.

"What did you think of our grandfather's picture, Sam?"

"To be honest, Charles, I can't believe how much I look like him; it's uncanny, though, until I moved into Primrose Cottage, I'd barely ever seen myself in a mirror. I believe the first time was when Charlie Chugg took me to Hollyford Farm to spruce me up for his wedding to Eveline Carter. He let me have a bath, cut my hair, and shaved off my beard. He couldn't believe the change in my appearance, so he took me upstairs to his brother's bedroom to let me see myself in the mirror. I have to say, you don't bear much resemblance to Ephraim yourself; perhaps you took after your grandmother. I didn't see her picture today; I don't think, did I, Margery?"

"No, there are a few, but my mother died quite young; I'll show you next time, Sam."

"Thank you. Robert and Margery suggested we come here today as they thought you'd like to see my father's gold watch and hear how it was given back to me recently. I'm not sure how much you know about what happened when Thomas ran off with his girlfriend, Gypsy Jane, but Betsey was able to fill in many of the details of that time. You probably don't know Betsey, but she's Annie's grandmother and the same age as you, I believe, Margery?"

"Yes, when Thomas took me riding, we often encountered Betsey on her travels. She had a hard life when she was young; bless her, and it's a wonder she survived. Her younger brother, Norman, was less fortunate. Anyway, Thomas befriended Betsey, and he was concerned about her. She often visited the gypsies begging for food, and I think it was one way he had an excuse to call and see Jane."

Sam reached into his pocket and withdrew the gold watch.

"Here it is, a real beauty. It's inscribed with the name Ambrose Fellwood and the date 1725. I think Ambrose was Ephraim's father, so he was Thomas' grandfather. Robert worked out that Thomas was only five when his grandfather died, but Betsey told us that Thomas remembered sitting on his grandfather's lap and playing with this watch, and so it was left to him."

"How did Betsey come by it? Did she steal it?"

Robert glanced angrily at his mother. "No, Mama, she did not steal it!"

He went on to tell his parents how Betsey had witnessed the fight between Thomas Fellwood and the miller, Jasper Morris, and how the poor man had lost his life when his head hit a stone. They were surprised to hear that Betsey had helped dispose of the body, saving Thomas from facing a possible murder charge.

"Not only that, but she was only six, and she kept that secret until it was finally revealed when she reached the age of twenty-one and was told Thomas had bequeathed a hundred guineas to her. Even then, Betsey only told her nearest and dearest to explain her inheritance. Before Jane left for France, she told Betsey Thomas had lost the watch in the fight and was upset about it, and Betsey returned to the scene and retrieved it from a bush. Despite her uncle facing a debtor's prison for defaulting on a loan, she never sold the watch but always kept it in the hope she could return it to Thomas one day. Of course, we now know that was never to be. I'm so pleased she came forward and told me her story. The watch is of sentimental value, but it was more important to me to hear how my father came to run away to France. By all accounts, he was happy there for a couple of years but drowned in a fishing accident, and his wife returned with me to the gypsies in England."

"Goodness, what a tale; I'm glad you have something so personal of your father's, Sam. I expect one day you'll want to pass it on to your son, Marrok. How is he, by the way? I heard Geoffrey Turner was operating on his broken leg?"

"Yes, that's right, he had the operation yesterday, and the doctor thinks he'll make a complete recovery, though it will take six months or so for it to heal properly. Geoffrey examined him again this morning before departing with his wife, Clara, for their home in Cullompton. They planned to call in at the Lodge House on the way to see Sabina's son, Danny. I don't know if you've met the child, but he was born with a cleft palate and two deformed feet. It's remarkable what the doctors have done to correct his mouth and one foot, and now they're considering one more operation on the other foot. I've met him a few times now, and he's quite a character; he took all the pain and discomfort in his stride and is so pleased with his appearance. He used to get teased mercilessly at school, I believe. He's an example to us all."

Charles and Eleanor were silent, realising Sam had no idea that Danny was, in fact, their child, rejected at birth because of his deformities. Aunty Margery was highly amused at the situation and could barely keep a smile from her face, but Robert swiftly moved the conversation along.

"Now, there are one or two things about the estate that I want to discuss with you all, so now is as good a time as any. Aunty Margery and you, Papa, will undoubtedly remember Ephraim Fellwood building the aqueduct and canal in the 1830s."

"Yes, my father was so excited about the venture; it was a ground-breaking project at the time and cost an enormous amount of money. My late husband, Clarence, provided a considerable amount of the money required when he bought shares in the scheme. Unfortunately, a lot of damage was done to the foundations of the aqueduct during a thunderstorm, and they were both so worried that they would never see a return on their money. It took a few years, but then it repaid them times over. Why do you mention it now, Robert?"

"I'm sorry to tell you this, but I plan to cease using the canal to transport goods soon and will close the business down."

"What! Oh no, it was my father's pride and joy."

"Yes, I know, and that's why I wanted to explain the matter to you. In its day, the canal was a marvellous feat of engineering, and it was much quicker to transport the goods on barges than by horse and cart on the roads. The roads are still poor these days, but they were much worse back then, so it made sense."

"So why close it?"

"Unfortunately, the canal has had its day, for since the railway came to Devon, that's the fastest and most economical method of transport by far. I've kept the canal open far longer than I should for sentimental reasons, but it's no good; I have to make the change and transport our goods by railway from now on. Other folk are doing the same, so we're losing customers, and the canal is no longer financially viable."

"I see; I can understand the logic behind your decision, unpalatable though it is. What will happen to the canal?"

"I have an idea that I wanted to run past you all, for you're all older and wiser than me. We seem to have an ever-growing number of city-dwellers coming to North Devon to take a holiday in the countryside and benefit from our clean air. They're glad to leave behind the smog of London and other cities and marvel at our coastline and scenery. I wondered if we could adapt a couple of the barges into pleasure boats like they have on the Thames. If we add rows of seats and a roof, the same donkeys or a shire horse could pull them along the towpath. When the canal was being built, Betsey came up with the idea of an additional food outlet at The Red Lion Inn to cater for the many workers the estate employed. Betsey's Kitchen is still making a profit, and the canal runs past the bottom of the orchard behind the inn. I haven't mentioned this to Annie yet, for I know she'll be so excited, but I reckon the inn could benefit from a lot of trade in the form of lunches, cream teas, and similar."

"What a wonderful idea; it's much better than letting the canal go to rack and ruin. Yes, I like that idea, Robert, and it would continue to employ the villagers. Whatever gave you the idea?"

"Last summer, after the twins had been born, I persuaded Annie to have a day out with me. We have so little time to ourselves these days. Anyway, after some persuasion, she agreed, and we rode to Ilfracombe and stayed the night at an inn there. She'd only been to the town once and loved the place, so I knew she'd enjoy it. The weather was warm and sunny, and we strolled along the seafront and then the pier, which was built about ten years ago; another amazing piece of engineering. Anyway, we carried on and came to the entrance of The Tunnels; I don't know if you've ever visited them?"

"Oh, yes, I have," exclaimed Lady Margery, "in fact, I've even bathed in the pools there."

"Good Lord! What in the sea?" Eleanor was astounded.

"Yes, shocking, isn't it? But it was amazing, and I loved every minute. It was so invigorating. Did you bathe, Robert?"

"No, but Annie wanted to, and I promised her we might return this year and do so."

"But it's so undignified. What do you wear, and what if someone sees you?"

"It's well organised. The six tunnels were originally dug through the cliffs around 1820 by hundreds of Welsh miners. The project cost a lot of money, but the tunnels provide direct access to the coves, both on foot and by carriage, and they have transformed the small fishing village into a popular seaside resort. Some magnificent houses have been built there now. By building walls out into the sea, bathing pools were formed and replenished with fresh seawater at each high tide. One pool, the Crewkhorne, is reserved for men, and the other at Wildersmouth is for ladies. The bathers are kept strictly apart, and the man I was talking to on our visit delighted in telling me that the men bathe in the nude."

Eleanor gasped in horror, and Lady Margery threw back her head and laughed.

"Yes, that's right, but don't worry, Eleanor, I didn't go that far. The ladies were wheeled down to the water's edge in bathing huts and could access the sea without anyone seeing. There was even a man on duty with a bugle, and he would raise the alarm if he spotted a man attempting to spy on the ladies. Swimming in the sea was so enjoyable, and I'd love to do it again, though, at my age, it's hardly advisable."

"Anyway, that's what's made me think of using the canal as a tourist attraction. I don't know whether the number of folk taking holidays will increase, but it seems to be all the rage now, and I think canal pleasure trips would be popular. I'm also investigating offering shooting parties and fishing at Hartford Manor. It's a pastime that's becoming popular, and it would be another attraction to offer to holidaymakers. We have acres of moorland unsuitable for farming but ideal for a day's shooting. All we need to do is rear some pheasants for the visitors to shoot, and there's already a lot of fish in Shebworthy Pond. We'd need to improve access and consider accommodation for the visitors."

"I suggest you talk to my estate manager, Robert, for we already offer shooting parties and fishing at Enderby, and you're right; it's a lucrative business. We offer accommodation in one wing of the house; it may be something you could consider here."

Glimpsing the angry expression on his mother's face, Robert hurriedly moved the conversation along.

"Thank you, Aunty Margery; I'll speak to your manager about that when I next see him, but one step at a time. I want to concentrate on the canal for now, but I'm glad you all seem to approve of my idea."

CHAPTER 27

EGGESFORD

Rosa let her guests sleep until they awoke naturally the next morning because she knew they were exhausted. She glanced in on them when she arose and envied them in their deep slumber; if only she could sleep like that. Sadly, those days were long gone, as the pain in her hip or the pressure from her bladder always meant she was up with the lark. At last, she heard them moving, and they clattered down the creaky old stairs.

"Good morning; did you sleep all right?"

"Oh, yes, and thank you for letting us stay. We've been lucky so far, for since we left home, we haven't had to sleep outside in the cold. We'll walk to Kings Nympton today and see if we can find work at the inn you mentioned. Hopefully, they'll feed us and provide shelter for the night."

"I hope they will; now, would you like a bowl of porridge for breakfast? It will warm your insides for the journey, and I've cut you a couple of cheese sandwiches to take with you for your dinner."

"Yes, please, and thank you again for your kindness."

Within minutes, they were enjoying a bowl of creamy porridge with a generous spoonful of honey drizzled across the top. Whilst they were eating, Rosa showed them where she had hidden the brooch.

"Now, only you and I know where it is, but later on, I'll tell Esther, my next-door neighbour, and if anything happens to me, she'll retrieve it and keep it for you. I'd love to offer you a home here with me, but I'm afraid I can't afford to feed and clothe you. Still, I've decided to sell my two fields to a local farmer soon, so I'll have more money then. He's wanted to buy them for years, but my Jim would never sell them while he was alive, for we managed all right with his wages. I've been considering selling them for a while, for I've no family, and the extra money would provide me with some comfort in my final years. Anyway, I'm rambling on, but I want you to know that if you can't find these relatives of yours or if they don't want anything to do with you, then come back here, and you can live with me. We'll manage somehow; that's if you'd like to."

"Oh, thank you so much, and it's the second offer we've had, as Mr March, the farmer at Newton St Cyres, said the same thing to us. I never knew people could be so kind, but we must try to find our relatives and meet up with my granny."

"Yes, of course, you must, and I hope it works out for you. Now, be careful as you go, and if you hear a cart or a stagecoach coming along the road, I should hide in the hedge in case it's Lady Grantley's men searching for you. Goodness, that lady knows how to harbour a grudge. She shouldn't seek revenge on you for her husband's infidelity. Still, there it is, and I wouldn't use your own names, either."

They left shortly after breakfast and were dismayed to find it was snowing. The cold easterly wind soon chilled them to the bone, and Millie tucked her arm through Jonathan's to encourage him onwards. Taking Rosa's warning to heart, they listened hard for the sound of hooves, but on such a dreary morning, there was little traffic, and they saw no one on foot. Jonathan was miserable and tired, and in truth, Millie, too, was feeling desperate, though she did her best to remain cheerful for her brother's sake.

Around them, the scenery was beautiful, with far-reaching views of the rural landscape. However, they were in no mood to appreciate it, for on a couple of occasions, when they heard a farm cart and a stagecoach approaching, they hid in the undergrowth and were soon wet through. Millie was torn between the desire not to be discovered by Lady Grantley's men and the chance of getting a lift on a cart to Coleton Mill.

Rosa had told them it was a walk of around five miles to the mill, and in the treacherous travelling conditions, it was nearly four hours before they spotted the imposing four-storey building. They approached cautiously, entered through an archway at the gatehouse, and then walked across a yard to the heavy oak door. Hoping to at least be able to rest and get warm, Millie anxiously lifted the heavy brass door knocker and let it fall a couple of times. The sound reverberated through the large hallway inside, and after a few minutes, a maid opened the door.

"Yes, can I help you?"

"Good afternoon, miss; my brother and I are walking to Kings Nympton and wondered if we might shelter here for a while. We're cold and wet and would be grateful to warm ourselves if you have a fire going."

"I'll have to ask the cook, so you'd better wait there."

She shut the door, leaving them to face the elements for several minutes before she returned.

"Yes, the master's out for the day, so she says to go around the back to the kitchen door. You'd better take off your boots, or no doubt you'll get an earful from cook; she hates muddy footprints on her clean floor."

"Oh, thank you so much."

Millie and Jonathan followed a path around the house and knocked on the back door. It was opened for them by a thin scullery maid, who told them her name was Edith. She admitted them to a boot room and, sure enough, told them to take off their shoes and follow her. The girl was only about eight years old and regarded them curiously.

"You look frozen; have you walked far?"

"Yes, about five miles from Eggesford."

They entered a large kitchen where the cook had her sleeves rolled up and was kneading pastry. It was a pleasant, clean, and well-stocked room, with crockery and utensils on wide shelves. Along one wall was an enormous range, and its heat hit them as soon as they entered. Several other maids were working at the long kitchen table, one spreading jam on a sponge, another chopping up onions, the pungent aroma causing tears to run down her cheeks. The cook glanced up at them.

"Hello, I'm Gracie Davidson, the cook, and I hear you'd like to warm yourselves; is that right?"

"Yes, ma'am, we've walked from Eggesford and need to get to Kings Nympton before dark, but it's such a cold day, and with all the snow, we're wet through."

"I can see that. Sit by the fire and take off those blankets you have draped around you. Edith, spread them on a clothes horse to let them dry out. I should take off your socks, too and spread them on the rack above the Bodley. Are you hungry?"

"Yes, but we have some cheese sandwiches if you don't mind us eating them here."

"No, that's all right, you carry on. The master is out today, and the housekeeper is entertaining a friend, so Edith can find you both a piece of cake if you like."

"Yes, thank you."

Millie and Jonathan gratefully sat as close to the range as they could, and seeing how uncomfortable they were, one of the maids opened the door to the fire so they could benefit from the direct heat. Within minutes, their hands and feet started to ache and tingle as they thawed out, and Jonathan began to cry with the pain. Millie took him on her knee and massaged his fingers and toes, ignoring the discomfort in her own extremities. The staff watched them with interest, wondering what they were doing walking alone in such weather. It was Edith, with her youthful curiosity, who posed the question.

"Why are you walking so far on such a cold day?"

"We're on our way to North Devon to stay with some relatives as our mother died recently."

"Oh, I'm sorry to hear that; I don't have a mum or a dad. Do you have a dad?"

"No, he's dead too. We have a granny, but she's ill, so she'll join us when she's better."

"Is it a long way to walk?"

"Yes, I think so; we don't know. We're asking the way as we go, but if we can get to Kings Nympton today, we've been told there's an inn, so we're hoping to find some work for a few days and somewhere to sleep."

The cook exclaimed aloud at this piece of news.

"Oh, well, good luck with that, my dears. The inn's called The Farmer's Arms, and a new owner has taken over recently. He's not popular with the locals, and he's upset quite a few of his staff with his manner; Jenny here, for one. Jenny, tell Millie and Jonathan what you know. Do you think they'll find work there?"

"Yes, I expect you will because several kitchen staff have sought other positions. Mr Higgins is not a local man, but he inherited the inn recently after his uncle died. He comes from Bristol and doesn't understand country life. All I'll say is, if you stay there, Millie, lock your bedroom door at night and make sure you're never alone with him, for he can't keep his hands to himself. You might be better off walking on to The Portsmouth Arms near Umberleigh. The landlord there is a much nicer man; I know him and his wife. If you mention my name, they'll treat you right."

"Oh, thanks for the warning, Jenny. Perhaps you're right, and we should try to get to the Portsmouth Arms. How far is it?"

"Kings Nympton is about a mile away, and The Portsmouth Arms is another three miles after that. Mind you, it will be unpleasant walking there in this weather. Mrs Davidson, couldn't Millie and Jonathan stay here for the night?"

"I wish I could say yes, my dears, and if it were up to me, it wouldn't be a problem, but our housekeeper is a stickler for the rules, and she'd never agree to it. I'd offer you to sleep in the mill, but her husband rules the roost there, and he's tarred with the same brush. No, you'll have to be on your way when you've finished eating, but I hope you feel better than when you came in."

"Yes, thank you so much for letting us eat our dinner here in the warmth. We'll finish this delicious cake and then be on our way again."

Jonathan was dismayed at his sister's words.

CHAPTER 28

KING'S NYMPTON

Millie and Jonathan pulled on their still-damp socks, and Millie pinned the blankets around their shoulders once more. The blankets had dried out slightly but were heavy from the moisture they contained, and they shivered. Thanking the cook and the kitchen staff for their hospitality, they donned their boots and resumed their journey.

The sky was leaden with dark, forbidding clouds, and they could see their breath in the air as they panted up a steep hill, the exertion warming them and bringing roses to their pale cheeks. Within a few hundred yards, it began to snow even more heavily, and they struggled to see the track before them. Millie was terrified they might get lost and die of the cold. Her granny had warned her of the dangers of resting too long in the bitter winter temperatures, and she was afraid if they stopped and fell asleep, they might never wake again. With that alarming thought in mind, she hurried her brother onwards, ignoring his increasing complaints. Suddenly, Millie pushed back her hood and listened. Although the snow deadened any sound, she was sure she could hear the distant sound of horses' hooves approaching. Whilst she would have been grateful for a lift to the next village, she was afraid to risk being seen in case the oncoming horses belonged to the men who were pursuing them.

"Quickly, Jonnie, hide in the bushes!"

She pulled her little brother to the side of the lane and into the undergrowth. Before joining him, she grabbed a fallen branch, hastily brushed the snow, obliterating their footsteps for the last few yards, and walked backwards to the hedge. She pulled Jonathan down to the ground, and they lay flat on their bellies and put their heads down. It was snowing heavily, and she hoped the horsemen would not notice that their footsteps did not continue. However, to her dismay, the two horsemen reined in their horses and stopped only a foot from where they lay.

"I don't know about you, Bill, but I'm fed up with this carry-on, and I bet her ladyship wouldn't want to be out in this weather. What chance do we stand of finding anybody in this blizzard? If those youngsters have any sense, they'll have found somewhere warm to wait until the weather improves. Shall we go back?"

"I know, mate, but you know what she's like, and she said if we didn't find them, then we could look for new jobs. I don't know about you, but I can't risk that, especially with no reference. I've got seven mouths to feed."

"Aye, I'm in the same boat, but I don't know where they can be. I mean, they're only youngsters and on foot. I don't see how they could have gotten this far; we're wasting our time."

"Someone must have helped them. They've either got a lift on a farm cart or someone's taken them in, and they're lying low. Either way, 'tis bad news for us, for as we all know, her ladyship's not a reasonable woman. Here, have a swig of this, Larry; it'll warm your belly. We'll come to The Farmer's Arms at Kings Nympton soon, but I can't stand the landlord there, so I reckon we should carry on to The Portsmouth Arms and stay there for the night. The ale's better there, too. We might as well get a night's rest and start again tomorrow; we aren't going to find anyone in the dark, and I wouldn't send a dog out in this weather."

After a few more minutes, the two men galloped off to the enormous relief of the children. They were wet from lying on the snow and shivering violently from the cold.

"Oh, Millie, I'm so cold; I can hardly feel my feet. Are we nearly there?" Jonnie's teeth were chattering as he spoke.

"I don't know, Jonnie; I certainly hope so. We must keep moving, though, or we could die from the cold. Come on, let's hurry and try to warm up a bit."

They trudged on, thoroughly miserable now, and after nearly an hour, were relieved to see a few buildings suddenly loom in front of them. Realising they had reached Kings Nympton, Millie urged Jonathan forward as she searched for the inn. She had hoped to push on to The Portsmouth Arms, as the young maid, Jenny, recommended, but it was impossible, for the snow was at least six inches deep and beginning to drift in the strong wind.

After a short distance, they heard the sign for The Farmer's Arms creaking as it was buffeted by the wind, and Millie was relieved to see a light shining through the window.

"Come on, Jonnie; we're here, and hopefully, we can stay the night; surely, no one will turn us away in this weather."

She pushed open the inn door and entered a cosy room where a log fire was burning brightly. Only a couple of men were present, and they regarded the two youngsters in surprise as they approached the man behind the bar. The innkeeper was around fifty with greying hair and beady, ferret-like eyes.

"Hello, sir; I wondered if me and my brother could stay here for the night if we do some work for you? We don't have much money, but the weather's so terrible we can't continue on our way."

"Where are you going on such a day? Do your parents know where you are?"

"We don't have any parents, sir, but we're travelling to some relatives in Umberleigh. Our Granny's unwell and will follow us as soon as she's feeling better."

Millie suddenly realised she didn't want to tell this man too much, but had to say something. According to the cook at Coleton Manor, Umberleigh was the next village after The Portsmouth Arms and was situated some seven miles away. She hoped the innkeeper didn't know many people in Umberleigh, but then remembered he was new to the area.

"All I can say is your granny must have been mad or desperate to send you out in a storm like this."

"She has typhoid, sir, and our parents died of it recently, so she wanted us out of the house in case we caught it. When we left Exeter a week ago, the weather wasn't as bad as this."

"Hmm, I see, and no, I don't suppose I can refuse you shelter in this weather, though I hope you're not bringing typhoid here. I'll take you to the kitchen, and you can sleep in front of the fire; will that suit you?"

"Oh, yes, we'll be grateful for anywhere in the warm, thank you; we're so wet and cold."

"Come through here, then, and I'll show you the way. I'm Simon Higgins, and luckily for you, I could do with some help; a couple of kitchen maids have left recently."

The man raised a section of the wooden counter and led the way to the kitchen. It was a large room and none too clean, but it was warm, and for that, they were grateful. At the sink, an elderly woman was peeling potatoes, and a young boy was feeding logs into the stove.

"Dora, I've said these two can shelter here for the night. Let them thaw out a bit and then put them to work." He turned his attention to the boy. "That's right, Luke, don't let that fire go out; get yourself to the woodshed and bring in as many logs as you can to keep the fires burning overnight. This lad can help you when he's warmed up a bit." He left abruptly to return to the bar.

The woman eyed the two visitors with suspicion and said nothing. The boy, too, seemed unwilling to talk to them, so Millie decided to break the ice.

"Hello, I'm Gertie, and this is my brother, Walter. Is it all right if we take off our wet things and hang them somewhere to dry?"

The woman nodded. "Yes, put them on that clothes horse, and they should dry overnight. Here, dry yourself with this towel."

Millie removed the blankets they wore over their coats and spread them on the wooden frame. She then helped Jonathan remove his jacket, boots, and wet socks. She rubbed his cold feet vigorously with the rough towel, and he wept as the feeling flooded painfully back into his fingers and toes. She fished in her sack, found him a dry pair of socks, and quickly put them on his feet.

"There, that's better; sit by the fire and get warm."

She turned her attention to the young boy running in and out of the kitchen with his arms full of logs, a cold draught entering the room every time he opened the door.

"Have you brought in enough logs, Luke, or shall I help you? I don't want Walter going out in the cold again, or he'll get his dry socks wet, and he doesn't have any more."

"Yes, we'll need a lot more to last until morning, for it isn't only this fire, 'tis the one in the bar and the ones upstairs in the bedrooms."

"All right, I'll help you before I take off my boots and coat. Walter, you stay there."

Millie was kept busy for the next half an hour or more, and by the time the woman said they had fetched enough, she was exhausted. At last, she took off her coat, removed her wet boots and socks and sat beside Jonathan, her wet skirt raised above her ankles as she tried to warm her frozen feet. The innkeeper returned and surveyed the baskets full of logs. He eyed Millie's delicate white ankles with interest, and she quickly lowered her skirt and blushed under his gaze.

"I suppose you two will want feeding; have you brought food with you?"

"No, sir, we've eaten all we had, but I've brought in the logs, and we'll do any other jobs you might have if you would give us some supper and breakfast, and then we can be on our way again tomorrow."

"Aye, all right. Dora, find these two something to eat before you go home with Luke and don't be late in the morning."

"Aye, sir, I'll do that."

When Simon Higgins returned to the bar, he found a party of four had arrived in their carriage. The man, woman, and their two children were bound for Barnstaple and had hoped to reach their destination before dark, but the treacherous weather had delayed them. From their dress and manner of speaking, the landlord could tell they were wealthy people who would probably not have chosen to stay at his establishment. Simon agreed the family could stay the night in one room and their driver could occupy another. He hastened to the kitchen to prevent Dora from going home, instructed her to prepare a meal for the travellers, and told Millie to help her. Business had been slow of late, and he was pleased to think he would be making a profit out of the inclement weather.

Once they had eaten, the travellers retired to their room, for the journey had exhausted them, and they wanted to put their two children to bed. Their carriage driver leaned against the bar and chatted with the innkeeper while downing several pints of ale and one or two whiskies.

"I was talking to a couple of blokes at our last stop in Crediton. They were asking folk if they'd seen two brats travelling on their own: a little boy and an older girl. The girl had stolen a brooch from some stately home in Brampford Speke, and they wanted to arrest her. I wouldn't want to be in her shoes if they caught her. They were a couple of unsavoury characters and not best pleased to be sent out on a fool's errand in weather like this. I hope they don't take their feelings out on the poor maid."

"How old were these children? Do you know?"

"From the description they gave, the lad was about five and small for his age, and the girl, a pretty lass by all accounts, was around fifteen, with long red hair. The men were employed by Lady Grantley and told not to return without the culprits if they valued their jobs, so they had no choice but to continue the search. They said there was a reward for anyone who could hand them in, so the lady must mean business."

"I'll keep an eye out for them, then. Where would someone claim this reward?"

"Oh, at the policeman's house in Crediton or Grantley Manor in Brampford Speke, I suppose. 'Twas a tidy sum they were offering; ten guineas, I believe, and that's not to be sneezed at in these hard times. Anyway, I'm ready for my bed. Those whiskies have warmed my insides nicely, so I'll wish you goodnight."

The driver was the last customer, and Simon smiled as he locked the front door. Without a doubt, the two children in his kitchen were the runaways with a price on their heads, and he was just the man to claim it. Inheriting the inn from his late uncle had proved to be a mixed blessing. Simon had been born and raised in Bristol and, accustomed to city living, he hated the country way of life. The inheritance had been timely, though, for he was out of work and unable to meet his substantial gambling debts, so it suited him well to disappear without a trace and leave his debts behind. However, the locals had not taken to him, and when word got around that he couldn't keep his hands to himself where the maids were concerned, he found most of his customers deserted him, inconvenient though it was to travel a further three miles to The Portsmouth Arms. His clientele had been reduced to a few elderly locals who were too old to contemplate such a journey.

Dora, the local woman who still worked for him, would have gone home by now and taken her grandson, Luke, with her. As she was in her seventies, Simon had no interest in her, and she had no choice but to continue working, for she had no other income. It was a pity the young maid had her brother with her, or Simon could have used her as he pleased, but even he drew the line at forcing a girl in front of a child. He perused the matter as he approached the kitchen door.

The room was dark, and he swung the lantern around and saw them huddled on a rag mat in front of the range. They were not asleep and stared at him with wide eyes, Millie feeling concerned as she remembered Jenny's warning.

"Ah, you're not asleep yet, then. I think I've been a bit mean, making you sleep on the floor. I've got a spare room you can have for the night. The fire's all laid, so it only needs a match, and the room will soon warm up. Come on, follow me upstairs."

"No, it's all right, Mr Higgins; we don't want to put you to any trouble. We're grateful to be here in the warmth. I feared we might perish in the storm."

"No, come on, I insist. I reckon you might be here for a day or two, for it's still snowing heavily. I'm not likely to get any travellers calling with the roads in the state they are, so you might as well use the beds as leave them empty. Tomorrow, you can earn your keep helping Dora. Bring your things with you."

Reluctantly, Millie and Jonathan picked up their belongings and followed the man up the stairs, and he led them along a landing to the farthest room. He opened the door and entered with the lantern, lighting a candle beside the double bed and then the fire.

"There, the room will soon warm up." He lifted Jonathan onto the bed. "There, that's more comfortable for you, isn't it?" The boy nodded.

Turning to Millie, he approached her, standing far closer than she liked.

"You seem nervous, my dear, but you have nothing to fear from me." He gently pushed a curl away from her face and held her chin. "You're a beautiful young lady; how old are you?"

"I'm fifteen, sir."

"Ah, such a tender age. Now, as I've been so kind to you and your brother, how about rewarding me with a little kiss to show your gratitude?"

Millie tried to move backwards but was pinned against a heavy oak dressing table.

"I'd rather not, sir, though I am grateful for your hospitality."

"Nonsense."

Simon suddenly pulled her towards him and covered her mouth with his, one hand wandering down over her buttocks and the other caressing her breast through her dress. As she struggled, Jonathan leapt from the bed and tried to pull the man away from his sister, but his efforts were in vain. Eventually, the innkeeper released her and stepped back, grinning.

"There, now, that didn't hurt, did it? And, by the way, I know you're runaways with a price on your head, so you'll be staying here until I can turn you in and collect the reward."

"But we haven't done anything wrong, mister. Lady Grantley has it in for us because she bears a grudge against our late mother."

"That's not my problem. I'm sorry if that's the situation, but you must try to convince the judge; I need to get my hands on that reward money. See me through the winter, that will. Now, get some rest, for I think you'll be here for a few days until the road to Crediton is passable anyway. I'm locking the door, so don't bother trying to escape, and if you start hollering and making a noise, I'll be back to give you a hiding." He winked at Millie. "And a little something extra for you, my lovely."

CHAPTER 29

HARTFORD

Geoffrey Turner called in to see Marrok on the day after his operation and was delighted to see a broad smile on his patient's face. Although the young man knew his leg would take some months to mend, he was relieved that he was already in far less pain. Now that his leg was immobilised, the bones were no longer grating together and causing him such terrible discomfort. The doctor assured him there should be no further complications and that a local doctor could remove the plaster cast when the time came.

Geoffrey also confirmed that Marrok could travel in the carriage to Primrose Cottage as soon as he felt strong enough. This was music to his patient's ears, for although he had enjoyed spending Christmas with the Fellwood family at Hartford Manor, he was keen to return to some normality as soon as possible. However, he wondered if that was even possible with so many changes in his life. It had been quite a step to move from a meagre and miserable existence in the workhouse to being positively spoilt for the last couple of weeks at Hartford Manor.

He knew his children, too, were struggling to adjust, for they had been through so much in the last few months.

First, they were forced to leave the only home they had ever known and then to suffer the hardships of the workhouse, but the worst thing by far was losing their mother to cholera. He knew he had not yet begun to grieve properly for his wife, for there had been so many other things to worry about. He missed Laura dreadfully and would gladly give up his newfound life of ease if he could only have her back. However, it was never to be, and he was grateful to have found his father. There was much to look forward to.

When Sam and Aunty Margery came to see him later in the day, he was pleased to tell them that he could travel to Primrose Cottage and would like to do so as soon as possible. Margery suggested that she and Sam travel back to Enderby the next day to make preparations for Marrok and his family. It would be necessary to make a few changes to accommodate them, for they had to consider the needs of Peter, Christopher, and Clarice Webber.

After leaving Marrok, Geoffrey and Clara said their goodbyes to Robert and Annie and thanked them for their hospitality over Christmas. They insisted the young couple visit them soon at their country house in Cullompton. The doctor planned to spend a few weeks relaxing there with his wife before returning to his lucrative practice in Harley Street. Although she missed her husband when he was away, Clara did not enjoy life in London, for as a severe asthma sufferer, she found the city's smog detrimental to her health. Instead, she busied herself by helping with several local charities and was well-known for her generosity with both time and money. Geoffrey returned home every couple of months, for he, too, preferred life in the countryside and, in the not-too-distant future, would retire there.

The carriage stopped outside the Lodge House, and the driver helped the elderly couple alight, saying he would stay with the horses. Liza saw the doctor and his wife arrive and welcomed them inside, where Sabina was sitting in an armchair nursing her new daughter.

"Hello, Sabina; you shouldn't be out of bed yet, my dear. It was a difficult birth, and you need to rest."

"Hello, Geoffrey, hello, Clara, thank you, but I'm fine. I'm so spoilt these days. In the past, I would probably have had to go back to work today if we wanted to eat. We're lucky nowadays not to have to worry about where our next meal comes from. Liza's not letting me do anything, so I am resting, but it's too much work for her to keep running up and down the stairs to attend to me."

"May I see the baby, please, Sabina?"

Clara stooped over the baby, and Sabina pulled back the shawl so the older woman could see the little girl better.

"Oh, she's beautiful, and I hear you've picked an unusual name, Katel, isn't it?"

"Yes, it's an old name I saw in Ned Carter's family bible, and I liked it. He says it's Cornish. Would you like to hold her?"

"Oh yes, please; we only had one son, Stephen, and I'm hoping for some grandchildren one day, but I would have loved a larger family; sadly, it wasn't to be."

Whilst Clara cooed over the new arrival, the doctor insisted Sabina return to her bedroom to allow him to examine her. Thankfully, after a few minutes, he was satisfied all was well and asked where Danny and the rest of the family were.

"Danny's in the dairy with Edward, feeding some hedgehogs they found; I'll give them a shout in a minute. Helen and Stephen are playing with their cousins at their Uncle Fred's house. Would you like a cup of tea whilst you're here?"

"Thank you, but no, I'll examine Danny's foot, and then we'll be on our way. It's not long since we enjoyed one of Maisie's delicious breakfasts with Annie and Robert."

Liza fetched Edward and Danny from the dairy, and Edward smiled shyly at the doctor and his wife. Danny, however, gave Geoffrey a wide grin and happily shook his hand.

"Now, young man, let me see you walk around the room so I can decide what to do about your other foot."

Danny proudly walked around as requested, and the doctor observed him, pleased to note his improved appearance since the operation on his cleft palate. One foot still turned in slightly, causing him to limp, though not nearly as badly as before the treatment to his other foot.

"That's so much better. Are you pleased with what we've done so far?"

"Oh, yes, especially my mouth, thank you; the boys at school don't tease me much anymore. I wish I could run faster, though."

"Would you like Doctor Brown to operate on your other foot? It will be your third operation, and I know it's not pleasant."

"Yes, please, I would like my other foot straightened. I don't like the operations, but the medicine you give me helps with the pain, and it's worth it in the end. This will be the last one, though, won't it?"

"Yes, I think one more operation will do the trick. You and Edward can play again now, and leave me and your mum to discuss the best time to do it. I think you might enjoy these."

The doctor reached into his pocket for the bag of toffees he kept for such occasions and offered one to each.

"Now, Sabina, we need to decide the best time to do this operation on Danny's foot. I wondered if he would want to go through it all again, for it's a painful experience, but I'm glad he's willing, and this one should be the last. You'll have your hands full for a few months with young Katel here; I wonder if Danny would be willing to come to London with Robert? If we leave it until March or April, the weather will be better for travelling."

"That might be a solution if he's happy with that, and Robert, too, of course. I wouldn't want to leave Katel for a few months, though I would rather be with him. Could his operation wait a year until the baby's older?"

"It could, but I'd prefer to do it sooner rather than later, and, of course, you might be with child again by then."

"Oh, dear, I hope not. I'm delighted to have given birth to a baby belonging to Arthur and me, but I'm hoping she'll be my last. After all, I have three grandchildren, and I'm getting a bit old for all this."

"Only time will tell. Now, I'll leave you to think about all this and discuss it with Robert, Annie, and Danny, and then you can let me know what you want to do. I'm sure Robert will write to me with your decision. Now, my dear, I'm afraid you'll have to return that baby to her mother, for it's time we were on our way."

Lady Margery and Sam enjoyed their carriage journey back to Enderby, discussing the changes needed at Primrose Cottage to accommodate Marrok and his family. The heavy snow that had hampered travel over Christmas was now a distant memory, though it had left the roads exceedingly muddy. Within a few hundred yards, the pair of grey horses was splattered with mud, and the grooms would have their work cut out later to return their coats to their former pristine condition. Thankfully, it was also much milder, and the driver was relieved not to sit in the bitter east wind, which had been prevalent all over the festive period.

"We need to think carefully about arranging the accommodation at Primrose Cottage, for I don't want to upset Peter, Christopher, and Clarice."

"I doubt you'll do that, Sam; they're all delighted to live there and think the world of you."

"Yes, I know, and I think of them as friends rather than servants, particularly Peter. There are six bedrooms, but at the moment, I have one. Peter has another, plus one as his art studio, and Christopher and Clarice are using two, one as a bedroom and one as a sitting room, so that only leaves one spare. What do you think I should do, Margery? Women are better at these things, and for most of my life, I lived in a gypsy wagon or a hut, so I know little about such matters."

"Well, you have five good-sized rooms downstairs, so if it were up to me, I'd suggest that Christopher and Clarice move downstairs to use two of them, and that will leave three bedrooms spare. That could be one for Jinnie and Eliza and one for Martin and Paul. The third one will eventually be for Marrok, but it will be better if he sleeps downstairs until his leg's healed. The kitchen is what it is, but you and Peter only need the sitting room, so if Christopher and Clarice have the study as their bedroom and the parlour as their sitting room, then Marrok can sleep in the dining room. It may be possible to temporarily move the dining table into your sitting room. It will only be for a few months."

"Yes, that should work; I hope it doesn't upset anyone."

"I'm sure it won't; shall I come to Primrose Cottage tomorrow, and we can run it past everyone together?"

"Yes, I'd be grateful; thank you, Margery."

The carriage stopped outside Primrose Cottage, and the driver helped Sam with his bags and then proceeded to take Lady Margery to Enderby House. After some refreshment, the driver started the journey back to Hartford Manor, hoping to get there before dusk.

The next day, as promised, Lady Margery arrived at Primrose Cottage. She had planned to walk the short distance, for she enjoyed seeing the changes in her gardens. However, it was raining heavily, and the elderly lady unashamedly instructed her staff to harness the horses so that she could travel comfortably in the carriage. Even so, she peered out of the window and was delighted to see swathes of snowdrops in tight buds on the banks.

At Primrose Cottage, Peter and Sam were waiting in the sitting room for her to arrive, and once she was settled, Clarice brought tea and cakes for them all to enjoy. She was encouraged by Peter to share the news that she and

Christopher were expecting their first child in June. Peter was proud that this would be his first great-grandchild.

Margery outlined her suggestion of how she thought Marrok and his children could be accommodated, and as Peter approved of her plan, they called Christopher and Clarice to join them. The young couple had no objections, and it was agreed that Margery would send some of her workers to the cottage the following day to help move all the furniture.

"Good, now that's all sorted out, Peter, we can move on to other matters. Did you get much painting done over Christmas?"

"Yes, I did; perhaps you might like to see my handiwork when we finish our tea."

Peter had produced a delightful painting of the snowy landscape around Primrose Cottage. He had skilfully captured the clear blue sky and the wintry sun shining on the icy pond. In the foreground, a couple of young deer were futilely seeking a little grass to eat, and a solitary robin was sitting on a gatepost.

"Oh, Peter, I think it's your best yet; it even makes me feel cold, and that robin is such a clever touch. With all the white and blue, that single splash of red on its breast brings the picture to life."

"Thank you. I had just enough paint left to finish it, but I need to buy more. Perhaps the next time one of you is travelling to Barnstaple, I might beg a lift in your carriage."

"Yes, I'm always game for a day out, Peter. Perhaps if we leave it for a few days until all the rooms here are ready for Marrok and his family, we can call at the Manor House to tell them. I want to go into Barnstaple anyway, to visit the Penrose alms-houses and the Alice Horwood ones. I have it in mind to build a few cottages here in Enderby and bequeath them to poor single women in the village, and I need to know more about what is entailed. When a farm labourer dies, his widow and family are often made homeless because the tied cottage is needed for the new worker. I want to help people in that situation and possibly a few destitute single mothers. I know society views them as wanton women, and their condition no one's fault but their own, but I know that sometimes their predicament is not of their making."

CHAPTER 30

HARTFORD

Having discussed his plans for the canal with his parents and Aunty Margery, Robert felt ready to tell Annie about his idea to convert the barges into pleasure boats. As he expected, she was wildly enthusiastic, particularly when he reminded her that the canal ran past the bottom of the meadow behind The Red Lion Inn.

"Oh, Robert, that would be an amazing opportunity for the inn to attract more trade, wouldn't it?"

"Yes, absolutely, and I'm hoping that if the venture proves profitable, it will compensate for the loss of revenue from carrying goods on the barges. I'm sure it's the right thing to do because more and more people are turning to the railway as it's cheaper and quicker. I've been thinking about it for a long time, but was reluctant to close the canal and let it become overgrown. It was my great-grandfather's pride and joy when it was built, and it caused him endless worry as to whether it would ever pay its way. It was an incredible resource at the time."

"Yes, it was, and with the promise of more custom from the additional workers employed to build it, my granny opened Betsey's Kitchen and saved the inn from being sold.

Well, that and Granny's inheritance from Thomas Fellwood. Do you think we could tell Granny and Grandad of your plans? They're giving up The Red Lion soon, and I'd like them to know. Uncle Fred and Aunty Charlotte, too."

"Yes, by all means. Now that I've made my decision, I want to get on with things, and I thought your Uncle Fred might be just the person to fit the barges with seats and add a roof. Shall we call on them this afternoon?

"Yes, I'd like that."

With the Christmas festivities over, Fred Carter had started renovating Bluebell Cottage and getting it ready for his parents to move into when they vacated The Red Lion. He was pleased that the tenants had moved out early, but found they had left the dwelling in quite a mess. The place was filthy, and before he could start replacing the rotting windows and back door, he had to clear up all the debris they had left behind. He had not been working long when his mother arrived to see how he was getting on.

"Oh, Fred, what a mess; it's worse than I thought when we looked around the other day. They'll be getting a piece of my tongue if I ever set eyes on them again. That's what comes of letting the place to foreigners."

"They weren't foreign, were they?"

"They certainly weren't locals. I think they were from Gloucester or some such place up north."

Fred chuckled at his mother's definition of foreigners: basically, anyone not from the village. However, he agreed with her in this case, for the cottage was in a terrible state.

"Leave the clearing up to me, and you make a start on whatever jobs you need to do to make it sound."

"That would help if you're sure. I'm going to replace the window frames, and I think I'd better make a new back door, too; this one's certainly seen better days."

"Yes, that door never did fit properly; it was always draughty, even when I was a child."

"I'm glad to have the chance to talk to you without Dad around. I've written to Uncle Silas and Uncle Barney about Dad's birthday, and I received a reply yesterday. They're both coming with Josie and Bronwen and will stay for a few days. It's up to you, but I wondered whether we could combine Dad's birthday party with a farewell party for when you leave the inn. Not only that, but it's your birthday a few days before Dad's, so there's quite a lot to celebrate. What do you think? We can have two parties if you like, but I doubt Silas and Barney will come again as it's a fair journey for them, and I thought you might like to have them here for both occasions."

"That's an excellent idea; let's do that. It's also our wedding anniversary on my birthday on the twenty-fourth of the month, and we can celebrate everything at the same time. We must say goodbye properly to all our loyal customers."

"Oh, I didn't know that; that's even more reason to have a party then. You've never mentioned your wedding anniversary before."

"It was such a long time ago, there's hardly anyone left to remember our wedding day. Anyway, in that case, I think we'd better tell your father about the party, but not that Silas, Josie, Barney and Bronwen are coming; then that will be a wonderful surprise for him. It's not long to Dad's birthday, though; do you think you can get the cottage ready in time?"

"I hope so, but if not, it doesn't matter if you and Dad stay on at the inn for a while; there's no rush for you to move out."

"No, I suppose not. What about the outbuildings behind the inn? How are you getting on with adapting them?"

"Yes, all right. I've cleared out the barn and made the necessary repairs. I might extend it eventually, but it'll do for now while we have so much else to do."

"Splendid. If you can finish the work in the cottage before Dad's birthday, Silas, Josie, Barney and Bronwen could stay here, and then they can show up at The Kitchen for the party later and surprise Ned. Once that's over, Ned and I can move in here, and you and Charlotte into the inn. You can take your time sprucing up your cottage, and when it's ready, we'll advertise for new tenants, but I hope we can find someone local to rent it this time."

"That sounds like a plan; now, do you know why Annie and Robert want to see us all this afternoon?"

"No, no idea at all; it all sounded quite intriguing, and I could tell Annie was excited; she never could hide her feelings. Perhaps she's expecting another baby. Anyway, time will tell. Are you going home before they arrive, or will you have some dinner here?"

"I'll have a pasty or something here, I think, then I can carry on working until the last minute. I told Charlotte to come here around two o'clock, so that should work out all right. I'll measure the door and window frames, and then I can make new ones back at the yard. We need to make the place more secure than it is."

"Right, I'll leave you to it now and go back and talk to Ned about having a party. I'm sure he'll be pleased; he likes a family get-together. You carry on with your repairs, and I'll come back again tomorrow and finish the cleaning. I might bring Sarah with me if she isn't too busy."

Robert and Annie arrived at The Red Lion Inn at two o'clock with Selina, Thomas, and David. Selina was wearing a new pair of boots purchased from Richard Martin, the local cordwainer, and also Sarah's father. The boots were beautifully made of the finest leather, and Selina showed them off proudly to Betsey and Ned, telling them she had walked all the way from the Manor House. Thomas and David were in their pram, and Annie lifted them out and took off their warm coats before handing each child to their great-grandparents for a cuddle. It wasn't long before

Charlotte also arrived with Rosella, Eddie, and the two babies, Doris and Nicholas, and Ned asked Eddie to go to the cottage next door and tell his father to stop work and come and have a cup of tea. Fred arrived, apologising for his scruffy work clothes and explaining that he was making the most of his time to get on with repairing the cottage. When they were all comfortably seated and Betsey had found some toys to amuse the children, they regarded Robert and Annie expectantly.

"Now, Robert, what is it you have to tell us? I can tell Annie's excited about something. As a child, I always knew if she had news to tell or had done something wrong."

"I never could hide anything from you, Gran; you've always read me like a book. Go on, Robert, tell them about your idea."

"I don't think it will surprise any of you to learn that the canal is no longer making a profit. It was a marvellous venture in its day, but nowadays folk prefer to use the railways because they can travel and transport their goods much quickly by train. I've been putting this decision off for a long time, but I must close the canal. It's simply a sign of the times, and you can't stop progress."

"I'm not surprised; in fact, Betsey and I have been expecting it for some time now, haven't we, love?"

"Yes, we used to get a lot of trade from the folk using the canal, but it's dropped off to next to nothing in recent years. It hasn't mattered much to us because the folk travelling by train also have to eat, so the Kitchen is still profitable. It seems an awful shame, though, because such a lot of work went into building the canal, and I know it was Ephraim Fellwood's pride and joy. What will happen to it?"

"That's been the problem; I've been trying to think what we could do with it. I didn't want to let it clog up with weeds and become an eyesore, and I think I've come up with a solution. Town folk like visiting Devon for their holidays, especially from cities like London. What with the smog and the stench from some of the rivers, they love the clean, fresh air of the countryside, and I think we can cash in on that. I want to convert the barges into pleasure boats and offer trips on the canal. The bathing pools at Ilfracombe gave me the idea when Annie and I visited last year. They were carved out in the 1820s and are a major tourist attraction. Ilfracombe has grown from a tiny fishing village into a popular seaside resort, and many grand houses have been built there. The town is prospering."

"That sounds like a wonderful idea, Robert, and I wish you every success with it, but what has it to do with any of us?"

"That's where you come in, Fred, because if I have my way, you'll be extremely busy. As a carpenter, I wondered if you could convert three barges into pleasure boats. They'll need roofs, rows of seats, and a general paint and tidy-up. Is that something you could do?"

"Yes, though it would take some time, and I'm already up to my eyes renovating the cottage next door for Mum and Dad to move into when we take over The Red Lion. Is there any rush?"

"Ideally, I'd like to get the boats ready by Easter; that's when the visitors will start arriving. Easter Sunday is on the twenty-fifth of April this year, so I'd like to start offering the trips from then onwards. I'm afraid your involvement doesn't end there, though, Fred."

"Oh, what else do you have in mind for me?"

"This is entirely up to you, of course, but the canal runs past the bottom of the meadow behind The Red Lion Inn, and if you built a jetty to allow the passengers on and off the boats, I reckon you'd do a roaring trade in cream teas, pasties, and the like. You could even put a few tables and chairs in the meadow to be used in warm weather."

"Oh, my, what a fantastic idea." Betsey's eyes shone as she took in the full potential of the venture. "Fred, it would be such a steady source of income, and I reckon the stagecoaches could be the next casualty of the railways. There are already fewer stagecoaches running than there were ten years ago, and that's the main business of the inn, so it would be wise to diversify. You should never put all your eggs in one basket."

"Your mother's right, lad, as she usually is. She's always had a phenomenal head for business, and it's too good an opportunity to miss. Perhaps you could employ another carpenter to help you. I've been thinking you won't be able to do everything when you take over the inn. Llewie's coming on, but he's only a lad and still learning his trade. I don't know if there's anyone suitable in the village, but you could advertise in Barnstaple to find the right man. You'll also need more staff at the inn if this works out. Maybe one of the new employees will have a family and like to rent your cottage when you've got it ready."

"Goodness, my head's in a spin. So many things are happening; what do you think, Charlotte?"

"I think it sounds like an amazing opportunity, Fred, and we should grasp it with both hands, but your dad's right; we'll need to employ more staff, for you can't do any more hours than you already are."

The conversation about the new venture continued for some time, and Betsey was delighted when all present agreed to stay for tea. She took the opportunity to tell them about the party she was planning.

"My birthday and our wedding anniversary are on the twenty-fourth of January, and Ned's seventy-fourth birthday is on the thirtieth. That's a Saturday this year, a perfect day for a party because folk can take it easy the next day on Sunday. We'll combine all those events with our farewell party at The Red Lion; it will be grand."

CHAPTER 31

KING'S NYMPTON

Millie spent a sleepless night worrying about their dilemma. She was concerned on two counts. Firstly, she didn't want to suffer any more of the landlord's unwanted attention, and secondly, how could she and Jonathan escape his clutches and avoid being handed over to the police? She had never thought Lady Grantley would put so much effort into pursuing them, but it seemed the lady's resentment ran deep, and she was determined to wreak vengeance on anyone involved with her husband. Millie tossed and turned as she considered various methods of escape and tried not to disturb Jonnie, who had fallen asleep as soon as his head touched the pillow. She decided that come morning, to explore if it was possible to climb out of the window or, failing that, run away when they went downstairs to help Dora and Luke with the chores. The problem was the snow; would it be too deep to go anywhere?

Finally, around four o'clock, sleep claimed her and she fell into a restless slumber. A couple of hours later, she was awakened by Jonathan shaking her shoulder.

"Millie, Millie, I need to pee."

Wearily, she opened her eyes and, for a moment or two, wondered where she was, then remembered their predicament.

"All right, Jonnie, hold on; I expect there will be a chamber pot under the bed."

Fortunately, there was, so Jonathan and then Millie relieved themselves, and she lifted him back into the warm bed. The fire had burned low during the night, and she quickly added some logs, then crossed to the window and peered out. However, it was still pitch-black outside, and she could see nothing, so she, too, climbed back into the bed.

"Millie, what are we going to do? Will we be sent to jail?"

"I hope not, Jonnie; we have to escape somehow. I hope the snow's gone by morning, but I don't think it will be. We might have to pretend to accept what's happening, then escape when we can."

It wasn't long before they heard a key in the lock, and the door opened, revealing Dora carrying a tray. Millie immediately sprang out of bed, planning to push past her, but Dora shook her head and viewed her with sad eyes.

"Don't bother trying to get past me, lass; the landlord's downstairs, and he'll stop you."

"Why have you brought us food? Don't we have to help you in the kitchen?"

"No, Mr Higgins says you're two runaways with a price on your head, and he's going to take you to Crediton to claim the reward as soon as the snow clears."

"Surely he doesn't need to keep us locked up here until then; we can't go anywhere because of the snow."

"No, I know, but we have some of the gentry staying, and he doesn't want to risk them seeing you."

"Oh, Dora, can you tell the visitors about us and ask them to rescue us? We haven't done anything wrong. The charges against us are all made up because Lady Grantley didn't like our mum."

"I'm sorry. I'd help you if I could, my dear, but I daren't. The money I get from this job is all I have to live on, and if I lose it, then me and Luke will starve. It's been up to me to raise him since his mother died, for we've not seen hide nor hair of his father since he was born."

"Is it still snowing?"

"No, it's stopped, but it's too deep to travel, though I don't think it's so cold this morning, so maybe it will thaw in a day or two. I don't think the folk in the carriage will be able to leave today, either, maybe tomorrow. Eat your porridge, and I'll be back for your tray later. I wish I could help you, but I can't."

As Millie and Jonathan sat in the bed, eating the porridge, her mind was working overtime to think of ways out of their predicament. As soon as it was light, she pushed open the window and saw they were in a room at the back of the inn. She could see a carriage in the yard below her, which looked like it belonged to someone wealthy. If only she could attract the passengers' attention, perhaps they would help her and Jonnie escape. However, the snow lay a foot deep on the ground, and she realised Dora was right and no one would be leaving that day.

They spent a dull morning lying in the bed, where it was the warmest. Fortunately, their blankets and coats had dried beside the fire overnight and would be ready to wear should they have the chance to escape. However, with their bags to carry, it would be difficult to creep away unseen, even if an opportunity did present itself.

Around midday, the landlord brought them a bowl of soup and a couple of thick slices of bread.

"Here's a tasty bowl of soup for your dinner. I'll say one thing about Dora: she's a good cook, so you won't starve while you're here."

"Please let us go, mister; we haven't stolen anything. Lady Grantley's telling lies."

"That's as maybe, and you must plead your case with the judge, but I need that reward money, so don't waste your time trying to dissuade me. In any case, with all this snow on the ground, you can't go anywhere today. I think it's beginning to thaw, though, so maybe tomorrow I can take you to the policeman in Crediton, and that means you and I can become better acquainted later, my dear; you must do something to earn your keep. I was planning on putting you both to work, but we have other customers staying, so I need to keep your presence here a secret, or they might want the reward money for themselves. I don't think they need it, mind, but folk never seem to have enough these days."

Millie racked her brain to think how she could prevent the innkeeper from taking advantage of her, and then a possible solution presented itself. Dora had emptied their chamber pot when she collected their breakfast tray, and when Millie felt the need to use it later, she was dismayed to find her period had started and her drawers and petticoat were saturated with blood. Desperately, she searched the heavy dressing table for something to absorb the blood, but it was empty. Dismayed, she rummaged in her sack, reluctantly retrieved her best petticoat, and put it between her legs.

When Dora arrived to collect their soup dishes, Millie explained what had happened and apologised for the mess, which was now also on the sheets.

"Oh, now that's more washing to do. As if I haven't got enough on my hands, the sheets will take days to dry in this cold weather. I'll fetch some rags for you, and then you can help me strip the bed."

Within minutes, Dora returned with some rags, and Millie attended to herself. She put on her only clean pair of drawers and asked Dora to let her wash the soiled ones and her petticoats.

"No, I can't let you out of this room. Give them here, and I'll wash them with the sheets. Come on; you can help me change the bedding."

As Millie helped Dora, she realised that her period might deter the landlord from taking her to his bed.

"Dora, will you make sure Mr Higgins sees the mess I've made, please?"

"Why would you want him to see? Oh, he's been trying it on, has he?"

"Yes, he kissed me last night and hinted earlier that he wants more than that tonight. I don't quite know what happens between a man and a woman, but I've seen animals mating, and I guess it's the same?"

"Oh, he's a despicable man to take advantage of a young girl like you, and yes, my dear, it's as you say. Don't worry. I'll make sure he knows what's happened, and he'll leave you alone if he has any manners at all."

"Thank you so much, Dora, and I'm sorry to have caused you extra work. What with travelling and everything, I forgot my period was due, and in any case, I'm not that regular, so I'm never sure when it will start."

Dora was as good as her word and entered the kitchen, grumbling loudly at the mess the girl had made. She displayed the heavily soiled drawers and petticoat and said she had never seen anything like it; you'd think the girl had been stabbed. There was so much blood.

Simon Higgins observed the laundry with distaste and told Dora to get on with her work and stop moaning.

Fortunately, Millie and Jonathan spent a peaceful night without any interference from the landlord. The girl was mightily relieved and thankfully caught up on some sleep from the previous night. When Dora brought their breakfast and more clean rags for Millie in the morning, she told them that the snow had melted considerably and the roads were clearing. She suspected Mr Higgins would take them both to Crediton later that day.

"What about the people in the carriage? Are they leaving today?"

"Yes, I've cooked them some breakfast, and they'll be on their way when they finish eating it. Why do you ask?"

"Oh, I just wondered. If those travellers can leave, then I expect you're right, and Mr Higgins will take us to Crediton today, especially as I'm no use to him now."

As soon as Dora left the room, Millie told Jonathan to eat his breakfast as quickly as possible. She hastily spooned the thick porridge into her mouth, then pulled a chair to the window, pushed it open wide, and perched her bottom on the wide window ledge.

"What are you doing? Shut the window; 'tis cold."

"No, I'm going to shout to the family that's leaving this morning; you never know, they might take pity on us. We've nothing to lose anyway."

By the time Millie heard voices in the yard, she was shivering violently from sitting on the window ledge in the bitter wind. Below her, the yard was a mess, with the quickly melting snow mixed with straw, dung, and mud. The carriage driver was harnessing the horses and preparing to resume his journey, and she decided to wait until his master appeared before drawing attention to herself. Ten minutes later, a lady emerged carrying a toddler and leading another small child by the hand. She was an attractive, well-dressed woman with blond curls. A few minutes later, her husband appeared, and Millie immediately began shouting.

"Sir, sir, up here, look. I need your help, please. The landlord is keeping me and my brother prisoner in this bedroom. Will you help us? He means to take advantage of me."

The gentleman looked up at the young girl in surprise.

"Why is he keeping you locked up? Where are your parents?"

"Our parents are dead, sir, and we're travelling to relatives in Barnstaple. We had to stop here because of the weather, and now Mr Higgins has locked us in and won't let us go. Oh, please help us, sir. I'm a virgin, and I'm frightened."

Simon Higgins appeared in the doorway and stared angrily at the girl sitting half in and half out of the window.

"Take no notice of the young maid, sir. They're two runaways, and the police are after them for stealing. Your driver told me so himself. I'm taking them to Crediton later today to claim the reward money."

The gentleman beckoned to his driver.

"Jed, what do you know of this?"

"I didn't know they were here, sir, but I did mention to Mr Higgins that some men in Crediton were asking if anyone had seen a small boy and a teenage girl. He said they were on the run from the police because the girl had stolen a brooch from Lady Grantley of Grantley Manor in Brampford Speke. A reward of ten guineas is being offered."

"I see." He craned his neck to glance up at Millie. "That puts a different slant on things, young lady; what do you have to say for yourself?"

"'Tis true the police are searching for us, sir, but we've done nothing wrong. Lady Grantley bears a grudge against my mother, and as she's dead, she's taking it out on us, but I swear to you, I've stolen nothing."

The lady in the carriage opened the door and spoke to her husband. She had not enjoyed her stay at the inn and felt uncomfortable with how the landlord's eyes had wandered over her body.

"Roger, I think we should take them with us. We can hand them over to the police if necessary."

"Yes, I agree. Landlord, we'll take them to Crediton and save you the journey."

"That's all very well, but I want to claim the reward money. I found them, not you, sir, and I'm entitled to claim it. I'm sure I need it more than you do, so no, thank you, kindly, but I'll take them to Crediton myself."

The gentleman glanced at his wife, noted her pursed lips, and smiled inwardly to himself; his wife was not one to be ignored.

"Very well, Mr Higgins; I agree, you are entitled to the reward money, so I'll pay it to you and take the children to

Crediton to claim the reward. That way, no one loses out. Is that acceptable to you?"

Millie was horrified to learn that she and Jonathan would still be turned over to the law. Nevertheless, she felt sure they would be safer with this family than with the lecherous landlord. She was relieved when Mr Higgins agreed and sent Dora to release them.

CHAPTER 32

KING'S NYMPTON

Millie and Jonathan hastily gathered their belongings and ran down the stairs. Millie took a moment to thank Dora for her kindness and then hurried outside to the waiting carriage. Simon Higgins sneered at her as she walked past him, and she felt a shiver run down her back at the thought of the fate that had nearly befallen her. The driver held the door open for them to climb into the carriage.

Once inside, the gentleman introduced himself as Sir Roger Everson and his wife, Lady Jasmine, and invited Millie to tell them her story. He listened carefully, then his eyes narrowed, and he interrupted her.

"Just a minute, you say Sir Edgar Grantley has died?"

"Yes, sir, a week or two ago."

"What happened to your granny? Did she die, too?"

"No, but she was seriously ill, and when she heard of the death of Sir Edgar, she insisted we run away, for she was afraid Lady Grantley would make trouble for us. She was too weak to leave her bed, so we had to leave her behind, but she hopes to follow us when she feels better."

"Where are you headed?"

"We're travelling to Hartford. Granny told us that our great-grandfather came from that village, and she thinks we may still have relatives there. We'll throw ourselves on their mercy and hope they'll take us in or offer us employment."

"I see; it sounds like a risky plan in these hard times. What will you do if they refuse to help you?"

"Fortunately, we have a couple of options. On our journey, we made friends with two families, and both have offered to give us a home if we're desperate, though neither can afford to do so. It's so generous of them."

"I see, and what of this brooch that Lady Lilliana says you stole? Do you have it?"

"I did have it, but it wasn't stolen, sir. It was given to my mother by Sir Edgar recently, following the death of his own mother. My granny gave it to me before I left home."

"So, where is it now?"

"I've left it with someone for safekeeping, for I knew if I were caught with it on my person, I would be found guilty of stealing it. I don't want the brooch, and I'm hoping I'll get the opportunity to return it to Lady Grantley one day, though I don't think she wants it; she just wants to make trouble for me. Will you hand us over to the policeman in Crediton, sir? I realise you need to claim the reward money."

Sir Roger smiled at the young girl's anxious face.

"No, my dear, it was your lucky day when we came along. Sir Edgar was a close friend of mine, and I'm distraught to hear he has passed away. I believe I once met your mother when she was young; indeed, you strongly resemble her. I often stayed at Grantley Manor in my youth, and Sir Edgar introduced me to her. She was beautiful, and I know he was besotted with her, so I believe your story is true. I've never taken to his wife, though no woman would like to be in her position. It was an unfortunate situation, and Sir Edgar should never have married her, but I'm afraid he was given no choice. You obviously don't know the road, but we're travelling in the opposite direction to Crediton and will arrive at Umberleigh in time for lunch."

"I'm sorry that man tried to force his attention on you, Millie; I must confess he made me feel uncomfortable, and I had Roger to protect me. When I heard what you said from the bedroom window, I was determined to get you away from him, even if you were a thief. I'm so pleased to discover you're not."

"Thank you so much for believing me, Lady Everson; it's such a relief to know we're not going to prison to await trial. Hopefully, the farther we get from Brampford Speke, the less likely we'll be apprehended."

"Yes, I hope so, and we can offer you a lift as far as Barnstaple. We will stay the night there, but then travel to Cornwall on a different road, so you'll have to make your own way from there. Does that please you?"

"Oh, yes, thank you so much, but what about the ten guineas you paid to Mr Higgins, sir? I'm afraid I can't pay you back."

"Don't worry about it; I can afford it, and Sir Edgar would be pleased to know I helped his son and daughter."

The rest of the journey was uneventful, and by late evening, the carriage arrived at The Fortescue Arms, an ancient hostelry in Barnstaple, where the family was to spend the night. Lady Jasmine was concerned about the two youngsters making their way in a strange town at night, and she arranged for them to have a bed in the servants' quarters. Millie and Jonathan were given breakfast in the morning and left before the Everson family was up. Millie was grateful to the couple but did not want to take advantage of their generosity. She checked how much money she had left and found it was barely enough for a meal. She decided to seek employment for a week or two and, if possible, purchase a ride on a cart to Hartford.

Barnstaple was a sizeable town, and they wandered down the road from the inn to an impressive square. There was a tall clock tower with a clock face on all four sides, and Millie noted that it was not yet eight o'clock and still dark.

It was a mild morning, and there was no trace of any snow left in the town where the heavy footfall and carriages had obliterated it. It was far too early to seek work in the shops, and she decided to explore.

Close to the clock tower was a beautiful fountain, and water was gushing from the mouths of four lions at the top. Around the wall that surrounded the base, more jets were shooting water upwards. Millie and Jonathan had never seen anything like it and were fascinated. Eventually, they turned away, and farther on, they could see the river and, in the near distance, the wide bridge that spanned it. There was also a railway bridge, built on tall iron legs, which ran adjacent to the road bridge, and as they watched, a train sped by and whistled to announce its arrival. They waved to it as it passed, and Millie thought that if only they could have stayed on the train, they would have avoided all the unpleasantness at Kings Nympton.

They wandered across the entrance of the road bridge and along the quay, where many people were bustling about their business. Two large ships were docked, their cargoes being unloaded, and despite the hour, The Star Inn and The Angel were already busy. They walked past an impressive statue of Queen Anne and on to where they could see a large lake with an island in the centre.

"It's a grand town, isn't it, Jonnie?"

"I've never seen so many people so early in the morning. Where are we going, Millie?"

"I'm not sure yet, but this seems to be the main street; let's go up here and see what shops there are. Oh, yes, it says it's the High Street, look. I need to find a job for a couple of weeks and somewhere for us to sleep tonight, and I think this street will be the most likely."

They continued up the busy street and came to a large building, which someone told them was the Pannier Market. It was a grand construction, and inside, many stalls were being set up selling every product imaginable. They strolled from one end to the other, amazed at the high ceiling and the pillars supporting it. Near the far end of the market, they exited and found themselves on another street, which a sign informed them was called Butchers Row. Turning right, they headed back toward the High Street again and were intrigued to find that butchers occupied all the shops down one side.

By the time they were back in the High Street, it was after nine o'clock, and once again turning to the right, they retraced their steps. Many customers were frequenting an inn called The Three Tuns, and Millie paused, wondering whether to enquire if any work was available. She became aware of two young women watching her and felt slightly uncomfortable. The women were curious about Millie's presence and sidled over.

"Not seen 'ee yer before, love. Lookin' fer business, is 'ee?"

"Um, I'm looking for work for a week or two to earn the fare to Hartford for me brother and me. Do you know where I might find a job?"

"If 'ee stand round yer long enough, especially wi' the young lad, ye'll certainly get offers, but they may not be the sort ye want. Yer not a prossie, then?"

"I don't know what a prossie is. I want a job cleaning, washing up, or something like that."

The women realised the girl was not trying to steal their business, and the elder of the two suddenly whispered in the other girl's ear, and she nodded.

"A prossie's a maid who grants favours to men fer money if 'ee know what I mean, and if 'ee 'ang about yer, particularly on a market day, then ye'll soon get picked up whether 'ee like it or not. If yer not careful, ye'll get taken to a brothel, and they'll make use of 'ee and the boy. A few of us women stick together and take care of one t'other though, and if 'ee like, us can offer 'ee a job for a week or two and somewhere fer 'ee and the boy to sleep. Is 'ee interested?"

"What would I have to do? I don't want to sell my body!"

"No, that's all right; I guessed ye'd say that. Yer both smartly dressed, so I reckon you've 'ad an easy life up to now, though what's brought 'ee yer might be a different story. No, us live with a woman called Fanny Prowse, and 'er lets us prossies 'ave the use of 'er 'ouse fer our business in return for part of our earnings. Quite a character is Fanny. Gettin' in the family way is an occupational 'azard for us, and us 'ave several brats between us. If 'er'd mind 'em, twould be perfect, but 'er's never sober enough to be any 'elp. I'm thinking 'ee could stay in the 'ouse and look after the little uns, which'd let all of us six maids go out to work. At the moment, one of us 'as to stay 'ome, and time's money. This way us could earn more. What do 'ee think? Is 'ee interested?"

Although Devon born and bred herself, Millie struggled to understand the broad dialect of the two prostitutes. She was aware she was taking a considerable risk by going with the women, for they might hand her over to a brothel owner anyway, and she hesitated.

"Look, I can see ye be worried, and so yer should be, but I think us can 'elp one t'other, and I promise ye'll come to no harm."

"All right, thank you. How much will you pay me?"

"That depends how much us earn, but shall us say yer bed and board fer a couple of weeks and enough money for two seats on a coach to Hartford, plus a few shillin's extra; does that sound agreeable?"

"Yes, thank you."

CHAPTER 33

BARNSTAPLE

The older of the two prostitutes led Millie and Jonathan back along the High Street and into a long alleyway. The stench of rubbish was overpowering, and the high-sided buildings made the alleyway dark and imposing. Sensing their apprehension, the woman glanced over her shoulder and smiled encouragingly at them, revealing a broken tooth.

"Look, I can see ye be frightened, and in yer situation, anybody would be, but 'ee be much safer coming wi' me than standing about on the streets. Yer just 'ave to trust me, but I 'ave daughters meself, and I'll look after 'ee. All right?"

Millie nodded, gripped Jonnie's hand tighter, and followed the scantily-clad woman. Although it was a comparatively mild morning, it was winter, and Millie was puzzled how the woman could withstand the cold in her skimpy clothes without even shivering.

They picked their way along the dim passageway, at one point stepping over the body of a dead black and white cat, and up ahead, they could see a lighter area. They stepped into a cobbled courtyard surrounded by houses, and the alleyway appeared to be the only entrance. The dwellings were in a poor state of repair; their paintwork was peeling, and a few windows were broken. One house was covered in thick ivy, which reached the roof. However, after the grim alleyway, the area was cleaner than Millie had expected, and outside one house, she was surprised to see a tiny but well-tended garden. At one end was a small holly tree, the weak winter sunshine glistening on the bright red berries and shiny green leaves, and at its roots, some pristine white snowdrops were already in bud in the sheltered spot.

The prostitute led them to the house next to the one with the garden and pushed open the grimy front door. As her eyes adjusted to the dim light, Millie saw they had entered directly into a sparsely furnished room. Numerous children were present; some were crawling around on the floor, a baby was asleep in a wooden box, and a middle-aged woman was sitting in the only chair, drinking something from a glass. She raised her eyes in surprise.

"What's 'ee doin' back so soon, Jess? 'Ave 'ee no customers s'morning?"

"Not found any yet, Liz, but 'tis a tad early for even the most randy of 'em, I guess."

"Who's this, then? A new prossie come to join us? The punters are goin' to love 'er, with her fiery red 'air and blue eyes. Take the custom away from the rest of us, 'er will."

"No, don't fret, Liz; this maid's lookin' fer work skivvying fer a week or two; ye can see her's no prossie. 'er wants a bed for 'erself and 'er brother and to earn a few shillings. If 'er minds the brats, us could all go out to work and earn more money. What do 'ee think?"

The woman eyed Millie up and down and then scrutinised Jonnie.

"Aye, that might work, an' I'd rather be out there earnin' than sittin' in yer wi' this lot all day. They don't need them smart clothes in yer, though. Get 'em off, you two, and us'll find 'ee somethin' else to wear."

Millie turned anxiously to the younger woman, whom she now knew to be called Jess, but before she could speak, Jess held up her hand.

"Look, maid, I know what yer goin' a say, but 'ee must do as Liz says. Yer about the same size as me, so us'll swap clothes; I'll attract a better class of punter, wearin' your togs, and us can sell the boy's clothes."

Seeing the expression on Liz's face, Millie could see she was determined to have their clothes, whether they agreed or not, so she removed her many layers of clothing and told Jonnie to do the same. Within minutes, both were attired in threadbare, ragged garments, which, to Millie's disgust, were none too clean and probably full of fleas.

"What's in yer bags? Be there somethin' there us can sell?"

"It's our best Sunday clothes."

"Well, that's a proper job; fetch a pretty penny they will, 'and 'em over."

Liz gathered the fine clothes and, delighted to be released from her child-minding duties, the older woman swigged the last of her drink and left with a wide grin on her face.

Jess swiftly led Millie around the rest of the house. There were four decent-sized bedrooms. In two, the floor was covered with numerous palliasses where the children and their mothers slept. The doors to the other two rooms were closed.

"Now, ye and yer brother will 'ave to squeeze in yer wi' the rest of us to sleep; 'twill be a bit of a squash, but us'll manage and at least 'twill be warm. That bedroom there belongs to Fanny, and 'er never shows 'er face 'til at least midday. 'Tis the smallest room, and 'er won't share, but that's fair enough cos 'tis er 'ouse. This other room is fer business, and Janie's entertaining one of 'er regulars in there at the moment, so keep out. Just one other thing ye need to keep on the right side of Liz. Fanny's 'er mother and Liz is 'er favourite, so what Liz says goes. Her isn't the easiest maid to get on wi', an' you can't trust 'er, so be careful what you tell 'er."

Leading the way back down the twisting staircase, the woman opened the door to another room with a large double bed. It was cleaner than the rest of the house and better furnished, with some drab pink curtains at the window. Jess advised that this room, too, was used for business and out of bounds to Millie and Jonathan. The rest of the house consisted of the room they entered from the street and a surprisingly spacious kitchen, which led into a backyard surrounded by a high wall.

Two washing lines stretched from the back wall of the house to two posts on the far wall. On one, nappies were blowing in the wind, and on the other were pegged long ribbons of something Millie was unable to identify.

"Now, over that wall, there be some lucky girls, for that's the Alice Horwood Free School. Some rich lady gave that property to charity years ago to be used as a school, and twenty young maids go there. They get their clothes and dinner for free and be taught more than most."

Millie pointed to the long ribbons floating gently in the wind.

"What are these things?"

Jess smirked. "Oh, they be the tools of our trade, me dear. Sheep's intestines; 'ave 'ee never seen 'em before?"

Millie shook her head.

"Like I told 'ee, in our business, one thing leads to another, and that's why there be so many brats. Some gentlemen like us to use these things to stop 'em from catchin' anythin' nasty from us maids, and it seems they also stop us gettin' in the family way quite so often. I don't know 'ow it works, but it certainly 'elps."

Seeing Millie's puzzled face, she continued.

"Us wash the intestines and dry 'em, then sew up one end and attach a long ribbon. The man puts it on 'is willie, before we, well, you know."

"What's the ribbon for?"

"Oh, the darned thing nearly always comes off at some point, so the ribbon's so us can pull it out afterwards. One of yer jobs will be to wash out the intestines. I won't lie, maid; 'tis a filthy job, but there 'tis. Still, there's none to do for a day or two cos Alice did 'em yesterday. Now, there's eleven brats' yer; the eldest is eight, and the youngest is only a few weeks old. Do 'ee know much about children?"

"Not much, but I've looked after Jonnie since he was a baby."

"That's good enough. Now, come and meet 'em all, though 'ee may not remember all their names. Doesn't matter."

Jess quickly introduced Millie and Jonnie. There were five boys and six girls, and they were all dressed in rags, similar to the ones they, too, were now wearing.

"Now, they be all at 'ome at the moment, but Andy, Ben, Eli, Amy, an' Nell, will go out to earn a few pennies 'ere an' there later. They run errands fer the butchers, an' the bakers, an' what 'ave you, an' pick a few pockets when they get the chance."

Millie was shocked to hear they were taught to steal, but said nothing and gave Jonnie a stern look, hoping he would keep quiet.

"They don't get nothin' to eat 'til dinner time, so don't let 'em tell 'ee different. Now, come into the kitchen, an' I'll show 'ee where everythin' is afore I go back out to work."

It didn't take long to show Millie where a large piece of cheese and a slightly stale loaf of bread resided in a cupboard. There was also a large jug of milk, which Jess explained was only for the two youngest; the rest were to make do with water.

"For the babby, pour some milk into that little teapot and fix this on the spout for 'im to suck."

"What is it?"

"Oh, 'tis a finger cut from a glove; it makes a decent teat an' does the job."

"Can't his mother feed him?"

"No, sadly 'er didn't make it, poor maid; 'er died in agony bringin' 'im into the world. Us should send 'im to the workhouse, but 'er was me best friend, and in a weak moment, I promised 'er I'd raise 'im. He's a month old and doin' all right, considering. Give some milk to Flora, too, 'er's me youngest and about six months old, bless 'er heart. I'm 'oping 'er'll be all right, 'cos as 'ee can see, Tim and May 'ave both got rickets and can't walk, though they be old enough. The old biddy next door reckons milk can stop 'em gettin' rickets."

"Is there anything else you want me and Jonnie to do?"

"The brats'll keep 'ee busy, I reckon, but there's some soap under the sink if ye feel like doin' some cleanin'. It could do with it, but none of us 'ave the time."

Jess quickly applied rouge to her already red cheeks and checked her appearance in a cracked mirror hanging lopsidedly on the wall. Patting her hair into place, she glanced over her shoulder at Millie.

"I'm usually out all day, 'specially today, bein' a Friday. 'Tis market day in the town, so a lot of business to be 'ad, but I'll come 'ome at dinner time to introduce 'ee to Fanny, else knowin' 'er, er'll show 'ee the door."

As the door closed behind Jess, the baby began to cry, and the eldest girl, Amy, went to the makeshift cot and lifted the child. She rocked the little boy confidently and raised her eyes to Millie.

"Ee wants feedin'; do 'ee want me to do it? I usually do if I'm yer."

"Yes, if you want to, I'll warm the milk."

"Nah, don't bother, 'e usually 'as it cold, an' 'e don't seem to mind."

Once the baby was fed, Amy helped Millie change the nappies of the three youngest children. She washed them in the sink and added them to the ones already blowing on the washing line. She was surprised the children demanded so little attention, for they had nothing to play with besides a few ancient bricks and a couple of rag dolls, but they seemed content to huddle together for warmth and stare into the distance.

"Amy, are any of you allowed outside to play?"

"Aye, them that can walk can go out in the courtyard, but there ain't much to do."

"Jonnie, it's a sunny day, and there's a piece of chalk in Gran's workbag. Do you want to show them how to play hopscotch?"

"Oh, us knaws 'ow to play 'opscotch, but us never 'ave any chalk. Shall I go out wi' 'em to keep an eye, or do 'ee want me to stay in yer?"

Millie found the piece of chalk and handed it to Amy. "No, you go out too, Amy, and enjoy yourself; I'll mind the babies."

The baby, now content with a full belly, was returned to his cot, and Millie sat on the floor for a few minutes, building the bricks for the younger children. Leaving them to play, she warmed some water on the old stove and sought out the large bar of soap Jess had mentioned. Under the sink, she also found a scrubbing brush and kept herself busy for the next couple of hours washing the many dishes stacked on the wooden draining board and then scrubbing the filthy kitchen floor.

CHAPTER 34

HARTFORD

Willie Carter stretched and lingered a few more minutes in his warm, cosy bed. It was still dark outside, but his body clock seldom let him down, and he knew it was time he was up. Willie had worked at Sugworthy Farm for several years, having started as a young lad. He remembered well the day he started work. His mother, Sabina, had sent him off to his first job on an empty stomach, for there was no food in the house and by midday, Willie was ravenous. He had stared wide-eyed at the amount of food the farmer's wife placed in front of him for dinner. He could still see it in his mind's eye: bacon, sausages, mushrooms, eggs, and fresh, crusty bread. He seemed to remember there had even been some delicious fried potatoes.

Sabina had been reluctant for him to leave home at all, but she was desperate, for after his father, Tom, died of consumption, there was little money coming in and even less food to feed her large family. Willie understood the situation and assured his mother he was ready to go out to work, and indeed, once he saw how much food was coming his way, he never looked back. The lunch placed before him that day would easily have fed his whole family.

Willie's employer, Tommy Houle, had been the tenant of Sugworthy Farm for over fifty years, having taken over from his father before him. He and his wife, Elizabeth, had hoped to raise a large family there, but unfortunately, it wasn't to be, and Elizabeth had passed away a few years earlier, leaving the devastated farmer alone. Tommy was a great bear of a man, well over six feet tall and with immense strength, but following the loss of his wife, the energy seemed to drain from his body, and he had no interest in life.

At just over two hundred acres, Sugworthy Farm was the smallest of the farms let to tenants by the Hartford Estate. It should have been making a substantial profit, for it was situated on a favourable site with flat, fertile fields and a plentiful water supply from the stream that ran through it. However, since Tommy had withdrawn into himself, things had been let go, and the neglect was beginning to show. It wasn't that Willie and the other farmhand didn't work hard, but Tommy was so uninterested in life that he gave them no instruction and, as likely as not, would forget to pay them at the end of the month. Several farm staff had become tired of this treatment and sought other positions, so the two loyal remaining workers were run off their feet.

After allowing himself five minutes to run through his tasks for the day in his mind, Willie heaved himself out of bed, lit a candle, and pulled on his clothes. He crossed the room and shook the other lad, who relied on Willie to wake him. Yawning, he left the tiny cottage that housed them and entered the largest shippen, where he surveyed a dozen cows that needed milking. It was a chilly morning, but better than it had been, for all the snow had finally melted.

He placed the lantern on the shelf where it usually resided, and one by one, the cows lumbered slowly to their feet. Collecting his three-legged milking stool, he turned his cap around the other way, nestled his head snugly against the first cow, and drew the milk from her udder in a gentle, rhythmic motion. Within minutes, the other farmhand joined him to help with the milking. That task done, the two men shovelled the dung that had accumulated overnight into a wheelbarrow and transported it to the dung heap in the yard.

The two men worked hard, moving from attending to the cows to cleaning out the stables and feeding the horses, pigs, and poultry. By nine o'clock, they were more than ready for breakfast and trooped back to the farmhouse where Florrie, the housekeeper, had cooked them bacon and eggs.

"No sign of Mr Houle this morning, Florrie?"

"No, I haven't seen hide nor hair of him yet, Willie. 'Tisn't right, though, you two doing all the work while he lies in bed all morning."

"No, but then he hasn't been too well, has he? Still, he's usually up by now; I'll see if he's all right." Willie left the kitchen, mounted the stairs, and knocked loudly on the old man's bedroom door. Receiving no answer, he opened the door and peered in. It was difficult to see much, for it was a dull morning, and the thick curtains were still drawn. He crossed the room and pulled them back, turning to survey the still figure huddled in the bed.

"Hello, Mr Houle, it's Willie. Are you all right?"

Tentatively, Willie pulled back the bedclothes and was shocked at the sight of his employer. He knew the man had lost weight, but lying in bed in only his nightshirt revealed how thin he had become. He gently shook the man by the shoulder, and the farmer groaned weakly.

"Morning, Mr Houle, it's Willie; 'tis time you were up."

The man's eyes flickered open momentarily, but there was no response, and Willie could not rouse him further. Retracing his footsteps to the kitchen, he told the others what he had found.

"Florrie, could you take a look at Mr Houle and see what you think? I reckon I'd better fetch Doctor Luckett because something's not right. I don't know what's wrong with him; perhaps he's had a heart attack. You do hear of such things happening. He was all right last night, wasn't he?"

"Aye, he had a tot of brandy afore he went to bed like he does sometimes, and I went to my room and left him to it. Mind you, he's in his late seventies, and he's not been himself."

Florrie could not rouse the farmer either, so Willie saddled up one of the farm horses and rode into Hartford to find the doctor. Fortunately, Doctor Luckett was at home and agreed to visit Sugworthy Farm immediately.

"Mr Houle's been ailing for some time, Willie, but I wasn't expecting this. He's been losing weight steadily for some months, and that could be due to his state of mind, since losing Elizabeth or something more sinister like cancer. It's difficult to know, and in either case, I can do little for the poor man. Anyway, I'll come and see him. Are you riding straight back to the farm now? If so, we can ride together."

"Thank you, doctor, and no, whilst I'm in the village, I want to call in on my mother and see my new baby sister. If possible, I'd also like to have a word with Robert Fellwood if he can spare me a few minutes. The farm hasn't been run properly for a while, and I think it's time he was made aware of the situation."

"Very well, if I don't see you at the farm, I'll leave instructions with Florrie about what needs to be done."

Willie remounted his horse and rode through the village to the Lodge House. However, he rode on past the house, thinking it best to call on Robert Fellwood first, for if he couldn't see him straight away, he could return later after visiting his mother. When he reached the Manor House, Willie was unsure how to enter the large building. He knew his sister, Annie, would tell him to use the front door, for now that she was married to the heir to the Hartford Estate, that would be appropriate. However, he wasn't comfortable with that idea, so he led his horse to the back of the house, left him with a stable lad, and knocked on the kitchen door. The cook, Maisie Jones, opened it, and she smiled at him in surprise.

"Hello, Willie; we don't see you here often. Your sister will grumble that you came to the back entrance."

"I know, Maisie, but I'd rather come in this way; knocking on the front door doesn't feel right. I'd like to see Annie while I'm here, but it's Robert I've come to have a word with; do you know if he's at home?"

"Yes, I think you're in luck, for I believe they're both in the sitting room playing with the children. Would you like me to take you there?"

"Yes, please; I think I know the way, but I'd feel more comfortable if you took me."

Robert was seated at the piano with Selina, trying to teach her a new tune, and Annie was sitting on the floor with David and Thomas, playing with some toys. They were surprised to see Willie, and Annie rose to her feet to hug him, and Selina shouted excitedly.

"Uncle Willie! I didn't know you were coming to see us. Would you like to hear the tune I can play on the piano?"

"Yes, indeed, I would, Selina. What's it called?"

"It's three blind mice. Shall we sing it while I play the tune?"

After a couple of lusty renditions of the nursery rhyme, Annie asked what had brought her brother to see them.

"I need to speak to you about Mr Houle, Robert; I'm afraid he's poorly, and I've had to fetch the doctor. He's been failing for some time, and this morning, when he didn't come down for breakfast, I went to his room and couldn't wake him. The doctor's on his way there now, but I don't know if he can do anything."

"Oh, dear, I'm sorry to hear that. I don't think Mr Houle's ever recovered from losing Elizabeth, and maybe never will. I believe they were married for over fifty years, and a loss like that is difficult to come to terms with. How are you managing without him?"

"That's just it, sir; sorry, Robert, we aren't managing. There's only me and one other labourer left working outside, and Mr Houle does next to nothing. The other workers have left because half the time, he forgets to pay us at the end of the month, and, of course, folk get fed up with it. I'm afraid since he lost Elizabeth, his heart's not been in it."

"No, I guessed as much, and he hasn't paid the rent for this quarter. Jack Bater was planning to visit him in the next week or two, for he's always paid on time. He's lived there so long, and his father and grandfather before him, that I wouldn't want to hassle him for the money, but it indicates that all is not as it should be. Can you carry on as you are for the time being while I sort something out?"

"Yes, I'll do my best, but I thought you should be aware of the situation. I have one suggestion that might help."

"Excellent; what is it?"

"My younger brother, Edward, is going on ten, and I know Uncle Charlie out at Hollyford Farm has taught him how to milk the cows. As you know, Edward's been deaf since birth and makes little progress at school; there isn't much point in his going. If he likes the idea, I wondered if I could take him to Sugworthy Farm to start work as a farm labourer. I know he's young, but he has such a way with animals, and not only do I think he'd love it, but I reckon he could be a big help. Since the family's been eating better, he's become a sturdy lad and is intelligent enough; it's just that he can't hear or speak."

"Oh, Willie, that's a wonderful idea. I think Edward would love that. Thank you for thinking of it."

"There's your answer, then, Willie. It doesn't matter what I think; Annie has decided for us. As it happens, I think it's a great idea, so please go ahead, and I'll ask Jack how much he should be paid."

After leaving the Manor House, delighted with the outcome of his visit, Willie rode to the Lodge House, where his mother and siblings were glad to see him.

"Oh, Willie, this is a nice surprise; what are you doing here?"

Willie hugged his mother and Liza and explained the reason for his visit.

"So, do you think Edward would like to become a farm labourer? I'd take care of him, Mum, but it would mean him leaving school."

"I think he'd love it. He doesn't do much at school, and it's no wonder when he can't hear what the teacher says. He lip-reads a bit, though, so we'll try to make him understand what you're suggesting. Anyway, come and see your new sister."

Katel had awoken for her feed, so whilst Sabina attended to her needs, Willie had a cup of tea and one of Liza's newly baked scones and spent some time chatting with Stephen, Helen, and Danny. He then turned his attention to Edward, who was watching all that was happening with interest. The boy took his elder brother by the arm and led him to the dairy, which still housed the young hedgehogs. Willie duly admired them and then held Edward by the shoulders and spoke clearly to him, using his hands to emphasise his words.

"Edward, will you come with me?"

He pointed to Edward and himself and then to the door.

"Will you ride on my horse with me?"

He made the motion of someone holding reins and galloping on a horse.

Edward looked puzzled, so Willie repeated his actions and mimed milking a cow. He pointed to Edward and then mimed milking a cow again. The young boy suddenly grinned and nodded his head.

Willie and Edward returned to the sitting room, where Sabina held the baby over her shoulder and patted her back to bring up her wind.

"I think he understands, Mum, and would like to go with me. Do you want to get a few clothes together for him?"

"Yes, I'll do that; here, take Katel and keep rubbing her back. She can get to know her eldest brother for a few minutes."

Taking Edward by the arm, she led him to the bedroom and packed a few spare clothes into a bag. She spoke to him slowly and repeated some of Willie's actions, and the boy nodded his head with a broad smile. However, when they returned to the kitchen, he took her arm and Stephen's and led them to the dairy. He pointed at the hedgehogs.

"Oh, he's trying to ask us to take care of them, Stephen. Will you do that for Edward? He can't take them with him on the horse."

"Yes, I'd love to. I've been helping Edward to look after them, anyway, so I know what to do."

Stephen nodded and smiled at his brother, and they rejoined Willie in the sitting room, where he was quite at home nursing the new baby. A little later, Willie and Edward mounted the horse and, with Edward clutching his bag of clothes, galloped back to Sugworthy Farm.

CHAPTER 35

HARTFORD

The past few weeks had been frantically busy for Fred and several other members of the Carter family. Leaving most of the day-to-day carpentry work to his son, Llewellyn, he had concentrated on renovating Bluebell Cottage, ready for his parents to move into. He was pleased with Llewie's progress, for although he was not yet fourteen, he was becoming skilled at carpentry and taking on more and more responsibility. A couple of days before the grand party, Fred escorted his mother to the cottage to see if his efforts met with her approval.

Taking Betsey's arm, Fred led her through the repaired garden gate and along the path to the new back door. On either side of the track, the garden had been forked over by Louis Blaquiere and was neat and tidy, though there was little to see other than winter jasmine and a few snowdrops so early in the year. Betsey admired the new door, painted a deep green, and as Fred led the way into the kitchen, she gasped in amazement, for he had worked wonders.

The kitchen walls had been lime-washed and were fresh and bright. Charlotte and Sarah had scrubbed the rough flagstones, which were cleaner than Betsey had ever seen them. The two windowpanes sparkled in the weak winter sun and were adorned by blue curtains donated by Annie from the Manor House and altered to fit by Fred's sister, Eveline. Best of all were the kitchen cupboards, which Betsey recognised from Fred's cottage. A bunch of early snowdrops in tight buds were on the table in a small pot.

"Oh, Fred, you have worked hard; it's wonderful, and thank you so much for the cupboards. How is Charlotte managing without them?"

"I've put up a couple of shelves for her to use for now. She doesn't mind; it's only for a week or two until we move into The Red Lion. Come on; there's more to see yet."

Fred led his mother through the rest of the cottage, and she was thrilled with the changes he had made. Although it was only partly furnished, she could see that it would be cosy and warm for her and Ned and, most importantly, so different from her childhood home.

"This is amazing, Fred. I hardly recognise the place; thank you so much. I think we'll be happy here. Where did you get the second double bed? There was only one here before."

"Good, I'm glad you're pleased with it, Mum. Yes, there was only one bed and a couple of palliasses. Annie let us have the other double bed and also some spare linen. Sarah and Charlotte came here yesterday for a final clean-through and to make up the beds because Silas, Josie, Barney and Bronwen are expected to arrive late tomorrow. I wrote to them and explained about the party and that we hoped to keep their visit a secret from Dad. Hopefully, they can sneak in here and keep out of the way until the party and then make a surprise appearance."

"That should be easy enough; Ned's not getting out and about much now, and it will be a lovely surprise for him. I can't wait to see them; it's been several years since we all got together, and we were so close in our youth."

The next day, a few minutes before the last stagecoach was due to arrive, Betsey carried a tray laden with a fresh pot of tea and a few scones to where Ned was resting in the sitting room. She told him she was feeling tired and that Sarah had insisted she put her feet up and rest. Betsey settled herself in her favourite armchair opposite her husband, added some milk to each cup, and poured them a strong cup of tea. She handed him a tea plate with a freshly buttered scone and put his tea beside him.

"There we are. Sarah's such a thoughtful girl; I can see why our William married her. I'll never forget how she treated his three children back along, but she regrets it now, and we all make mistakes. I don't know how I would manage without her these days. Do you fancy a game of cards when we've eaten our scones? It's ages since we played."

"What a splendid idea, Betsey. I'd love that. I get so bored sitting around these days. Shall we play old maid or perhaps cribbage? I'd love a game of whist, but we need four people for that."

"Oh, let's have a game of cribbage; I'll find the pegboard."

The sitting room window faced onto the back garden of the inn, and Betsey knew there was little chance of Ned seeing the passengers alight from the stagecoach if she kept him occupied for the next hour or so.

In the bar, Fred was waiting to welcome his two uncles and aunts and was enjoying a tankard of ale. He didn't have to wait long, for the stagecoach arrived half an hour earlier than usual, and he was relieved his mother had left to keep his father occupied. He went out to greet the visitors.

"Hello, everyone; it's wonderful to see you all."

He warmly shook the hands of his Uncles, Silas and Barney, and kissed the hands of his two aunts.

"My goodness, Fred, it is you, isn't it? I shudder to think how many years it's been since I last saw you. I have to say you're so like your father in his younger days."

"Yes, Uncle Barney, it's me, and you're not the first to say that. Now, would you follow me to the cottage next door, please? As you know, we're trying to keep your arrival a secret from Dad until the party, so we've made up beds for you to sleep there. I'll arrange for your luggage to be taken there later."

The four visitors hastily followed Fred, and Barney exclaimed at the improvements made to the cottage.

"Oh, my, this is not how I remember the place at all. What an improvement. Does no one live here?"

"No, not at the moment. It's been rented out for some years, but the last tenants moved out a month ago and left it in quite a mess. As I told you in my letter, Dad's a bit under the weather, so he and Mum will retire soon and live here. I've spent the last few weeks doing the place up for them. Now, the fire's lit, and I believe Sarah has stocked the larder with a few essentials, and there's a rabbit pie and some potatoes in the oven."

"Thank you; it smells wonderful, but tell me more about Ned. Is he seriously ill?"

"Well, to see him, you wouldn't think there's anything wrong, but it's his heart. It's weak, and there's nothing the doctor can do; it's just a symptom of age. The doctor says that if he rests and takes it easy, he should have a few more years, but he gets short of breath with any exertion. He finds it frustrating, and I don't think he's the easiest patient to care for. Mum and Dad got us all together recently and said they wanted Charlotte and me to take over The Red Lion. George wasn't best pleased at first, as he's the eldest son, but even he could see he would be a terrible landlord. I mean, he's strictly religious and a teetotaller, and that's not the makings of a successful innkeeper."

Silas laughed. "No, that wouldn't work at all. I wish you all the luck in the world, Fred, but 'tis hard work, as Josie and I know; still, we had some happy times here with Betsey and Ned, and I can't wait to see Ned's face when he sees all of us."

"I'll leave you to settle in and have a bite to eat, and I'll see you at the party tomorrow night. Mum will be here to see you before too long."

The visitors were eating the last of their delicious tea when they heard a gentle knock on the door, and it opened to reveal Betsey. As she took in their presence, she grinned and, within minutes, was embraced in a warm hug from her brother, Barney.

"Oh, Betsey, it's so good to see you. How are you?"

"I'm very well, thank you, and it's lovely to see you all. How wonderful that we're all together again. What times we had, eh?"

The next hour sped by as the relatives caught up with each other's news. Silas and Josie reported having a new granddaughter, making eight grandchildren from their three daughters and one son. However, Barney and Bronwen easily surpassed that number by telling Betsey all about their eighteen grandchildren and three great-grandchildren from their seven children.

"What a large family we have, and how interesting it is to hear all your news. I can't wait to see Ned's face when you walk in tomorrow."

Barney followed Betsey as she left the kitchen and placed his arm around her shoulder.

"Is everything all right? Will Ned be all right with all the excitement?"

"Oh, now you've worried me, but I think he'll be all right. It's so frustrating for him to live like an invalid, but that's what he is now, whether he likes it or not. We're lucky that we can retire and pass the inn on to Fred and Charlotte. It's time we took life a bit easier, and I must admit I'm looking forward to it, though I wish Ned were in better health. Still, the doctor says that if he's careful not to overdo it, he should be fine for a few years."

"That's good, and you've both certainly earned the right to take things easy; you've worked so hard all your life.

You're looking good, though, and I'm pleased to see it. Did you ever hear any more about our beloved father?"

"No, I never saw or heard from him again. The last we heard was when Becky Chown left him and returned to Hartford. It didn't take her long to see through him, and she was lucky to have somewhere else to go. Her mother took her back, though I don't think she was happy about the situation, and the villagers gave Becky a hard time for the rest of her life. She never married; I don't think she could trust anyone after her experience of living with Dad. He ruined her life, too. How about you? Did you ever hear what happened to him?"

"No, like you, I've never heard any more, and for that, I'm glad. I could never have forgiven Dad for abandoning you and Norman. The only reason I ever wanted to see him again was to give him the hiding I once promised him."

"Ah, well, it's all water under the bridge now, but like you, I've never forgiven him for causing Norman to die."

With tears in their eyes, the two siblings hugged each other in silence.

The next day passed in a blur as the Carter family prepared for the party in Betsey's Kitchen. A long trestle table was positioned down one side and covered with snowy white tablecloths in readiness for all the food. Josie and Bronwen joined Sarah in Betsey's Kitchen and helped her to bake pasties, sausage rolls, and scones.

Betsey would dearly have liked to join them but was fearful Ned might also wander out there if she did. That being a risk she was unwilling to take, she stayed in the kitchen, prepared a giant tureen of leek and potato soup, and baked some fresh bread rolls to accompany it.

It was very much a family effort, and George's wife, Mary Ann, was contributing a couple of trifles and some leftover Christmas puddings. Eveline had baked two fruit cakes and jam sponges, and Sabina and Liza made four bacon and cheese quiches. At Annie's request, Maisie had poached a whole salmon and roasted four chickens and a ham on the spit. Many villagers had been invited, and Betsey worried there would not be enough room for them all. She decided to lay out more tables and food in the bar of the inn so folk could socialise and wander from one area to another. Fortunately, the weather had become mild over the last few days, and there was no sign of rain.

The party began at six o'clock, and Betsey insisted that Ned remain seated to welcome their guests. She was worried that all the excitement might be too much for his heart, but he waved her worries away and told her that if he couldn't attend his own party, life was not worth living anyway. By half past six, most of the guests had arrived and were served a glass of cider or ale and one or two with Madeira wine. Ned was sitting in his chair with a broad smile, surveying the many people around him. They were all dear to him: customers, friends, and family. When the door opened once more, he glanced up, wondering who else could be coming, and his eyes nearly popped out of his head as they rested on the dear face of his brother, Silas.

"Oh, Silas, what a lovely surprise. And Josie, too, how lovely to see you."

As the two brothers embraced, Ned caught sight of Barney and Bronwen.

"Oh, good heavens, you're both here too! How wonderful to see you all."

Ned was quite overcome, and with tears running down his cheeks, he glanced at Betsey.

"I shall have a word with you later, my dear, about keeping this news from me. Is there anyone else to come that I don't know about?"

"No, that's it, now; isn't it grand that we're all together again in Betsey's Kitchen?"

"That's not quite all, Mum; there is one more surprise for both of you. Do you know who this is?"

A middle-aged woman entered the room and greeted the curious couple.

"Hello, Uncle Ned and Auntie Betsey; I wonder if you know who I am? Mind you, it must be fifty years or so since you last saw me, and I've changed a bit. I'm Amy, and I was born here at the inn. What a long time ago that was, and I'm a granny myself now."

Betsey and Ned hugged their new guest.

"Oh, Amy, I'm so pleased to see you again. I remember when Silas and Josie left here with you on a cart and all their possessions. You were only a baby, and it broke Uncle Mal and Auntie Kezzie's hearts when you went. Auntie Kezzie filled a bed warmer with hot coals from the fire to keep you all warm on the journey. I can't believe we've barely seen you since that day, but how did you get here? Did you travel today?"

"No, I came with the others yesterday, but I got off the stagecoach in the village before it got here, and I've been staying at Uncle Fred's cottage. We wanted it to be a surprise for both of you."

The party was a huge success; the ale and the wine flowed, the food was delicious, and Eveline played the piano, keeping most folk dancing until the early hours of the morning. At half past ten, Betsey could see that Ned was flagging.

"Come on, Ned, shall we go to bed? It will be one of the last times we'll sleep here in The Red Lion."

"Yes, I think I'd better get some rest, for I'm feeling gone in. I'd love to stay to the end and whirl you around the dance floor like I used to."

"I know you would, my love, and that would be grand, but as long as you're still here to cuddle me before we settle down to sleep, that's all I ask. In any case, it's not only you that's getting older, you know; I'm tired too."

It was another half an hour before they managed to tear themselves away from all the guests, and gratefully climbed the stairs, and settled down for the night.

CHAPTER 36

HARTFORD

Willie Carter was the first to leave the party at The Red Lion Inn, and, unlike most of the guests, he had consumed only a meagre quantity of ale. His employer, Mr Houle, was seriously ill, and Willie had promised Florrie he would not be late home. The housekeeper was struggling to keep her eyes open as she heard the sound of Willie's horse clattering across the cobbles. She was thankful, for the last few days had been difficult.

Doctor Luckett had visited the farm a few times and was convinced the elderly farmer had suffered a massive heart attack from which he was unlikely to recover. When he divulged this information to Willie and Florrie, they thought it was probably for the best and what Mr Houle would want. The doctor agreed with them. He was unsure whether the poor man's lack of appetite and lethargy was caused by his immense grief at losing his wife or if there was some other cause, but the man had clearly lost the will to live. Willie found Florrie sitting by her employer's bedside.

"Hello, Willie; thanks for coming back early. 'Tis good of you. Did you have a nice time?"

"Aye, it was a splendid party, and I reckon it'll go on for some hours yet. Most villagers were there, and I suspect there'll be some sore heads in the morning. Has there been any change?"

"No, he's not stirred. I suspect the poor man's not long for this world."

"You get off to bed now, then. You've been sitting with him all day and must be exhausted."

"I can't deny that I am, lad, but then, so must you be."

"I'm all right and a bit younger than you."

"That you are, lad, that you are. What about Edward? Did you bring him back with you?"

"No, I told him I'd fetch him tomorrow; there was no need for him to miss his grandparents' party. That sort of celebration doesn't happen often, and he's only a boy."

" Quite right; he's a sturdy lad for his age, and I think he'll be a big help. Well, if you're sure, I'll get off to my bed, but call me if you need me."

Willie sat beside the bed and watched the old man's chest slowly rise and fall. In his opinion, the farmer's breathing seemed shallower than earlier, and he wondered if the end was near. However, it was after five o'clock in the morning before Tommy Houle took his last breath. Willie felt sad but also relieved, for the poor man had been so miserable since losing his wife that Willie knew this was what he would have wanted. Willie pulled the sheet up over Tom's face and, knowing there was no time for sleep, went to the kitchen and made himself a cup of tea. After drinking it, he woke the other labourer and told him to get on with the day's work while he rode to Hartford to see Fred Carter about a coffin.

Willie was surprised to see his Uncle Fred and cousin, Llewellyn, up and about, for it was barely seven o'clock, and he was sure they must have been late to bed.

"Hello Willie, what brings you here so early? I didn't see you leave the party last night; did you stay at your mum's house?"

"No, I left early and returned to Sugworthy Farm because Mr Houle was so ill. I told Florrie I wouldn't stay too long, and that's why I'm here; I'm afraid he died early this morning."

"Oh, dear, that is sad, though I suspect it's a happy release, as they say. The last time I saw him, he was so down in the mouth. I think he's probably glad to be reunited with Elizabeth."

"Aye, we all think so, too. Anyway, could you sort out a coffin, please?"

"Yes, of course. Llewie, do you want to stay here and work, or would you like to ride out to the farm to measure up for the coffin? You've got to do it sometime. Mr Houle was a huge man, and I don't think we have anything here that will be big enough."

"I'll ride to the farm if it's all right with you, Dad. I've seen a few dead bodies now, and I'm getting used to it."

"All right then; measure carefully, though. You know what I'm always telling you. Measure twice, cut once."

"Aye, I know. You tell me every single time. Can I ride back with you, Willie? I don't see much of you these days, and it would be nice to catch up."

"Aye, I'd like that; I expect Florrie will have laid the body out by the time we get back. I must visit the Manor House first to tell Robert about Mr Houle, and then I'll collect Edward, and he can ride back behind me. I'll probably be an hour or two."

Leaving the carpenter's yard, Willie remounted his horse and galloped to the Manor House. This time, he was saved from deciding which door to use as Robert appeared from the woods and walked towards the front door with his dog.

"Hello, Willie; how are you? I can probably guess why you're here."

"I'm fine, thank you, and yes, Mr Houle died earlier this morning; I thought you should know."

"Thank you. Well, it wasn't unexpected. How old was he? Do you know?"

"Florrie thinks he was seventy-eight or thereabouts. I've asked Uncle Fred to provide a coffin, and Llewie will ride back with me later to measure the body. I'll be taking Edward back with me, too; I let him stay at Mum's house last night so he could enjoy the party."

"How's it working out with Edward?"

"Yes, it's going well. He loves it, and he's a natural with the animals; they all seem to love him for some reason. The other farmhand has taken to him, too, so that's good. Edward's been milking six cows every morning and night since I took him to the farm, so it's a huge help. It means we can get on with something else."

"Have you had any sleep or breakfast?"

"Not much sleep, though I dozed in the chair while I was sitting with Mr Houle. I didn't intend to, but I couldn't keep my eyes open. I'll be all right, though; 'tis not the first time I've been up all night; it often happens when a cow's calving or we're lambing. I didn't stay to have any breakfast; it didn't seem right."

"I'm sure Tommy would have told you to eat your breakfast, but no matter, you can have some with me."

An hour or so later, Willie, feeling much better for having eaten, left Hartford Manor, collected Edward from the Lodge House, and called for Llewie to ride back to Sugworthy Farm together. Robert was thoughtful as he asked one of the servants to find Jack Bater and ask him to come to his study.

Jack Bater had been the estate manager at the Manor for many years. He had been there all his working life and, at nearly seventy, would soon be thinking of retirement. He had started working on the estate as a stable lad in 1830 when he was fourteen, and Robert's great-grandfather, Ephraim, was the Lord of the Manor. That had been in the good old days, for Ephraim took an interest in everything and everyone on the estate and had soon noticed the boy's potential. By the time of Ephraim's death in 1840, the estate had passed to his son, Joshua, and Jack had progressed to the position of groom. Again, Jack enjoyed working with his master, and by the time of Joshua's untimely death, caused by an unfortunate riding accident in 1868, Jack had achieved the prestigious position of estate manager. The next few years were more difficult for the new Lord, Robert's father, Charles, who took little interest in the estate and begrudged spending any money. However, when Charles was forced to relinquish his position because of ill health, Jack's life became considerably more pleasant, for he had always liked Robert, having known him since he was born. Between them, many improvements had been made to the farming practices and the working conditions for the farm labourers.

"Hello, Jack; thanks for coming so quickly. I hope I haven't dragged you away from something important?"

"No, it's all right, sir; how can I help?"

"It's not unexpected news, Jack, but Tommy Houle has passed away, and we must decide what to do. As I understand it, the farm is short-handed and not running smoothly. Annie's brother, Willie, is doing an amazing job holding everything together, but he's working all the hours God sends, and he won't be able to keep that up forever."

"I'm sorry to hear that, and yes, I know there are problems. Willie confided in me some time ago, and I know more farm labourers have left since then. Are you thinking of letting Willie take over the farm? I mean, he is your brother-in-law."

"Yes, I know, and I have been wondering about that, but I think he's too young to be a tenant farmer. The only farm hand that's left follows his lead, but there will need to be several new workers. I suspect older men might not take kindly to being ordered about by a teenager, particularly if they think he got the farm because of his connection to me. What do you think?"

"I think you're right, sir. One day, Willie will make an excellent tenant farmer, for he's a hard worker and a conscientious lad, but as you say, he's too young at the moment. He could be considered for the position of manager, though, if we get the right man in as a tenant. Do you have anyone else in mind?"

"I do, though it may not work out. Did you know that Sam found his missing son recently?"

"Yes, I heard about that; how wonderful for both of them."

"His son's called Marrok, and his background is in farming. I thought he might be a suitable tenant for Sugworthy Farm. He was raised as a gypsy until his early teens, but since then, he's made his living working on farms. I understand that until recently, he was in a well-paid job with a tied cottage on a farm in South Molton. Then he fell while helping to thatch a roof and broke his leg. The farmer had no choice but to lay him off, and he and his family ended up in the workhouse, where, sadly, his wife died of cholera. After Sam found him, they all stayed with us over Christmas, though I don't suppose you met him, for he couldn't go far on his crutches."

"No, I didn't meet him, but I heard the tale about his discovery. Are you sure he'd be the right man for the job?"

"No, I don't know much about him, so we need to make a few enquiries. Perhaps you could visit the farm in South Molton and ask the farmer what he thinks. If you get a favourable report, then I could visit Marrok at Primrose Cottage in Enderby, where he's living with his father, and put the offer to him. If the farmer has any misgivings, we'll have to think of someone else. Please keep it to yourself, though, Jack, because I know what Annie's like, and she always wants to help anyone in the family. In the meantime, can we do anything to help Willie?"

"Yes, I can spare a couple of workers for a month or two. It's winter, so there are no harvests to worry about, and we won't be ploughing until March. The lambing will start soon, though, and Willie will have that problem, too, so we'll have to manage. If I send him two experienced workers, that should help."

CHAPTER 37

BARNSTAPLE

Living in Pengelly Court was quite an eye-opener for Millie and Jonathan, but they were well-treated, given enough to eat, and not harmed. The women tended to rise late in the mornings, for they knew there would be little trade early in the day, and they usually needed to sleep off the effects of the alcohol and drugs they relied on to cope with their sordid lives. They would leave the house late in the morning and then come home around tea time for their main meal before going out again to work the night shift.

Millie and Jonathan were fascinated by Fanny Prowse, the landlady of the house. No one knew how old Fanny was or how she had come to own the house, but she was quite a character. Her plump face was lined with wrinkles and fine red lines, and her large, slightly purple nose was a testament to her life of alcoholism. She had wispy white hair, thinning on the top and barely hiding her shiny scalp. She was seldom seen outside the house without her faded yellow bonnet tied with ribbons under her chin. A prostitute herself in her younger days, three of the girls were her daughters, and she did her best to keep them as safe as possible. Fanny knew enough muscle around the town to frighten off any men with ideas of becoming the girls' pimp, and few would dare to cross her.

At first, Millie and Jonathan were frightened of this formidable lady, for her language was ripe, with every other word an obscenity, but one day, when Jonnie was suffering from an earache, she mixed up a potion to ease the pain, then cuddled him on her lap until he fell asleep. She was the same with all the youngsters, and Millie thought the old lady loved them more than their mothers.

The working girls found most of their trade on the quayside, for voyages could last several months, and when the ships docked, the sailors usually had one thing on their minds. The prostitutes frequented the many inns along the quay and in the town, though by law, they were only allowed to stay inside for fifteen minutes to have one drink, for soliciting was illegal. One enterprising landlord had got around this irritating problem by having a hole knocked through his garden wall, allowing his customers to step through, partake of a lady's pleasure, and then return to their tankard of ale.

Once her looks had deserted her, Fanny made herself useful by keeping a watchful eye out for the peelers. She wore a whistle on a ribbon around her neck, and three quick blasts warned any prostitutes nearby that the police were about. A few years ago, this had been a valuable practice, but in recent times, Fanny was usually so drunk that she blew her whistle whenever the urge took her, and this caused no end of disruption in the hidden alleyways and doorways of the town.

The only person that Millie didn't get along with was Liz, Fanny's eldest daughter. The girl did everything she could to please the older woman, but it was plain that Liz didn't like her, perhaps because her mother, Fanny, was often singing Millie's praises. The house was cleaner than it had ever been, and whilst the other prostitutes were grateful for Millie's efforts, Liz made her life as difficult as possible, delighting in trudging mud through the house without wiping her feet and leaving dishes strewn everywhere. Taking Jess's advice, Millie did not complain and tried to avoid the unpleasant woman if possible.

Millie did her best to improve the lives of the children in her own way. One day, she bathed them all, one after another, in the old tin bath that hung on a rusty nail in the outhouse. They were unsure about it at first, but then enjoyed themselves when Jonathan showed them how to blow bubbles with the soap. She also taught them a few nursery rhymes, and one toddler, in particular, loved having Millie touch each of her toes and recite the verse, 'This little piggy'.

Millie also encouraged them to play outside on dry days, for none of them went to school, and she thought the fresh air would be beneficial. She carried the two suffering with rickets outside and sat them on a blanket so they could at least watch the others play. The piece of chalk she had provided for hopscotch did not last long, and when a heavy downpour obliterated the chalk marks, that game was no longer possible. However, having been to school, Millie knew several games to play, and one, which became a firm favourite, was 'oranges and lemons'.

"Come on, Andy and Ben, raise your arms to make an arch; that's right. Now, we'll all sing the rhyme I've taught you, and you two move your arms up and down to chop off someone's head as they pass through; then, they will be the 'chopper' for the next game."

In taking the children outside to play, Millie got to know the neighbour with the attractive, tiny front garden. Alice Brown was an elderly lady who did not seem to fit into the surroundings where she now found herself, and Millie enjoyed chatting with her. Alice was an educated woman and would not be drawn on the circumstances that led to her living where she did, but she took more pride in her house than most in the courtyard. Her windows were always sparkling clean, the step scrubbed, and the garden well-tended. Millie confided her story to Alice, and the old lady advised her to keep the details from Liz at all costs and to escape the run-down area as soon as possible.

The one job Millie hated was washing the sheep's intestines. It was a filthy, stinking task as they were full of half-digested food and had to be rinsed many times, the smell making her gag. Her other job was to sew the ends of sections of the intestines and leave a pile ready for the girls. The makeshift condoms did not last long, so a regular supply was needed. When Millie asked Jess why they got through so many, she explained that with use, they soon tended to crack and become useless.

One morning, Millie sent the children out to play, intending to clean the kitchen thoroughly. Jonnie had a bad cold, so she let him stay inside with her, and the pair were enjoying a few rare moments alone. Millie was scrubbing the floor when the front door opened, and Liz staggered in, very drunk despite the early hour. Behind her was a plump man with a ruddy complexion, and his eyes gleamed when he surveyed Millie's shapely bottom as she worked hard on her hands and knees.

"Why, Liz, you didn't tell me you had a new maid here, and, no disrespect, love, but I think I might like to explore pastures new, if you know what I mean. What's your name, my lovely?"

"No, Ted; yer wasting yer time, there, mate. 'er's no prossie, 'er's just our cleaner and far too 'igh and mighty for the likes of ye. Ye'll 'ave to make do wi' me, though I'm not sure I'm willin' now if yer so picky. I've always been good enough for 'ee before."

Millie was embarrassed as the man's eyes explored every inch of her body, and he held out his hand to help her up.

"No need to be frightened of me, my love, and if 'tis your first time, why that's even better, and I'll be kind. I know my manners, and I can be a gentleman when I want to be. Whatever this lot is paying you to clean, I'll pay you far more to spend an hour or two with me. What do you say?"

"No, thank you. I appreciate the offer, but I'm happy doing the cleaning. My brother and I aren't staying here long, just a few days, so that I can earn some money."

"See, Ted, I told 'ee; 'er be too good for the likes of ye. I don't quite know what's goin' on wi' 'er and 'er brother, but I reckon there's more to it than meets the eye. 'er don't belong yer and that I do know. Now, do 'ee want my body or not? Time's money, and if yer not keen, I'll get out and find someone who is."

"Aw, Liz, don't be like that; you know I've always had a soft spot for you. 'Tis nothing personal, and yes, of course, I want your lovely body."

He took the older woman's hand and led her into the downstairs bedroom. As he closed the door, he winked at Millie and whispered. "Let me know if you change your mind."

Millie was determined not to be around when the man left the building, so ten minutes later, she abandoned her chores and knocked on Alice's door, taking Jonnie with her. The old lady answered the door and smiled.

"Hello, Millie, this is a nice surprise; is everything all right?"

"Yes, thank you, Alice, but if it isn't too much trouble, could Jonnie and I come in for a few minutes?"

"Oh, yes, please do; I'd love the company, my dear. Come in, and I'll make us a cup of tea."

The other children were playing in the courtyard, and Millie knew they would be safe with Amy looking after them. She told the girl where she was going and where to find her if needed. Millie had never been in Alice's house before and was not surprised to find it was sparkling clean and comfortably furnished.

"Oh, Alice, what a cosy house you have. You know, I don't want to pry, but I don't think you belong in Pengelly Court."

"No, I have known a better life, Millie, it's true, but I'm happy enough here, and although the area is a bit run down, the folk are friendly enough, and it's the last place anyone would look for me. I don't want to talk about my past, my dear, but I think you and I are in the same boat, both fleeing from something or someone unpleasant. Anyway, sit down and make yourselves comfortable. Would you like a piece of my jam sponge, Jonnie, and a glass of milk?"

"Oh, yes, please."

"Good; if you'd like to sit at the kitchen table, I'll fetch it for you, and you can draw me a picture while your sister and I have a chat. I have a slate and some chalk here in the cupboard."

When Jonnie was settled, Alice brought Millie a piece of cake and a cup of tea.

"Now, what's upset you this morning? You looked anxious when I opened the door."

Millie explained what had happened, and Alice sat in a chair where she could see out of the window.

"I'll sit here and see if I know the man you're talking about, and like I've told you before, you're best not to let Liz know anything about you. I get the feeling she would sell her own mother for the price of a tot of gin. Do you have enough money to move on yet? It might be for the best, given the circumstances."

"I'm not sure, but I've been here a couple of weeks and haven't been paid anything. I think you're right, though, Alice, and perhaps it is time we were on our way."

"Yes, you should ask Jess for your wages. She's a good sort, though I expect she's hoping you'll stay; she was singing your praises the other day, and even Fanny seems to have taken a liking to you. Oh, now, just a minute, Liz's visitor is leaving, and yes, I do know him. It's not good news, I'm afraid, Millie, for he's a constable. Hopefully, word about you has not spread this far, but given that it's a wealthy lady who's looking for you, it might have. I think you could be in danger and should be on your way as soon as possible."

CHAPTER 38

BARNSTAPLE

Reluctantly, Millie and Jonnie left Alice's house and returned next door. Millie was relieved Liz was not home and had presumably gone out looking for another punter. Until now, the girl had felt relatively safe, but she now felt uncomfortable and couldn't wait until she and Jonnie could be on their way again. Pushing aside her anxieties, she got on with peeling turnips, carrots and swede to make a stew for their tea. Fanny had brought home a breast of lamb the day before, and Millie hoped to make it stretch further by adding lots of vegetables. She was pleased when Jess was the first to come home that day and plucked up the courage to ask about her wages.

"Jess, I'm sorry to ask, but have I earned enough money yet to pay the fare to Hartford?"

"Ah, I was wonderin' when ye'd ask, Millie. Aye, of course, ye 'ave, but to tell 'ee the truth, us'd like 'ee and Jonnie to stay, especially the children. Ye've worked wonders with 'em since ye's been yer, though yer only a chit of a girl. Us'll miss 'ee if ye go; any chance ye'd stay?"

"'Tis kind of you, but I must try to find our relatives in Hartford, for I promised Gran that I would, and she might even be there by now, waiting for us."

"I thought ye'd say that. Well, yer free to go whenever ye want; us'd never keep 'ee yer against yer will. Remember, though, if it doesn't work out in Hartford, ye can always come back yer. Us wouldn't make 'ee go on the game, I promise, but us love 'aving 'ee yer lookin' after us. Yer gettin' to be a good cook, too. I reckon even Fanny 'as a soft spot for 'ee."

"Thank you, Jess; I can't believe how several strangers have offered to take us in if we're desperate, but I have to keep my promise."

"Aye, I know 'ee do. Now look, take yer wages, but would 'ee stay another week or two 'til us can find someone to replace 'ee? I had a chat with the girls t'other day, and us decided that if 'ee did go, then us'd find someone else cos this arrangement's worked well. I think the only one who isn't too keen on 'ee is Liz, and I don't know why 'tis, but er's a funny maid sometimes."

The words were barely spoken by Jess when the door opened, and Liz walked in. Jess looked anxious, wondering if Liz had overheard her words, but it appeared not.

"Ah, Liz, 'ave 'ee 'ad a good day?"

"Not bad, though Ted would have preferred Millie's company to mine."

Liz glared at Millie, and Jess tried to make light of the situation.

"Oh well, I expect he'd prefer Millie to any of us, Liz. I wouldn't be offended by that; after all, 'er's less than 'alf our age, so 'tis understandable. Ye don't need to fret about it though, cos Millie's decided 'tis time 'er and Jonnie went on their way. Us knew 'er'd only be yer fer a week or two, but 'er's agreed to stay 'til us can find someone to replace 'er."

Liz glanced at Millie. "This is a bit sudden, Millie; is it cos Ted took a fancy to 'ee? Or is there something else worrying 'ee?"

"No, we only intended to stay for a couple of weeks, anyway, Liz, so now we need to be on our way."

"Well, 'tis good of 'ee to stay 'til us find someone else. I may not be yer biggest fan, but I've liked not 'aving to do any 'ousework or look after the little uns. And ye'll stay another week or two, then?"

"Yes, we're in no big hurry."

In the early hours of the morning, Millie woke Jonathan, and, as quietly as possible, they picked their way between all the sleeping bodies lying on the palliasses on the floor. As they passed Jess, she opened her eyes and looked at them in puzzlement.

"What's the matter, Millie? Is something wrong?"

"It's Jonnie; he feels sick. Lamb never did agree with him, and that stew was quite greasy. I'm going to take him downstairs. I don't want him to be sick in here."

"Oh, all right; I hope ye soon feel better, Jonnie." Jess turned over and was asleep again in minutes.

In the kitchen, Millie hesitated, wondering whether to retrieve her sack and Emily's workbag from the cupboard under the stairs. However, she didn't want to risk waking anyone and decided not to bother. Liz had sold every stitch of their clothing, and all they owned were the threadbare rags they stood in. There was little enough food in the house, and she decided to leave empty-handed. Quietly, she and Jonathan eased open the front door and stepped into the courtyard. As arranged earlier in the day, Millie tapped lightly on Alice's door and was admitted straight away.

"Any problems?"

"No. I don't think so, though Liz seemed a bit suspicious at teatime. I wonder if Ted does know about us?"

"It's safer if you don't wait to find out. I can just see Liz and Ted sharing the reward that's offered for you."

"Yes, I suppose so, but I feel guilty because Jess paid me my wages without question and asked me to stay until they can find someone else to do the cleaning and look after the children. I said I would, and now I'm going to let her down."

"Well, that's a shame, but I don't think you can risk it. Now, come through the house and out the back gate. I've already spoken to Anna, the headmistress of the Alice Horwood School, and explained the situation. She's happy for you to stay there for a few days until you can get away. You can trust her; she's been a good friend to me."

However, they hadn't even left the house before they heard a disturbance outside. Alice hurried upstairs to her bedroom and peered out carefully from behind the curtains. She was dismayed to see two constables outside, hammering on the door of the neighbouring house. One of the constables was Ted. She hurried back downstairs and waved her hands at Millie and Jonathan.

"Quickly, go out the back gate and across the alleyway. The gate opposite will be unlocked. Go through and lock it behind you. My friend, Anna, is expecting you, and she'll take care of you. I won't come with you because it won't take them long to guess you've made a run for it. No doubt they'll want to look in here; they know we're friends."

Millie hastily hugged the old lady and ran through the backyard and across the alleyway, pulling Jonathan by the hand. As Alice had said, the gate was unlocked, though Millie had to pull it hard as the old hinges were rusty. It squeaked loudly, and the girl hoped and prayed no one had heard it. Once through the gate, she pushed the bolts across and heard Alice do the same to her gate.

It was bitterly cold, and they shivered; the thin rags they wore were inadequate to keep them warm. Luckily, there was a little light from the full moon, and Millie and Jonathan picked their way across the cobbled courtyard to the back door. She knocked gently, not wanting to make too much noise, and was relieved when the door was opened, and a middle-aged woman bade them enter.

"Hello, you must be Millie and Jonathan. Alice has told me all about you. Please come this way."

"Thank you so much for sheltering us, ma'am. As it turns out, we escaped with only minutes to spare. Two constables are knocking on the door of Fanny's house, and they must be looking for us; 'tis too much of a coincidence."

"Yes, I expect they are, my dear, but not to worry, you'll be safe here. Now, we need to be quiet, for six young maids are asleep upstairs, and we don't want to awaken them. The fewer people who know of your whereabouts, the better. I use a small boxroom upstairs as a storeroom, and I thought you could hide there for a few days. No one else goes in there except me. Most of our pupils live with their families and attend school daily, but six are orphans, so they stay here with me. Follow me."

The room was tiny, but Anna had placed a large palliasse in the middle of the floor amidst all the boxes she stored there, and there were a couple of blankets.

"Now, do you think you can sleep there all right?"

"Yes, thank you so much. Hopefully, we can be on our way in a day or two; I have enough money for a stagecoach ride to Hartford."

"That's good; now settle down and get some rest, and I'll bring you some breakfast in the morning. There's a bedpan there if you need one. Good night."

Next door, there was pandemonium in Fanny's house as Liz admitted the two constables and pointed them in the direction of the room where Millie and Jonathan slept. Within seconds, the household was awake, the frightened children crying, and the prostitutes grumbling at being disturbed. The only one who slept blissfully on was Fanny, and her loud snores could be heard through the bedroom door. Liz was furious when they discovered the empty bed where Millie and Jonathan should have been sleeping.

"Where is 'em? I saw 'em go to bed only a few hours ago. Does anyone know where they be?"

"Millie got out of bed to take Jonnie downstairs because he felt sick, and her didn't want him to make a mess in the bedroom. T'wasn't long ago, so I expect they be out in the yard. If they be, there's no back exit, so they'll still be there. Why's 'ee looking for 'em anyway, and what's it got to do with ye, Liz?"

"Oh, Jess, don't come the innocent with me. I think ye've known all along they be on the run from the police; why else would 'em be living yer with the likes of us? 'Tis obvious the maid thinks 'er's better than us. Were 'ee planning on keeping the reward fer yerself?"

"No, Liz; I didn't know they was on the run, and even if I 'ad, I certainly wouldn't 'ave squealed on 'em. How could 'ee, after all Millie's done fer us."

"I didn't know 'til Ted came yer earlier and saw Millie. Then, when he see'd Jonnie, he put two and two together and realised who they be. 'Twas nothing to do with me; all the police stations round yer 'ave been asked to keep an eye out for 'em. Millie's wanted for thieving a precious brooch from some rich lady."

"Well, I don't believe that for a minute; Millie's no thief, and if there's a reward, I'll bet you were 'oping to claim it and share it with Ted."

Despite Jess's protests, the two constables insisted on searching the house from top to bottom, even waking Fanny, who was furious. When she heard what was going on, she scowled at her eldest daughter, and if looks could kill, Liz would surely have dropped dead. When the entire house and the backyard had been searched, the constables questioned the children and asked them if Millie was friendly with any of the neighbours. Liz's daughter, Amy, soon provided the information that Millie and Jonathan had visited Alice Brown earlier in the day.

Within minutes, the two men were knocking on Alice's door, and she took her time before answering the door in her nightgown and rubbing the sleep from her eyes. When they explained the purpose of their visit, she gave them a piece of her mind for waking her and assured them she was not sheltering any fugitives. They, however, refused to believe her and insisted on searching the house and the backyard. When they saw the back gate leading into the alleyway, they opened it and peered outside. However, they soon realised that the two youngsters could have entered any one of several properties or escaped down the alleyway and gone on their way.

The following day, Anna woke the two runaways early and brought them a bowl of porridge each. She sat on a wooden box in one corner of the room and chatted to them whilst they ate.

"I think travelling on the stagecoach to Hartford is too dangerous. The constables know where you're heading and that you have the money for the fare. They'll undoubtedly be watching all the transport to Hartford for some time. I don't know whom you've upset, but they must be rich and influential for the police to go to all this trouble. I think the best thing is for you to lie low here for a day or two and let me see if I can make other arrangements to get you to Hartford. Would you like me to do that?"

"Oh, yes, please, and for what it's worth, we haven't stolen anything; the charges against us are all made up."

"Yes, I know; Alice has told me your story, and I believe you. Now, a friend of mine is a farmer from Hartford who usually comes to the market on a Friday. He calls in here first and lets me have my pick of his produce before he goes to the Pannier Market. I'm sure if I ask him, he'll give you a ride on his cart back to Hartford. If he comes around the back, we can hide you under some blankets until you are clear of the town. It certainly won't be as comfortable as riding in the stagecoach, but to be honest, dressed as you are, I suspect they wouldn't let you inside anyway. I think they'd make you ride on the roof."

"Oh, that would be wonderful, thank you, and, yes, I know we look scruffy, but Liz sold all our clothes, and these rags are all we have now."

"Very well, I'll see what I can do. In the meantime, I'll bring you a few books and a slate and chalk and perhaps that will help you to pass the time."

Around three o'clock on Friday afternoon, Anna came to fetch Millie and Jonathan from the bedroom. Most of the pupils had gone home from school for the weekend, and she'd settled the six that lived there in the front parlour with a piece of cake and a mug of milk, a reward for working so hard during the week. The children were surprised by this, but none queried their good fortune.

Anna hustled Millie and Jonathan outside to the lane, where a horse and cart were waiting. The farmer had made a space in the middle of his remaining produce, and they lay down, and Anna covered them with two blankets, which she told them they could keep. Telling them to stay where they were, the farmer clicked his tongue, and they were soon on their way. It was not until they reached Braunton, some four miles from Barnstaple, that Charlie Chugg called over his shoulder and told them they could come out and sit beside him. On the journey, the pair told him their story and asked if he knew of a family called Lovering.

"No, I don't know of any Loverings in Hartford, but it's a sprawling village, and I was at sea for many years, so I'm probably not the best person to ask. Where would you like me to drop you off?"

"We don't know, but perhaps in the middle of the village?"

"Yes, all right; we'll go past one of the inns called The Three Pigeons, so I'll drop you there, and you can ask around. If you get no luck there, I'd try the vicar or the other inn, The Red Lion. My wife's parents own it."

Around three hours later, Charlie drew the horse to a halt outside The Three Pigeons Inn and announced they were in Hartford. Millie thanked the driver and pushed a florin into his hand.

"No, I don't want your money, my dear; I was glad to help, and I hope you find your kin soon. You keep it; I reckon you need it more than me."

"Thank you so much, Mr Chugg; we're grateful."

As the farmer went on his way, Jonnie pulled on his sister's arm.

"What are we going to do now, Millie? Can we get something to eat? I'm starving."

"Yes, I think we'll get something to eat at this inn and ask if anyone there knows of a family called Lovering."

It wasn't long before the pair were enjoying a hearty beef stew with some slightly stale crusty bread. When the serving girl came to clear their plates, Millie asked if she knew anyone called Lovering living in the village. The girl was unable to help but said she would ask the landlord. However, she returned saying he couldn't help either and that he had lived there for ten years or more, but had never known anyone by that name. Disheartened, Millie asked for directions to the rectory to see if the vicar could help them. Fortunately, the Reverend Rees was at home and willingly received them, listening closely to their sad tale. However, unfortunately, he, too, was unable to help. He wished them luck in their search and said they must excuse him, for he had parishioners to visit. By this time, it was late evening, dark, and beginning to rain.

"Millie, where are we going to sleep? I'm cold and tired."

"I don't know, but we must find somewhere out of this rain. I hoped the vicar might offer us a bed for the night."

Leaving the rectory, they wandered into the adjacent churchyard, and Millie tried the handle of the heavy oak church door.

"Oh, that's good; it's unlocked; we can spend the night in here."

"But there are no beds."

"No, I know, but at least we're out of the rain and can sleep on the pews. It's only for tonight; if we can't find the Loverings tomorrow, I'll get a job and somewhere better to sleep. Gran told me if all else failed, to find a church to sleep in."

The pews were made of wood, and the seats were covered with a thin layer of material. Millie settled Jonathan on one of them and tucked one of the kneelers behind his head.

"There, that kneeling cushion will make a pillow, and I'll cover you up with your blanket. Are you all right?"

The boy nodded but then clutched his sister's arm, his eyes wide.

"Millie, you don't think there are ghosts in here, do you?"

"No, of course not. Come on; we'll cuddle up together."

It wasn't long before Jonnie was fast asleep, for lying partly on his sister, he was reasonably warm and comfortable. However, for Mille, tired though she was, sleep was elusive, and she heard the church clock strike every hour until just before dawn, when she finally fell into an exhausted sleep.

CHAPTER 39

HARTFORD

Willie, Edward, and Llewellyn enjoyed their ride back to Sugworthy Farm, racing over the moorland and letting the horses have their heads. Llewellyn easily reached the farm first and reined in his horse, laughing, as he waited for Willie and Edward to catch him up.

"Never mind, Willie; you were never going to win that race, were you? Not with your horse carrying two. Still, I enjoyed it, and by the grin on Edward's face, so did he. I've not had the chance to go riding for a long time."

They left Edward to attend to the horses, and Willie led Llewie into the old farmhouse. Florrie was in the kitchen peeling potatoes, and she eyed Llewie with suspicion.

"I can't believe your father has sent you here to measure up poor Mr Houle's body; you're only a lad. What on earth was he thinking of?"

"Tisn't the first dead body I've measured, ma'am, and I know what I'm doing. Dad says I've got to learn. Can you take me to the body, please?"

Still tutting to herself, Florrie led the way to the bedroom where she had washed the body, and Mr Houle was now attired in his Sunday best. She had carefully brushed his hair and laid his hands on his chest, and he looked peaceful. She had placed bunches of snowdrops in glass jars on the dressing table and the windowsill, and some holly with bright red berries on the bedside table.

"Oh, you've done a lovely job of laying him out, Florrie," exclaimed Willie, "I'm surprised you found any flowers at this time of year."

"There's not much around, 'tis true, but he liked snowdrops, did Tommy, and I thought 'twas better than nothing. When you return to the village, Llewie, can you put the word around that folk can come here to see him and pay their respects?"

"Yes, I will. Now, I'll measure the body. We'll need to make a coffin from scratch because he's such a tall man. We usually keep a couple of coffins ready, but they're not big enough for him. Not to worry, I'll get straight onto it when I get home and return with it in a couple of days, ready to transport him to the church for the funeral. Do you know when it will be yet?"

"The vicar's coming here this afternoon to talk about that, but hopefully in a few days. 'Tis better to get it over and done with as soon as possible. Willie, did Master Robert say who'll be taking over here?"

"No, he said he'd discuss it with Jack Bater and let us know, but in the meantime, Jack's going to send over a couple of labourers to help out, and I'm glad about that, for we certainly need them."

"I hope whoever it is wants to keep us on. You never know when a farm changes hands; we could all be out on our ear in a week."

"Don't worry; I'm sure Robert won't let that happen. He's a fair man."

"Aye, I certainly hope so; I'm too old to be traipsing around the countryside seeking work."

Jack Bater had taken Robert's advice and was visiting The Red Lion Inn. He was enjoying one of Betsey's hot pasties and a pint of ale while waiting for Louis Blaquiere to have time for a chat. After twenty minutes or so, when the visiting stagecoach had left, the young man joined him.

"Can I buy you an ale, Louis?"

"I wouldn't say no, Jack; I've been rushed off my feet for the last couple of hours. What can I help you with?"

"Master Robert wants to help Marrok find work when his leg's healed, but he's a thorough man and would like to find someone to provide a reference. After all, although they're related, no one knows much about the young man. How long have you known him?"

"We worked together on a farm in South Molton for a couple of years, and I can assure you he's honest and trustworthy, despite his gypsy background. He's a hard worker and good company. It's a shame that everything went wrong for the farmer and then for Marrok and me."

"Why, what happened?"

"I took some colts to the Barnstaple market for Mr Fisher and then came here to Hartford. He'd agreed I could take a few days off work to visit our family grave in the churchyard here. I expect you've heard how I was set upon and robbed?" Louis glanced at Jack and raised his eyebrows, and Jack nodded. "I was knocked unconscious, and when I came around, I'd lost my memory. If it wasn't for Charlotte and Fred Carter, I doubt I'd be here to tell the tale."

"Yes, I've heard all about that; Hartford has few secrets."

"No, and I didn't know where to go or what to do, but luckily, Betsey and Ned offered me work here for a few weeks. It wasn't until the christening of Mr Fellwood's twins that Liza Hammett, a woman in the village, thought she recognised me, and it turned out she once knew my parents. Once she told me a few things, my memory came flooding back, and I remembered I used to work at Mr Fisher's farm in South Molton. As soon as I could, I went to see him and his wife, Nancy, to pay them what I owed, and they told me what had been happening in my absence. They'd had a run of bad luck; a rogue dog savaged their flock of sheep, and they all had to be destroyed. Then, their other farm labourer, Mark Fellwood, was mending the thatch on their roof, and he slipped and fell and broke his leg. Poor Mr Fisher felt awful about it, but he had to let him go, and Mark, his wife, Laura, and the four children ended up in the workhouse. Poor Laura died of cholera after a couple of weeks there."

"That is a sad tale, Louis. Are you going back to work on the farm in South Molton?"

"No, Mr Fisher's taken on new workers, and in any case, I'm settled here now. I love talking to Liza; she recognised me and is like a mother to me now. I've nearly finished paying Mr Fisher the money stolen from me; in fact, if you're going to see him, perhaps you could take my last payment and save me the journey?"

"Yes, I will; thank you so much for your help. I'm going to ride out to see the Fishers tomorrow."

"Remember me to them, please, and like I say, I'm sure Mr Fisher will give Marrok a glowing reference; he should do, anyway."

The following day, Jack Bater was up and about early as usual, and once he had made sure everything was running smoothly on the Hartford estate, he saddled up a horse and set off for South Molton. There had been a hard frost earlier in the day, but now the weak winter sun shone from a clear blue sky, and he was looking forward to the ride.

He had never visited South Molton before and was pleased Louis had been able to provide him with directions. From Barnstaple, he took the main road to Taunton, passing through several villages, including Landkey, Swimbridge, and Filleigh. His route took him past Castle Hill House, a grand building, and the country house of the Fortescue family. He seemed to remember that the Fortescues were somehow related to the Fellwoods and decided to mention it to Robert when he returned.

South Molton was a sizeable town, and when he noticed that it was market day, he decided to do as Robert had suggested and stop for an hour to explore. Leaving his horse tied up outside The George Hotel, he wandered through the town and soon found the pannier market. Though not quite as large as the one in Barnstaple, it was an impressive building, providing shelter for the many folk selling their produce. The market was crowded, and he enjoyed strolling through it before returning to The George Hotel, where he enjoyed a tankard of ale and some bread and cheese.

Refreshed, he was soon on his way and, within half an hour, arrived at the farm owned by Willy and Nancy Fisher. As he trotted into the farmyard, a middle-aged man came out of the barn to greet him. The introductions over, Willy invited Jack inside for a pot of tea, and despite his protests that he had recently eaten, Nancy pressed him to have a piece of fruit cake. Willy and Nancy could not sing the praises of Marrok Fellwood loudly enough and were delighted to hear the young man had been dealt a stroke of luck.

"Aw, I'm so pleased to hear he's come into some money. He deserves it, for he's had a hard life and is the sort of fellow who'd do anything for anybody. What a shame he didn't find all this out when his poor wife was still alive. It makes me feel a bit better, though, for I hated having to let him go. If you see him, would you tell him how pleased we are for him?"

"Aye, I will. I'm not likely to see Marrok myself, but I'll mention your good wishes to Mr Fellwood, and I'm sure he'll pass them on. Before I go, I have some money here for you from Louis Blaquiere. I believe it will clear the debt he owes you."

"Oh, yes, it will, and can you thank Louis? He was also a reliable man, and the best recommendation I can give for him and Mark is to say I would employ them both again tomorrow. Mark will be more than capable of managing a farm; he's worked on farms all his life, I believe, and has a real feel for the work."

Jack left the farm pleased that he could return to Hartford with such positive news for his employer.

Once Robert had received the glowing report about Marrok's character and abilities from Jack, he confided his plans for Sugworthy Farm to Annie. He was surprised when she seemed a little annoyed.

"I thought you'd be pleased?"

"Oh, I am pleased for Marrok, but I was hoping you'd offer it to Willie. He's worked there for years and has held the place together since Mr Houle lost his wife, and I think his loyalty should be rewarded."

"I did consider offering it to Willie, but I discussed it with Jack, and we both think he's too young to be the tenant of a property as large as Sugworthy Farm. If Marrok decides to accept the offer, then I'm going to suggest to him that he make Willie the manager. He's still young for that, too, but he is experienced, and as you say, his loyalty should be rewarded. Are you happy with that?"

Annie put her arms around her husband's neck and kissed him on the lips. He responded and drew her to him, wondering if she would try to change his mind.

"Yes, and I think it would be ideal for Marrok and his family. I'm sure Willie will be delighted to be made up to manager, and as you say, he is young."

Robert heaved a sigh of relief.

"Thank goodness, I thought you were trying to change my mind."

"Can't I kiss you without having an ulterior motive?"

"You can kiss me any time you like; you know that. Are you busy for the next hour or so?"

Annie giggled as he lifted her off her feet and laid her on the bed.

A couple of days later, Robert and Annie, accompanied by Selina, Thomas, and David, set off in their carriage for a visit to Enderby House and Primrose Cottage. They called at Enderby House first, for they knew if Aunty Margery got to hear they had visited Primrose Cottage without calling in to see her, there would be hell to pay. However, the butler told them that Lady Margery was, in fact, already at Primrose Cottage, painting with Mr Webber for the afternoon.

They arrived to find Sam and Marrok enjoying a game of cards in the sitting room, and within minutes of their arrival, Lady Margery and Peter Webber abandoned their painting session and joined them. Eliza, Jinnie, and Martin were all at Enderby School, but Paul was delighted to find he had an unexpected playmate, and he and Selina scurried off to his bedroom, where he had quite an array of new toys.

"It's so delightful to see you all, my dears; is this a social visit, or do you have some news?"

"It's both, Aunty Margery. I have some news to discuss with Marrok, but when Annie heard I was coming here, she wanted to join me."

"If you have something to discuss with Marrok, I'll leave you all to it and see you later, Sam."

"No, it's all right, Peter; we think of you as one of the family now, and I'm sure you can keep our discussion to yourself for the time being."

"Oh, aye, you need to have no worries on that score; I know how to keep me mouth shut."

"I'm intrigued, Robert; what do you want to talk to me about?"

Robert explained about Mr Houle's death and how he was seeking a new tenant for Sugworthy Farm.

"It's a farm of around two hundred acres with some of the most fertile land on the estate, but I'm afraid Mr Houle has let matters slide for the last few years. Jack and I knew of the situation, but his family had farmed there for at least three generations, and we didn't have the heart to evict him. Mr Houle has no one related to him to take over, but, fortunately, Annie's brother, Willie, has worked there since he was a lad, and he's tried hard to hold things together."

"So, presumably, you'll offer the tenancy to Willie? I mean, he is your brother-in-law. What has all this to do with me?"

"I'd like to offer the tenancy to you, Marrok. It has a spacious farmhouse and would be ideal for you and your family. You'll need something to do, and according to Louis Blaquiere and Willy and Nancy Fisher, I'll not find a more reliable, honest and hardworking man."

"Oh, my goodness, are you serious?"

"I wouldn't joke about such a matter; are you interested?"

"Interested? It would be a dream come true, but my leg is not yet mended."

"No, I realise that, but you could move in soon to get a feel for the place and get to know Willie and the others. Jack's sent a couple of our labourers to help out for the next few months so they can manage for a while."

Robert glanced at Annie. "There is one thing I should mention, or I'll never hear the end of it from my wife. I'd like you to offer Willie the job of farm manager and raise his wages accordingly. He's young, even for that role, but I think he deserves recognition for his hard work, and he'll be a godsend to you until you're fit."

"I don't know what to say, and, yes, I'd be happy for Willie to be promoted to farm manager. I met him at Christmas, and we chatted about farming matters. Thank you so much, Robert; I can't believe it."

"It seems only right, doesn't it, for you are a Fellwood and deserve a bit of luck. What do you think, Sam?"

The beaming smile on Sam's wrinkled old face said it all.

CHAPTER 40

HARTFORD

It seemed to Millie that she had only been asleep for a few minutes when she felt someone shaking her arm. Wearily, she opened her eyes and was astonished to find the vicar staring down at her.

"Good morning, my dear. I'm sorry to awaken you, but you can't sleep in the church. Some women are coming in soon to clean the place, and they won't think much of you sleeping on the pews. I presume you didn't find your relatives?"

"No, I'm afraid not, vicar, but we'll continue our search today."

"Well, I've been here for several years, and I think I know everyone in the parish. I'm pretty sure there are no families here named Lovering. What are you going to do if you can't find them?"

"I'll try to find a job and somewhere we can sleep for at least a few weeks. We came in here to sleep last night because it was dark and starting to rain, and we had nowhere else to go. My gran said anyone could seek refuge in a church."

"That's true, and I'm glad you spent the night under cover, but I think it might be best if I take you both to the workhouse in Barnstaple; at least you'll be fed and have shelter there."

"Thank you for the offer, sir, but I want to trace our relatives, and if we can't find them, I'd rather find employment."

"Suit yourself, but if you change your mind, come to the rectory tomorrow, and I'll take you into Barnstaple myself; I'm going there anyway. I can't take you today because I have a funeral this afternoon. For now, come with me, and I'll get my housekeeper to give you some breakfast."

Millie and Jonathan were grateful to the vicar, for the housekeeper provided them with a large bowl of porridge each and some bread and cheese for their dinner. Leaving the rectory, Millie once more turned into the churchyard, for although the housekeeper did not know of anyone called Lovering, she had suggested they look at the gravestones to see if the family members they sought had died.

The grass was wet beneath their feet as they trudged up and down the numerous rows of tombstones. Many graves had no stone, and Millie thought it would be just their luck that the graves they sought were unmarked. To make the task quicker, they split up and each searched an area on either side of the path that ran through the middle. She wondered whether this was a good idea, as although Jonnie had learnt his letters, he could not read. She told him to show her any graves he found with a name beginning with the letter L, and he seemed to enjoy the task. It was not easy, for the graves were somewhat haphazard and not arranged in straight lines, and it was a large churchyard, but after half an hour, Jonnie shouted triumphantly.

"Millie, come here! I think I've found it. Look!"

Millie joined her brother and gazed at the weathered gravestone that marked the last resting place of Ellen Lovering, who died on the twenty-fifth day of September in

1820, some sixty-six years earlier. A further inscription revealed that her three-year-old son, Norman, had died in 1821 and was laid to rest with his mother. The grave was neatly trimmed, and a bunch of snowdrops, surrounded by moss, was positioned at the foot of the stone.

"Do you think they're our relatives, Millie?"

"Yes, I expect so; I wonder if there are any members of their family left alive. It's strange because this gravestone doesn't look nearly seventy years old. Also, if there are no Loverings left alive in the village, then who's tending the grave? There must be someone who still cares. I suppose it could be someone who was called Lovering and then married, or a friend of the family. I'm pleased we found this, Jonnie; I think there is someone still living here that's related to the Lovering family; all we have to do is find them."

They continued scouring the graveyard in case there were more Lovering graves, but found none. By then, it was lunchtime, and they ate their bread and cheese in the church porch, not daring to venture inside the church again. Leaving the churchyard, they went to the village pump and took turns to pump the handle whilst the other held their mouth under the spout.

"Look, there's a shop; I reckon that would be a good place to ask. They must know a lot of people."

They entered the shop, which had the name George W Carter above the door, and found two young girls serving behind the counter.

"I'm wondering if you can help us, please?"

"Yes, if we can; what do you want?"

"We're searching for some relatives of ours who used to live in this village. They were called Lovering. Do you know anyone by that name?"

The two girls glanced at each other and shook their heads, and then one answered.

"No, I don't think so, and yet I've heard that name somewhere. Have you, Harriet?"

"Hmm, no, I don't think so."

"There's a grave in the churchyard of two Loverings. The name on the stone is Ellen Lovering, who died in 1820, and her son, Norman, is buried with her. He died when he was only three. Someone's tending the grave because there's a bunch of snowdrops on it."

"That's it! Yes, I remember now. One day, I walked around the churchyard with Gran, and she stopped to put some flowers on the grave. I think Ellen Lovering was her mother, and Norman was her younger brother. Dad would know for certain, but he's at the Barnstaple shop today."

"Oh, that's wonderful; could you introduce us to your granny, please?"

"Yes, of course; she and my grandad run The Red Lion Inn, but there's no point in me taking you there at the moment because I know she's attending a funeral in the churchyard this afternoon."

When the news of Tommy Houle's death reached The Red Lion Inn, Barney and Silas decided to stay a few more days to attend his funeral. They had known the farmer since childhood and wanted to pay their respects. The service was well attended, and Tommy was laid to rest in the same grave as his wife, Elizabeth, once more reunited. There was no wake, for Tommy left no known relatives, and as the farm had not been paying its way in recent years, he was not expected to leave a great deal of money. His will had not yet been read, but most folk thought he would reward his loyal housekeeper, Florrie, and maybe Willie Carter.

After the service, the mourners began to drift away and go about their business, but Barney, Silas, and Betsey strolled through the churchyard, pointing out the graves of folk they had known over the years. Betsey had persuaded Ned not to attend the funeral, although he would have liked to, and, not knowing Tommy, Bronwen and Josie had decided to stay at the inn and keep him company.

Naturally, once out of the church, Barney and Betsey made a beeline for the grave of their mother and brother, and on the way, they passed that of Becky Chown, who was buried with her parents. The tomb was overgrown, and the gravestone was covered in ivy, making it difficult to read the inscription.

"There's no one who cares what happens to that grave, is there? Serves her right; I never forgave her, you know. Norman might still be alive if it weren't for her enticing our father away."

"Aw, Betsey, it wasn't just her fault, was it? Dad had much to answer for; you know what he was like."

"Yes, I know what he was like, but what woman would knowingly run away with a man who'd abandoned his two youngsters and left them to their fate? Good heavens, I was only six, and Norman was three. 'Tis no thanks to her that I'm here today."

Realising the depth of Betsey's feelings, Barney put his arm around his sister and urged her forward.

"Come on; let's pay our respects to Mum and Norman."

The grave wasn't far from that of Becky Chown, and all three stood there silently for a few moments, each lost in their thoughts. It was Barney who broke the silence first. He still had his arm around Betsey, and he gave her a squeeze, noting the tears shining in her eyes like jewels.

"It's a grand headstone and must have cost you a lot of money, but it was worth every penny. Mum would love it, especially the angel on it."

"Yes, it was one of the first things I did when I inherited that money from Thomas Fellwood. I paid off Uncle Mal's debts on The Red Lion Inn and repaired the roof of Betsey's Kitchen, then Ned insisted I should spend some money on myself, and all I wanted was to put a headstone here so they're never forgotten. Oh dear, it's starting to rain." Barney helped Betsey to put her shawl over her head.

The trio were so engrossed in the past that they did not notice Betsey's granddaughter, Theresa Carter, approaching, accompanied by a young boy and girl.

"Hello, Gran, Uncle Barney, and Uncle Silas. I'm sorry to intrude, but could I have a word, please?"

Theresa could see that she had not arrived at a good moment, for all three standing by the graveside had sombre expressions, and her granny was holding a handkerchief to her tear-streaked cheeks.

"Of course, you can, my dear; we were on a trip down memory lane and not all of them were pleasant. How can we help you?"

"It's handy you're standing by this grave, Gran, because this is Millie and her brother, Jonathan, and they are looking for relatives of the Lovering family that once lived in Hartford. They found this grave and could see someone was tending it, so they came to the shop to find out more. I know this grave is important to you, but I can't remember the connection. Was Ellen Lovering your mother?"

"Yes, she was, and Norman was our younger brother, but I don't know of any other Loverings, and I'm pretty sure Dad was an only child. I don't know of any other relatives. Whom is it you're trying to find, my dears?"

The sudden rainy squall stopped as quickly as it had started, and Betsey removed her shawl from her head and put her handkerchief away. She turned from the grave to face the two youngsters and smiled kindly at them, but her expression turned to one of concern as their faces paled, and the girl gasped.

"What's wrong, my dears? You look like you have seen a ghost!"

"I'm sorry; it's just the shock of seeing you. You're the spitting image of our granny."

"Am I? How strange. What's she called?"

"Emily Gibbs."

"I don't know anyone by that name, but why are you looking for the Lovering family? Perhaps that will shed some light on the situation."

"Well, it's a long story, and the only name we have is Adam Lovering; he was our great-grandfather." Amid gasps of amazement, Millie reached into her pocket. "This is the only thing I have that was his. I'm told he always smoked this pipe; it has his initials carved on the bowl."

She withdrew an old brown pipe, and etched into the side of the bowl were the initials A.L.

CHAPTER 41

HARTFORD

There was a stunned silence as Betsey, Barney, and Silas tried to take in what the girl was saying. The colour had drained from Betsey's face, and she was as white as a sheet. Theresa rushed to her side.

"Gran, are you all right? Who was Adam Lovering?"

"He was mine and Barney's father, but all our siblings died. How can you two be related to him?"

"Betsey, we can't sort this out here. Let's go to The Red Lion and listen to their story; I think Ned should hear this, too."

"Yes, let's do that, Uncle Barney. Gran needs to sit down; do you want me to come?"

Though genuinely concerned for her granny, Theresa was intrigued and dearly wanted to hear Millie tell her tale.

"Yes, you come too, my love; no doubt you'd like to know what's going on. Will you be missed in the shop, though?"

"No, it's all right; Harriet can manage for a while, and Dad should be back from the Barnstaple shop soon."

Together, they walked slowly back to the inn, and Betsey led them into the sitting room where Ned, Bronwen, and Josie were enjoying a pot of tea. As soon as Ned saw Betsey's face, he could see something had upset her, and rising slowly to his feet, he put his arm around her and glanced curiously around the room.

"Who's upset Betsey? They'll have me to reckon with."

Betsey laid her hand on his arm.

"It's all right, Ned; no one has upset me, but I've had a bit of a shock. These two youngsters are looking for relatives of the Lovering family, and they reckon my dad, Adam, was their great-grandfather. We need to hear them out and get to the bottom of this. Please sit down, everyone. Josie, could you ask Sarah to bring in some more tea and a bite to eat? I expect this lad's hungry; boys usually are."

When they were finally settled and Sarah had provided them with some light refreshments, Betsey urged Millie to tell her story.

"Come on, then, lass, you tell us your side of things, and then we'll tell you ours. As you will have gathered, Adam Lovering was the father of Barney and me."

Holding Jonathan's hand for support, Millie nervously began to tell her story.

"My gran is called Emily Gibbs, and she was the daughter of Adam Lovering and his wife, Greta. They lived in a village called Brampford Speke, not far from Exeter, and that's where Jonnie and I have travelled from. I don't think they were married long before Adam died, and Greta and her daughter, Emily, were put into the workhouse. My gran can barely remember her mother, who died when she was four. Gran spent her childhood in the workhouse until she was sent to work in a bakery when she was about twelve. At the bakery, she met my grandfather, Lenny Gibbs, and eventually, they got married and had one daughter, our mother, Rosemary. I never knew my grandfather, as he had passed away before I was born."

"Goodness me, I never thought for a moment that Dad would go on to have more children. But then, he would, wouldn't he? We should have known he'd spend little time mourning our mother."

Bronwen squeezed Barney's arm, and Ned tightened his arm around Betsey's shoulders.

"We are related to you, then?"

"Yes, lass, from what you've told us, I think I'm your great-aunt, and my brother, Barney, is your great-uncle. Your granny, Emily, is our half-sister."

"Oh, thank goodness; Gran will be so pleased we've found you."

"I don't understand why you've come looking for us, and where are your parents? You're no age to travel so far on your own; why, Exeter must be a good fifty miles from here. How did you get here?"

"It's a long story, and I won't lie; Gran's hoping you'll take us in or at least offer me a job."

Ned looked shocked and not best pleased.

"That's a lot to ask of strangers, my dear; why can't your parents or granny look after you?"

"Unfortunately, they can't. A few weeks ago, our mother, Rosemary, died of typhoid. Many people in our village were stricken with the disease, and when we left her, our gran was also seriously ill. That's why she wasn't able to come with us. We've walked a lot of the way from Brampford Speke, travelling a few miles a day. It's been hard, especially for Jonathan. I found work at a couple of places for a week or two, here and there, to get enough money for food and somewhere to sleep. Hubert March, a kindly farmer that Gran was in the workhouse with as a child, put us up for a couple of nights over Christmas, and his son, Vivian, paid for us to travel on the train for a few miles from Crediton to Eggesford."

"It sounds as if you've had a terrible time of it, my dear, and I'm sorry you've lost your mother, but what was your gran thinking of to send you off on such a journey on your own, and in the middle of winter too; it doesn't make sense."

Millie's head dropped, and tears glistened on her cheeks when she eventually continued.

"There's more I need to tell you, I'm afraid. I had to go on the run to escape the police. They're pursuing us to arrest me for stealing a valuable brooch taken from Lady Grantley of Grantley Manor in Brampford Speke."

"Oh, my God, how much worse can this get? Do you still have the brooch?"

"Yes and no; it's being kept for me by a lady we met on our travels, but I want you to know I did not steal it."

Betsey moved from Ned's embrace and went to sit next to Millie. She took the troubled girl's hand in hers and held it.

"Go on, lass, take your time. Tell us what happened, and where's your father in all of this?"

"My mother, Rosemary, never married. As a child, she lived on the Grantley Estate in a tied cottage, as my grandfather, Lenny, worked there as a farm labourer. Rosemary grew up playing with Edgar Grantley, the heir to the estate; then, he was sent away to school, and they lost touch with each other for several years. By the time he returned home, she was working as a tweeny at the Manor, and he soon noticed her, for she was beautiful. You can guess the rest: they continued their friendship, which became a romance, but Sir Edgar knew he could never marry her. His marriage had been arranged, almost from birth, and he was forced to marry a lady called Lilliana; I don't think I ever knew her maiden name."

"A common story, I'm afraid, and a sad one, and I suppose your mother became pregnant with you, and that was the last she heard from him?"

"No, that's not it at all. I didn't know any of this until after my mother died and Gran told us we must run away. No, Sir Edgar married Lilliana because he had no choice, but he refused to give my mother up. After my grandad, Lenny, died, Sir Edgar allowed my gran to continue living in the tied cottage. He supported us financially, and the affair with my mother carried on for years, in fact, until the day he died, and despite them trying to avoid another pregnancy, eventually, Jonathan was born."

"Did his wife not mind that he had a mistress? I know some ladies willingly turn a blind eye, but I couldn't live with it myself."

"Yes, Lilliana did mind. She minded very much, particularly as theirs was a childless marriage, and she had always longed for a family. Naturally, she wanted to know why Sir Edgar allowed my granny and mother to continue living in the tied cottage after my grandad died. Normally, if a farm worker dies, his family must vacate the tied cottage to leave it free for a new worker. Gran said that Sir Edgar was honest with his wife and told her about Mum, but said he'd never give her up, and she would have to live with it. You can imagine how hard it was for her to know her husband had fathered two bastards but given her no children."

"That's completely understandable, and I sympathise with the poor woman; no wife should be asked to live like that, but it's her husband at fault here, not you or your gran. Why is he not still looking after you?"

"He died of typhoid on the same day as our mother. We had met Sir Edgar, but never knew he was our father until after they were dead. Gran said she and Mum wondered why he hadn't called with any money for a couple of weeks, and now we know it was because he was too ill."

"So, where does the brooch come into it?"

"The brooch once belonged to Sir Edgar's mother, Lady Melissa, and when she passed away recently, he gave it to our mother as a gift. He made no secret of it from his wife, Lilliana. She knew all about it and was furious, but he insisted that although she could have all the other jewellery, he wanted this one item passed on to his only daughter. Gran was cross with my mum for accepting it, for she knew it could only lead to trouble.

"When Gran heard that Sir Edgar had passed away, she knew Lilliana would want revenge for all the humiliation she had suffered over the years and would most likely turn us out of our cottage. Gran was worried that she might not stop there, but also make trouble for me over the brooch. Gran insisted we leave that same night despite the bitter weather. She pinned the brooch onto my bodice so no one could see it, packed us up with food and as many clothes as we could wear or carry, and sent us on our way. She thought I could sell the brooch if I were desperate, though she said I'd have to be very careful about it.

"I wanted Gran to come with us, but she was so weak she could barely walk, so it was impossible. She planned to ask a neighbour to take her to the workhouse in Exeter the next day rather than give Lady Grantley the pleasure of turning her out onto the street. Gran promised that when she was stronger, she would follow us here. I hoped she might have arrived before us, but I'm sure you would have said if you'd seen her."

"My word, what a tale. No, I'm sorry, but we haven't seen your gran. So, where's the brooch now?"

"When Vivian March dropped us off in Crediton, we were approached by a policeman searching for two runaways. He suspected it was us because we carried bags and had blankets around us. Luckily, Mr March came out of the shop he had been in and saw what was happening. He pretended we were his children and scolded us for getting off his cart. He asked the policeman what was going on, and he said he was looking for a girl and a boy about our age because the girl had stolen a valuable brooch from Grantley Manor. Mr March wished him luck in his search, and we drove off. To help us on our way, he took us to the railway station and paid for us to travel a few miles to Eggesford on the train. He thought it was unlikely anyone would be searching for us that far from Brampford Speke."

"You've been leading a charmed life by the sound of it."

"Yes, it's been a nightmare, but I promised Gran I'd take care of Jonnie and get us to Hartford to try to find our kin. You see, not only is Lady Grantley bitter that we exist at all, but we're the only descendants of Sir Edgar, though Gran said we would never be recognised as such, seeing as we're illegitimate."

"So, what have you done with the brooch?"

"On the train, we were befriended by an elderly lady called Rosa Baker, who told us she was also getting off at Eggesford station. It was helpful because we didn't know where to get off, and she said to follow her. When we left the train, I helped her carry her heavy shopping up a steep hill to her cottage, and she asked us in. We chatted with Rosa for a while and told her we were heading for Hartford. By this time, it was late afternoon and nearly dark, so she suggested that if we cleaned her house for her, she would cook us our tea, and we could stay the night. She suffers from arthritis and can't do the cleaning herself, and she thought it would be safer for us to continue our journey in the morning in daylight."

"That was kind of her."

"Yes, it was, and she was so pleased we cleaned her house; she said if we couldn't find our family, to go back to her, and she'd let us live with her. The elder Mr March said the same, although I don't think either could afford more mouths to feed."

"I'm pleased to hear that, but where's the brooch now? As long as it's in your possession, you'll look guilty of stealing it."

"Yes, I know. We told Rosa that our names were Gertie and Walter because we didn't want her to know the police were searching for us, but after tea, she said she didn't think they were our real names, and she thought we might be called Millie and Jonathan Gibbs. It was quite a shock, but she assured us our secret was safe with her. She said she'd treated herself to a bun and a cup of tea in the bakery in Crediton, and two men came in asking if anyone had seen two youngsters matching our description because the girl was wanted for theft. When she told us that, I showed her the brooch and asked her if she would keep it safe for me. I knew that if we were caught, and it was found on my bodice, then I'd be found guilty and sent to jail or even hanged."

"Dear me, that was trusting of you, Millie; I hope she's an honest woman. What was the brooch like?"

"I think Rosa's trustworthy, but it doesn't matter because the brooch is useless to me; I can never wear it, and I'd probably get caught if I tried to sell it. I'd gladly give it back to Lady Grantley, although Sir Edgar gave it to my mother. It is beautiful. It has a large blue stone in the middle, which I think is a sapphire, and it's surrounded by tiny diamonds. Gran said it's worth a small fortune, but it's not the money that Lady Grantley's interested in; it's revenge."

"Yes, I can see that, and in some ways, I can understand it, but she's wrong to take it out on you two, for none of it's your fault."

Betsey was staring intently at Ned, trying to ask a question with her eyes. He knew what she was thinking and gave his head an almost imperceptible shake.

"Now, just to put your minds at rest, you two will sleep here tonight, and your bellies will be full, so don't worry. This is all quite a shock and a lot for us to take in, so we need to think about what we all do now."

"Oh, thank you ever so much … Aunty Betsey," Millie said the name cautiously, "we had such a miserable night last night, sleeping on a pew in the church, and it was so cold."

"You poor lass, come here and give me a cuddle; I don't think you're too big for one. How old are you, anyway?"

"I'm fifteen, and Jonnie's five."

Betsey put her arms around them both and held them close, glaring at her husband over their heads. Ned knew a difficult conversation lay ahead.

CHAPTER 42

HARTFORD

Betsey escorted Millie and Jonathan to the inn's kitchen and introduced them to Sarah, Louis, and Bentley. She informed Sarah that they were her niece and nephew and that they would be staying for a couple of nights.

"Perhaps you could make up the smallest bedroom for them, please, Sarah? I think all the others are in use, but there are two single beds, and I'm sure they won't mind sharing. When you've done that, I think they might benefit from a bath."

She glanced enquiringly at Millie.

"Oh yes, thank you. I'd love a bath. So would you, wouldn't you, Jonnie?"

To Betsey's amusement, she elbowed her brother sharply, and he quickly responded.

"Oh, yes, please; I'd love a bath."

Betsey ruffled his hair. "You don't need to pretend with me, young man; I've never met a boy your age yet who wanted a bath. Nevertheless, I think you could do with one. Sarah, there are quite a lot of clothes from one grandchild or another in the corner cupboard of my bedroom; see if you can find something clean for each of them to wear, will you, while we get their clothes washed? Sarah will find you a hot meal when you've had your baths. In the meantime, Jonnie, I think Bentley would love to show you his toys and play with you, and Millie, I'm going to ask Theresa to keep you company for a while; she's not much older than you. I'll see you both later."

Betsey returned to the sitting room and noticed that the conversation had ended abruptly at her arrival.

"No need to ask what's been discussed in my absence, then. I can hear you all now. 'Betsey will want to take them in; you know what she's like. We mustn't let her, though; she's retiring to take things easy.' How am I doing so far?"

They all laughed, even Ned. "Spot on, my dear; it's all true, though, isn't it? None of us has the heart to turn them away, but the whole point of us retiring is for us to do less and enjoy our last years, which doesn't include raising another two children."

"I'm not stupid, and I understand your concerns, but I think this could work in our favour. At the moment, although I work hard at the inn, I have help with all the household chores like washing, cooking, and cleaning. When we move to the cottage, quite rightly, it will all fall to me, for you need to do as little as possible. It seems to me that if we let Millie and Jonathan move in with us, it will solve two problems. It will give them a roof over their heads and a safe place to live, and I'll have someone to help me around the house. Millie is old enough to take care of herself and her brother, and I'm sure they'll be so grateful not to be turned out onto the streets that they'll give us no trouble. Millie could work a few hours here at The Red Lion, and Jonnie will be splendid company for Bentley."

"That's as maybe, but the girl's wanted for theft, and that trouble could still find her, even here. For someone as well placed as Lady Grantley, she'll have the money to advertise in the newspapers if she so wishes, and there's always someone willing to tell tales for financial gain."

"Yes, that's true enough, but from what Millie's told us, there's no proof, and the brooch can stay where it is for now. As Millie says, she can't wear it or sell it, so although it may be beautiful, it's no use to her, and if that woman sells it, I don't see how the trail will lead here. In any case, when we tell Annie all of this, no doubt Robert could intervene and see justice was done."

Ned looked at his wife impatiently. "You always have an answer for everything, don't you?"

Betsey refused to be riled and grinned at him. "It's lucky for you, I do, Ned Carter, and you know it. But I'll tell you something now, for even if it wasn't convenient for us to take them in, I couldn't turn them away. I've been in the same position as they now find themselves, and if it weren't for the generosity of Aunty Kezzie and Uncle Mal, I would have been forced onto the streets or into the workhouse. I couldn't do that to a member of my family, however far removed they are. We don't know the full story of what happened to my father, and we probably never will, but I doubt he's innocent in all of this."

"No, probably not, and, as usual, you make a good point. There won't be enough room for Millie and Jonathan to live with us in Bluebell Cottage, though, you do know that."

"No, there won't, though my parents lived there with three children. All we need to do is rent out Bluebell Cottage instead and move into Fred's place when he and his family come here. It will be a better solution because Bluebell Cottage is ready to let, and if we move into his cottage, Fred can take his time moving his business here."

Ned threw up his hands. "See what I mean, an answer for everything."

They all laughed at him, for they could see that, as usual, Betsey was going to get her own way. However, Ned had one last missile to throw, and he chuckled.

"Good luck with asking Fred to move those heavy oak cupboards you're so fond of back to his place again, my dear; 'tis not a conversation I'd want to have."

The following day, Betsey and Ned ate breakfast with Millie and Jonathan. They had explained the situation to Sarah and Louis the night before and advised them of their plans. That being the case, Sarah made sure Betsey and Ned had some time alone with the two runaways.

Betsey served her visitors a bowl of thick, creamy porridge liberally topped with some runny honey from her bees.

"Did you sleep well?" Were you warm enough?"

"Oh, yes, thank you so much. It was such a treat to sleep in a warm and comfy bed, wasn't it, Jonnie?"

The boy nodded, then turned his bright blue eyes anxiously to Ned.

"Do we have to leave here this morning, mister, and walk somewhere else?"

Millie became still and studied her plate, and Ned had to swallow hard before answering the child. He realised that Betsey had been right all along. He could not turn these two waifs away and make them live on the streets.

"No, lad, you're with your family now. No more walking the streets for you."

Millie burst into tears at this news, and it was only seconds before her brother joined her.

Betsey gathered them both once more to her ample bosom. "Now, what's all this about? I thought you'd be pleased?"

"Oh, Aunty Betsey and Uncle Ned, is it all right to call you that? We're so pleased; I can't tell you how much."

"Yes, Millie, I insist you call us that. Now, the next few days, or weeks, will be a bit hectic because there was a lot going on in this family, even before you put in an appearance, so bear with us, but it will all be sorted out eventually."

"Oh, thank you so much; you don't know what this means to us."

"Actually, I do, my dear, but that's a story for another day. In the meantime, just to put you in the picture, Ned and I are going to retire from The Red Lion soon, and our son, Fred and his wife, Charlotte, will take over. We'll live in their cottage, and you'll move in with us. You can both help around the place, and Millie, we thought maybe you could work a few hours here at the inn."

"Oh, yes, anything. I promise we'll never be a burden to you, and we'll work hard."

"I'm sure you will, my dear. Why don't you go to the rectory this morning and tell the vicar your news? I'm sure he'll be pleased to know you've found your family, and there's no need to take you to the workhouse."

As the two children left the kitchen, Ned took Betsey into his arms.

"Well done, love. You always know best, don't you? I should know by now. I'm such a silly old fool sometimes. At least now we can settle down to enjoy a quiet and peaceful retirement."

Betsey went quiet for a moment, and then, holding him close, she whispered.

"Yes, Ned, but there is one more thing I have to do."

He pulled apart and held her at arm's length, looking into her eyes anxiously.

"What now?"

"Oh, Ned, isn't it obvious? I have to find Emily!"

AUTHOR'S NOTE

Thank you so much for reading my book. I do hope you enjoyed it. If you believe this book is worth sharing, please consider posting a review on Amazon or Goodreads.

An honest review is the highest compliment you can pay to any author and is much appreciated.

You can follow me on Facebook, Twitter and Instagram. If you want to learn more about me and my books and keep up to date with new releases, please join my mailing list here: https://marciaclayton.co.uk/

Thank you.

Marcia

About The Author

Marcia Clayton writes historical fiction with a sprinkling of romance and mystery in a heart-warming family saga that stretches from the Regency period through to Victorian times.

A farmer's daughter, Marcia, was born in North Devon, a rural and picturesque area in the far South West of England. When she left school at sixteen, Marcia worked in a bank for several years until she married her husband, Bryan, and then stayed at home for a few years to care for her three sons, Stuart, Paul and David.

Now a grandmother, Marcia enjoys spending time with her family and friends. She's a keen researcher of family history, and this hobby inspired some of the characters in her books. A keen gardener, Marcia grows many of her own vegetables. She is also an avid reader and enjoys historical fiction, romance, and crime books.

Marcia has written seven books in the historical family saga, "The Hartford Manor Series". You can read her free short story, "Amelia", a spin-off tale from the first book, "The Mazzard Tree". Amelia, a little orphan girl of 4, is abandoned in Victorian London with her brothers, Joseph and Matthew. To find out what happens to her, download the story here: https://marciaclayton.co.uk/amelia-free-download/ In addition to writing books, Marcia produces blogs to share with her readers in a monthly newsletter. If you would like to join Marcia's mailing list, you can subscribe here: https://marciaclayton.co.uk/

Betsey

The Prequel to the Hartford Manor Series

1820 North Devon, England

Betsey, a sadly neglected child, is shouldering responsibilities far beyond her years. As she does her best to care for her little brother, Norman, she is befriended by Gypsy Freda, an old woman whose family is camped nearby. Freda's granddaughter, Jane, is also fond of the little girl and is concerned about her.

Thomas, the second son of Lord Fellwood, happens across the gypsy camp and becomes besotted with Jane. However, Jasper Morris, the local miller, also has designs on the young gypsy, and inevitably, the two men do not see eye to eye.

Betsey is drawn into their rivalry for the attention of the beautiful young woman, and she finds herself promising to keep a dangerous secret for many years to come.

The Mazzard Tree

Book One in The Hartford Manor Series

1880 North Devon, England

Annie Carter is a farm labourer's daughter, and life is a continual struggle for survival. When her father dies of consumption, her mother, Sabina, is left with seven hungry mouths to feed and another child on the way. To save them from the workhouse or starvation, Annie steals vegetables from the Manor House garden, risking jail or transportation. Unknown to her, she is watched by Robert, the wealthy heir to the Hartford Estate, but far from turning her in, he befriends her.

Despite their different social backgrounds, Annie and Robert develop feelings they know can have no future. Harry Rudd, the village blacksmith, has long admired Annie, and when he proposes, her mother urges her to accept. She reminds Annie that, as a kitchen maid, she will never be allowed to marry Robert. Harry is a good man, and Annie is fond of him. Her head knows what she should do, but will her heart listen?

Set against the harsh background of the rough, class-divided society of Victorian England, this heart-warming and captivating novel portrays a young woman who uses her determination and willpower to defy the circumstances of her birth in her search for happiness.

The Angel Maker

Book Two in The Hartford Manor Series

1884 North Devon, England

When carpenter Fred Carter finds a young woman in dire straits by the roadside, he takes her to the local inn, where she gives birth to a daughter. Charlotte Mackie is an unmarried mother and has run away from home, where she would have no sympathy from her strict parents. A few days later, Fred takes Charlotte to her aunt's house and does not expect to see her again.

When their paths unexpectedly cross, Fred finds Charlotte is distraught as her aunt has arranged an adoption behind her back. Charlotte is desperate to find her baby, and Fred promises to help.

However, they are unprepared for the sinister discoveries that lie before them. Set alongside the absorbing detail of country life and budding village romances, dark forces are at work which ultimately test the bravery and resourcefulness of the whole community.

The Angel Maker is the sequel to The Mazzard Tree, and the second novel in a compelling series which follows the lives and loves of the villagers of Hartford. A rare treat for lovers of historical fiction.

The Rabbit's Foot

Book Three in The Hartford Manor Series

1885 North Devon, England

Mr Edward Snell was more than a little curious when Robert Fellwood, the heir to Hartford Manor, and Lady Margery, his elderly aunt, begged an audience on a Saturday morning. However, being such valued clients, the solicitor was happy to oblige. As his clerk showed the visitors in, he was intrigued to see them followed by an older man who, though respectably dressed, had something of a vagrant about him. The crisp suit in which he was attired could not disguise his weather-beaten face or his missing teeth.

Robert introduced his Uncle Sam and explained he had come to claim his inheritance. The solicitor was old enough to remember the extensive search for Thomas Fellwood when his father, Ephraim, died in 1840. However, that was some forty-five years ago, and the young man had never been found. Yet, here was Sam, who claimed to be Thomas Fellwood's son, and even more surprising was the fact that the Fellwood family appeared to have accepted him as such.

The Rabbit's Foot tells the tale of how an old man who has spent his life with barely a penny to his name suddenly finds himself rich beyond his wildest dreams. However, there is only one thing that Sam Fellwood truly wants, and that is to be reunited with his son, Marrok, whom he abandoned at the age of five.

A Woman Scorned

Book Five in The Hartford Manor Series

1886 North Devon, England

Lady Lilliana Grantley has been seriously ill with typhoid, a disease that recently claimed her husband Edgar's life and that of his long-time lover, Rosemary Gibbs. Now recovering at last, the lady wastes no tears on her husband but is determined to wreak revenge on his two illegitimate children.

Embarrassed for years by his affair with Rosemary, a childhood sweetheart living nearby, she has falsely accused Sir Edgar's daughter, Millicent, of the theft of a precious brooch and wants to see her jailed or hanged.

Fortunately for Millie and her little brother, Jonathan, their granny, Emily, insisted they leave home as soon as she heard of Sir Edgar's death, for she knew his widow would seek revenge. The old lady was soon proved right, and Lady Lilliana, furious that the two youngsters were nowhere to be found, evicted the old woman despite the fact that she, too, was dangerously ill.

After a long and hazardous journey to North Devon, Millie and Jonathan were united with some long-lost family members who made them welcome and gave them a home. However, aware that Lady Lilliana has put a price on Millie's head, they know they are not yet out of danger. Despite this, they are determined to find their granny, Emily, who seems to have disappeared.

Aided by her long-time lover, Sir Clive Robinson, Lady Lilliana is determined to find Millie and Jonnie and get them out of her life once and for all, but how far will the embittered woman go?

Annie's Secret

Book Six in The Hartford Manor Series

North Devon, England, 1887

When Lady Eleanor Fellwood gave birth to a badly deformed baby, she insisted that the child be adopted as far away as possible. However, that proved difficult to accomplish, and so, in return for payment, Sabina Carter, an impoverished widow living locally, agreed to raise the little boy as a foundling. The child's father, Lord Charles Fellwood of Hartford Manor, warned Sabina that the matter must be treated in the strictest confidence or her family would be evicted from their home. As far as Lady Eleanor was concerned, the child was being cared for miles away.

All was well for several years until fate took a hand and, against his parents' wishes, Robert Fellwood, the heir to the Hartford Estate, married Sabina's daughter, Annie. Robert arranged for his mother-in-law, Sabina, and her family to reside in the Lodge House, situated at the end of the Manor House driveway. A house that Lady Eleanor passed regularly, and it was not long before she spotted Danny's dark curls among the Carter redheads. As she looked into the child's eyes and noted his disabilities, she recognised her son.

Now, at seven years old, Danny has had numerous operations to correct his disabilities and is a happy, healthy child. However, his presence is a source of constant anguish for his birth mother as, day after day, she watches him play in the garden. Her husband, Charles, and son, Robert, are aghast when she announces that she wants him back! An impossible situation for all concerned, and a rift develops between Robert and Annie as he struggles to find a solution to suit everyone.

Over the years, Lady Eleanor has steadfastly refused to acknowledge her daughter-in-law, for she disapproves of Annie's lower-class origins. When a freak accident forces the two women to spend time together, they inevitably find themselves drawn into conversation. Before long, the years of pent-up resentment and family secrets surface as home truths are aired.

Will the two women be rescued from their precarious situation unscathed? And, if so, will the family survive the scandal that is about to be unleashed?